D0847730

THE DEFECTOR

ALSO BY CHRIS HADFIELD

FICTION

The Apollo Murders

NONFICTION

An Astronaut's Guide to Life on Earth

You Are Here: Around the World in 92 Minutes

FOR YOUNGER READERS

The Darkest Dark

THE DEFECTOR

A NOVEL

CHRIS HADFIELD

MULHOLLAND BOOKS
LITTLE, BROWN AND COMPANY
NEW YORK BOSTON LONDON

Mulholland Books / Little, Brown and Company
Hachette Book Group
1290 Avenue of the Americas, New York, NY 10104
littlebrown.com

First United States Edition, October 2023
Published simultaneously in Canada by Random House Canada, October 2023

Mulholland Books is an imprint of Little, Brown and Company, a division of Hachette Book Group, Inc. The Mulholland Books name and logo are trademarks of Hachette Book Group, Inc.

ISBN 9780316565028
Library of Congress Control Number: 2023941643

Printing 1, 2023

LSC-C

Printed in the United States of America

To Henry and Poppy,
my steadfast book-writing companions.

A man who lies to himself and listens to his own lie comes to a point where he does not discern any truth.
—FYODOR DOSTOEVSKY, *The Brothers Karamazov*

All warfare is based on deception.
—SUN TZU, *The Art of War*

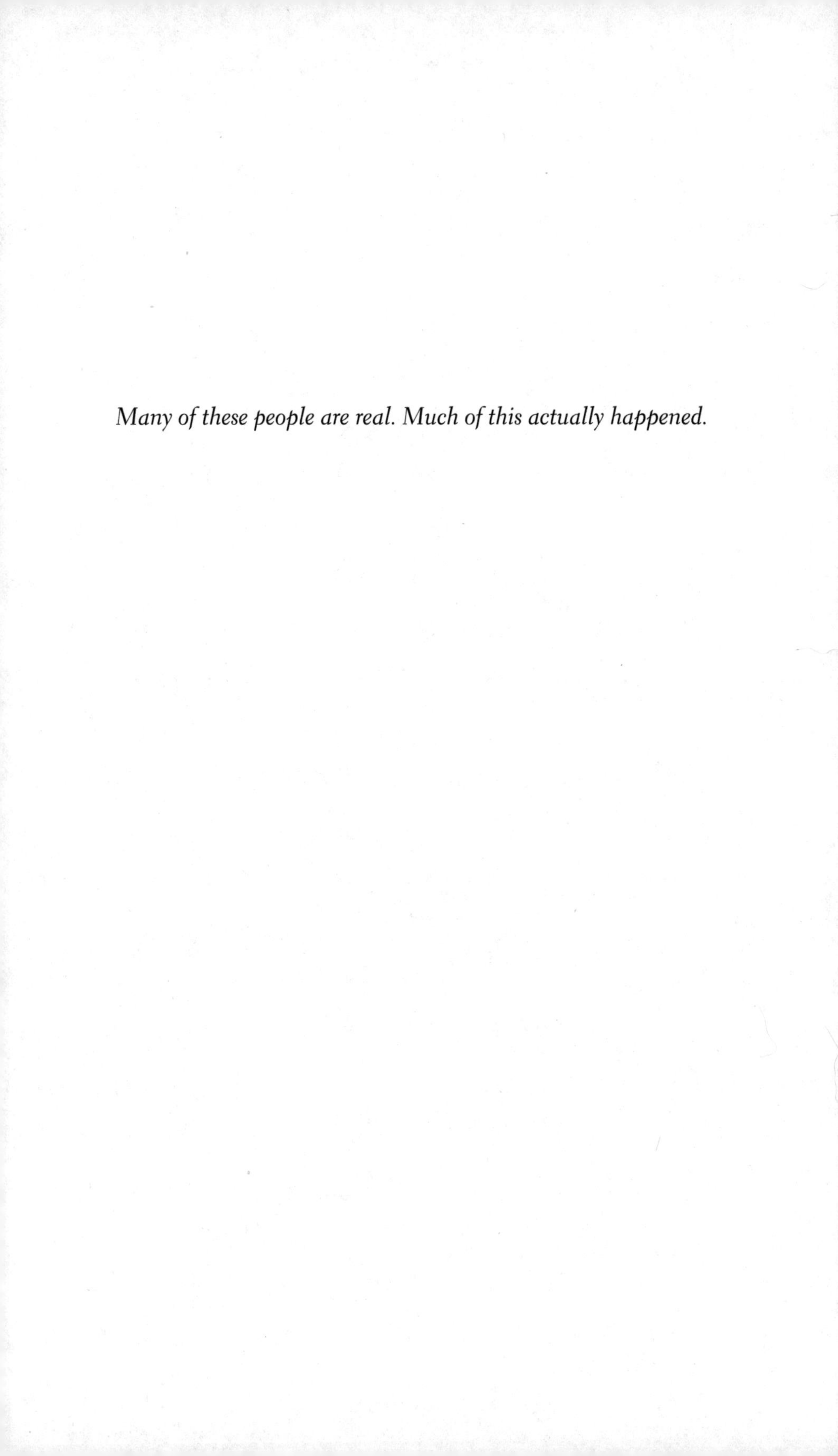

Many of these people are real. Much of this actually happened.

PROLOGUE

North Vietnam, June 1965

"Contact ten left, low, Kaz!" The voice from the back seat of the F-4B Phantom was clipped, urgent. "Looks like it's moving west, away from us."

"What range, Toad?"

Kaz Zemeckis, the pilot, craned his neck, looking down through the thick windscreen, trying to see past the Phantom's bulbous black nose. He was the lead on this combat air patrol, flying off the aircraft carrier USS *Independence*, stationed a hundred miles off the coast of Vietnam in the Gulf of Tonkin. Providing top cover against enemy fighters.

Pedro Tostado, long since nicknamed Toad, was head-down behind him, working the radar. "It's intermittent, too much ground clutter." Toad was Kaz's RIO, his Radar Intercept Officer.

Kaz glanced left. His wingman was just beyond his Phantom's wingtip, another pale-gray F-4B with a Jolly Rogers skull-and-crossbones painted on the tail, holding loose formation. Its pilot was looking back at him, waiting for direction.

Toad's voice rose in pitch: "Bogey's turned hard back into us, Kaz, solid lock now! Eighteen miles!"

"Copy."

Kaz turned his whole helmet towards his wingman and made a brush-off motion with his gloved left hand while porpoising the plane slightly. A clear signal. The other Phantom immediately banked crisply away, its glossy white belly revealed, moving out to tactical formation at the same altitude, still abreast but a mile distant. Close enough to keep sight, but with room to maneuver independently in case there was a dogfight.

Kaz pushed a button on the throttle to transmit on their discrete frequency. "Victory Flight, jettison tanks." With an unidentified fighter pointing at them, neither of the jets needed the added weight and drag of their external gas tanks if they had to engage. And there were plenty more tanks stored back on their aircraft carrier. Kaz reached forward, selected centerline, and pushed the red button on his stick to pickle off the tank. He and Toad felt the slight lurch as the plane got lighter.

The wingman's voice came harshly into their helmets. "Two has contact left eleven low, maybe a pair of bogeys, climbing towards us now!"

Kaz dropped the Phantom's nose to point where he expected the enemy planes would be; a mile to his left, the wingman did the same. Two F-4Bs moving at Mach 0.9, 90 percent of the speed of sound, covering a mile every six seconds. They had their missiles armed, but they needed to visually identify the targets before the US Navy's Rules of Engagement would allow them to fire. They knew the Soviet-made fighters didn't have missiles, only 20- and 30-millimeter plane-mounted guns. Minimal threat head-on.

Both pilots urgently scanned the hazy, humid air in front of them, looking for the telltale silver of MiGs against the green-brown of North Vietnam.

Toad spoke. "Locked bogey descending now, Kaz! Looks like they're dropping back down into the weeds again!"

Why would they do that?

Suddenly Kaz knew. He whipped his helmeted head around, squinting against the brightness, searching the blue of the sky beside and behind them for movement. He raised his left hand to block the glare and saw a metallic flash.

"Bandits, seven o'clock high!" he yelled into his mic. "Two, extend out, I'm breaking left!"

Flames instantly leapt from his wingman's exhaust as the pilot slammed the Phantom's throttles into full afterburner and pushed on his stick to get to zero g, minimizing drag, maximizing acceleration. To outrun the enemy's guns, and then be able to pitch back in and fire missiles.

Kaz buried his stick in his lap and pushed both throttles into max afterburner, his arms and back straining to haul the big jet around to face the threat. Both he and Toad grunted as they fiercely clenched the muscles of their legs and lower bodies to squeeze the blood up into their heads against the heavy eight-g turning force.

At the edges of his graying vision Kaz saw small balls of fireworks arcing down towards his canopy. "Tracers!" he yelled, and rolled as he pulled to avoid the line of gunfire coming from the North Vietnamese fighters. The Phantom climbed as the enemy planes descended, whipping past each other in the blue.

"MiG-17s!" Kaz and Toad yelled, recognizing the swept wings, rounded tips, triple wing fences and high T-tails of the Soviet fighter. Both men rapidly processed the mental image of color details and markings, and Kaz got it first. "Not Chinese, North Vietnamese," he said, twisting his head to follow their descent behind him. Some of his early dogfights had been with MiG-15s of the Chinese Air Force. "I see two of them, descending and running!" He rolled and pulled, bringing the Phantom around again to seek a missile solution.

It had been a classic aerial gunfighter tactic, choreographed by the Vietnamese People's Air Force ground control radars: wait until the American fighters are headed inland, send two decoys at low altitude to distract them while two fighters, maneuvering from high altitude, come straight out of the Sun for a strafing pass, and then all four would dive away, too close to the ground for US missiles to follow.

Kaz kept his eyes glued to the retreating silver shapes, lining the Phantom up so Toad could get a radar relock. As soon as he called it, Kaz took triggers and sent one of his AIM-7D Sparrow radar-seeking missiles to chase the MiGs down.

It was all he could do, and Kaz silently cursed the arrogance of the politicians who had decided that the F-4 didn't need a gun. Defense Secretary McNamara had said putting guns on fighter jets would be like using "bows and arrows in modern warfare." *Asshole*, Kaz thought, not for the first time, waiting to see a flash of the missile detonating.

Nothing. *Either the MiGs got too low or the Sparrow didn't fuse.*

But staring hard, Kaz saw the flashing planform of one of the MiGs against the green, pitching back up towards them. "One MiG's headed back our way, Toad!"

"I have him locked. Shoot!" Toad yelled. Kaz squeezed the trigger again and a second Sparrow raced away, its small brain frantically solving angles as it homed in on the Phantom's reflected radar signal. The MiG was head-on now, and Kaz willed the missile to work. He saw an explosion of white, but the growing silver shape of the Soviet jet didn't change. "Fused late!" Toad called, and tracers zipped past just to Kaz's left. He rolled 90 and jinked hard, clenching his teeth, but he felt no impact of bullets as the MiG flashed past. Kaz reversed his roll to watch the MiG push over and dive away again.

But it didn't dive. Instead of using its remaining speed to lower the nose and accelerate to safety, the pilot did something with the MiG that Kaz hadn't seen before. First he pitched hard and yawed the plane one way, and then he slammed rapidly the other direction, reversing and somehow pointing exactly back towards Kaz in one wild, seemingly barely controlled maneuver. Tracers raced towards Kaz across the void between them.

"Shit!"

Reacting immediately, Kaz did something jet fighter pilots never do and jammed his stick hard forward. The Phantom was rated for not only eight positive but also three negative g, but pilots didn't like using it because it pivoted the plane blindly down belly first, where they couldn't see. With Kaz's maneuver all the loose maps and checklists and floor dirt slammed up into the canopy, and Kaz and Toad's shins whammed into the bottom of the instrument panel, blood rushing to their head, the whole world seeming upside down. Kaz forcefully held the stick in position for three long seconds, ignoring the disruption to the fuel and oil systems of the plane, and then rolled 90 degrees left and pulled, hard.

Shoot at that! he thought.

He and Toad looked over their shoulders, scanning the sky where the MiG had to be, and were relieved to spot it, down low now, running away.

The wingman's voice came over his headset. "Two's inbound. Didn't get a good firing solution!" With the speed and multi-plane confusion of the engagement, that didn't surprise Kaz.

"Copy Victory Two," he said, "they're bugging out under you. I'm rolling out headed one zero zero, four twenty knots at five thousand feet. You're cleared to rejoin." The wingman acknowledged with a double mic click, and Kaz and Toad's heads stayed on a swivel, checking six to make sure the MiGs didn't come after them again. They didn't expect it: the MiG-17F with its afterburner was notoriously fuel-hungry and often ran short.

As the two Phantoms went feet-wet again out over the Gulf of Tonkin, cruising slower to save fuel as they headed towards the relative safety of the arresting cable waiting for them on the deck of the USS *Independence*, Kaz kept thinking about the maneuver he had just seen.

Where did that pilot learn to do that?

THE

DEFECTION

1

Syria, October 5, 1973

It was a simple mission, to a man of his abilities.

Get assigned to fly the right jet, follow the route, save enough fuel, avoid ground fire and find someplace to land.

Raz plyunut, he'd thought to himself. As easy as spitting.

He hated Syria. The place was a hellhole, compared to Moscow. Everything was brown and filthy, all the way to the hazy, rocky hills that surrounded the Tiyas T-4 Military Airbase. Even when it rained, as it had the evening before, it was just grimy mist falling onto sand. Like warm, dirty sweat from the sky, leaving smeared streaks on everything that was parked outside.

But his jet was inside, protected by an arched shelter that had been hardened against missile strikes and thickly covered with sand to avoid the prying eyes of satellites. There were no hangar doors at either end, so he could start engines, taxi out and get airborne swiftly, and get back inside just as quickly after landing.

His flying boots echoed oddly off the curved walls as he walked towards his hulking silver-and-black jet. A tall, thin yellow ladder, balanced on its tripod base, showed the way up to the cockpit. He hung his helmet on the side hook and stepped back to look at the airplane. One careful walk-around, a last chance to check all systems before takeoff.

Two things about the MiG-25 always caught his attention. The first was the bizarrely tall and thin tires. It was as if they'd been taken from some oversized off-road motorcycle and mistakenly attached to this flying machine. The bright-green hubs of the inner wheels added to the incongruity. He kicked the black rubber as he walked past, like he always did.

For luck.

The other strangeness was the enormity of the engine intakes. Yawning black rectangles, bigger than any jet he'd ever flown, leaning forward like giant shoulder pads on either side of the cockpit. Empty great mouths that could gulp down air fast enough to feed the two voracious Tumansky R-15B-300 engines within. After years of flying MiG-25s, Grief knew the deafening whistling sound they made as well as he knew his own voice.

As a test pilot, he'd pushed the plane to find its limits of speed and altitude, clawing a record-breaking 37 kilometers up above greater Moscow to where he'd seen the blackness of the sky above and the curvature of the Soviet Union below. His squadron mates had nicknamed him "Griffon" after the highest-flying of all birds, the griffon vulture. The name had soon been shortened to just one harsh Russian syllable. "Grief."

The cool of the desert night had soaked into the hardened aircraft shelter's walls and the metal of the jet, but the day's heat was already starting to blow in through the open doors. He could feel it on his hands and head; the rest of his body was encased in the tightly laced pressure suit he wore to protect himself from the thinness of the air at the extreme altitudes that this MiG-25 could reach. The same sort of suit that cosmonauts wore. He liked the feel of smooth pressure against his skin.

Completing his preflight inspection, Grief pulled his helmet off the hook, put it on with hoses dangling and started up the skinny ladder.

The Americans called the jet Foxbat. The first letter *F* had been designated for fighter aircraft in the Western military naming system, and predecessor MiGs had been clumsily nicknamed Fagot, Fresco, Fishbed and Flogger. Grief had seen the words in American reporting and disliked the lack of avian poetry; he was glad they'd chosen better this time. The actual foxbat was a flier, one of the largest bats in the world, with keen eyesight and the ability to fly stealthily and far.

The MiG-25 Foxbat was still the best in the world at what it did. The Mikoyan-Gurevich design engineers had been tasked in 1959 with intercepting and shooting down the new Cold War American high-altitude supersonic bombers and spy planes, and that deadly purpose had shaped everything: the big radar dish in the nose, oversized wings optimized for lift in thin air, underwing racks for multiple air-to-air missiles, and big enough fuel tanks to give long range. Mikhail Gurevich himself, late in his career, had taken charge of designing it, and the end product had made him proud; the Foxbat was a crowning glory that could cruise high in the stratosphere at Mach 2.8, nearly three times the speed of sound. Even faster in an emergency.

Halfway up the ladder, next to the large "18" stenciled on the side, Grief paused, and looked to his left. Holding on securely with his right hand, he swung his bare left wide to touch the plane's silver skin. He liked feeling the deep cold of the stainless steel against his palm, knowing the metal would be able to withstand the intense heat of the upcoming high-speed flight. The sharp leading edges of the wings would get hottest of all, pushing air abruptly out of the way; they were made of titanium.

The metal surfaces inside the cockpit were painted green, the same reliable anti-rust green the Soviet builders at aircraft factory Plant Number 21 in Gorky had used on the tall wheels. The flight instruments and controls were black, and the weaponry buttons were yellow, blue and red. As Grief clambered over the side rail into the jet's single seat, he glanced around, checking switch positions. As a test pilot he'd helped design the layout and he took comfort in the functional familiarity.

His hands easily found the four heavy straps that attached his harness to the KM-1 ejection seat, pulling and clipping them securely, then tightening. He plugged in his cooling, comm and oxygen hoses and clicked his helmet into place, feeling as he always did, like he was somehow transplanting himself into a more powerful host body.

Like the legendary Griffon, with the physique of a lion and the head, wings and talons of an eagle. The ultimate New Soviet Man.

The Foxbat was already alive around him. Its navigations system took time to align; the groundcrew had connected a thick power cable an hour previously, allowing the gyroscopes and racks of vacuum tubes to warm up. Grief's eyes flicked across the cockpit instruments, confirming that everything was lit and working.

The Soviet Air Forces had decreed that checklists weren't allowed during combat missions in case the plane was shot down or the pilot had to eject. He reached into his leg pocket and pulled out the single permitted sheet of cryptic, handwritten notes, with key timings, frequencies and navigation coordinates, plus a detailed map that spanned from the Turkish border to Cairo. Centered on Israel. The flight suit that he wore over his pressure suit had a metal clip on the right thigh, and he tucked the two papers securely into place.

He checked his watch, comparing it with the clock mounted in the instrument panel above his left knee; still 20 minutes until takeoff. With engine start and taxi time, that gave him five extra minutes. He held up an open hand so the groundcrew could see all five digits and nodded once. The airmen nodded back, understanding. No reason to waste fuel by starting before the allotted time.

He had woken early that morning, getting up at five a.m. for his regular dawn run on the airfield, his blood quickening and his mind emptying as he pushed the pace. Then back for breakfast at the Syrian Arab Air Force's makeshift *leotchick stolovaya*, the pilots' canteen. Lamb stew, rice, flatbread, and sweet tea to wash down the yellow vitamin pills provided by the Soviet medical doctor, who also gave him the required health check. Nothing unusual.

Four minutes to start. He'd been anticipating this day for months. When he'd seen on the roster that he was assigned to fly plane number 18, with its peculiar capabilities, the excitement of it had started a low, burning feeling in his stomach. He could feel his heart beating faster now and was glad the doctor wasn't watching.

Three minutes. He was in Syria at the direct request of the country's president, Hafez al-Assad, to Soviet General Secretary Leonid Brezhnev. Tensions with Israel were near breaking point, and Assad had secretly asked for aircraft and pilots that could photograph what the Jews were up to. Sadat had kicked all Soviet pilots and technicians out of Egypt a year earlier in a pique of tactical nationalism, but Assad wasn't as worried about upsetting the Americans. War was brewing, and he needed to know what the MiG-25s could show him.

Two minutes. Grief flicked up the top paper on his knee to have a final look at the map underneath. His fingertip traced the route that was programmed in the Foxbat's nav system: climb just south of Homs across Lake Qatina, stay north of Lebanon, arc hard left at the coast to photograph down the length of Israel, reverse right over the Med for a second look up the coast, and recover back to Tiyas T-4. He leaned close to remind himself of the road that defined the Lebanese border.

Sixty seconds. Time to think of the machine. He reviewed the memorized starting procedures, and quickly ran through probable failures like engine fire or abnormal oil pressure, and what his immediate responses would be. He knew the jet intimately.

The second hand on his watch ticked past the 12. Grief raised his right hand over his head with one finger pointed skyward and made a tight spinning motion, signaling engine start.

Time to fly.

2

The Israeli Coast

When the missile warning came, it was a pleasant surprise.

Cruising at 73,000 feet, 22 kilometers above the glinting Mediterranean shoreline, racing through the thin air at nearly three times the speed of sound, Grief was supposed to have been safely above any weapon the Israelis could fire at him. But the big radar dish in his jet's nose had detected the two enemy aircraft far below, flying faster than normal, and he'd watched with interest as the blips suddenly pulled up hard to point at him, their altitude numbers rapidly climbing. The radar warning tones in his helmet had instantly become higher and more urgent.

He leaned to his left and peered down hard, scanning the blue of the water and the brown of the land for a telltale new trace of white smoke.

There it was. Unmistakable. A harsh line painted pale against the earth as the AIM-7 Sparrow missile's rocket engine burned hot, trying to solve the angles and get the missile high and fast enough to do damage. To him. Get it close enough for the proximity fuses on the missile's sides to detect his jet and explode the 90-pound warhead in a destructive spreading hail of metal rods. A simple and deadly design, now racing purposefully up towards him.

He threw three switches, getting ready. A second thought occurred to him, and his left hand tensed on the throttle.

He looked intently out through the thick plexiglass of the canopy. At the exact moment he judged the missile was at its closest—he could actually see the white glint of the Sparrow itself supersonically in the sky nearing to him—his hands moved swiftly, taking action.

Oddly, he smiled.

3

Tel Aviv, Israel

It was excellent beach weather.

A light wind off the Mediterranean, clear blue sky, the big thermometer on the breakwall already showing 28 Celsius. Kaz did the math. Eighty-two degrees. Nice. The beach was emptier than normal too, which he appreciated. It was the day before Yom Kippur, the end of Jewish High Holy Days, and many people were home in celebration.

“Get you another drink, Laura?”

The woman turned in her striped beach chair towards him, her face shaded by large round sunglasses and an oversized straw hat. She held out her empty glass. “Sure! More lemonade would be great.”

Kaz padded up across the warming sand to the Hilton beachside bar and got them two refills. He turned and paused as his eye caught a long-tailed kite in the sky, a child and her father running along the shore to keep it aloft in the gentle breeze.

When he got back to Laura, he found her watching the kite as well. She smiled at him as he handed her the drink. “I’m really glad we came, Kaz.”

Kaz smiled back—he was too. He had family in Israel, relatives who had fled Lithuania during the war, people and a country he'd never visited. He and Laura had rented a small car and taken day trips, navigating the narrow roads to meet Zemeckis second cousins and elderly aunts who called him Kazimieras, smiling as he struggled to communicate with his few words of Hebrew as they looked through photo albums together. They'd drunk endless cups of strong coffee and toasted new family connections with small glasses of plum brandy.

The vacation was a reward. Kaz and Laura worked in Houston, Texas, and had been deeply involved in Apollo 18, NASA's ill-fated last voyage to the Moon. US astronauts and Soviet cosmonauts had died under circumstances that needed to remain secret for national security's sake. When the seemingly endless classified debriefs and scientific analyses had finally wound down, they'd both needed a break.

Mostly, they were in Israel to be together. They'd been dating for nearly eight months, and when they'd transferred to board the big, new El Al 747 in New York for the long flight to Tel Aviv, it had felt like an important next step for them both.

Kaz took a sip, watching Laura still gazing up at the kite. The small white bikini hugged her long, lithe body; her thick black hair was unruly under the hat. They'd never been able to spend so many consecutive days together, and he'd relished every one of them.

"What's that, Kaz?" Laura said.

She was pointing into the sky above the kite. Kaz squinted against the bright sun, his good right eye instantly watering at the glare; he'd lost his left eye as a US Navy test pilot in a birdstrike. He spotted a high, straight contrail, moving fast down the coast, but couldn't see the jet that was creating it.

She noticed where he was looking, and said, "No, there. Look lower."

Just visible against the blue, arcing up towards the high contrail, was a new line of white. He scanned the sky, but couldn't see the jet that had launched the missile. *Likely an F-4.*

"That looks serious, Laura," he said, still tracking the contrails. "Most probably an Israeli Phantom firing an AIM-7 missile up at a Soviet MiG-25 reconnaissance plane."

No way it will reach it, he thought. He'd fired AIM-7s and knew their performance limits. The missile had fared very disappointingly in Vietnam. *Just the Israeli Air Force warning the Russians off.*

Now, post–engine burnout, the missile became invisible as it coasted higher, steering autonomously with small aerodynamic fins, refining its radar-guided aim towards the target. Kaz counted seconds in his head, guessing on altitudes and distances. He figured if there was no explosion by the time he got to 20, it would be a clean miss.

"What are you seeing, Kaz?"

He raised a hand, palm open, asking her to wait as he counted.

When he reached 17, he swore. The MiG-25's contrail had visibly changed thickness, and then stopped.

Kaz turned to Laura, frowning. "We need to go," he said.

4

Eastern Mediterranean Sea

It was Catherine the Great who had been the first to station Russian ships off the coast of what would become the state of Israel. From her subarctic capital in Saint Petersburg in 1769, she had ordered Russian naval forces to sail through the Straits of Gibraltar and into the Mediterranean, to tactically support—and win—a key eastern land battle.

On this October Friday, two centuries later, as Grief's MiG-25 was racing south towards Tel Aviv, a high antenna on a Soviet ship named the *Krasny Krim* had seen the distinctive radar return signal and was now tracking it.

For an aircraft at 72,000 feet, the ship's tall MR-310 Angara-A radar antenna had direct line-of-sight well beyond the visible curve of the Earth's horizon. The captain of the *Krasny Krim*—"Red Crimea"—had been carefully steering a course well clear of the coastal waters and now he listened to his electronics officer's update.

"That high-flier has steadied on a north-to-south track, Captain, altitude 22 kilometers, speed 825 meters per second." He checked his conversion table. "Mach 2.8."

The captain nodded. *One of ours, no question.* He drummed his fingers lightly on the fake leather armrest of his command chair. The cat-and-mouse game of the Cold War navies was delicate, and demanded patience. The Soviet Mediterranean Squadron had 52 ships and submarines patrolling on high alert due to the Arab-Israeli tensions, against 48 vessels of the US Sixth Fleet, including two aircraft carriers. A force deployment capability the Soviet Union lacked.

"Any threats?"

"Da, Captain, the Israelis have several mid-altitude fighters airborne, as usual." The tech watched his scope intently, evaluating the blips, looking for telltale signs. A flash of new data registered as one of the targets showed a rapid Doppler shift. "An Israeli jet has fired a missile." His voice remained calm; no air-to-air missile had ever reached the Soviet MiG-25 overflights.

The captain peered eastward through the ship's large, square side window, seeing nothing but sea and sky. *No surprise. We're 150 kilometers away.* He waited.

"Captain, I'm seeing something unusual." A different tone in the tech's voice.

Several seconds passed. "What is it?" the captain tersely demanded.

"I see two returns now, and a rapid deceleration." The tech's eyebrows drew together as he stared at his screen, willing it to give him better data. Different data. "Also descent, Captain."

He turned to face the man in the chair.

"I think the Jews hit our plane!"

5

Washington, DC

Ten a.m. in Tel Aviv was four a.m. in Washington, so when Kaz hurriedly dialed long-distance direct to Sam Phillips's office, the night desk answered. A male voice with the flat vowels of a Michigan accent sounded bored and robotic.

"Andrews Air Force Base, United States Air Force Systems Command, please state your name and rank." USAF standard protocol: get the facts out front.

"This is Commander Kazimieras Zemeckis, US Navy. I've worked with General Phillips and need to get a message to him ASAP."

A pause. General Sam Phillips headed the entire Command. Not a typical phone request.

"I copy, Commander Zemeckis. This is Master Sergeant Henderson. Do you have access to a secure line?"

"I'm in a hotel room in Tel Aviv, Master Sergeant." He read the phone and room number off the center of the dial. "Please tell the general that it's urgent, concerning an air combat event I just witnessed." He'd been thinking about next steps as he and Laura had hurried up from the beach. "I'll contact the US embassy here in Tel Aviv and can be over there within fifteen minutes." He'd noticed the embassy while driving, and knew it wasn't far.

"Sounds good, Commander. Please call this number again when you get there. I'll have more info by then."

Laura drove him to the embassy, and realized she must be looking worried when Kaz paused as he was climbing out of the passenger seat, leaned in and kissed her. "I'll call you as soon as I'm done."

She watched him walk up to the uniformed Marine at the door, fish in his pocket and then hold out his passport and Navy ID. The Marine scrutinized them carefully, then saluted and pushed a button. The door swung open, and Kaz disappeared inside.

As she pulled away from the curb, twisting in her seat to hook a U-turn back to the Hilton, Laura swore loudly. "Damn!" There was always news of conflict in Israel, and it had made her quietly hesitant about them traveling here. This was definitely not the way she'd wanted their first vacation together to go.

As she picked up speed back along the narrow road, she sighed. *What can I expect with a man who always seems to run towards a crisis?*

It took several urgent explanations for Kaz to work his way up through the embassy's approval layers, and he glanced at his watch as a staffer finally sat him in a secure room, handing him an oversized handset, dialing. It was already 10:45. He listened to a series of clicks and noises, and then heard Master Sergeant Henderson's voice. Distorted by encryption, but clearly not nearly so bored this time.

"Commander, General Phillips is expecting your call, let me patch you through." Kaz heard a succession of low tones, and then ringing on the other end. With a sharp click, the general picked up.

"Kaz, good morning. I hear you're in Israel." The distinctive, calm voice oddly digitized, but immediately recognizable.

"Yes, sir, sorry for the early hour. I'm on vacation, but I saw something from the beach in Tel Aviv just under an hour ago that you and Washington will be interested in." He described exactly what he'd seen, and his appraisal of what had happened.

Phillips had been director of the National Security Agency. After a birdstrike had partially blinded Kaz and put an end to his test flying, Phillips had recruited him to work in electro-optics and high-altitude intelligence gathering. Now, as the recently assigned commander of USAF Systems Command, Phillips was responsible for research and development of all new weapons for the US Air Force and its Foreign Technology Division. The MiG-25 Foxbat was still a prime Soviet threat.

The general gave a low whistle. "Worth getting me up for, Kaz." A short pause as he thought. Phillips had been an air combat fighter pilot in World War II. "Did you see any ensuing smoke trail or crash?"

"No, sir, though it could have splashed well out in the water, or somewhere farther inland. The Foxbats cruise up over 70K, and that's a long way to fall." He paused. "Didn't see a parachute either."

"I'm going to call my contacts in the Israeli Air Force there, and get Washington woken up to the news too. If Israel has found a way to knock down MiG-25s, we need to know about it. And if the wreckage has anything worth salvaging, I want to see it."

Phillips said, "Give me your hotel info," and after he had copied it down, he paused. "Kaz, I may need you to go look at things there for me. You have time to do that?" Phrased as a question, it was undeniably an order.

"Yes, sir. I've already visited all my relatives here, and we only had beach time planned for the last couple days. Can extend as needed."

"Good. This'll likely get taken out of my hands pretty quick by the State Department, but I'll be in touch soon."

6

Israeli Air Force Command Center

The Air Force reaction to the airborne intruder had been by the book.

When the high-flying MiG-25 had first entered Israeli airspace, the northern region air defense technician had assessed it on her green-and-black radarscope, recognized the distinctive trajectory and speed, and marked it with a hostile tracking number, instantly alerting IAF command and control center operations, near Tel Aviv. Two airborne combat patrol jets, F-4 Phantoms, already orbiting in a high, fast racetrack pattern north of the city, rapidly received a hot vector from their tactical controller. They turned hard and climbed to get a radar lock-on, pushing to full afterburner to accelerate into a favorable geometry to release their missiles. Permission to fire was rapidly transmitted, and at the optimum moment the lead F-4 pilot squeezed the trigger on his control stick and called, "Fox One, Fox One, Fox One," watching as his radar-guided Sparrow missile raced from under his wing, arcing sharply skyward.

In the darkened operations room, the F-4's tactical controller scanned his radar screen as the high-speed missile tracked upwards.

Ever since the first MiG-25 had flown high over Israel, the combined fighter weapons team had been working on how to shoot them down, but with no luck so far. He watched the blips move rapidly towards each other, counting under his breath, assessing speed and altitude. Expecting another miss, as it was an intercept beyond the capability of the missile.

But this time he saw something different.

Where there had been two blips, there were suddenly three. The speed readout of the Soviet jet instantly dropped, and he stared in surprise as two distinct radar returns plummeted down through the atmosphere. He pushed the transmit button under his foot, his hands adjusting the screen for maximum resolution.

"Kurnas flight, I show a potential hit! What are you seeing?"

Both Phantom crews, pilots in front and weapons operators in back, had been staring upwards.

"We haven't seen any explosion, but the MiG's contrail has stopped," the lead pilot replied, and quickly checked with his backseater. "We're tracking it rapidly falling now, maneuvering in for a visual ID." He turned the jet to intercept and glanced at his fuel remaining. "We're at Joker fuel, coming out of AB." He pulled the throttles back out of afterburner, as the fuel level had dropped to the point where they had to end tactical maneuvering. "Should have enough for a quick look."

"Copy, Kurnas flight, let us know what you see." The controller thought further. "Tell us if you see a parachute."

The two Phantoms flew west, out over the water, closing on the radar returns, all eyes straining forward.

"Tally ho! Left eleven thirty, slightly low, descending rapidly." The flight lead corrected left and dropped his nose to cover the remaining distance. "Looks largely intact, nose low." He scanned quickly around for the source of the second radar return but saw nothing. He warned his wingman. "Coming right, let's yo-yo up and come back down to intercept." He wrestled the Phantom up and inverted, paused as he judged relative motion, and then pulled hard down. "Closing now."

The controller watched the screen as the blips merged, the wingman remaining behind and clear, in missile firing position. He suppressed the urge to ask what they were seeing, letting them do their job, picturing their actions.

Finally, the lead pilot reported.

"Okay, the MiG looks intact, the canopy's still in place, and I can see the pilot. He's not moving, and we're still diving." He quickly glanced inside his cockpit, assessing speed versus altitude. "I'll need to pull out soon."

"Copy, plan to stay on station as long as fuel allows." If the MiG crashed into the sea, they would want to get high-speed ships there ASAP to retrieve any useful debris.

"Wait, the MiG is maneuvering now!" The controller could hear the urgency in the pilot's voice, and then the strain of heavy g-forces in the F-4. "I'm turning with him. He's leveling off, rolling out towards shore!"

The controller's mind raced. *What is the MiG doing?* His superior in the command center had been listening and watching, and his voice now cut in. "Kurnas flight, does the MiG have weapons?"

The pilot had been thinking ahead as well. "Nothing under the wings or belly—she's clean." He pushed his throttles up to get closer. *Could this pilot be some sort of kamikaze, planning to crash into a ground target?*

The superior spoke again, urgently. "Get your AIM-9s locked on, and stand by for fire command."

The Phantom's back-seater had already locked up the MiG's engines as a heat source, and the pilot heard the steady tone. "Roger, we're locked on and have a firing solution."

In the command center, they watched the MiG's new heading steady out on the screen, and quickly assessed the ground track. The senior officer spoke. "Looks like he's headed for Lod airport! Maybe strafing or an intentional crash. The second you see any hostile action, you are cleared to fire."

The pilot looked again at his dwindling fuel. "Wilco, cleared to fire."

The MiG suddenly loomed large in his window, and he yanked his throttles back and moved his thumb to deploy full speed brakes to keep from overrunning. The Soviet jet's gear doors abruptly opened and the wheels pivoted down into view.

"He's dropped his landing gear! The MiG is lining up to land on runway zero eight at Lod!"

7

Israeli Airspace, West of Tel Aviv

Shock waves are fickle things.

As the MiG-25 Foxbat had raced through the high, thin air, pushed by its huge afterburners, it was traveling almost three times faster than the speed of sound, covering a mile every two seconds. An observer floating under a high-flying balloon wouldn't have heard the jet coming. Only as it flashed past would the roaring sound of wind and engine arrive, trailing an invisible, deafening wake.

Like an unseen hammer, the shock wave was the leading edge of that wake. The sonic boom the balloonists would feel was the pressure change, rattling their eardrums as all the pent-up energy hit them in an instant.

But the MiG's giant engines needed air to mix with its fuel to burn, and that air had to be slowed from supersonic speed to pass through the motor without blowing out the internal fire. The Soviet engineers at the OKB-300 Tumansky Design Bureau in Moscow had carefully shaped the huge, square engine intakes, testing them in factory wind tunnels. They'd found that if they placed the sharp metal lip at just the right angle, a shock wave could be controlled so that it stayed in front of the engine—a protective layer to slow the howling wind. On the inside of the intake, they'd installed a metal ramp that moved automatically to adjust secondary shock waves, further slowing the air, and thickening it. By the time it reached the spinning blades of the engine's first-stage compressor, the air was moving far slower than sound, and ready for smooth burning.

Until Grief moved his left hand on the throttles.

It was something his instructors, back when he'd first qualified to fly a supersonic plane, had warned against. Sudden changes in the throttle position at high Mach could demand more than the slow-moving mechanical intakes could deliver. The carefully controlled shock waves might shift, allowing the high-pressure air deep inside the motor to backfire, blowing out the front, unstarting the engine and potentially vibrating the spinning compressor blades beyond their limits, breaking hot metal off into a pinwheeling maelstrom of self-destruction.

The lesson had been hammered into every Soviet fighter pilot since Ivan Fyodorov had first broken the sound barrier in 1948: when you're going supersonic, move all controls carefully or bad things will happen.

Yet, staring down through the thick curve of his canopy, when he judged that the Israeli missile was as close as it would get, Grief yanked both engines' throttles all the way back until they hit the IDLE stop.

He was instantly thrown forward, and despite the sound-deadening layers of his helmet and earphones, he could hear the repeated, deep bangs of the engines' compressors stalling in protest. Up through his ejection seat he felt the jet shuddering at the abuse. Ignoring it, he pushed his body back hard against the backrest to stabilize himself and then reached forward with his right hand, flicked up a red cover and pushed the recessed button underneath.

For the long reconnaissance flights down to the Egyptian border and back, the Foxbat couldn't carry enough fuel in its internal tanks. A large, double-pointed silver cylinder had been added under the jet's belly to feed extra fuel into the system. When Grief pushed the button, emergency pyrotechnic charges fired, instantly releasing and jettisoning the external tank. It pivoted nose-down and tumbled clear, trailing a thin white plume from its hastily disconnected feedlines.

Hopefully enough distraction for everyone's radars. Now to fly this thing, he thought.

His eyes flicked to the airspeed indicator, then the altimeter. In the thin upper atmosphere the jet had already slowed to barely flyable airspeed, and he eased the control stick forward to drop the nose and accelerate. From test flying experience he'd been confident the engines could take the sudden deceleration and the huge twin tails would keep him flying straight, but controlling the heavy jet now required finesse. He kept the nose coming down until he was sure he was in stable flight.

Grief turned his head to the left and looked down at the Israeli coast. He could just make out a sliver of brown beach between the blue of the Med and the gray-brown sprawl of Tel Aviv.

He needed a place to land. And fast.

During previous overflights he'd scanned the length of Israel and had seen a triangle of big runways at a major airport near Tel Aviv. It looked like a mix of military and civilian operations, with jets parked on the ramp and many large, square hangars visible.

One will have its doors open.

His altitude was plummeting. The radar warning alarms were squawking in his headset as the Israeli Air Force defense systems tracked him. He let the big jet fall, not turning towards land yet, hoping to appear less threatening. As he descended near-vertical through 5,000 meters, he judged that it was time. He moved the stick left and pulled, turning to align with the longest of the runways, the one running east-west.

He ticked through his biggest unknowns. *Would the Jews shoot a surface-to-air missile at him? Could he avoid other aircraft using the airport? Would the surface wind be strongly the wrong way, making him land too fast for the runway length?* He'd thought through all three in advance and had done everything he could to mitigate risk. *Now isn't the time for worrying, it is time to react to what actually happens.* To be a superb pilot.

He'd flown many aircraft with malfunctioning engines during flight test, where the approach and landing were essentially just a controlled glide to touchdown, with no chance to try again. He'd decided that would be his best option today, visually judging height versus speed, evaluating ahead to where his flight path would hit the ground. He'd already asked a lot of the engines and didn't want to have to count on them to extend his glide, or to level off. Unless he needed to do so.

Grief nodded to himself. The buildings of Tel Aviv were getting bigger at a rate that felt familiar, and a quick cross-check of height and speed confirmed it. *Pakah vsyo horashow.*

So far so good.

"El Al zero two, we show you ten back, no other traffic, winds two-four-zero at one-six, altimeter one-zero-one-three-point-two, cleared to land runway two-six." The Lod airport controller's voice was calm, at ease with the familiarity and the good weather he could see out his tower windows.

"Tel Aviv tower, El Al two copies, cleared to land two-six." With 16 knots blowing in from the Mediterranean, the Boeing 747 captain could feel his big jet buffeting slightly in the turbulence. He smiled. After 14 monotonous hours flying from New York, the small bumps made the plane feel alive again in his hands. He glanced at the instrument landing system needles, showing he was on glide slope, and then looked out the forward windows, managing the momentum of his 200-ton jet and 400 passengers, getting ready to touch down smoothly on the 12,000-foot-long runway. He'd already dropped the landing gear, and the plane rumbled with the added drag and turbulence.

Tower broke back in, urgently. "El Al zero two, go around, I say again, go around!"

The captain frowned and glanced at his first officer as he pushed the four throttles forward and waited until speed and altitude started increasing to raise his gear. The FO reset the flaps and then spoke to the tower. "El Al zero two's on the go-around."

"Tower copies El Al zero two, immediate left turn heading two-three-zero, expedite climb to five thousand." Belatedly, the controller gave a reason for the disruption. "We have pop-up head-on traffic inbound, looks like they're doing an emergency landing on zero eight. Sorry for the last-minute call, El Al two, but they're not on freq."

The 747 had four flight crew, and as the captain racked the plane to the left, all eight eyes were scanning hard right, looking for the offending aircraft. The FO spotted it first and transmitted. "We have the traffic, tower, El Al two is clear." He pointed with his right hand at the small silver silhouette. "Looks like a fighter, coming in fast."

All their heads turned to follow as it neared, the captain rolling out and leveling off. "What is that?" he asked. All the pilots had served in the Israeli Air Force, and stared hard, trying to identify the unexpected jet.

The first officer had the best view.

"That jet has twin tails! I think it's a MiG-25!"

Grief watched as the jumbo jet changed heading and climbed out of his path. He'd kept his speed up to minimize exposure time to any twitchy air defense crews and now reached to slam down his landing gear handle, and then flaps. His throttles were still at idle, and he lowered the nose to burn off the final excess speed prior to the runway. The other plane had been landing from the opposite direction, so he knew he'd have a tailwind, and thus high touchdown speed. The tires had a limit, and he couldn't afford to have the rubber self-destruct during this landing. He flew low across several roads and fields, and then the barbed wire fence of the airport property flashed by underneath. The huge painted "08" on the runway flicked by below him as he flared, still going far too fast. He held the jet just off the ground, willing it to slow down. He reached with his left hand and grabbed the drag parachute handle to be ready.

The distance-to-go markers showed 5,000 feet remaining, and he was going to need all of it.

Now, he decided. He released the back pressure on the stick and let the jet fall the final meter to the runway, simultaneously opening his speed brake and moving the chute handle. The plane skittered along, heavy with forward inertia, and the nose jerked left and right as the cross-shaped drag chute unfurled and snapped open behind him. He tightened his fingers carefully on the brake lever, careful not to skid, squeezing harder and pulling back on the stick as he got it under control. The end of the long runway was approaching fast, but he'd judged it right, and he was at high taxiing speed as the runway ran out at a turnoff to the right. He pushed carefully on the right rudder pedal and the jet sluggishly responded, wheelbarrowing but staying in control.

Grief exhaled with satisfaction. *Now to park, fast.*

Ahead to his right, he saw multiple jets on a wide paved apron, with several massive hangars behind them. The nearest had its huge doors rolled open, and he could see aircraft on maintenance stands inside. He pointed his nose directly at the opening, and moved his throttles forward, asking his engines for one more favor. They responded with an increased whine, and he felt the push to hold max taxi speed.

The drag chute was yanking him sideways in the wind. He danced on the pedals, working rudder, nose wheel steering and brake to keep straight. Cutting diagonally across the pavement, he held speed as long as he could, then yanked the throttles to IDLE and hand-braked, hard. As the jet rolled into the relative darkness of the hangar, he steered into an open space between parked machinery and people, raised the finger lifts, chopped the throttles to OFF and stopped.

Safe, for the moment. Out of sight of prying eyes on the ground or satellites passing overhead.

Time to raise his hands, climb out of the cooling jet and convince the Israelis that what they needed to do now was to stage a crash.

8

Israeli Defense Forces Headquarters, Tel Aviv

Golda Meir was worried.

It had already been one of the most intense days of her long political career, one that had driven her to smoke continuously. The situation was as serious as she'd seen in her four years as Israel's prime minister. And it looked as though things might soon get drastically worse.

She took another long, deep drag on her unfiltered Chesterfield cigarette, her soft, wrinkled cheeks hollowing as she inhaled. In addition to a rapid, recent buildup of enemy troops along Israel's borders, Mossad agents in Syria had reported that the Soviets had brought in transport jets to evacuate their embassy families and nonessential personnel from Damascus. The last time that had happened had been just before the Six-Day War, seven years earlier.

She felt sick to her stomach with the seriousness of the threat to her country. *I need clarity!* she thought, as she sat in a high-backed chair in "the Pit," deep underground—the nation's war room.

Meir looked at the men surrounding her.

"Moshe—what do you recommend?"

Moshe Dayan was her defense minister, a lean, balding combat veteran who'd lost an eye in 1941 when a Vichy rifle bullet had shattered his binoculars, destroying his left eye socket. He habitually wore a black eye patch over the ugly wound.

"We're fine, Golda." An easy smile creased Dayan's face, the taut skin wrinkling around his good eye. "The Arabs are just posturing, pretending to be soldiers again." The Syrian and Egyptian armies had massed troops along the Golan Heights to the northeast and the Suez Canal to the southwest. "It's their standard autumn military exercise, undertaken when it's not so hot out for them. They'll rattle their swords, tell each other how brave they are and then go home." He snorted, showing a flash of crooked teeth. "Like always."

Then why do I feel this rising panic? Meir shook her head slowly. It was Yom Kippur Eve, the holiest day of the year, and her country was going quiet. Everyone would soon be home or in synagogue. Military staffing along the borders was minimal, and to call up the reserves now would come at a heavy political cost, especially with an election looming at month's end.

Her chief of staff, Dado Elazar, was watching her troubled face. Like all the other men in the room, he was military, but he'd learned to listen to her differing, civilian intuition. And she was the boss. He decided to offer an option.

"Even with the enemy buildup, Golda, our intelligence will give us at least a day's warning before any attack. But we could have a partial reserves call-up, just in case. And do it now, before everyone gets settled for Yom Kippur."

She looked away, picturing what that would mean. Young men and women pulled abruptly from their plans and their families, a confusing scramble to meet an uncertain threat. They'd done it back in May, in response to Egypt's spring maneuvers, and had suffered serious political damage from being unnecessarily alarmist.

She exhaled slowly, the smoke stinging her eyes and causing her to squint. *One day's notice, guaranteed. Okay. But everyone in government will be at home and unavailable.*

She made up her mind, and looked past Dayan to Elazar.

"No action for now, but I need special permission to be able to call up the reserves without the normal process." She raised her chin towards the man with the eye patch. "Just Moshe and myself to have complete authority."

Elazar looked around the room at the country's senior leadership and saw no objections. "I'll get a resolution typed up and signed."

Golda thought further. "And I need the Americans to clearly warn off the Soviets for us. Bad enough that Brezhnev is giving so many weapons to our enemies, but I definitely don't want any Russian soldiers or advisors on our borders. Get the request to Kissinger as soon as possible, through the US ambassador. What's this new one's name—Keating?"

Elazar nodded, reaching for the phone next to him, but just before he lifted the handset, it rang. He picked it up and Golda watched as her chief of staff's black eyebrows showed surprise, and then furrowed. As he asked several rapid-fire questions, the men near him eavesdropped, but she was too far away to hear.

"What is it, Dado?" she asked impatiently as he replaced the handset.

He looked at her and spoke for the whole room to hear, incredulity in his voice. "A Syrian MiG-25 reconnaissance jet has made an emergency landing at Lod airport!"

There was a hush as everyone assessed the significance. Golda, the lifelong politician, saw it first.

"Forget my last request! Dado, get Keating to come meet with me soon as possible!" She took a last deep drag, holding the smoke in her lungs as she stubbed the butt out in her full ashtray. When she spoke again, it streamed from her nose and mouth.

"And bring me the pilot!"

9

Israel Aircraft Industries Hangar 4, Lod Airport

"What the hell?"

The high-pitched whine of engines out on the ramp had sounded normal enough, but when unfamiliar brakes squealed loudly inside the hangar, the airframe technician pulled his head out of the Nesher aircraft's wheel well. He'd been replacing a hydraulic line in the Israeli-built fighter, but now wiped his hands hurriedly on his coveralls, jamming fingertips into his ears to block the deafening racket. He watched the pilot lean forward in the cockpit with the effort of final braking, make a couple of quick hand movements down out of sight, and then the engines wound down into silence. With no jet exhaust to support it, the plane's drag chute fell to the concrete floor at the hangar entrance. The technician stared in amazement.

The plane was huge, pale gray, and had a red star on the tail.

Like all Israelis, he'd served three years of compulsory military service, and immediately identified the jet as a MiG-25 Foxbat. He'd been working alone in the hangar, and now he backed rapidly to the red phone on the wall. As he grabbed the handset and impatiently waited for someone to pick up on the other end, he watched the MiG's canopy open.

A voice, in Hebrew. "Lod Airport Emergency Services, state the nature of your call."

After he urgently described the situation, the voice told him to stay clear and await the security team that had already been dispatched by the control tower. As he hung up, he could hear multiple sirens getting louder outside. There was the sound of braking, a clatter of boots and shouted voices, and armed men burst into the hangar. One of them cautiously approached the front of the MiG, and began yelling at the pilot in Russian.

With the canopy now fully open to the side, and his helmet visor rotated up, the pilot raised his hands.

The armed soldier yelled again, and the pilot answered. After a few seconds the soldier looked around, caught the technician's eye and waved him to approach. "Get a ladder up to the cockpit!"

This plane is taller than ours, the technician thought, and ran to the corner of the hangar where painters had been working, returning with their aluminum extension ladder. The soldier jerked his head towards the MiG, and the tech nervously maneuvered the paint-splattered ladder into place, clattering it against the curve of the unfamiliar fuselage, happy that it was just long enough. One further jerk of the soldier's head, and the tech retreated to a spot against the hangar wall, glad to be farther away.

Several soldiers moved to covering positions, as their leader yelled more instructions in Russian. The tech saw the pilot nod in response and then reach down, unstrapping. Grabbing the canopy rail, the Soviet pulled himself up until he was standing on the ejection seat and raised both hands again when the soldier yelled at him. A second soldier noisily climbed the ladder, quickly looked around the cockpit, then roughly turned the pilot left and right, inspecting the pressure suit. He looked down and nodded to his leader.

Checking for booby traps, the technician thought.

The soldier descended the ladder, swung his Uzi machine gun off his back to point up at the pilot, and waited.

Grief lowered his arms, turned and carefully climbed down the narrow ladder, clumsy in the stiff suit. As soon as his feet touched the hangar floor, the soldier grabbed him by the shoulder and forced him down onto his stomach. He turned his head inside his helmet, his cheek jammed against the padded inner lining. He felt his feet get kicked apart, and then hands moving through all his pockets, finding and removing the pistol that all Soviet fighter pilots carried. Satisfied, the soldier stepped back, and Grief saw the boots of the leader stop beside him. His Russian was terse and accented. *Moldovan Jew*, Grief thought.

"What is your name, and why did you land on Israeli soil?"

Grief answered loudly from his uncomfortable position. "Abramovich, Alexander Vasilyevich, Colonel in the Russian Air Forces, Honored Test Pilot of the USSR."

He paused, careful to pronounce the next words slowly and clearly to be sure the soldier understood the significance of his response.

"I have secrets of great value, am defecting to the United States of America, and I need to speak to your superiors immediately."

He added the phrase he'd prepared that he knew would get a response.

"And I am Jewish."

10

US Embassy, Tel Aviv

Ambassador Kenneth Keating almost missed connecting the dots.

He'd only been posted to Israel in August, and was just now getting comfortable navigating the people, the labyrinthine corridors with locked security areas and the underground listening rooms of this US embassy. His embassy. The urgent telephone summons from the Israeli chief of staff was highly unusual, and he'd hastily called his senior personnel into his upper-floor office for their suggestions before he responded to it.

His second secretary spoke first. "As we briefed you this morning, Ken, the Egyptians and the Syrians have unusually large numbers of troops massing along Israel's borders. Our satellites are seeing bigger numbers than for previous fall training exercises." He looked down, eyes wandering across the coffee cups and ashtrays as he thought. He looked back up at the ambassador and shrugged, offering his conclusion. "Meir wants Nixon to do something and will be asking you for help."

Keating nodded. He'd served in India during World War II, rising to brigadier general before going into politics and then serving as a New

York appeals judge. His recent time as Nixon's ambassador to India had taught him much about wielding US power abroad.

"Any guesses what she'll want?"

His second spoke again. "Most likely to have Kissinger warn off the Soviets. Ever since Sadat threw the Russians out of Egypt a year ago, they've been itching for increased influence in the Middle East. Meir believes that the Israeli Defense Forces can handle the Arabs themselves, but not if the Soviets become directly involved."

Keating turned and looked out his office window at the blue of the Mediterranean. He still wore his hair parted neatly down the middle, as he had since he was a teenager, and his fingers unconsciously ran through one side, then the other, stroking the rich thickness of it, now pure white.

His consular affairs chief was frowning. "Ken, we had someone come in unannounced this morning, a US Navy officer on vacation here, who urgently requested a secure line through to the head of Air Force Systems Command." His frown deepened. "He'd seen something he needed to report. He seemed pretty connected."

"You think it's related?"

"Possibly. He said something about an unusual contrail and potentially significant new air combat capability." He tipped his head to one side. "Might explain the urgency of the call from Prime Minister Meir. Maybe she knows whatever has happened has given her leverage, something we could use." He glanced at his watch. "The Navy guy may still be in the building."

Ken Keating's eyebrows went up, black under the white hair. "Bring him to me, ASAP."

Part of the embassy's purpose was to project American values abroad, and that included Ambassador Keating's official car. His Marine driver skillfully maneuvered the oversized black Ford LTD through Tel Aviv's narrow streets, as the ambassador and Kaz conferred in the back seat. The State Department had called Keating during their hasty meeting at the embassy and, on General Sam Phillips's insistence, strongly recommended that Kaz accompany Keating to talk with Prime Minister Meir.

"Tell me again why shooting down one of these airplanes is so important?" Keating said.

"There's nothing like the MiG-25 Foxbat in the world, sir. It's a high-speed intelligence-gathering platform, and it's also the main threat to shoot down our SR-71 reconnaissance Blackbirds. In fact, the new fighter that the Air Force is developing, the F-15, is being built purely to be able to counter it." He paused to make sure Keating understood. "The MiG-25 flies so high and fast that we haven't been able to touch it. If the Israelis found a way to knock one down, we need to know how. It would change our tactics globally."

Keating nodded while assessing the man next to him, dressed for a vacation in cotton slacks, loafers and a button-up short-sleeved shirt, but unquestionably a Navy commander.

They were driving to an address Keating hadn't recognized. He guessed it would be a Mossad safe house, bland from the outside but secure and fully wired for sound within. As the driver pulled up to a detached home on the outskirts of Tel Aviv, his suspicions were confirmed. A guard leaned into the car to check identification, then waved them through the gated entrance. A second guard held up his hand for the driver to park and stay put, as he opened the rear door for the ambassador and Kaz.

"Follow me, please."

Kaz glanced around as they walked across the small courtyard. A few other official-looking cars were tightly parked in the short driveway, including a Land Rover marked as "Lod Airport Security."

That's interesting.

The guard opened the door and led them down a tiled hall and into a side room, asking them to please sit and wait. His English was good, the Israeli accent thick. All the other doors in the hallway had been closed, and as the guard left, he closed their door behind him.

Both men stayed silent.

After several minutes, the door opened abruptly and a grandmotherly woman in a drab, faded dress and heavy shoes came in, followed by a balding man in fatigues, wearing a black eye patch. The two Americans rose to their feet, and the woman nodded at Keating. "Thank you, Ambassador, for coming on short notice." She looked at Kaz, holding his gaze for a moment. "Let's sit," she said. Her accent surprised Kaz—she spoke English like she came from the American Midwest.

An aide placed coffees in front of the four of them, and the prime minister pulled an ashtray close, lighting a cigarette. Meir took a long, deep drag, and spoke as she exhaled.

"Ambassador, I won't mince words. Israel is currently under serious threat. I'm certain your intelligence people have told you of the Arab forces that are massing along our borders. It is a grave time for my country, and we need our closest ally, the United States of America, to stand strong on our behalf."

She took another drag, glancing at Moshe Dayan, whose single eye was studying Kaz.

A small smile played on her lips. "I see you have not come alone today, Ambassador."

"Yes, Prime Minister, this is Kazimieras Zemeckis, detailed to my staff, here to advise me." Generally true, but no mention of military rank.

She looked closely at Kaz. "Zemeckis is often a Lithuanian Jewish name." She waited.

"Yes, ma'am, my parents emigrated to New York just before the war, and joined the Litvak Jewish community there."

She nodded, absorbing the information, then said, "Welcome to Israel."

She turned again to face Keating. "Ambassador, I request that you ask your president to speak directly with the Soviets, with Brezhnev, and warn him not to interfere with what the Arabs are up to this time." She paused for effect. "Superpower to superpower."

Keating made a point of checking his watch. "It is just eight a.m. now in Washington, Prime Minister. I will pass your message on as soon as I get back to the embassy. I am certain Mr. Nixon will fully understand your situation and comply to the best of his ability as President of the United States."

Meir nodded. "That is all that I can ask. Thank you." She looked at Moshe Dayan. His turn.

Dayan spoke to Kaz. "As a man who wears an eye patch, I sometimes notice things others might not. Do you mind if I ask how you lost your left eye?"

Kaz shrugged. "It was in an accident, sir, but fortunately the doctors could rebuild my eye socket, and it holds this glass eye well in place." During his long convalescence he'd read about Moshe Dayan, and he knew that the damage to Dayan's eye had been much more severe. "I'm sorry they couldn't do the same for you."

Dayan's turn to shrug, and his right lip raised in a crooked smile. "It was a long time ago, and my new wife says the patch makes me look more dashing." The smile faded, and he tipped his head slightly. "Commander, I need to ask, what is your security clearance level?" His use of Kaz's rank made clear that Israeli intelligence had done their homework when the US embassy had added him to the list of meeting attendees.

Kaz held his gaze, eyeball to eyeball. "Top secret, sir, same as the ambassador."

Dayan looked back to Golda Meir. She stubbed out her cigarette, her expression thoughtful.

"I have one other key request of your president, Mr. Ambassador," she said to Keating. "If the Arabs do decide to attack this time, Israel will need rapid resupply. Our armaments are insufficient for any sort of extended combat, especially on two fronts." She raised her shoulders slightly. "We are very small, and America is very big."

When Keating began to reply, she held up a nicotine-stained hand to stop him. "I am not simply asking. I have something of great value to your country. Please tell President Nixon that I am willing to trade a unique asset, if it comes to that."

Golda Meir waited.

Kaz got what she meant, and he sat back abruptly.

Meir glanced at Kaz, then back at Keating, watching for him to figure it out, almost smiling.

When Keating didn't respond, she ended the meeting. "Minister Dayan and I must get back to our cabinet meetings, and the urgent business of defending our country. Thank you, Ambassador, for coming today. And please let us know as soon as you hear back from my friend, Mr. Nixon."

Dayan was already up and moving to open the door as Meir rose, nodded at both Americans and walked out. Dayan smiled at them both, teeth showing, as he closed the door.

As soon as they were back in the security of their car, Keating turned to Kaz. "What did she mean, 'something of great value'? It looked to me like maybe you understood."

Kaz pointed back at the parked Land Rover as they drove out through the gate. "That Soviet jet didn't crash. It *landed*! I was puzzled as to why I hadn't seen a flash of missile impact or any smoke trail as the jet fell. I just figured it had somehow been disabled without burning." He shook his head. "But I didn't see any smoke rising from a crash site either. That much fuel and metal hitting the land or the water should have exploded on impact."

He met Keating's eyes. "Those two weren't behaving like people begging for a big favor. It was more like they were working from a position of strength. I saw that Lod airport truck parked outside and so it clicked. I think that MiG-25 is somewhere out of sight at the Lod airport, and"—he looked back at the building they had just left—"its pilot is inside that safe house."

11

Soviet Air Forces Headquarters, Moscow

Sitting at his broad mahogany desk, Pavel Stepanovich Kutakhov, Marshal of Aviation, Great Patriotic War fighter ace and commander of the Soviet Air Forces, held the two flimsy pieces of paper in his thick hands, his brooding eyes flicking between them.

One of his MiG-25s was missing over Israel. The captain of a destroyer in the Mediterranean had radioed an urgently encoded message describing what he'd seen, and the groundcrew commander at the Syrian air base had sent an encrypted telex an hour later, per strict procedures, to report that a fighter aircraft hadn't returned.

How could this have happened?

Kutakhov felt a wave of sadness, and anger, as he always did when an airplane crashed. Far worse, in this case, because the jet was a classified asset.

What to do first? He looked out his window at Moscow's gray October sky. *Confirmation*, he decided.

The Israeli embassy in Moscow had been sitting empty since the Soviet Union had severed ties with the country at the end of the 1967

Middle East war, so approaching the Jews directly was going to be tricky, and political. *Better to get the truth from an independent source.*

Kutakhov picked up his phone handset and dialed the commander of the Zenit spy satellite fleet. He needed detailed imagery of the potential crash area, and fast, to see what had happened. If the MiG-25 had splashed into the water, the resulting oil slick and debris field would dissipate quickly; if it had struck land, the Israelis would be stripping the site already.

The Zenit satellites were as simple as the Soviets could make them. Tough spheres, two and a half meters across, weighing a little over two tons, they housed superb cameras and lenses, and orbited the Earth for up to two weeks at a time. From an altitude of two or three hundred kilometers, they could photograph details on the ground as small as one meter. Plenty accurate to identify crash site debris.

The commander told Kutakhov that a Zenit-2M had launched two days ago and was due for deorbit in four days. A more modern, lower-altitude Zenit-4MK was being prepared for launch the next day, and would return with its images in a week.

Too slow!

When he pushed for more, he was relieved to hear that a third Zenit-4MK had launched from the Plesetsk Cosmodrome nearly two weeks previously, had recently overflown Israel and was now being prepared for deorbit. He requested expedited processing of the imagery to be delivered to him personally, and hung up, satisfied.

His next call was to his counterpart at the KGB. Perhaps their spies in Israel had information, or could access any reported crash sites? If the pilot had ejected, or there was salvageable debris from the crash, rapid Soviet action on location would be critical. When the spymaster picked up, Kutakhov explained what he wanted, passed on the estimated crash location and promised immediate updates to the KGB as information became available.

Kutakhov hung up, took a deep breath and let it out slowly before he made the least desirable call.

Through the earpiece he could hear the phone ringing at the desk of his *zampolit*—the top political officer assigned to the Soviet Air Forces. When the officer brusquely answered, Kutakhov quickly summarized the news, outlined his actions so far and gave his estimation of the fallout from the potential scenarios. The voice on the other end asked the marshal to repeat several points, often interrupting him to take the time he needed to make notes. More probing questions carried a strong undercurrent of disappointment that the commander of the Soviet Air Forces had allowed such a thing to happen. After the officer extracted a clear promise from Kutakhov to pass on all significant new information as it arrived, he hung up without a goodbye. Just a click, then the dial tone.

Kutakhov replaced the handset in its cradle, shaking his head. This was delicate, and there were going to be far too many meetings, with too many self-important fingers in the pie.

Just before he slipped the two pages back into their top-secret folder, he paused to imagine what the MiG pilot must have experienced. Kutakhov loved flying, and still maintained pilot currency with weekly flights in the two-seat L-39s at nearby Ramenskoye airfield. Had the death been instantaneous, like the deaths of so many of his squadron friends in the war? Had the pilot somehow survived ejection at such great speed and altitude, and landed alive? Was he now cruelly injured and hiding in the dry, scrubby hills of the Israeli near desert, or floating in the sea? Or had he been taken prisoner, and was about to undergo the worst the Mossad could inflict, trying to wring the secrets of the MiG-25 and Soviet flying doctrine from him?

Death, he decided. *I hope it was a quick death.*

Kutakhov closed and resealed the folder and moved on to the next emergency in his inbox.

12

Mossad Safe House, Tel Aviv

The tone of the voice was gentle, conversational. "Tell me again, Colonel Abramovich. Why did you choose to land your aircraft at Lod airport?"

Grief looked calmly at his questioner, a smiling, soft-spoken man, lean and relaxed in casual civilian clothes. *My interrogator*, he corrected. *Don't let his friendly manner disarm you.* Grief repeated what he'd told each increasingly senior Israeli official who'd asked.

"I'm a Jew who would like to defect to the United States of America, and I offer the MiG-25 and the knowledge inside my head in exchange."

The cigarettes and water that had been offered to Grief lay untouched on the table in what both men recognized as a careful courtship dance.

"But why the United States?" The interrogator smiled more widely and waved his hand in a sweeping gesture. "Israel is a beautiful new country and welcomes Soviet Jews." His Russian was unaccented and flawless.

Grief smiled tightly back. "America calls itself the land of opportunity. We hear that, even in Moscow." He shrugged. "They have more to offer a man with my skills. I want a new life there."

The soldiers at Lod airport had methodically stripped him down to his underwear and socks, making certain he was wearing no weapons or booby traps. They'd roughly dressed him in ill-fitting coveralls, handcuffed and hooded him before loading him into a truck. The hood and cuffs had only come off when he'd gotten to this room.

"A new life," the Mossad interrogator repeated. "What do you want in that new life?"

Grief raised his chin. "What do I want?" He allowed a small smile to tug the corners of his mouth. "Since I was a small boy, I've simply wanted to fly. To fly the best airplanes in the world. Our Soviet planes have strengths, but they are crude copies built by unimaginative bureaucrats." He lifted his hands. "I am a pilot to my core. I have much to offer, and America builds the best planes."

The Mossad interrogator nodded, thinking, *Maybe some honesty there, but I don't like volunteer defectors.* He switched tack.

"What of your family, Alexander? May I call you Alexander?"

Grief lost the smile. "My parents are long dead. I was their only child, and I am single."

A slow nod. The interrogator had checked and there was no mark from a wedding ring on his hand. "But what of Russia? What of the Soviet Union, your homeland?"

Grief exhaled, shaking his head slightly. "I am deeply tired of all the political meddling in Air Forces matters, of incompetence getting rewarded, of uncomprehending centralized power making repeated bad decisions." Looking directly at the Mossad man, he spoke with sudden heat. "I've had a lifetime of it and now I want better."

The Israeli raised his eyebrows. "America has its problems too. Their president is being investigated for corruption and illegal actions."

The Russian snorted. "All politicians are corrupt. At least in America he can *be* investigated."

A shift. "What do you know for sure of America, Alexander?"

Grief nodded, then dropped his eyes to the table as he said, "I was selected as a pilot to be at the Paris Air Show back in June. For the first time I saw our planes sitting right next to theirs. Ours were so dumpy in comparison, like Zolushka's ugly stepsisters." He shook his head. "I watched an American Navy pilot fly his F-14 in an amazing display and saw their new F-15 and F-16 mock-ups. And I had to watch as our ham-fisted incompetents crashed a beautiful new Tu-144, killing not just themselves but some people on the ground, there in front of everyone."

Keep him heated. A concerned frown. "Why did it crash?"

"They'd modified the Tupolev's flight control laws without ever properly testing the result, in a vain effort to get better performance. They let political pressure from Moscow tell them what to do with an airplane!" Grief's indignation was real. "It changed the response of the forward canard, and the pitch rate pulled them into a deep stall with not enough altitude to recover." He paused, taking the time to gather himself. "I knew Kozlov, the pilot, of course. He pulled so hard trying to recover that it tore the left wing off. Idiocy, in front of the world. I want to be done with it."

Grief shifted in his chair, suddenly aware he needed to gain back some control.

"How are you staging the crash of my jet so it fools Moscow?"

The Mossad man tipped his head. "We're taking care of it. Your flight path was far enough off the coast that we chose a crash at sea. There are Israeli ships out there now, circling an oil slick, and they'll find some small burned actual pieces of your jet that we can offer to Moscow." He smiled. "It's over a thousand meters deep, and we control our waters."

Grief nodded. A crash at sea made sense; he would have done the same. Too many spies on the land.

He waited.

"What of money, Alexander? Do you want to be a rich man?"

Grief smiled, this time broadly. "The Americans dropped pamphlets in Korea, offering fifty thousand dollars to any pilot who would bring them a MiG-15. All Soviet pilots know of this. That was over twenty years ago, and I have just delivered a far more important jet. I'm not interested in being wealthy. But I'm certain I will be well taken care of."

"And what about your religion? The United States is not as openly anti-Semitic as your Soviet masters, but trust me, it's no walk in the park there for a Jew with your ambitions."

"With the knowledge I have in my head to trade, and the opportunity to fly their planes, I'm willing to risk it," Grief said.

The Israeli frowned. "It will not be easy, convincing my Israeli masters to let you go to the Americans. It will take time, and will need approval at the highest level."

Grief nodded, once. "I know."

But that wasn't all he knew. He had chosen the timing of his defection carefully.

He'd be going to America soon. Israel's hand was about to be forced.

In the adjoining room, seated in chairs side by side, Golda Meir and Moshe Dayan watched the interrogation through mirrored glass. The men's voices sounded distorted coming through the wall-mounted speaker, so even though both politicians had been raised by Russian-speaking parents, they found the conversation somewhat hard to understand. But the exact words didn't matter: they were listening primarily to get a feel for the Russian pilot's emotions and authenticity. Behind the two of them, an interpreter quietly murmured exactly what was being said.

After several minutes, Golda had made up her mind, and turned to Dayan.

"What do you think, Moshe?"

Dayan turned towards her, listened for several more seconds, and then nodded.

"He tells a convincing story. I wouldn't trust him for a long time yet, but that can be dealt with. The hard facts are that he has brought us an unparalleled asset, and undoubtedly has useful intelligence to reveal."

She kept looking at him, the speaker noise rising and falling, the interpreter droning.

"Do you believe he's Jewish?"

Dayan shrugged. "I'm a pragmatist, Golda. He says his last name is Abramovich, and pronounces it like a Russian Jew would. But under Stalin's purges and Khrushchev and Brezhnev's alignment with the Arabs, there wouldn't have been much room in the Soviet Union for him to be all that Jewish, especially as a military pilot." He smiled a little. "If I were him, I would have said I was Jewish too. Why not?"

Golda sighed. She didn't disagree. "He and his plane are valuable to us for several reasons. We already are home to so many expatriate Russian Jews, he'd soon be comfortable here if he is indeed a Jew. But like so many, he wants to go to America."

She turned and looked back through the thick glass at the balding Russian. She saw a medium-sized man, lean, with a cleft chin and a wide, feminine mouth. An unremarkable man in a pivotal circumstance.

"And sending him there may do Israel the most good."

13

Tel Aviv Beach, Israel

Kaz strode quickly along the Tel Aviv seaside boardwalk, deep in thought. He'd decided to cover the mile from the embassy to the Hilton on foot, needing time to think after another briefing with General Phillips in Washington, and drafting a summary letter with the ambassador for President Nixon. As he walked, he dodged the casually strolling couples and teenagers who were heading to spend Yom Kippur Eve at the beach.

He exited the tenth-floor elevator in the Hilton, walked down the blue-carpeted hallway and knocked on the matching blue door. He heard Laura's muffled "Just a minute," watched as the peephole briefly darkened, and then came the rattling of chains and clunking as she pulled the door open. She had changed into jeans and a T-shirt, her backlit hair an unruly cloud in the humidity.

"You were gone a long time," she said.

He nodded. "Yeah, I'm really sorry, Laura, it got way more complicated than I expected." He stepped inside and hugged and kissed her, kicking the door closed behind him. "Did you eat lunch?"

"I ordered us some room service, but when it hit two, I ate." She disentangled herself and pointed at the balcony. "It's still out there."

"Great, thanks," Kaz said, walking across the room and out into the afternoon sun. He sat and poured himself a cold coffee from the pot on the small table.

"Should I order some fresh?"

Laura shook her head, taking the seat facing him. "Tell me what happened!"

Kaz filled her in between sips of coffee and bites of dried-out club sandwich.

"You met Golda Meir? Holy cow! What's she like?"

"She looks like any other Jewish grandmother, right down to the housedress and cardigan sweater, but she's as whip smart as you'd expect, and is clearly accustomed to wielding power." He took a bite and spoke around the mouthful. "And keeping secrets."

He met Laura's warm, wide-set brown eyes. She was a civilian geologist with NASA, an expert in the samples the Apollo crews had brought back from the Moon. "I can't tell you everything that was discussed, because of the military security clearance levels."

Laura nodded. "Of course. But can you tell me what's going to happen next, with us at least?"

Kaz frowned, took a cold sip and set the coffee cup down. "Not something I want to happen, but I don't see any way around it. I've been asked by Washington to stay here to help clear this up. It's likely going to take several days." He shrugged regretfully. "Sorry, Laura, but you're going to have to fly home tomorrow night without me."

"Yeah, I was figuring that might happen." She smiled at him. "The price I pay for dating the Six Million Dollar Man." When they'd watched the TV movie together in Texas, she'd teased him about being another ex-astronaut who'd also lost an eye in a flying accident. She looked out at the sun across the water. "Still have time for the pool, or the beach?"

Ambassador Keating had promised to contact him as soon as there were any developments, but otherwise he was free. He could leave word with the front desk as to where they could find him.

He looked at her and smiled. “Sure! And how about I help you back into your bikini first?”

14

Yom Kippur, October 6, 1973

Golda Meir's phone rang shrilly by her bedside. As usual, at the Sabbath, she had stayed at her three-room flat on Baron Hirsch Street Row in Ramat Aviv. Since it was Yom Kippur, she had eaten before sunset with her son's family at his place next door, and then stayed up late talking with her daughter. Swearing, she fumbled in the dark for the handset, and blinked as she clicked on the small bedside light.

"Yes?"

"Golda, I am very sorry to waken you so early, but I have urgent news." General Yisrael Leor, her senior military aide, paused for a moment to make sure she was fully awake.

She pulled herself to a half-sitting position on her pillow, feeling a rising dread. "Go ahead, General, I am listening."

"We have authoritative intelligence that the Arabs will attack today, at sunset, invading our country in an act of war."

"Authoritative? What's the source?"

"Zvi has been talking at length with the Angel. He is convinced." Zvi Zamir was the director of Mossad, Israel's national intelligence agency.

Golda shook her head to try to clear it. The effects of the radiation treatment she was secretly receiving for her spreading lymphatic cancer were like a constant fog. "Isn't Zvi in Paris?"

"He was, but he flew to London last night to meet the source in person."

The source, code name Angel, was Ashraf Marwan, the playboy son-in-law of former Egyptian president Gamal Abdel Nasser. A very connected Mossad-paid informant who had passed on valuable information several times before.

Golda glanced at her window, trying to gather her thoughts, seeing only darkness. "What time is it?"

"It's four a.m., Golda."

She took a deep breath and coughed involuntarily. *Zvi Zamir is certain it will be war, so that's enough,* she thought. *Time for action.*

"Call all senior staff to a meeting at my office. I'll need a car here in forty-five minutes to take me there. Call up reserves and mobilize forces, urgently. Contact Ambassador Dinitz and get him on a plane to the US ASAP—I need him face-to-face with the Americans. Tell Zvi I want him back here from London. And get the US ambassador—Keating—and his advisor back in to see me as soon as he wakes up."

"Yes, Prime Minister."

Golda quickly considered the probable reactions of the military men who advised and surrounded her. The men she counted on, and ultimately commanded.

"And, Yisrael, this is of utmost importance: strongly reiterate to everyone you talk to that we must *not* strike first. It will be tempting, but the Angel has been wrong before, and we cannot be seen as the aggressor in this, no matter what. American support will depend on it."

General Leor read back her instructions, and they ended the call.

Meir pulled the thin sheet down, welcoming the still, warm air of the lingering night on her aching, 75-year-old legs. She painfully rolled onto one hip and sat up on the side of her bed, rested a moment, then pushed with both arms until she was standing unsteadily on her bare feet. A wave of nausea passed over her.

The day had begun.

15

Prime Minister's Office, Tel Aviv

I'm in a ghost town, Kaz thought.

A phone call from the embassy had awoken him early, and the ambassador's car had swung by to pick him up at the Hilton 20 minutes later. Tucked into the corner of the driver's windshield was a large placard in Hebrew and English, permitting the car to be driven on the deserted streets of Tel Aviv on the country's holiest day, Yom Kippur.

Inside the sedan were Ambassador Keating in the back seat with Kaz, and his deputy, Nicholas Veliotes, sitting up front with the driver. For a time all three of them sat in silence, looking out at the spectacle of an almost empty city, all shops closed and dark, with only a few people visible, walking to synagogue.

Keating spoke. "Nick, say again what the Israelis told you on the phone?"

"They said there'd been a significant intelligence development overnight, and that the prime minister needed to talk with you, urgently." He nodded at Kaz. "They asked for Commander Zemeckis to be there as well."

Keating pondered that. "Any guesses as to what the intel might be?"

Veliotes figured the ambassador, though new, should be able to guess on his own, but as a career diplomat he also knew to appear deferential, always, to the latest man from Washington.

"The Israelis have extensive listening posts and wiretaps, deep into Syria and Egypt. Perhaps they've heard something definitive about an attack. But with it being the Highest Holy Day here, and with the fasting and other constraints of Ramadan on the Arab side, it's unlikely there will be any military action today." It was the tenth day of the Muslim month of Ramadan, a time for believers to focus on mercy and charity. *A very unlikely time to start a war*, Veliotes thought.

Kaz said, "Something must have tripped a wire. Otherwise, she wouldn't have called us in so early on this of all days. And it must involve that MiG-25, or she wouldn't have asked for me."

Keating nodded. "We'll find out soon enough." He peered over Veliotes's shoulder, through the windshield. "One advantage of Yom Kippur, we've made great time."

The car pulled up in front of a building that looked as though it belonged in nineteenth-century central Europe. As Kaz got out, he stopped to look at its dappled, light-gray stucco walls, partially obscured by thick ivy and capped with a red slate roof. The trim was cream colored with pale-green shutters. Ornate cast-iron railings with the Israeli menorah emblem enclosed a small, buttressed balcony on the second floor, flanked by porthole windows. Veliotes saw him staring.

"It was built by German Christian Templars in 1930." He smiled indulgently. "Israel has a complicated history."

Kaz spotted two men smoking and talking vehemently on the small balcony, and the silhouettes of several more within. A young soldier noted the US flags on the embassy car, checked the men's passports against a list on his clipboard and waved them through the single arched doorway.

Inside was mayhem.

As deputy ambassador, Veliotes had been in the building several times, and led them through the crush of people and up a narrow side staircase, into an equally crowded second-floor conference room. As soon as definitive word of impending war had come from the head of the Mossad, General Dado Elazar had activated the telephone tree connecting all Israeli Defense Forces commanding officers. The room's long central table was surrounded by angry-sounding and largely unshaven men, most in hastily donned fatigues. Keating and Kaz squeezed into a spot by a curtained window while Veliotes threaded his way towards the prime minister's office door, at the far end of the room.

A large silver coffee urn had been set up near them, and Kaz went over to fill two Styrofoam cups, scanning the big corkboard on the wall beside him. A young woman was neatly thumbtacking a fresh slip of paper to it, adding to a column already in place. On the left side of the board was a map of the region, with a thicket of symbols and labels, all in Hebrew, tacked along the Egyptian and Syrian borders: Golan Heights to the northeast, Sinai Desert and Suez Canal to the southwest. Israel was a small, narrow country squeezed between Jordan and the sea. *Tough to defend*, Kaz thought.

Everyone was smoking, and a yellow-gray haze filled the room. Kaz turned back to the ambassador, eye stinging, grateful for the slight flow of fresh air coming through the open window. He handed him a coffee, then had to raise his voice to ask, "Do you read Hebrew?"

Keating shook his head. "I've learned the alphabet, but there wasn't time for language school before Nixon posted me here in August." He nodded towards his deputy, who was speaking with someone through the partially opened door. "Nick, of course, is fluent." He stared at the other men. "I wish I knew what they were saying."

Kaz took a sip of coffee, which was strong and extra hot. Occasional snippets of English punctuated the rapid-fire conversations around them, but not enough for him to follow. But the tone was urgent, opinionated—these were leaders trying to convince each other and themselves what actions they should take, what orders they needed to give.

Veliotes beckoned from the far door. Time to meet Prime Minister Meir again.

She was seated behind a square brown desk, whose top was glass-covered and darkly reflected her somber expression. She looked up as the men came in.

"Mr. Ambassador, thank you for coming on such short notice." Meir nodded at Veliotes and Kaz, then met Keating's eyes. "I think you know most everyone here."

The small office had a simple leather sofa and chair for visitors, but all the men in the room were standing. Indicating each one with a small thrust of her chin, Meir said, "Mordechai and Avraham, my advisors, and Abba Eban, my minister of foreign affairs." The men nodded at each other. *All civilians*, Kaz noted. Standing beside Meir in the space behind her desk was a bulky man with heavy-rimmed glasses, a trim mustache and a comb-over. "And your opposite number, my ambassador to the United States, Simcha Dinitz."

Keating and Dinitz had met in the course of their duties, and nodded at each other, Dinitz blinking behind the thick lenses, his forehead deeply creased in concern.

Meir said, "Let me get straight to the point, Mr. Ambassador. Our intelligence operatives are certain that the Egyptian and Syrian armies are going to simultaneously attack Israel at sundown today." The news was a bombshell, and she held Keating's gaze. "We have confirmation from multiple sources. As of this morning, my country is readying for imminent war."

Keating's mouth hung open. Nick Veliotes's eyes went round behind his glasses.

Meir tipped her chin towards the closed door. "My military advisors want to attack now, while we still have an advantage." She glanced at the pack of cigarettes on the desktop, next to the full ashtray, but didn't reach for it. "Preemptive action was key in minimizing our loss of life and swiftly winning the war in 1967." She let the words hang.

Keating began to speak, but Meir raised a hand to stop him, and then retrieved and lit another cigarette. As she drew the smoke into her lungs, the hot red flare of flame lit the deep bags under her squinting eyes. After she exhaled, she said, "But I have overruled them. I want to make this perfectly clear, to your president and to the world. The Arabs are the aggressors here, and Israel will not strike first. Those orders have already gone out."

Keating nodded. "Understood."

Kaz was rapidly analyzing the situation. *Was the Soviet's MiG-25 defection somehow part of this?*

"This morning I have asked the families living in the Golan Heights to bring their children southward, to safety." She glanced at the thin watch on her puffy wrist. "And even though it is Yom Kippur, our holiest Day of Atonement, word is being spread in the synagogues to call up the reserves." She slowly shook her head, clearly loathing the necessity. "I am tearing young men away from their families on our most sacred day, and many of them are likely to be killed."

She pointed her cigarette at her watch. "But there is a slim chance that it is not too late to avoid this war. In Washington it is just 3:45 a.m. I need you, please, to send an urgent message to your president and Mr. Kissinger and ask them to try and talk the Arabs out of their folly. To pull every string they can to avoid unnecessary bloodshed. To please use their hotline to the Soviets to persuade them also to apply immediate pressure on Syria and Egypt."

A small, tired smile crossed her face. "But you can't be a Jew without being a realist. War is probably inevitable, and we *will* fight to defend ourselves, and our homeland. This battle, which we did not start, will go poorly for the Arab aggressors."

Kaz heard the steel in her voice.

She turned her gaze to Veliotes. "Egypt's Sadat is behind this aggression. He wants battle—he needs it—to try and regain the territory and honor his country lost in 1967, and to tilt the playing field of power in the Middle East." She took a last drag, and stubbed out the butt, adding it to the mound in the ashtray. "In the north, Assad is mostly hungry for territory, and the tactical advantage of Syria controlling the Golan Heights."

She looked back at Keating. "What this all means is that the war is likely to be protracted. As I told you yesterday, Israel can protect herself for now, but very soon we will need more weapons. More surface-to-air missiles, more Sidewinders, and more jet fighters. Even more tanks." Her eyes closed as the horrific image of a burning tank, with young Israelis inside, flashed through her mind. She shook her head to clear it.

"We are America's strongest ally in this part of the world, and Mr. Kissinger will understand that resupplying Israel is a good plan. But our oil-rich neighbors undoubtedly will use this excuse to restrict the world's oil supply and heighten their power." She took a deep breath, then had to stifle a cough. "I know I am asking a lot, and there will be those in the US who oppose the idea of helping us."

For the first time, she looked directly at Kaz. "This is why I asked Commander Zemeckis to join us. We have something of great military significance to offer in return, as I also hinted yesterday." She quickly summarized details of the MiG-25 pilot's defection the day before, and that they had staged a crash to allay Soviet suspicion.

Meir sounded rueful. "My Air Force generals are yelling at me, because they want to take that plane to pieces and learn everything about it."

I bet that's already happened, Kaz guessed.

"But please make this clear to your president, and your Air Force. I am willing to hand a Soviet MiG-25, and the senior test pilot that defected with it, to you on a platter." Her expression was deadly serious. "I need that resupply to begin immediately."

Did she say the defector was a senior test pilot? Could she have that right?

She held his gaze for a few seconds for emphasis, and then sat back, lighting another cigarette. Glancing at Ambassador Dinitz beside her, she said, "Simcha will be on the next plane out of Lod to Washington, to be able to pass all this directly to Mr. Kissinger, and to be our main point of contact there throughout the war. But I urgently need you to please summarize our conversation for your president, and let him know I am willing to talk directly if he wants." The haze of the new smoke rose around her head, Dinitz squinting resignedly behind his glasses. "Are there any questions?"

Keating shook his head no, but Kaz had a thought, and spoke up.

"Could I ask Ambassador Dinitz for a small favor?"

16

US Embassy, Tel Aviv

- S E C R E T -

FLASH
061033Z OCT 73
FM AMEMBASSY TEL AVIV
TO SECSTATE WASHDC FLASH 9988
SUBJECT: GOI CONCERN ABOUT POSSIBLE SYRIAN AND EGYPTIAN ATTACK TODAY

1. AT PRIME MINISTER'S URGENT REQUEST, I MET WITH HER AT HER TEL AVIV OFFICE THIS MORNING AT 09:45. I WAS ACCOMPANIED BY DCM, USN CDR ZEMECKIS, AMB DINITZ, MORDECHAI GAZIT OF PM'S OFFICE AND AVRAHAM KIDRON, DIRGEN MFA EBAN ALSO PRESENT.
2. MRS MEIR INITIATED CONVERSATION BY NOTING THAT THE SYRIAN AND EGYPTIAN SITUATION HAD BECOME VERY SERIOUS WITHIN THE LAST 12 HOURS. ISRAEL HAS "CONFIRMATION FROM MULTIPLE SOURCES" THAT SYRIA AND

EGYPT ARE PLANNING A COORDINATED ATTACK AGAINST ISRAEL TODAY AT SUNDOWN. AS A RESULT, ISRAEL IS "READYING FOR IMMINENT WAR."

3. IN VIEW OF THE FOREGOING, SAID MRS. MEIR, ISRAEL WANTED THE URGENT HELP OF THE US IN TRYING TO HEAD OFF HOSTILITIES. SHE ASKED IF WE WOULD PASS ON TO THE SOVIETS AND EGYPTIANS, ASAP, THAT ISRAEL IS NOT PLANNING A PREEMPTIVE ATTACK ON SYRIA OR EGYPT. IT IS DEPLOYING ITS FORCES TO PROTECT ITSELF IN CASE OF ATTACK AND, ON A CONTINGENCY BASIS, IS CALLING UP RESERVES.

4. MRS. MEIR URGENTLY REQUESTS US MILITARY RESUPPLY SOONEST. SHE IS WILLING TO TRADE RARE ASSET OF A RECENTLY DEFECTED SOVIET PILOT AND MIG-25 FOXBAT FOR EXPEDITED SHIPMENT.

5. AMB. DINITZ WILL LEAVE FOR WASHINGTON ON FIRST AVAILABLE PLANE. HE SHOULD BE THERE WITH RESUPPLY DETAILS TOMORROW AT LATEST.

6. IF POSSIBLE, I WOULD LIKE TO GIVE SOME KIND OF REPLY TO PM WITHIN NEXT FEW HOURS.

KEATING

BT

- S E C R E T -

17

Waldorf Astoria Hotel, New York

The hotel room door slammed open.

"Time to get up, sir, there's going to be war!" Henry Kissinger's assistant, Joe Sisco, fumbled along the wall in the dark for the light switch and flipped it on.

The United States Secretary of State, squinting at the sudden light, reached blindly towards his bedside table and retrieved his glasses. He grabbed a second pillow and propped himself to a sitting position, pulling his knees up in front of him as a makeshift desk, and reached out wordlessly for the folder Sisco was holding. Opening it on his knees, Kissinger read the flash message, tracing each line of the flimsy teletyped page with a blunt finger. Without moving, his gaze still on the paper, he thought for a full 45 seconds, then raised his head.

"Is Ambassador Dobrynin still here in the hotel, Joe?"

Sisco nodded. The United Nations Security Council had been meeting, and the Soviet ambassador had also stayed in the Waldorf, a short limo ride to UN headquarters.

"Yep, I already asked the front desk. He's planning to head back to Washington today."

"Please go knock on his door, apologize for the early hour, and ask him to meet me in our conference room as soon as he can."

Kissinger turned and peered at the bedside clock and frowned. Lunchtime in Israel. Afternoon in Moscow. The message had said the Arab attack would come at sunset.

"I'll be there making phone calls as soon as I get dressed."

18

North of Cairo, Egypt

At his official residence on the edge of the Nile, Anwar Sadat had chosen his outfit carefully. Despite being the elected, civilian president of Egypt, he'd decided that today of all days called for a military uniform. And not a formal dress uniform, with its dark colors and peaked cap—this was a time to dress like a fighting soldier. His sand-colored fatigues carried the epaulets with the gold laurel and curved swords of the supreme commander of Egypt's armed forces, and on his chest were three rows of ribbons proclaiming his accumulated bravery. He smiled wryly. A long time since his cadet days at the Royal Military Academy. And his time in a British jail.

His wife, Jehan, worriedly kissed him and squeezed his arm as he prepared to leave the house. She'd watched the accumulating strain on her husband's face since he'd warned the Soviets a few days earlier, to when he'd briefed his full cabinet in secret just yesterday. Years of preparation, all leading to this day.

Sadat's car and driver were waiting outside to take him to Center Ten, the Egyptian Army central headquarters. He'd already passed word through military command that the men could break their Ramadan fast and eat. They would need their strength.

He had chosen the name of the operation carefully: Badr. A homage to the historic battle in 624 where Muhammad and his young Muslim army had defeated the Quraysh. Auspiciously, also during Ramadan.

As the armored car entered the ancient and congested city streets of Cairo, Sadat checked his watch: ten minutes to two. A thought occurred to him, and he pushed the small button on his car door to roll down the plate glass side window. Over the purr of the car's engine, he could make out a low rumbling. The distant, deep-throated roar of many jets in full afterburner, taking off and maneuvering over the city, getting into proper formation to attack the Israeli fortifications along the Suez Canal. What the Jews called their Bar Lev Line, a visible, persistent insult since the war of 1967.

Sadat closed the window and smiled. He and the generals had planned and practiced for years, conducting exercises aimed at success today. Egypt's heavily armed forces were massed in position, with deep reserves of Soviet-made tanks, artillery and surface-to-air missiles. And they had several tricks up their sleeve that were going to stun the hated Jews. After a lifetime of revolution, gathering of power, political maneuvers and meticulous preparation, he had brought the country to the brink of war. A war they would win.

Operation Badr was about to begin.

19

The Hilton Hotel, Tel Aviv

Laura's suitcase was open on the bed, and Kaz was at the closet, pulling her dresses off the hangers. She'd bought several souvenirs and was trying to hurriedly fit the more fragile items in so they wouldn't get broken in transit.

"Do you know what sort of plane I'm flying on?"

Kaz walked over and laid the bundle of clothes next to the suitcase. "Ambassador Dinitz didn't say. But my guess is a 707-320. Their Air Force has them, and so does El Al. They've got the range to make it nonstop to Washington."

Laura picked up her holiday dresses and laid them flat across the full suitcase, tucking them in around the edges. "We didn't have enough days for me to wear them all," she said, mostly to herself. She flipped the lid into place and Kaz helped her pull on the heavy zipper. She asked, "Where do I get the info to make the flight connection to Houston?"

"As soon as you're safely on your way, I'm going to head back to the embassy and call General Phillips. He'll confirm that someone is there to meet you when you land, escort you through to the civilian terminal and get you a ticket home to Houston. I'll make sure they're holding up a sign with your name." A thought occurred to him, and he quickly rummaged through his own satchel until he found a set of car keys. "I almost forgot—you'll need these to drive yourself home from long-term parking at Intercontinental." He handed them to her, then checked his watch. "Got everything? Passport? Driver's license? Toiletries?" He glanced towards the bathroom.

Laura felt a spike of irritation. She knew the embassy car was waiting at the hotel entrance to take her to the military airfield, but she didn't like being rushed.

She raised an eyebrow at Kaz. "Yes, Dad," she said, then calmed herself down and found a smile for him. "Okay, let's go. I don't want to keep the Israeli ambassador waiting."

Kaz waved as the black, US-flagged sedan pulled away from the curb. *Good,* he thought. *She'll make it out before the war starts.* As soon as the car was out of sight, he turned and started walking along the boardwalk towards the US embassy, ticking through the list in his head, confirming that he'd done all that needed doing.

There were more people at the beach than he'd expected, and he realized that most Israelis didn't yet know what was likely to happen at the borders of their country at sunset.

As he walked, he heard a distant wailing from within the city. Almost immediately, a loudspeaker on a nearby concrete telephone pole began blaring an alarm, followed by the answering call of multiple sirens, up and down the beach. People on the beach were standing, looking shoreward, hurrying to gather their things.

That's an air-raid siren! Kaz glanced at his watch. Just two o'clock. The intel had said sunset.

He stopped for a moment to scan the sky over the city and out across the sea. He'd just put Laura in a car headed for Lod airport. Would they directly attack Tel Aviv? What would their targets be?

Kaz broke into a run.

20

Over the Mediterranean Sea

The Egyptian pilot squeezed the control yoke as he urgently scanned ahead across the empty blue water, then rechecked his altimeter.

"Steady at five hundred meters!"

His heavy Tu-16 bomber hadn't been designed to fly this fast, this low. He fought to hold his altitude: just high enough for the navigator to get a good lock on the target, but low enough to avoid early detection by Israeli radars. Fortunately, turbulence was light. He concentrated on maintaining exact speed and height, just the way he'd practiced with his Russian flight instructors.

His crew only had one chance to do this right, it was nearly two o'clock, and the eyes of Egypt were upon them.

"I have radar lock!" The navigator behind him moved his control wheel and carefully pressed the designator to pass the steering information to the missile, attached under the bomber's right wing. He watched his display as they raced towards the coast at 800 kilometers per hour, waiting for the release line that marked the point when the missile could reach the target on its own. Despite the vibration of the jet and howling of the wind, the stopwatch hands seemed to crawl.

Suddenly, it was time. "Release in ten seconds, arming now!" The navigator raised a cover and clicked the switch forward, then poised his thumb, bracing his hand with his fingers. One step away.

"Three, two, one, fire!" He jammed down hard on the red button. The electrical signal raced through the simple circuitry and out to the hardpoint rack under the wing. Heavy solenoids sprang to life, slamming full throw to their release position. Holding arms clicked back, umbilicals unplugged, and the AS-5 air-to-surface missile fell away.

The bomber lurched violently as it abruptly shed over two tons of weight off its right side. But the pilot had been anticipating the left roll and used it to start his turn back towards Egypt. Towards safety.

As he turned, he looked across the water at the other bomber in the formation and saw it release its missile. *Excellent!* he thought. *We have both been successful.*

Inside the AS-5 missiles, a small delay timer had begun when the electrical umbilicals had unplugged, allowing three seconds for the missile to fall clear of the mother ship. At the three-second mark, both missiles' rocket motors exploded into life, slamming the weapons forward, up to their design cruising speed of 1,200 kilometers per hour. Then half of the rocket motors shut down, balancing just enough thrust to hold speed and conserve fuel.

Two airplane-sized cruise missiles, each armed with half a ton of high explosive, guided relentlessly by their inertial systems.

Aimed directly at Tel Aviv.

"Lizard Flight! We have multiple pop-up bogeys, bearing two two zero, range three zero miles, low altitude, heading northeast at Mach 0.97. You are cleared to engage."

The Israeli air weapons controller spoke in Hebrew, her voice crisp. Urgent. Her commander, sitting in the center of the ops room, was on the hotline to Tel Aviv air defense, warning them to sound the air-raid sirens.

"Lizard Flight copies, engaging." Major Eitan Carmi moved the control column of his Mirage III smoothly left so his wingman could follow and pulled hard to turn the jet. At the speed of sound, covering 30 miles didn't take very long. He scanned his radar screen.

His wingman spoke first. "Contact, Lead! Looks like two targets in trail, range twenty miles."

"Copy." The two green blips had just appeared on his own screen. "I'll take the leader, you take trailer."

"Roger." Both men focused on their radar displays while arming their air-to-air missiles.

As soon as they crossed the coast and were out over water, Major Carmi spoke. "My tanks are empty, plan to jettison if we engage." The big external fuel tanks mounted under the wings of the jets would be a liability if they got into a dogfight. He heard two quick radio clicks from his wingman.

He glanced left and confirmed the other Mirage a mile to his left, then heard him call. "Lead, I see my bogey dropping back."

A glance at the radar showed one target still racing towards them, the other rapidly slowing. *Odd tactic*, Carmi thought.

"Stay locked to him, Two, I'm almost in range on the leader."

Click click.

"Dash 2 has disappeared, Lead. My guess is they're Kelts, and mine splashed." *Kelt* was the Western name for the Soviet AS-5 cruise missile, notorious for malfunctions.

"Roger Two, eyeballs out." Carmi didn't want to get surprised. Staring intently through his windscreen, he spotted a white speck coming at them across the water.

"Tally ho, twelve o'clock low." He peered closer. "Agreed, looks like a single Kelt." *Time to maneuver.* He reached across the cockpit, threw an arming switch and pushed a button. He felt the jet shrug and lighten as the two empty fuel tanks fell away into the sea.

Mounted farther out on each wing was a Sidewinder missile, whose heat-seeking nose scanned for the high temperature exhaust of the

AS-5. He pulled his jet smoothly up into the vertical, rolled and yanked to point his nose directly at the Kelt's exhaust. When his sensor finally locked on, a distinctive grinding tone filled his helmet.

"Lizard One is Fox Two!" he transmitted as his thumb pushed the firing button on the stick. Instantly, a white streak of smoke erupted from his wing, racing down towards the sea, leaving a weaving trail as it maneuvered. *Just like a sidewinder snake*, Carmi thought.

A sudden bright flash appeared as the missile triggered its proximity warhead, followed by a secondary explosion and then black smoke, debris now falling towards the water.

"Control, Lizard One, splash one bogey, looking for the second. Visual confirmation—a Kelt."

The radar technician, who had been staying silent, letting the pilots do their job, now said, "Roger, Lizard Flight, we saw the second target slow and disappear, concur it probably malfunctioned. Copy bogey was a Kelt. No other traffic in your area. Good flying."

"Thanks." Carmi rocked his wings several times, a visual signal for his wingman to join back up, and then set a steady turn back towards Hatzor, their home air base. "What else are you seeing?"

The radar tech had been watching the other screens around her and listening to the rapid-fire chatter of comms. "Lizard Flight, we need you to return to base ASAP for a hot pit and reload." She shook her head. She'd expected her shift on Yom Kippur to be dead quiet.

"All available aircraft are being scrambled immediately on General Peled's orders. The whole country is under attack."

21

Lod Airport

Kaz stared intently through the car's windshield. The unexpected call-up of 100,000 soldiers had started to clog Tel Aviv's streets as people scrambled for taxis and buses. Many were headed to their staging points on motorcycles and bicycles, some even jogging, a country responding to the urgent radio appeal.

No MiGs, and no smoke, Kaz thought with relief, as the car approached a large hangar at Lod airport. Sitting beside him was the US air attaché, Colonel Billy Forsman.

"I'm sure she'll be fine," Forsman said. "The Israelis know how to keep flying in wartime. They've had practice." Forsman, who had flown combat missions in Korea and Vietnam, had been attached to the US embassy a year earlier. All military aviation that affected the United States was his responsibility, including the airborne resupply that was about to begin.

And the immediate task of figuring out how to get the MiG-25 and its pilot safely to the United States.

At the embassy, Kaz had called General Phillips at his home in Washington and learned that President Nixon, following Kissinger's advice, had already quietly directed the US Air Force to get the wheels turning on the airlift Golda Meir had asked for. It was going to take a few days until that could begin, but for now, Kaz was focused on just one airplane.

As soon as the driver put the car into park, Kaz had his door open and was striding towards the flight line, Forsman right behind him. An IAF soldier, machine gun slung at his hip, held up his hand to stop the two men to confirm they were on the restricted access list to the hangar.

As the soldier called for confirmation on his walkie-talkie, Kaz heard jet engines getting louder, echoing around the buildings. He couldn't see the airport runways, and the looming bulk of the hangar blocked most of the sky.

"Dammit, is that the ambassador's plane only taking off now?"

Hangar access approval crackled through on the soldier's radio, and he'd heard Kaz ask the question.

"Yes, that's the ambassador leaving." In the gap between the hangars, they spotted the silver-gray 707 climbing away. As Kaz watched, it stayed low and turned to head northwest. He pictured the map in his head: out over empty sea, splitting the airspace to stay clear of Egypt and Syria, tracking just south of Cyprus. Then westward towards the US.

He took a deep breath in and then blew the tension out. Laura was safely clear.

Billy Forsman had been watching him. "Good to move on to the next problem?"

Kaz nodded, and the two men followed the soldier to a side door in the hangar.

"Can you believe this thing?"

Kaz and Billy were up on the broad back of the MiG-25, standing between the tall, vertical twin tails. Ladders were propped against the fuselage, and temporary storage racks were arrayed along both sides.

Like a newly dead carcass in the jungle, the Soviet jet was being torn apart by teeming parasitic life, a hungry ecosystem taking fast advantage of an unexpected richness. Technicians from Israel Aerospace Industries had carefully unscrewed and removed all the access panels, and avionics experts from the Israeli Air Force had been peering into the jet's recesses, deciphering purposes, carefully applying power, capturing cipher code settings and radio frequencies. Learning everything they could about a threat they'd only seen, and feared, from a distance.

But that work had been interrupted for Yom Kippur, and the two Americans were alone in the hangar except for a single security guard.

Kaz knelt and ran his hand over the upper skin of the fuselage, tapping the metal, feeling it with his fingertips. "It's just stainless steel, and they've hand-welded it!"

Billy Forsman bent to trace an uneven weld. The blobs of metal where a Soviet welder had joined the steel skin plates had only been rough-ground smooth before being painted over with gray.

Forsman shook his head. "I thought it would be all titanium!" He looked at the machine in amazement. So different from the F-80 and Phantoms that he'd flown, and what he'd been told of the Soviet interceptor's technology. "And they've used non-flush rivets and screws." Parallel twin lines of the fasteners bulged up everywhere on the aircraft, like scars from stitches made by a careless surgeon.

Kaz looked back across the top of the MiG, picturing the airflow over the surface, imagining the Russian engineers' logic. "They were saving money, keeping it simple." He glanced out along the front of the wing, and pointed. "There, you can see they used titanium where the leading edge gets hot at Mach 3." He looked down at his feet. "But back here, where the air is just flowing by, they didn't care." He looked closer. "Fitting these steel plates and welding each one into place . . . this was put together by a low-tech but manually skilled workforce, cranking out these monsters on an assembly line."

He looked at Billy. "How are we going to get this beast to its new home?"

He shone a flashlight he'd grabbed from a toolbox down into the gaps where the Israelis had removed the wing and tail joining cover plates. He saw large shackles and trunnion pins, and a maze of connecting wires and hydraulic lines. But all possible to disconnect. He mentally paced the width of the MiG and pictured the biggest of the USAF transport aircraft.

"Think it'll fit inside a C-5?"

"I need to check for sure, but I think so. They can carry a quarter-million pounds, so weight won't be a factor." Billy walked to the back of the jet, stopping just short of the afterburner nozzles, turned, and paced methodically forward to the cockpit. Eyeballing the remaining length to the tip of the pitot tube at the front, he tallied it up.

"My guess is it's seventy-five or eighty feet long. With the wings, stabs and tail removed, the C-5 should handle it easily." Billy smiled. "Could probably take two of them if they've got any more to give."

Kaz looked at him. "You ever been to where they're going to take this thing, in Nevada?" General Phillips had told Kaz the stateside destination.

Forsman shook his head. "No, I'm just a regular line fighter pilot. No secret stuff for me." He smiled ruefully. "And besides, all I'm flying these days is a desk."

Kaz nodded, then walked forward past Billy to peer into the cockpit. He spoke, mostly to himself: "General Phillips has big plans for this bird."

22

Gagarin Cosmonaut Training Center, Star City, Soviet Union

It was centrifuge-riding day, and Svetlana Gromova didn't like it.

She'd awoken early in her seventh-floor apartment in Dom 2, the cosmonauts' residence at Zvyozdny Gorodok—Star City, 40 kilometers east of Moscow. She did her morning routine of simple calisthenics and stretching in her living room, showered, dressed in her blue tracksuit and walked the five minutes through the forest to the fliers' cafeteria, next to the headquarters building. For cosmonauts training for a launch, meal seating was assigned by table, but as a recent returnee from spaceflight, she sat alone. As the sole woman in the Soviet cosmonaut corps, she preferred it.

Svetlana ate lightly. Centrifuges could be brutal.

All cosmonaut training events began with a daily physical, and she and the nurse in the medical building went through the motions with bored efficiency: thermometer under the tongue, blood pressure cuff, stethoscope for heartbeat and breathing, attach the ECG pads, perfunctory questions, and the requisite signature in the green baize book.

Does anyone ever check that book? Svetlana wondered for the umpteenth time. No matter. It was the nurse's job, and as a military test pilot it was nice to confirm she was healthy. Again.

The TsF-7 centrifuge technicians were waiting for her and gave her their oft-repeated briefing: it would be a standard atmospheric re-entry profile, and then ballistic, simulating a Soyuz capsule control system failure. They stressed that the first run would be four g, squishing her into her seat liner at four times her normal weight, and the ballistic run would be eight or nine. Their faces were stern with the seriousness of their work.

If you only knew what I've already been through, Svetlana thought. The Soviet media had made a huge deal of her recent spaceflight heroics, the first Soviet and only woman to have walked on the Moon, outwitting the Americans, Brezhnev pinning a Hero of the Soviet Union gold star on her chest. But they had given little mention to the reality of the Apollo capsule's high-g re-entry into the Pacific Ocean. And as a Soviet Air Forces test pilot, she had often pulled eight g in the MiGs she'd flown. Yet riding passively in a centrifuge made it feel worse, somehow, with the lack of piloting control. And for someone with her background, the only purpose the exercise served was to check a box in somebody's training matrix schedule.

At the end of the lecture, the senior centrifuge tech asked her, "Gatova? Are you ready?"

"Da, gatova," Svetlana said, nodding.

Strap-in was the most realistic part of the whole thing. The seat and harness were reasonable replicas of the ones in the Soyuz, and she appreciated the chance to reacquaint herself with the straps and buckles. Her hands moved in familiar ways, clicking into place and cinching tight, making sure the comm and biomed cables were attached.

With a final check the senior tech nodded, closed and latched the hatch, pulled the access ladder to the edge of the circular room, and exited through a flush-mounted door. After a brief pause Svetlana heard his voice through the ear cups of her leather cap.

"Nominal profile beginning."

"Gatova."

Behind her seat, Svetlana heard the distinctive sounds of large electrical motors coming to life. The simulator smelled faintly of high-voltage ozone and stale male sweat. She focused on the lights and simulated instruments in front of her as she felt the mechanism lurch, and then begin to move. Spinning the low-fidelity Soyuz cockpit on the end of a long arm, the gimbal gradually pivoted outwards, to align the acceleration and make the ride feel as realistic as possible.

"Two g's," came the voice. Svetlana felt herself starting to be squeezed down into the shape of the seat, which pushed back uncomfortably at her neck and lower back. Like all equipment, it was proportioned for the male physique, not hers. She stayed silent.

"Three g's." In truth, she found g-forces pleasant. Like being wrapped in heavy blankets.

"Four g's, holding for ninety seconds." She glanced around the cockpit and moved her arm as if selecting switches. It was hard to point a finger accurately under g, so good to practice.

"Slowing now."

She felt the g's diminishing, as if someone had taken their foot off the gas pedal. As usual, there was a tumbling sensation inside her head that blurred her vision momentarily as the sim swung back towards its resting position. With a clunk, motion stopped, and the low hum of the motors ceased.

Silence.

There was an unusually long pause, and then the door in the wall banged open. The tech hurried over with the ladder, climbed it, opened her hatch and abruptly reached in to start to unstrap her.

Svetlana frowned. Had the machine broken? It regularly did, and she didn't want to have to go through this rigamarole again. "What's going on? Why are we not doing the ballistic profile?"

The tech undid the last of her connections. He met her eyes briefly. "Headquarters called me. They need to see you. Right now."

The hallway outside the Star City director's office had a high, arched ceiling with tall windows at each end, letting light shine down the worn red paisley carpet that ran the length of the narrow-hardwood floor. Potted spider plants spilled off the windowsills, warmed by the radiators mounted flush in the plaster walls. The tall, pale beechwood door that led to General Beregovoy's office was closed.

Svetlana had hurried from the centrifuge building, turning over in her mind possible reasons for such a summons. There had been endless requests for her to appear at public events since her spaceflight, and she hoped this wasn't yet another urgent order from the Kremlin to go stand somewhere, be handed flowers and repeat the same sincerely self-effacing speech. All while wearing the triumphant, earnest smile of the New Soviet Woman.

She smirked at herself. *Get over it. You walked on the Moon, girl.*

As she climbed the headquarters stairs and turned the corner into the hallway, she saw two other cosmonauts waiting outside the door: Alexei Leonov, already nearly bald but compensating with wide sideburns, and quiet Valery Kubasov, his dark hair combed in a high cowlick.

Interesting these two are here, Svetlana thought.

Alexei's face creased in one of his habitual wide smiles. "Privyet, Sveta," he said, his eyes twinkling as he looked at her and realized what this summons might mean. Three cosmonauts unexpectedly waiting outside the boss's office. He made a small joke. "Maybe we're all getting medals."

The door opened and Director Beregovoy's secretary apologized quietly for keeping them waiting. From behind her came a deep male voice.

"Come in, come in! And Vera, get coffees."

Lieutenant General Georgy Beregovoy, wide-shouldered in his Air Forces uniform, got up from behind his broad desk and came to welcome the cosmonauts. He shook hands with Leonov and Kubasov and nodded at Svetlana with a slight bow.

"Sit, sit!" he said, waving his hand at the pale rectangular table that abutted his desk front.

The general had been a Great Patriotic War fighter pilot and test pilot, and was already a Hero of the Soviet Union before he had flown solo in space, five years earlier. He found his new job of running the Cosmonaut Center often very political and trouble-filled, but not today.

He looked at the three cosmonauts in turn, as Vera placed instant coffees on the table in front of each of them.

"Alexei, Valery, Svetlana." He paused, savoring the moment. "You remember how, last year, the American president, Richard Nixon, came to Moscow in May?" A small smile ticked at the corner of his mouth. "Like most state visits, it was mostly *pokazookha*—noise and window dressing. But while the president was here, he and Premier Kosygin signed a document that is now going to be very important in your lives."

He made eye contact with each of them, smiling broadly.

"Today, I'm assigning you three to be the crew of a space mission like no other. You will fly a Soyuz to orbit, and dock with an American Apollo spaceship, meeting with a troika of NASA astronauts out in the cosmos, in peace and friendship!" He addressed Leonov, using his full patronymic to mark the formality of the occasion. "Alexei Arkhipovich, you will be the commander of the mission we are calling Soyuz-Apollo!" He reached down to yank open his lower left desk drawer and pulled out an angular flask of amber liquid. "Vera, bring us the best crystal!" He looked fondly at the bottle. "I've been saving this cognac for a truly special occasion, and this is it!"

As the general poured, Svetlana looked at each of her new crewmates' faces. She liked these two men, especially Alexei. He had been the world's first spacewalker and was respected by all. Valery, an earnest civilian engineer, hadn't yet flown in space, but he had always treated her politely.

As she raised the long-stemmed glass to her lips, joining in the first of what would be many toasts, she felt a deep rush of excitement and satisfaction. The best day in a cosmonaut's life.

I'm going to space again!

23

En Route to Nellis Air Force Base, Las Vegas, Nevada

Why are military transport planes always so damned cold?

Kaz pulled the rough blue USAF blanket more tightly around himself and tried to find a less uncomfortable position in his backwards-facing seat. The metal floor was especially frigid, so he was sitting cross-legged with his feet up.

And the stink! He blew out through his nose to try to clear it. The toilets were at the front of the C-5A Galaxy, just ahead of the three rows of seats, and the smell of chemicals and human waste wafted through the cavernous transport's interior every time someone opened the bathroom door.

This gigantic US Air Force cargo airplane had been the first of many to arrive in Israel, loaded with Sidewinder and SAM missiles—Nixon's resupply for the now-raging war. It had taxied right up to the Israel Aircraft Industries hangar, parking with its nose stuck inside to hide what it was unloading from prying eyes. And from Soviet satellites.

Like some giant fish yawning, the Galaxy's entire front rotated up out of the way for ease of loading, and at the tail, the lower aft section of the fuselage rotated down as a vehicle ramp. The crew had rolled the racks of missiles out the back, at night, emptying the cavernous hold for the return trip.

The loadmaster had shaken his head when he'd seen that a MiG-25 was his return cargo, but he had found a way to tow the Soviet jet inside and winch it securely into place, with its detached wings and tails strapped into the makeshift Israeli racks, cinched tightly alongside. With no windows in the C-5, the Foxbat had been the only real thing for Kaz to look at during the cautious, fighter-escorted flight down the center of the Mediterranean, from Tel Aviv to Lajes in Portugal's Azores, where they had refueled, and on to the 4,000-mile great-circle leg to Las Vegas. An extra-long flight for the C-5A, close to max range.

But good to be headed home.

Kaz glanced at the other passengers, sprawled and dozing under blankets across the mostly empty seats. The Air Force hadn't been sure of what to expect and had sent some muscle in addition to the plane's normal flight crew. Four large men from the USAF Security Police Force sat at the ends of the row ahead of him, taking turns sleeping and keeping an eye on the two people centered between them: the Russian pilot who had defected, leaning back in his chair, self-assured and still, and the thickly bespectacled CIA handler sitting beside him. As Kaz watched, the CIA man restlessly shifted position, as he'd been doing the whole flight. *Feeling the pressure of the big assignment*, Kaz guessed.

Kaz looked down at the paperback in his hands, titled *Очень Приятно: Beginner's Russian*, given to him at his request by the embassy staff in Tel Aviv. Kaz's Lithuanian parents had spoken a Yiddish dialect to each other at home while he was growing up, and he hoped maybe that had preset his brain to learn some Russian. Reading the book, he'd treated the symbols of the Cyrillic alphabet as a new code to crack; he was relieved to find that the pronunciation turned out to be very phonetic, at least. *Just another useful skill to learn,* he told himself. But he'd made little progress so far.

In Tel Aviv, when the Mossad had brought the Russian onto the plane shortly before takeoff, the CIA officer had asked Kaz and the crew to keep their distance—not even speak to them. But as the hours had dragged on, and while they'd stretched their legs during the refueling stop in the Azores, the handler had relaxed a bit, introducing himself as Bill Thompson. A Soviet specialist, he'd explained, which is why he'd gotten the current assignment. The security men had kept the Russian pilot inside the plane; he'd been docile and cooperative.

Tired of reading the theory, Kaz decided to take advantage of the opportunity and try out his few Russian words. He put the book down, got up out of his seat, keeping his blanket draped over his shoulders, and walked around beside the CIA officer's row. At first, it looked to Kaz like Bill Thompson was falling asleep, the eyes behind the glasses unfocused and staring at nothing. But then he noticed the way Thompson reflexively clenched and rubbed his hands. *Definitely awake and thinking about something that's bugging him.* Kaz moved into Thompson's line of vision and caught his eye, pointing to the empty seat next to him. Thompson shrugged, so Kaz squeezed past the security guards and sat. He had to yell slightly to be heard above the unending din of the plane. The Russian dozed, two seats over.

"You bored yet, Bill?"

A resigned smile. "Sure am." Thompson glanced at his watch. "Six hours down, should be about three to go."

Kaz nodded. He'd been up to the cockpit a couple of times, as they'd cleared the Mediterranean, and again as they'd crossed over Nova Scotia into North America.

"It'll be good to get to Vegas." He'd seen the officer talking quietly with the Soviet. "You must speak Russian?"

Bill Thompson looked at him. He had a sharp, angular face behind the heavy-framed glasses; his thick brown mustache and longish hair, combed straight back and high off his forehead, set him apart from the military men seated around them.

"A bit." *Standard CIA understatement,* Kaz thought. Thompson had noted the book Kaz had been reading. "Tee gavareesh?"

The Russian sounds sat in Kaz's head, uncomprehended, but from the questioning tone Kaz guessed Bill was asking if he also spoke Russian. He smiled ruefully and replied, "Nyet."

Hearing words in his native language, the Soviet pilot opened his eyes and leaned forward slowly to look at them, his face impassive. His gaze alternated between the two men and his guards.

Kaz asked Bill, "Mind if I say a few things to the Russian? Does he speak any English?"

Thompson shrugged, his pale-brown eyes unblinking behind the thick lenses. "He only speaks Russian. I'll translate as needed."

Kaz grinned. "I'll need a lot." He leaned forward in his seat to make eye contact with the man, deciding to follow what the language book had suggested as an opening gambit for beginners.

"Minyah zavoot Kaz." My name is Kaz.

The Soviet's expression didn't change as he enunciated a Russian self-introduction in response. "I am called Alexander." He paused with a very slight shrug. "Sascha." The standard diminutive.

Kaz went with the predictable next sentence from the book: the weather. "It's cold, Sascha."

Sascha smiled slightly. "Da, Kaz."

Kaz gestured with his chin towards the MiG-25 and turned to Bill for help. "That's a beautiful airplane," he said in English, and the CIA man translated. Pilot talk. A common language.

The Russian's eyes followed. "Agreed."

Kaz decided to work on vocabulary as an easy way to start to get to know the man, and he pointed to the wings. "What are those called in Russian?"

Glad for the small distraction after all the boredom, the two aviators talked in growing detail about the airplane in front of them, Kaz repeating the simpler Russian sounds, and asking technical questions that the Russian was glad to answer. Kaz spoke about some of the flying he'd done, and Alexander described his early test flights in the Foxbat, and what it was like to fly.

The CIA officer patiently translated, visibly bored. In a lull, he made a small dig at Kaz. "Uncle Sam will be pleased that we've gone to all this trouble to bring a Navy pilot his own personal Russian tutor."

When the conversation with the Russian petered out, Thompson got up and followed Kaz to get a fresh coffee at the large aluminum urn built into the plane's galley. The remaining uneaten boxed meals that had been loaded in the Azores were stacked and strapped down on the narrow, polished aluminum counter.

"Where are you taking him in Vegas?" Kaz asked.

"We have a place not far." An uninformative CIA stock reply, as Kaz had expected. No point asking the man his impressions and thoughts on the Russian, he decided.

Thompson asked, "You getting off at Nellis?"

Kaz shook his head. They were offloading the defector and his attendants at Nellis Air Force Base, on the outskirts of Las Vegas, so the CIA could begin their interrogation and debriefing. But Kaz had been asked to stay onboard by General Phillips, the head of USAF Systems Command and thus the new owner of the MiG-25.

Kaz pointed at the Foxbat with his Styrofoam coffee cup. "Nope, I'm sticking with the main cargo through to its final destination."

Seventy miles northwest of Nellis, to a lakebed air base in the Nevada desert.

Groom Lake.

24

Groom Lake, Nevada

It was a nothing place, really.

A small, flat valley in the high, dry Nevada desert, nearly a mile above sea level. A place of rattlesnakes and blowing sand.

When rare rains did fall, they had no place to flow to. The water drained intermittently into a central, brackish low spot, and evaporated to nothingness under the relentless sun, leaving a hard, baked, flat pan of accumulated sand and salt.

Without good water, the high valley was ignored as a settling place by the First Peoples, the Newe. Just one ridgeline to the east, the Pahranagat River slowly flowed towards the south, providing a more hospitable place to live. The Newe would only travel around the high, salty lakebed on hunting expeditions, pursuing pronghorn antelope and, if they were lucky, bighorn sheep or even elk, in the surrounding ridges.

The first Europeans to spend time there were mining prospectors from the English Groome Lead Mines company, and they were the ones who ironically named the barren salt flat "Groom Lake." They sat in their gritty tent and raised unclean whisky glasses to the time-honored place-naming tradition that had given the world Greenland and the Cape of Good Hope—titles to justify being there, far from home, and to lure the unknowing.

Not much lived close to Groom Lake itself. Anything that survived had to know how to endure blistering summers, frigid winters and perpetual drought. Creosote bushes, with their tiny, waxy, water-stingy leaves and long roots, dotted the gray-brown sand. Each bush was defended by a small horned lizard, fiercely protecting its shade. Fist-sized spadefoot toads buried themselves many feet deep in the dirt after each rain, surviving the endless dryness by absorbing the soil's water into their salty blood, directly through their skin.

Not an easy place. A nothing place. But a good place for keeping secrets.

The Central Intelligence Agency had many secrets to keep, some of them too big to easily hide. In the Cold War world of nuclear escalation, the agency had sent their officers across America, looking for good locations for clandestine activities.

On April 12, 1955, eight years after the CIA was created and six years to the day before Soviet astronaut Yuri Gagarin was the first to fly in space, CIA officer Richard Bissell, looking down from a small, V-tailed Beech Bonanza scouting plane, spotted Groom Lake. He had the pilot note the exact location and then circle it a few times as he stared out the side window, taking multiple pictures with his Kodak Pony 35-millimeter camera. He could imagine the dry lakebed as a natural runway, a place for covert experimentation and tests, far from prying eyes. He noted the surrounding hills, which further blocked the view.

"Perfect," he said, the word drowned out in the noisy cockpit. He'd needed a home for a project he had to run, code-named AQUATONE. Now to make it happen.

The Atomic Energy Commission already controlled 1,400 square miles of the remote Nevada desert and it had been testing nuclear bombs there for the past four years. Groom Lake was situated just to the northeast of the AEC's Nevada Proving Grounds, and Richard Bissell, photos in hand, requested the AEC acquire the extra land, an innocent-looking empty rectangle grafted onto the AEC's territory like an afterthought. The national importance of the secret operation that Bissell was directing persuaded them. With a stroke of a pen, the 38,400 acres were his.

Bissell's Project AQUATONE had one purpose: to develop a new airplane. One that could fly higher than surface-to-air missiles and cover long distances. A plane that could take detailed photos of secret installations deep inside Cold War enemy territory. A plane like no other.

Richard M. Bissell Jr., PhD, was in charge of the U-2. And now he had Groom Lake.

Money was plentiful, so progress was swift. Bissell gave an immediate green light for bulldozers to start carving access roads across the desert, connecting Groom Lake to Nevada State Route 25, and he partnered with the US Air Force to help build the secret base and test the airplanes. Cargo aircraft landed daily on the natural lakebed, and trucks arrived continuously on the new roads. Within three months they had dug wells, paved a runway, installed fuel storage tanks, and built three hangars, a control tower, trailer housing for test personnel and a mess hall. In true Air Force fashion, they even built a movie theater and a volleyball court, and dug a small swimming pool. Groom Lake was up and running as the U-2 test site.

But the CIA and the USAF didn't actually build airplanes themselves; that was the job of private companies. Richard Bissell had contracted Lockheed, based in Burbank, California, to build the U-2. Its Skunk Works was renowned for building the P-38 Lightning during the war and the revolutionary P-80 Shooting Star jet-powered fighter, both unique designs completed in record time. The engineers of the Lockheed Skunk Works, under the leadership of Kelly Johnson, not only knew how to work fast, they knew how to keep a secret.

Yet even with the temptation of movies, swimming and volleyball, not many Lockheed employees wanted to move from California to Groom Lake. Kelly Johnson, subconsciously echoing the optimistic

English prospectors of a hundred years previously, started calling it Paradise Ranch. It was neither, but it stuck, and quickly got shortened to "the Ranch." And for the more poetically minded and sardonic temporary residents, sometimes even Dreamland.

Such names worked for Lockheed, but they weren't suitable for federal government officialdom. The CIA and the USAF needed a name that was more serious, one that could be easily referenced in government documents yet wouldn't reveal the secret nature of the project, or even the location. Bissell and his team looked at what the AEC had used for its Proving Grounds, and liked the innocuous idea of simply calling the subdivided rectangles an "Area" along with a number, starting with Area 1. They especially liked that the AEC had left many numbers out to amplify the vagueness and obfuscation. They noted that the highest number the AEC had used was for Area 30, and that Groom Lake was next to Area 15. They reversed the numbers, leaving more room for confusion.

CIA officer Richard Bissell created Area 51.

Groom Lake. Paradise Ranch. Dreamland.

A nothing place, indeed.

25

Area 51, Nevada

"Cowboy 446 heavy, Dreamland Ground, exit runway 32 on the left just before the lakebed. You're cleared to taxi to the large hangars. You'll see the doors are open. Welcome to the Ranch."

Kaz was in the jump seat of the C-5A cockpit, listening to the radio communications on a spare headset. They'd invited him up for the short hop from Nellis.

"Dreamland Ground, Cowboy 446 heavy, wilco, thanks." The C-5's captain's voice was calm and professional, but all five men in the cockpit were staring out the windows. None of them had landed at Area 51 before.

The captain carefully taxied his 250-ton plane towards the hangars. A marshaler was waiting with batons in his hands and waved the C-5 along the painted yellow taxi line, through the turn, to put the nose exactly into the center of the hangar. Groundcrew walked by each wing-tip, ensuring clearance of the giant aircraft.

The marshaler raised the batons slowly to arms' length, sweeping them in big arcs, deliberately crossing them above his head at just the right moment. The captain smoothly applied toe pressure to the brakes and the C-5 stopped. His crew went through the shutdown checks, chopping all four engines to off, the harsh, echoing sound suddenly gone in the cavernous building.

The MiG-25 was safely at its new home in America.

And still a secret.

“Identification, please.”

An armed security guard had climbed aboard the C-5 and was checking each of the crew’s names against a list on his clipboard. He frowned as he looked at Kaz’s civilian clothes, and then at his passport and Navy ID card. All other nonspecific crew had gotten off at Nellis.

“You part of the C-5’s personnel?”

Kaz shook his head. “Nope, here on special assignment from USAF Systems Command.” He pointed at the MiG-25. “Ensuring safe delivery of that.”

The guard glanced at the jet. He was [illegible] an EG&G contractor, one of the many Edgerton, [illegible] and Grier employees ensuring strict rule enforceme[illegible] nuclear test site. Area 51 had the tightest securi[illegible] his job seriously. He peered closely at the phot[illegible] up at his face for several long seconds and rechecked [illegible] his list. Satisfied, he made a small, neat check mark and wordlessly handed the card and passport back.

We’re not in Kansas anymore, Kaz thought.

A tall man with long sideburns and thick eyebrows stuck his head through the plane’s side door. “You boys done running the gauntlet yet?”

He was smiling, but the guard frowned at him anyway. “All security checks complete,” he said stiffly, and squeezed past him and down the airstairs.

The man was dressed in an orange flight suit and blue flight jacket. His smile got broader as he peered into the transport’s cargo hold. “And what have you brought me here?”

The C-5's flight crew were working to pivot open the front of the plane for unloading. Kaz walked over and stuck out his hand. "Navy Commander Kaz Zemeckis, babysitter to that MiG."

Lanky black hair matched the sideburns that framed a flattened nose. "Colonel Irv Williams, Detachment Commander for the MiG pilots here." As they shook hands, Kaz noticed two patches on Williams's Nomex jacket: a supersonic plane with a slide rule, indicating he was a USAF Test Pilot School graduate, and a blue scorpion on a red mushroom cloud, with "DET 1, 57 FWW" underneath.

"MiG pilots?" Kaz looked past Williams into the otherwise empty hangar. Area 51 was a well-kept secret even inside the military, and especially when it came to non–US Air Force pilots. "What all do you have here to fly, Colonel?"

Williams shrugged. "Call me Irv. Looks like we've got a few minutes until the crew is ready to unload your plane, Kaz. Wanna go have a look?"

They exited the hangar through a side door, and Kaz had to shield his face against the sudden searing brightness of the desert sun. As they crossed the gap towards a matching door in the adjacent hangar, the wind pelted them with dust. Williams pulled the door open and they stepped inside, glad for the shelter.

As Kaz's eye adjusted to the darkness, he saw the looming shapes of several jets. The nearest one had the familiar large central star and adjoining stripes of the US Air Force roundel painted on the side of the nose, but the silhouette was odd. He realized with a start that it was a MiG-21. Looking beyond it, he spotted the distinctive high, angular tails of a MiG-17 and a MiG-19.

"Last time I saw these was over Vietnam!"

Kaz had stopped walking and Irv was standing beside him, smiling at his reaction.

"Yep. We acquired the 21 several years ago when an Iraqi defected into Israel, and the 19 and 17s came from various places. As soon as they got here, the techs took them apart to see how they ticked, put them back together, fueled them up, and we started flying them." He glanced down at his Det-1 unit badge. "First it was just Air Force, but we've started letting you Navy pukes in on it now too. It really helps with training realism, and our kill ratio in Vietnam suddenly got a lot better." Irv opened a switch panel on the wall and threw some circuit breakers. Overhead lights clicked on low, started buzzing and then got brighter.

Kaz had heard rumors through the Navy grapevine of guys flying MiGs, and he was fascinated to see them up close. The MiGs' skin was bare silver metal, and they still had a red Soviet star high on their tails. He ran his hand along the MiG-21 wing's sharp leading edge.

"How does it fly?" The fundamental pilot question.

"Better than we thought," Irv said. "Really simple flight controls and systems, and with that delta wing shape, it'll give you one bat turn that'll water your eyes." He looked at Kaz. "That's how we started killing them with F-4s. Feint to get them to commit to that one turn, force them slow, then stay fast and slash in with AIM-9s or guns." He considered, then asked, "You a test pilot?"

Kaz nodded. "Navy school, class 38. But I hit a seagull with an F-4 in '68, it came through the windscreen, took out my left eye." He shrugged. "The Navy lets me ride in two-seaters now."

Irv stared at Kaz's face. "So is that a fake eyeball?"

Kaz nodded, smiled and wiggled his eyebrows. "Good match, right?"

Irv whistled low. "That must have been tough to go through." All pilots feared having their ability to fly taken away from them. And blindness was a nightmare for people who relied on sharp vision.

"Yep, but shit happens and you move on. Now I deliver MiG-25s to Air Force dweebs at Dreamland."

"Touché," Irv said. "How long you staying with us?"

"Just until we get the MiG-25 unloaded and the paperwork signed over. I'm Houston-based and haven't been home for a while." He considered what to reveal about the Soviet pilot defector, and decided it was better to say nothing, given the CIA hadn't yet decided what they were going to do with him. "I'll be heading out as soon as the C-5 is unloaded and ready to go. But the folks in Washington hinted they may send me back here."

They walked back towards the door, and Irv threw the switches to shut off the hangar lights. "When you do, bring your flight suit. We've got some two-seaters here, and you'll want to see that MiG-25 flying up close."

26

Johnson Space Center, Houston, Texas

A pilot's medical clearance is an ephemeral and precious thing. Granted by a doctor, it gives the pilot permission to fly—the ultimate ticket to ride. Take it away and a pilot is grounded, forbidden to do the very thing that defines them as a pilot. And ever since the accident, where a seagull had smashed through the windscreen of his fast-flying F-4 Phantom and destroyed Kaz's left eye, he'd lost that medical permission. Without the standard binocular vision deemed necessary by the US Navy's medicos to safely judge distance and control an aircraft, he was earthbound.

But in Washington, General Sam Phillips, former director of the Apollo program and now in charge of USAF Systems Command, had decided to change that. He had recruited Kaz into electro-optics intelligence after the accident, and then had assigned him to support Apollo 18, where Kaz's insights had been vital. He wanted to reward Kaz for the work he'd done, and the personal risks he'd taken at splashdown in the Pacific. And as Phillips's man on the ground with the MiG-25 at Groom Lake, he wanted Kaz flying.

Sam Phillips had been a fighter pilot during World War II and knew of several extremely effective one-eyed pilots. Wiley Post had set a speed record flying solo around the world and became the first man to fly up to 50,000 feet, all with one functioning eyeball. Adolf Galland had shards of glass in one eye that rendered it virtually blind, yet he had been a Luftwaffe fighter ace with 705 combat missions. Japanese fighter pilot Saburō Sakai had sustained serious eye damage in combat yet had returned successfully to solo flight again in battle. And in Canada, Flying Officer Syd Burrows had lost an eye to a birdstrike in an F-86, yet had regained his medical and flown a full military career afterwards.

Sam knew that all it would take to grant the clearance was the right doctor, and then the military and NASA to agree. A longtime veteran of getting things done in Washington, he called in favors from his counterparts at the US Navy, and spoke with the current administrator of NASA, Jim Fletcher. After some cajoling, they agreed that they would permit Kaz to fly, only in the well-proven NASA T-38 and in peacetime, if he could get a flight surgeon to certify that his remaining vision and depth perception were adequate.

Pulling the last of the necessary strings, Sam Phillips had called NASA's Chief Astronaut and longtime friend Al Shepard, to set an appointment for Kaz with a suitable doctor for when he returned from Israel. Before he'd become America's first astronaut and had walked on the Moon, Al Shepard had been a Navy test pilot, and he immediately understood how important and useful it would be to get Kaz flying jets again.

Not just flying.

Piloting.

The Johnson Space Center, 25 miles southeast of Houston, Texas, was the home of American human spaceflight. It's where the NASA astronauts trained, where Mission Control was based, and where Kaz had worked for the past year, after he was detailed by the Navy and General Phillips to support Apollo 18. Built like a university campus, JSC had a large park in its central quadrangle, surrounded by blocky, looming, white-stuccoed buildings that housed simulators, classrooms, technical development labs and Mission Control itself. Spread low across the north end of the square was a two-story glassed structure, prosaically named Building 8. The second floor was used for photo processing, carefully developing and interpreting every inch of film brought back from the Moon by the Apollo astronauts. Directly below it, on the ground floor, was the JSC Clinic, where doctors tested and verified the health of returning astronauts and evaluated upcoming crews for flight readiness.

A couple of days after he'd delivered the cargo of secrets to Area 51, Kaz sat in an examination room, stripped to his underwear and slightly cold in the air-conditioning, undergoing his annual pilot physical. Depressing his tongue with a wooden spatula, Dr. JW McKinley, NASA Flight Surgeon, instructed him, "Say ahhh."

Kaz obliged.

Dr. McKinley grunted, withdrew the spatula, set it on the polished aluminum side table and started a hands-on physical examination. He steadied both sides of Kaz's head in his fingertips, his thumbs probing under the chin, feeling for the lymph nodes.

"Rumor has it you've been assigned to something classified, Kaz."

The two men had gotten to know each other well during Apollo 18. JW McKinley was short, strongly built, with thick black hair cut short above his black-framed glasses. He moved Kaz's head left and right, evaluating skin tone. "Wherever it is, must be sunny."

Kaz smiled. "Laura and I were on holiday in Israel, JW. I tan easily."

JW grunted again. He knew that Laura, a NASA planetary geologist, had gotten back to JSC nearly a week ago, and on her own.

Next, he raised and lowered Kaz's arms individually, a hand resting on the shoulder to feel for normal motion. He paused and looked at the wound on Kaz's left upper arm, tipping his head back to see clearly through his bifocals. Kaz had sustained it during the altercation in the water after Apollo 18's splashdown, and JW had been the one who helped pull Kaz to safety.

"Much pain?"

Kaz shook his head. It had been eight months. "I forgot it was there." Standard pilot answer.

JW took his stethoscope from around his neck, put the earpieces into place, rubbed the silver bell end on his palm for a few seconds to warm it and asked Kaz for deep breaths. He listened attentively to heart and lungs at various locations across Kaz's chest and back. The nurse had measured Kaz's blood pressure and pulse earlier, the results neatly written on the summary sheet. The doctor grunted a third time.

"You're disgustingly healthy." Like the rest of his family, JW put on weight easily, requiring strict diet and exercise, and he envied the tall, lean body in front of him.

Pulling on a rubber glove, JW said, "Stand up, Kaz, let's get the compulsories over with." Kaz had been in military aviation his entire adult life, and the pattern was familiar. He stood, pulled his undershorts down and turned his head.

JW said, "Cough."

Kaz forced a cough, and JW felt for asymmetry or hernia. Finding nothing, he raised a finger, squirted some lube on it and gestured for Kaz to turn around. Without being asked, Kaz bent over and grabbed for his ankles. JW inserted a finger and felt efficiently for the smooth, hard shape of a healthy prostate. He pulled his finger out, snapped the glove off into the garbage can, handed Kaz a Kleenex and asked him to sit again.

JW took a small triangular rubber hammer from a side table. "You been flying that little Cessna much?" He tapped just below Kaz's left kneecap, and the leg pulsed in response.

Kaz rented a house in an airport community west of JSC called Polly Ranch, which had come with a small Cessna 170 taildragger, and he and JW had flown together. For civilian private pilots, the FAA allowed one-eyed flying.

"Not enough," Kaz replied. "Too much travel."

JW looked at him steadily for a few seconds. "Well, maybe today we can get you flying something more high-performance."

He turned to flick off the room lights and pointed to a spotlit eye chart on the far wall. "No need for you to cover an eye. What's the lowest line you can read?"

Kaz, as usual, could easily make out the row second from the bottom.

"L P C T Z B D F E O."

"Yep. How about the bottom row?"

Kaz blinked and concentrated.

"Z O." He paused, squinting and blinking again. "Maybe a C, looks like an E and then an F or a P. Then L D, maybe an F and an E, plus a T." He relaxed. He knew the bottom line was just for bonus points. But today's stakes were high.

JW shook his head, reaching for an ophthalmoscope, which looked like a silver flashlight with a small black block on the end. "Here I am needing glasses to see anything, while your one naked eyeball got almost everything on the 20/10 row. Nothing wrong with your acuity, which is good." He moved closer to Kaz, turned on the scope and looked through it into Kaz's eye. He moved his thumb to adjust the brightness.

Kaz's field of vision filled with the dazzle of the light. "See what I'm thinking, Doc?"

JW ignored him. "Just stare at the eye chart." As Kaz held his eye still, JW swapped the device's small internal lenses and filters to inspect the structure of Kaz's eye, including the pattern of blood vessels and the optic nerve ending across the back, in the retina.

He leaned back, satisfied, and reached to turn on the room light. "All looks good." He turned to pick up an apparatus off the side table, a flat black oblong that looked like an elementary school writing slate. "Put on your shirt and pants if you're cold, Kaz, and let's have a look at your depth perception."

Kaz stood, pulled his shirt on over his head and redonned his slacks. He sat back down, still barefoot, facing JW. The device the doctor was holding was one he hadn't seen before.

"How's that work, Doc?" His tone was casual, but both men knew what the stakes were. The examination so far had been standard. This was the test that mattered, and Kaz wanted to know all he could in advance. Every pilot's physical was a contest to be won. Even to cheat if necessary.

"It's not something I normally use." He brought the window in the device close to Kaz's face. "Just look at the bars in the center and tell me which one of the three appears like it's closest or farthest from you."

Kaz blinked to clear his vision and then focused on the illuminated oblong in the center of the device. He saw three vertical bars of different thicknesses against a pinkish background. They looked perfectly aligned.

"Are we ready to start, Doc?"

JW paused for a couple of seconds, watching him. "Yep, go ahead."

Holding perfectly still, Kaz concentrated harder. He opened his eye wide, and then squinted, but the bars looked unchanged. Three obstinate little black strips against the pink. All that stood between him and flying jets again.

Kaz had a thought. "Can I move my head left and right a bit, like I do in the cockpit?"

JW considered briefly and nodded. A reasonable request for a one-eyed pilot. "Yep."

Kaz tipped his head and shifted in his seat, as if he was looking through the windscreen of a T-38, around the curve of the instrument panel.

That was better. "I see three parallel bars beside each other. The one on the left looks farther away."

JW reached to move a lever on the back of the device, and then flipped the whole thing upside down. "How about now?"

Kaz reassessed. "The one on the left looks closer now, and it's the skinniest bar."

JW moved the device's control and flipped it upside down again. "And now?"

The difference seemed to be getting less each time. Kaz concentrated, picking out the subtle difference. "The medium one's on the left, and it looks closer."

JW moved the lever again. "What do you see now?"

Kaz looked back and forth across the three lines, detecting a possible, barely perceptible difference. "The center one looks thickest, and is farther back," he said, more decisively than he felt.

"Last one," JW said, moving the control and inverting the device once more.

Try as he might, Kaz saw no differences. "They all look the same now." *Shit*, he thought.

"Take your time."

Kaz leaned back and blinked a couple of times, and then fully closed his eyes, consciously relaxing and moving them left and right under the lids. He could feel the motion of both his glass eye and his real one through the muscles and eyelid nerves; each different, but familiar.

He opened both, sat forward and looked hard. He felt more than saw an asymmetry in the pattern, and suspected he was imagining a difference. *Were the two on the right protruding?* He cursed himself silently for not doing his homework—maybe in the final image on this test they were all the same!

Nah, he decided. It would be like the eye chart. The last one would be to highlight pilots with exceptional vision.

Life was about decisions. "The left one is behind the other two."

JW set the device on the side table and looked over his bifocals into Kaz's apparently impassive face. The men had different roles to play, and each took his job seriously.

"Correct," JW said. "You've only got one peeper, Kaz, but it's a beauty. If you can show the flight instructors out at Ellington that you can fly their jets, I have no medical objection, and will do my damnedest to convince NASA's Aerospace Medicine Board."

His face broke into a wide smile, his big square teeth flashing white. As a NASA flight surgeon, he had back-seat privileges in the T-38.

"Just promise you'll take me flying once in a while."

27

Houston

Kaz came to meet Laura directly from Ellington Field. After JW had cleared him, Al Shepard had insisted Kaz get his front-seat checkout flights with a T-38 instructor done immediately, so no one in Washington had a chance to change their mind. Kaz had been quietly worried that his single eyeball wouldn't actually be good enough, despite passing the tests, and once he had completed his first flight—with multiple landings around the traffic pattern and no problem touching down on the numbers every time—he felt a huge sense of relief.

He and Laura were sitting in a small Mexican restaurant on the east side of downtown Houston. The owner, Mama Ninfa, had greeted them warmly at the door and seated them at one of her ten tables.

Laura was wearing a UCLA sweatshirt against the cool of the Houston early winter, with large, feathery earrings helping to hold back her long black hair. Ninfa's was open to the street on one side, and the swirling air kept her hair in constant, gentle motion.

It was their first real chance to talk since their hasty separation in Tel Aviv, and now that he was seated, Kaz realized that for the first time in a long while he was feeling awkward with Laura. He found himself inadvertently opening with an oddly formal question.

"So what's new in the Lunar Laboratory?"

She snorted. "Rocks can wait, buster. It's been a week, and I'm more interested in what all you've been up to. What happened after I left Israel? Besides the war, I mean, which is just awful."

A week? Had it been that long? Phoning her from Israel had been out of the question, and using an outside phone line for a personal call had been forbidden at Groom Lake. He decided to take the easiest way out.

"I'm sorry, Laura, but I can't tell you. Even where I've been is classified."

She watched his face as he spoke, and believed him, of course. But she decided to tease him anyway.

"Military man on a secret mission?"

He gave her a half smile. "Yeah, something like that."

She squinted and pursed her lips in a caricature of thought. "Well, let me guess, and I'll watch your good eye for tics to gauge whether I'm on the right track. When the helpless damsel was whisked out of harm's way in Tel Aviv, you were hot on the trail of a Soviet plane that had been shot down. You must have spent several more days in Israel"—she paused to stare intently at his face—"and then flew back stateside on a, what—a military transport?"

Kaz kept his expression neutral.

Laura squinted some more. "Aha, I'm right!"

Kaz frowned. "How do you know you're right?"

"Your face is an open book, Kaz," she said, then leaned back, laughing. "Nah, I'm just guessing. I know you need to keep secrets."

Mama Ninfa swept up to their table, her hands full of thick crockery plates laden with tortillas, grilled skirt steak, fried peppers and onions. Her accent was pure Rio Grande Texan. "Fresh tortillas, I make them myself in the back!" She looked at their table. "More tea?"

Kaz and Laura nodded, and she returned with a pitcher, refilling their tall plastic glasses. After one last check that everything was in place, she smiled at them and turned to greet another customer.

Kaz had been considering how much he really could tell Laura. One thing he did need to let her know. "Looks like my time will be split between Houston and elsewhere for a while." He grimaced. "Mostly elsewhere, I'm afraid."

Laura shrugged, her smile fading. "Well, let's make the most of the Houston part," she said. She'd piled beef strips, onions and peppers onto a soft tortilla and rolled it into a tube, and now took a large bite. As she chewed, her eyes lit up. "This is delicious!" she said around the mouthful.

Kaz did the same, adding some green hot sauce from a jar on the table. The mixture of textures and tastes burst in his mouth. The sauce was spicier than he'd expected, and his eye watered. He took a long pull on his iced tea before he said, "Did you hear the news?"

"What news?"

"I thought JW might have mentioned it. He cleared me to fly front-seat T-38. Even solo!"

"Wow, that's great! Have you been flying yet? How does it feel?"

He chewed slowly, taking the time to consider the last part of her question.

"I had my first flight today. I'd forgotten just how good it feels, Laura. Riding in the back is okay, but being the one making all the decisions and controlling the plane is totally different. It's been so long since the accident, I'd sort of pushed it out of my mind. Like I'd let a part of myself just lapse." He smiled. "I may still be one-eyed, but it makes me feel whole again."

She looked away and then back, her eyes sparkling. "So, now that you'll have an empty back seat, any chance you can take a motivated NASA lunar geologist for a ride?"

"I will if they'll let me. But I'm pretty certain there's some sort of list of who's allowed."

Laura gave him a mock pout. "You flyboys get all the fun!"

Kaz frowned slightly, remembering a previous conversation they'd had. "Any word on whether NASA is going to recruit women astronauts for the Space Shuttle?"

"Not yet," Laura said, suddenly serious. "But the new Equal Employment Opportunity Act is going to be hard for them to ignore. NASA employs over four thousand women—most of them secretaries. Only about three hundred are in science and engineering." She took another bite, chewed, swallowed. "Still, that's a lot more than there were ten years ago. I'm thinking my chances are improving. And rumors are they won't recruit until 1977 or so, so that gives me four years to get my act together. And for NASA to keep evolving."

Kaz nodded. His years as a Navy combat and test pilot had been all-male, but he knew several civilian female pilots. And the cosmonaut Svetlana Gromova sure had proven that women have what it takes.

"Have they said what skills they'll be looking for?"

She nodded. "My background won't let me be a Shuttle commander or pilot; those will still need to be test pilots. But they've created roles called mission and payload specialists, for doing experiments and helping operate the vehicle." She looked at him squarely. "Want to know what I've been thinking?"

"Always."

She shook her head quickly. "Always? Kaz, that really wouldn't be wise. What I meant was, the Space Shuttle is going to have a crew of as many as seven astronauts. I bet the pilot and commander will mostly be flying the ship, and that's going to open up spacewalking to the mission specialists." She paused briefly. "People like me. That's what I'm going for."

"A space walk. That'd be very cool. I'm envious."

Laura tipped her head and surveyed him. "Hey, if they're letting you fly front-seat T-38, maybe there's an astronaut shot for you too?"

Kaz laughed. "No way. It was a big stretch for them to let me back in as a pilot, and the Navy isn't even doing that, just NASA in their

T-38s." But her words echoed in his head. He hadn't considered it. *Is that even possible?*

Laura was watching him closely and smiled at what she saw. "So now we're both on the outside, looking in through tiny new doors that are just opening."

She wiggled her eyebrows at him.

"Race you to the Moon."

THE

SECRET

28

Baikal-1, Semipalatinsk Nuclear Test Site, Kazakhstan, January 1973

It was a lousy weekly commute, but she was used to it.

Wake up well before dawn in her small apartment in Kurchatov, dress in layers against the eternal winds of the Kazakh steppe, grab the breakfast of bread, dried sausage and cheese she'd packed the night before, fill her chai thermos from the kettle, and then stand outside and wait.

On the street in front of her place, Irina quickly lit her first cigarette of the day, cupping her hands against the cold gusts coming off the Irtysh River, sucking the hot, dry smoke deep into her lungs, grateful for the instant warmth. She glanced at her watch and then leaned around the protective corner of her building, relieved to spot headlights bobbing towards her on the uneven street.

Good, she thought. *He's not late this time.*

The small van pulled up next to her in the darkness. The bulbous contours and industrial-brown factory paint had long since led to the vans being nicknamed "bukhanka," after their resemblance to the traditional Russian loaves of bread. The other passengers, dimly visible through the fogged windows, all knew Irina got carsick and had left the front right seat empty for her, as usual. She yanked the door open and climbed up and in, the sour smell of the people and their cigarette smoke filling her nose. Without a word, the driver released the clutch and pulled away from the curb, the small engine whining loudly against the sudden acceleration. They snaked through the early morning streets, drove out from under the arched sign across the road proclaiming Kurchatov and headed west, into the emptiness of the treeless steppe. A few taillights were visible ahead of them, following the narrow main road towards the same destination, an hour away, bringing the scientists from their weekend apartments out to where they worked all week, at Baikal-1. The Soviet Union's laboratory for testing nuclear rocket engines. A cluster of buildings hidden deep in the heart of the Semipalatinsk nuclear test complex.

Irina took a final drag on her cigarette and then cracked her window open, flicking the butt out into the dawn's gathering light. She leaned back and closed her eyes, trying to ignore the rocking motion of the van as she thought about the week's work that lay ahead.

What they were trying to do was revolutionary, and elegantly simple: use the incredible power of the atom as the core of a compact, light motor to drive a spaceship. Carry a supercooled tank of liquid hydrogen, heat the fluid in the nuclear reactor and blast it out the exhaust nozzle at incredible speed. Since rocket effectiveness depended most on exhaust velocity, it would be the most efficient space engine ever built.

But there were problems. Many problems. Irina opened her eyes and absently watched the featureless steppe grasses flick by through the fogged-up side window.

How to control the nuclear reaction? They were using a zirconium hydride neutron moderator, and beryllium reflector control drums, but the radioactivity changed the very nature of so many metals.

And if you let the reaction get just a bit too hot, everything melts.

She closed her eyes again, visualizing it. They were already piping the coldness of the hydrogen through all the surrounding structure and even the exhaust nozzle itself, but it was such a delicate balance. The hydrogen ended up being heated to almost 3,000 degrees Celsius, where it needed a special additive just to keep it from reacting with the core materials. If there was any sort of pump failure, the vital engine parts turned to liquid. Or worse, the reactor itself would run away catastrophically.

But the prize! A nuclear rocket engine would be light and efficient enough to maneuver a spaceship around all orbits, to access any satellite, and to move easily between the Earth and the Moon. The planetary scientists were keenly interested in using Irina's engine to explore robotically across the solar system, suddenly freed to visit the distant planets and their moons that had been out of reach. With the goal—the dream that inspired Irina most—to take a Soviet crew rapidly and safely to Mars.

But it was the Soviet military that was funding Baikal-1. The generals wanted an engine that would allow them to move their spacecraft at will in Earth orbit, maneuvering large spy cameras and anti-satellite weapons. To gain not just air superiority but technological and tactical space superiority. Something no other nation on Earth could yet do, not even the Americans.

The demands on Irina and her team were extreme, both politically and practically.

Irina opened her eyes again, resisting the urge to light another cigarette and queasily rejecting the idea of eating any of her sack breakfast. She tried not to watch the hypnotic rise and fall of the telephone line, suspended on an endless, regular picket of cement poles. Their destination was still invisible against the morning horizon.

She and her team, and everyone working at the Baikal-1 experimental facility, had to find a way to test everything and not expose themselves to too much radiation. The remote location allowed them to vent the radioactive exhaust downwind into the atmosphere, where it could spread and dilute to harmless levels across the empty steppe. But after each full-up test, they had to wait a month for the radiation levels to drop low enough to reenter the test chamber itself. A month of analysis and preparation for the next test. Slow, methodical research, learning and moving towards the ultimate goal.

Irina gave in, reaching across to the van's center console to push in the lighter. As it heated, she retrieved a fresh Prima from her pack. She preferred the taste of the Kiev-grown tobacco over the roughness of the local cigarettes. The lighter popped out with a metallic thump, and she yanked it out, squinting against the red-glowing heat as she lit the cigarette. She pushed the lighter back into place and inhaled deeply.

She could feel the nicotine sharpen her mind.

One of the hardest problems with the nuclear rocket engine was start-up. She thought about what she'd just done to ignite her cigarette: the delicate balance of creating the right conditions to begin the thermal reaction yet controlling and protecting it to get to the desired steady state. She took another drag and glanced at the bulky bulge between herself and the driver that concealed the van's motor, picturing the continuous explosions and spinning machinery of the four-cylinder internal combustion engine hidden there. The automotive engineers had figured out how to reliably start and control those motors. She was certain it hadn't been easy for them.

Through the windshield, she was just now able to pick out the low shapes of Baikal-1 in the far distance. She smiled as she thought, *I'm smarter than an automotive engineer.* She had a doctorate in nuclear physics from the Moscow Engineering Physics Institute.

As the van slowed to turn off onto the long, pothole-filled road to the test facility, Irina bent to gather her things.

We can solve this. She sat back up, correcting that thought. *I can solve this.*

The wind. Irina hated it. But given she lived and worked on the steppes of eastern Kazakhstan, there was no avoiding it. The nearest upwind tree was well beyond the horizon, and the empty flatness stretched for thousands of kilometers.

The wind really couldn't help itself. But she hated it all the same.

Bits of dust pelted her face, carried by the gusting, unstoppable air whipping in from the northwest. *Same direction as Moscow*, she thought, with some irony. What had Shakespeare said? *The ill wind that blows no good.* Especially true today, given that she and her test team had been summoned by the powers that be, and were now standing outside in that ill wind, waiting.

The inspection delegation from Moscow had been scheduled to arrive at 15:00, helicoptered out to the Baikal-1 nuclear test site after they'd landed at Semey airport. But it was 15:15, and still no sign of a chopper. Her group huddled in the lee of their laboratory building, smoking, chatting and inwardly cursing the lost time.

Irina looked again to the eastern horizon, dreading the helicopter's arrival. She and her team had just run another major engine firing. She'd thought they'd finally figured out why all the previous tests had stopped prematurely. But within seconds of beginning to flow the compressed hydrogen gas through the nuclear rocket engine test rig, the automatic sensors had tripped and shut it down. Again. That meant another long delay, as they were going to have to analyze the dozens of strip charts and instrument-monitoring camera films of high-speed data, all while waiting for the radioactivity in the IVG-1 reactor test chamber to dissipate enough to go in and start taking the equipment apart.

Irina inhaled the cold air deeply, held it for a few seconds and sighed loudly. Before she took another breath, she heard the familiar whup-whup-whup of heavy helicopter blades, then saw the fat, insect-like shape of an Mi-8 transport approaching from behind the tall cranes over the test chamber.

"Rebyata!" she called. Guys!

The group chucked their cigarettes, quieted and formed up in a reasonably straight line. Everyone was wearing clean blue lab coats per her direction, all eyes on the noisy, massive helicopter as it approached nose-high and landed on its wide, squat tires. The steady whine of the twin turbines suddenly lowered in pitch, and as the five spinning blades slowed, the side door was thrown open, a short ladder pivoted out and a crewman stepped down quickly, turning and waiting to help the passengers disembark.

Irina knew a few of the people who worked in their overseeing organization and hoped to see a friendly face. This team was only going to be on the ground for about an hour—they certainly didn't want to spend the night in such a place as Baikal-1—so she needed to make as good an impression as quickly as she could.

She'd been so hopeful. In the reports she'd read from international conferences, she was sure they were ahead of the Americans in this race, especially in the critical technology of carbide fuels. But time after time they were being defeated by what seemed like simple things. The valves that had to open and close properly under super-cold conditions kept failing, and the storage tank insulation was insufficient. She was a nuclear engineer, not a plumber! Why couldn't anyone across the whole, glorious Soviet Union manufacture pipes and pressure vessels that worked with liquid hydrogen? It was the most basic atom that existed—the very first one listed in Mendeleev's table of elements!

With a start, she realized the entire group was already out of the helo and walking towards her: four men, one in uniform and three wearing dark suits and hats. No faces she recognized.

Her boss, the test site director, stepped forward to meet the men, his hand outstretched, and the lead visitor shook it, unsmiling against the wind. After a few words of welcome the director turned and gestured at Irina, and all four men started walking towards her.

The two with the thick glasses were undoubtedly from the Nuclear Test Office, her immediate superiors in Moscow. The tall man in uniform, his dark-blue serge cap low on his head to keep it from flying off, was Air Forces. Two stripes and three stars on his sleeve—a colonel.

The fourth man was clearly the leader, broad-shouldered and wearing a visibly better topcoat than the other civilians. *KGB*, Irina decided. *Why is he here?*

He stopped in front of her, the other three men remaining a pace behind. Irina knew he wouldn't shake a woman's hand, and it didn't occur to him to, so she kept her arm at her side.

He spoke. "Academician Irina Moldova?"

"Da, tovarisch." *KGB for sure. He knows my name and didn't give me his.*

The man had a flat, clipped way of talking. "We have traveled all the way from Moscow today, and will be returning tonight, so we have less than an hour." He nodded towards the test site director, who was hovering to his right. "The director tells me you have recently completed a test, and we would like to see your progress."

Irina couldn't help a quick glance at the director. *Thanks for nothing,* she thought.

"Da, tovarisch," she repeated. She gestured at the line of men and women beside her. "These are my coworkers, and we've been looking forward to your inspection."

The man's eyes didn't leave hers. The silence grew awkward, and Irina ended it by turning towards the building behind her.

"I suggest we get in out of the wind, and begin by looking at the Control Room."

After giving them a perfunctory tour of the consoles, gauges and recording equipment where her team monitored the tests and performed their core work, Irina realized the visiting men didn't want to see hardware but were waiting to receive a detailed briefing on the status of the project. There was a small meeting room off to the side of the central test and control chamber, where her team typically relaxed, drank tea and coffee, and discussed their progress in a quieter setting. She held the door for the four men, then pushed chairs into position and cleared papers from the table as they poured themselves tea from the samovar in the corner and sat. Her director stood, leaning on the door frame. Irina refilled a communal bowl with crisp dried sesame bread, set it in the center of the small table and then walked around to stand next to a large picture on the wall—a blow-up of a hand-drawn, color-coded schematic of a nuclear rocket engine.

She looked at the men watching her, and her mouth went dry. She wished she'd gotten herself a tea as well.

Para, she thought. *It's time to take this bull by the horns. I'm the expert here.*

"Gentlemen, thank you for traveling all this way. I am happy to report that we are making excellent progress. We have recently completed our latest test. As expected, we face new challenges with each new stage, and each one we meet teaches us something important."

She pointed at the wall schematic. "Let's look at spaceflight nuclear rocketry basics. This blue tank on the left is full of liquid hydrogen, our fuel, which needs insulation to keep it very cold, below minus 253 Celsius. It's pumped through these lines here"—she traced the blue outer lines to a large cone-shaped object on the right—"to the rocket exhaust nozzle. The hydrogen cools the nozzle on its way to the central engine." She tapped the center of the drawing. "Here is the nuclear reactor, where the reaction is controlled by these beryllium rods, shown in black."

She paused, surveying the four faces. They were all watching her intently. *Good*, she thought. *Let's focus.*

"The big advantage of this nuclear-powered space rocket engine is that it can create thrust over twice as efficiently as all current in-orbit rockets, and it could work for months, or even years." She paused, to emphasize to these men the part she was sure would interest them the most. "This would enable large, high-resolution Soviet observation satellites to change orbit at will, to rapidly photograph the Earth's tactical hotspots as they happened. And with it, the Air Forces could maneuver next to American spy satellites, to better understand the technology and, if needed, disable or destroy them."

The Air Forces colonel waved his hand impatiently and spoke. "Yes, we know all that, of course. But what of your testing? How close are you to a functioning engine?"

Men always acted as if they knew what was going on. She'd learned long ago it was better to clarify, and she carried on, unperturbed.

"The key component, our reactor, works. Our choice of carbide fuel elements is the correct one, as it stays unaffected by the high radiation and hydrogen itself. We have read in international journals that the Americans are using graphite, which they will inevitably find only works for shorter periods."

She tapped the blue lines running from the hydrogen tank. "Our problem is feeding the cryogenic hydrogen rapidly and continuously to the engine. It requires new technologies in non-brittle metals, extremely efficient insulation and fast-moving supercooled valves." She pointed at the arrows showing where the blue hydrogen flowed into the orange-red heat of the reactor. "Our latest test had an early shutdown as these feed valves couldn't move quickly enough to properly start and sustain the reaction."

The two bespectacled men from the Moscow Nuclear Test Office knew the problem well. It had been a key issue for years, and so their facial expressions hadn't changed. But the KGB man had stared at the Air Forces officer for several seconds, and now turned to Irina.

"So what is your plan to solve these problems and accelerate progress?"

Irina held his gaze. Her team had been in touch with universities and research institutes all across the Soviet Union and had made inquiries with the propulsion arm of the Soviet Navy, given their expertise in nuclear-powered submarines and the recently converted *Lenin* icebreaker. No one had the specific technology they needed.

"It is our biggest obstacle, tovarisch." She gestured out through the door, to the people sitting at the test consoles, reviewing the latest data. "My team is working in our machine shops here to build what we need, but our facilities are limited, and our staff is small."

In the evenings in her small apartment, Irina had read and reread the unclassified technical reports that came from the other nuclear-capable nations, trying to look between the lines at what they were actually up to, and how they might be solving the problems common to them all.

She nodded at the two men in back and voiced her conclusions from that reading. "I'm certain my esteemed colleagues from the Institute would agree that the Americans are the world leaders in this and that, given the length and scope of their testing, they have demonstrated that they have found solutions." She shrugged. "Unfortunately, that work is highly classified and unavailable to us."

The colonel was about to say something, but Irina raised a finger to emphasize what she wanted to say before he spoke.

"Recently, I have read that the US president, Richard Nixon, has canceled funding for their equivalent program to ours, what they call NERVA. The article said it was due to budgetary pressures, and their new focus on a different type of spaceship, a reusable shuttle, that will follow their Apollo lunar program."

This was her moment, and the words came out in a rush.

"That cancellation has given us a tactical advantage. The Americans are stepping away from nuclear rocket propulsion just when we are surging ahead. And like all canceled programs, it's inevitably going to lead to more lax security in their reporting. I have instructed my staff, and spoken with all my colleagues across the Soviet Union, to be on the lookout for new publications that contain answers to our problems."

She looked first at the colonel and then met the eyes of the KGB man. "What will make our engine work is to uncover what the Americans have been working on, out in the desert in their state of Nevada."

There! She'd said it. And hopefully to the right people.

She and her Baikal-1 team would do their part, and well. But she needed these two men sitting in her small briefing room to do theirs.

29

Spring Mountain Ranch, Nevada, October 1973

The United States Central Intelligence Agency maintains safe houses all around the world. Typically, they choose an unassuming private home or apartment in a good location and buy it using a dummy corporation. It's then available for clandestine meetings, or as an emergency bolt-hole or staging location for informants and spies.

The CIA also keeps several of these houses inside the United States, in places where national security issues overlap with international concerns. In the 1960s, with the rapidly growing torrent of gambling money pouring through Las Vegas, the Mafia and foreign interests had moved in to take their share. The CIA decided it was time to purchase a private location nearby, and called on a seemingly unlikely longtime ally to buy it: billionaire Howard Hughes.

A keen American patriot, Hughes was willing to finance activities that he judged were good for the country. With his multiple businesses, his reclusive and eccentric public persona, and his pattern of capricious, seemingly illogical decisions, Hughes provided perfect cover for multiple CIA operations. When an aging movie starlet named Vera Krupp put her 500-acre ranch, nestled in the hills on the outskirts of Las Vegas, up for sale, no one batted an eye when the Hughes Tool Company bought it. The cover story for the gossip sheets was that Hughes was trying to entice his estranged wife, Jean Peters, to join him in Vegas, where he was buying multiple properties and living in the Desert Inn Hotel.

The reality was that the CIA had funneled money to Hughes to make the purchase, and the ranch house's thick sandstone walls and out-of-the-way location in the Red Rock Hills made it ideal as a Sin City CIA safe house.

A perfect place to debrief a Soviet defector.

The CIA officer, Bill Thompson, picked Kaz up at Las Vegas McCarran airport after his commercial flight from Houston landed. Thompson drove north and west, angling them through the downtown gambling district. As they cruised along Las Vegas Boulevard, passing the glittering casinos, Kaz studied the long strip of oversized signs with their outlandish hotel fronts, and the crowds milling between them. Obviously fun for a lot of people, he knew, but not for him. Didn't people wonder where all the money came from? Why take risks you can't control?

Thompson saw where Kaz was looking, and misinterpreted, smiling knowingly. "Exciting, isn't it?"

Kaz looked across the seat at the man's thick glasses and combed-back hair, one knee bobbing as he drove. He didn't like Thompson's restless arrogance, but it wasn't his job to judge who the CIA hired.

"You like gambling, Bill?"

The CIA man frowned. "What, you don't?"

Kaz shook his head, and the ensuing silence hung between them. Kaz looked back outside.

"I hear you're staying with us for a few days." Thompson sounded less than thrilled at the prospect.

Kaz nodded. "General Phillips briefed me that things have been going well here, and he asked me to get the Russian pilot to Groom Lake, in place there with the MiG-25, as soon as you folks are done vetting him."

In truth, General Phillips had asked Kaz to try to hurry the process. In an intense week of activity, the technicians at Groom Lake had stripped the MiG-25 and rebuilt it, and it was almost ready to fly. "It's unique to have an experienced test pilot along with the airframe, especially given that the Soviets don't know we have it. The general wants us to take full advantage, and quickly. I'm here to help your process in any way I can, then move him as soon as you give the green light that he's for real. Hopefully, it won't take too much longer."

Bill Thompson glanced at Kaz, assessing. "So far, we're not seeing any problems. Our friends in the Mossad had given him a good going-over before they passed him on. They were obviously distracted by the outbreak of the war, but they didn't see any reason to doubt his story." Bright desert sunlight reflected off his thick glasses as he faced front again. "The fact that he delivered a top-end asset like the MiG-25, unasked, went a long way towards establishing his credibility." Thompson turned left onto Charleston Boulevard, heading straight west. "We agree with the Israelis, but of course we need to be extra-careful."

As they drove out of the city, the pavement gave way to dirt roads, and the government sedan began to climb into the hills. The sudden transition surprised Kaz; from the blaring Strip and the green lawns of suburbia, instantly into the empty dryness and scrub bush of the desert. Like driving from one movie set onto another.

In the distance Kaz spotted a cluster of green at the base of reddish rock outcroppings, and then the narrow road they were following crossed under a large wrought iron sign. A white pickup truck with the "H-T" of the Hughes Tool logo on the door was parked by the sign's support pillars. A thickset man in civilian clothes, leaning on the truck, made eye contact with Thompson and waved them through.

Kaz read the overhead sign aloud—"Spring Mountain Ranch"—and turned to Thompson. "I'm guessing the CIA didn't name it."

Thompson smiled thinly. "Maintaining the image."

They pulled up next to a rambling ranch house, surrounded by trees and white picket fencing. It was styled to look like a barn, with fieldstone lower walls, red vertical clapboard and white-trimmed windows. Extra gables in the cedar shake roof added to the countrified feel. Thompson parked beside two other nondescript sedans. As he got out of the car, Kaz noted several outbuildings, and a second white pickup and driver next to what looked like a small stable.

"How's security?" he asked.

"Tight and real quiet," Bill responded. "Right after Mr. Hughes bought it back in '67 there were apparently lots of looky-loos, but now, next to no one comes around. As far as the public knows, this place is used for Hughes company mid-level management meetings and overnights." He shrugged. "Nice and boring."

He unlocked the trunk, and Kaz retrieved his well-traveled suitcase.

Thompson gestured at the other cars. "Staff comes out every day to clean and cook. You hungry?"

The ranch house was bigger inside than Kaz expected, with pine floors, rough stone walls and a vaulted, wood-timbered ceiling. Looking out through the tall windows, he was surprised to see that the building enclosed a white, brushed-concrete deck and a large, bootprint-shaped swimming pool. He glanced at Thompson, raising an eyebrow.

The CIA officer smirked. "Job's gotta have a few perks." He pointed past the open kitchen at the end of the great room. "Bedrooms are down the hall there. Yours is second on the right."

Kaz looked in the other direction, where a single story jutted past the far end of the pool.

"That where you're debriefing the Russian?"

Thompson nodded, checking his watch. "They should be breaking for lunch soon. We'll eat out on the deck."

Kaz walked past two uniformed Hispanic women who were making sandwiches in the kitchen and counted doors. His small bedroom was carpeted in gray, and had dark wooden furniture and a single four-poster bed. The walls were smooth, off-white plaster, and hung with pictures of horses. When he joined Thompson by the pool, several other people were seated at the patio tables. Kaz nodded at the Russian, took an empty seat near him and said, "Dobry dyen, Sascha." Good day.

Grief recognized him and nodded. "Privyet, Kaz." Greetings.

Thompson sat down with them, to translate, and Kaz glanced at him, asking, "All right to talk about the MiG-25?"

"Sure, just not where it is or what the plans are, for now."

The two cooks set large plates of sandwiches on the tables, along with a bowl of potato salad and side plates of pickles and cheese. They put a pitcher of lemonade in each table's center, and took coffee orders.

Kaz took a sandwich, looked at Thompson, who nodded, and then looked at Grief.

"When did you first fly the MiG-25, Sascha?"

Thompson reached to serve himself as he interpreted for the two pilots.

Grief took a long drink of the lemonade and sat back into his wicker chair, savoring the tart liquid.

"I was thirsty. Been talking all morning." He looked relaxed, bemused, and his Russian was deep and guttural. He stretched, flexing his wide shoulders under the plaid short-sleeved shirt they'd provided for him. "First MiG-25 flight? That was in"—he looked into the distance—"1965. I was one of the early test pilots of the Ye-155-P1 interceptor model, doing envelope clearance." He smiled. "High and fast."

Kaz took the bait, asking the obvious pilot question. "How high and how fast?"

Grief stared at Kaz for a few seconds, evaluating. "What have you flown?"

"I'm Navy," Kaz said. "So standard basic training on the T-34 propeller two-seater, and then the T-2 trainer jet, then the F-11, and on to the F-4 Phantom." He paused while a cook set a black coffee in front of him. "I flew Phantoms off the ship in Vietnam, and then went to Test Pilot School, flew a variety of things there."

Grief nodded. "The Phantom. Top speed Mach 2.2, max altitude 18,000 meters?"

Kaz smiled, converting meters to feet. "Yeah, that's about right. I've had one up just a little over Mach 2.2, and on a good day you could get it a little higher, lob it up to 65,000 feet or so."

"Yes, but with that wing and tail design, at high angle of attack, it would want to roll and spin," Grief responded. "That heavy plane, hard to get control back, no?"

Thompson had to stop eating to concentrate on conveying the terminology.

Kaz acknowledged the expertise. "Yep, the flat spin is impossible to get out of. So we're careful with the Phantom at high altitude."

The Russian shrugged, going back to the original question. "I've had a MiG-25 beyond Mach 3 and flew it up over 36 kilometers." He thought for a second as he did the conversion for Kaz. "One hundred and twenty thousand feet."

Kaz whistled. No American jet could get close to that height. "What's the sky look like up there?"

Grief's smile was prideful. "Black. All of the blue is below you. In the distance, I could see the curve of Earth's horizon."

Thompson translated quickly and then seized the moment to take a big mouthful of potato salad, as everyone tried to picture what the Russian had just described.

Kaz swallowed a bite of his egg salad sandwich and washed it down with some coffee. "Almost makes you a cosmonaut."

Grief shook his head. "Cosmonauts don't fly anything." He waited until he swallowed to clarify. "They're just passengers, along for the ride. That doesn't interest me. Real pilots like to be in control."

Kaz smiled. "Spam in a can." Thompson frowned at the expression, and Kaz explained. "A lot of our test pilots feel the same way. They describe our astronauts as a lump of processed meat inside a metal container."

When Thompson relayed that to the Russian, Grief laughed, showing a flash of gold in his teeth. "We have the same thing in the Soviet Union—we call it tushonka." He chuckled and repeated the sound of Kaz's words to himself. "Spem ina ken."

Kaz was sure the CIA debriefing team had already dug into it carefully, but he decided to just ask directly. "Do you speak any English, Sascha?"

Grief answered in English before Thompson spoke. "A leetle beet, Kaz. From school." He rolled the *r* in the word "from."

Kaz nodded. The Air Force would need to provide a full-time translator and English teacher once the CIA had finished their work.

Grief turned from Kaz to Bill Thompson, reverting to Russian again. Thompson listened intently, wringing his hands restlessly at whatever the Soviet was saying. When he was done, Thompson nodded and translated so everyone could hear.

"What Grief is saying is even in the Soviet Union they know of Las Vegas. Their leaders often mention it as the symbol of all that is wrong with decadent America." Thompson looked at the CIA debriefing officers at the adjoining table. "He wants to know when we will trust him enough to go on an excursion together? An official training trip on Yankee culture?" Grief was smiling as Thompson concluded. "He says that test pilots have to be good gamblers. He'd like to see some of that terrible decadence for himself."

In the beginning the Americans had watched him every second, with someone always assigned to be next to him, guarding his bedroom door, ensuring that his movements were confined to the joined buildings. He hadn't wanted to be detected checking, so Grief simply assumed that his room was bugged; he was careful to say nothing aloud when he was alone. When he'd tried to open the single window, subtly, as though he was just staring out the window while leaning on the sill, he was unsurprised to find that it couldn't be opened.

In Russia, Grief habitually ran outdoors for fitness, and at first Bill Thompson had said no to his regular requests. But after settling into the routine for a few days, Thompson had relented, provided him with recently bought shoes, shorts, a T-shirt and tracksuit. Thompson was also a distance runner, so he escorted Grief himself every morning, ensuring that, as they ran, they kept to trails within direct sight of the buildings, and nowhere near the entrance road and gate. And the perpetual guard there.

Grief studied Bill as they ran together and could detect no concealed weapons. But with the wide, empty scrubland and no other buildings even visible, the opportunity for anyone to escape anywhere on foot was minimal.

He evaluated the CIA personnel as a mixture of smart interrogators and dumber guards, but all of them careful and dogmatic about following the rules. A group of unimaginative men, naturally and professionally watchful of each other. He'd tried engaging a few of them in casual conversation, but they stayed mute. He assumed, given this assignment, that at least some understood Russian, but no one gave that away.

His handler spoke Grief's language flawlessly, but since their first conversation on the plane, he'd given Grief no hint of how, or where, he had learned it. Grief found Thompson curiously hard to read, with his expressionless face half-covered by the thick glasses, and his perpetual nervous tic of wringing his hands. The American had an aloof quietness that never changed, showing zero warmth or empathy towards him.

The only wild cards were the temporary staff, the women who came daily to cook and clean, who provided a potential link to the outside. Over several days, Grief unobtrusively watched them. They spoke heavily accented English—first language Spanish, he guessed—when they exchanged words with anyone besides each other. Simple workers, with simple tasks. *Lesser-order people, worthy of no respect.* He noted that two pairs of women alternated days, but decided it made no difference. Unless something unusual happened, there would be no reason for him to communicate privately with them.

Besides, Grief was just being watchful. Thus far, the defection was proceeding as he had expected, and now he must simply wait.

30

Spring Mountain Ranch

The television in the main room was on, the volume up as a few of the CIA men perched on the surrounding sofas, intently watching an evening NBA game. The non–basketball fans had retreated to the deck around the pool or the surrounding buildings. Grief, an early riser, had already gone to bed, as usual.

Kaz and Bill Thompson were at the small table at the other end of the central area, in what the previous actress owner had described as the sun nook. Each man had an open beer in front of him.

Bill watched as Kaz delicately rubbed one of his eyes. "Tired?"

Kaz smiled and lowered his hand, tipping his chin towards the hallway. "Yep, that horse-themed bedroom is calling to me." He took a sip of his beer and regarded Bill for a few seconds. "Does the CIA teach you more about Russia than just the language?"

Bill frowned, his heavy glasses shifting slightly. "What do you mean?"

"I'm trying to understand what makes Sascha tick." *And other Russians too.* He hitched in his chair, putting his weight on an elbow. "At the Academy and in the Navy, the Soviet Union has always been portrayed simply as 'the enemy.' A malevolent monolith, some big bear lurking just beyond the horizon. There hasn't been much nuance." He shrugged. "Makes it easier for everyone in the military, I'm sure, but not very insightful. I was thinking maybe the CIA taught you guys to go deeper. 'Know thine enemy,' and all that."

"Yeah, in fact they do," Bill said. "At the Farm they give us a required reading list."

Kaz rolled the beer bottle in his fingers. "Any chance you could give me the CliffsNotes?"

There was a tinny series of shouts from the television, followed by a deep murmur of disapproval from the gathered men. Bill waited until it quieted.

"Sure. Russia's different, Kaz. Think about it. Here in America and in places like Australia and Japan, we have the oceans, and most of Europe has the Alps or a coastline that helps protect them. But Russia has no natural borders, so over their thousand-year history they've been repeatedly invaded by their enemies." He held up both hands so he could count on his fingers and thumbs. "Genghis Khan and his Mongol Horde, the Teutons, the Ottomans, the Poles, the Swedes, Napoleon, the Japanese, Hitler." He looked at his hands, rubbed them over each other in that odd way he had and then dropped them. "Huge losses of life too, extreme numbers, especially early on. Heck, in World War II alone we figure they lost over twenty-five million people." He paused, considering. "Imagine how we'd be if that was our history."

Kaz nodded but stayed silent. *When an expert is willing to teach you something, listen.*

"Russia also never had a Renaissance and all the cultural underpinnings of Western humanism that came with that. The complicated European Enlightenment that the Italians started, and the French and Germans continued along with the English, who then spread it all around their colonialized world, just never happened in Russia." Thompson was gazing over Kaz's head now, focused on his thoughts. "I was posted to the embassy in Moscow a few years back and saw it for myself. The Russians have operated on a feudal loyalty to strongmen leaders right from the beginning, and they still do, right up until today's Soviet Union." He nodded down the hall towards Grief's bedroom. "Some might say there's much to be admired in that kind of loyalty, but it's a pretty foreign idea here, where everybody behaves as if they are the makers of their own destiny, deluded as that can also be. Our man has a lot to unlearn if he's ever going to accept and fit into the cult of the individual that's normal here."

Thompson smiled self-consciously and picked up his beer. "After that lecture, I need a drink!" He took a swig and then wiped the wet from his mustache, staring across the room at his men, their focused faces blue in the light from the television. "Did you know that the original founders of Russia were Vikings? They led the Kievan Rus tribe—that's actually where the word 'Russian' came from." He looked back at Kaz. "That, coupled with the endless violent invasions and the lack of moderating cultural influences . . . it's as if the whole country had a long, brutalized childhood." He shrugged. "It's no excuse, but it helps me understand the behavior of the Soviets I deal with. And the men who lead them."

He exhaled and focused an intense, unblinking, guarded stare on Kaz. "Heavy stuff for a tired military man to take onboard."

Kaz shook his head. "Not at all, Bill. It's clarifying."

The CIA man looked at his near-empty beer bottle. "Okay, one last thought, then I'm done with my sermon. Average Russians think all Western leaders are weak. Sascha likely extrapolates that weakness to me and you. It's as if power and fate are the same thing in the Russian mind." A pause. "They have an old saying: 'Beat your own so that strangers are afraid of you.'" He cocked his head and looked hard at Kaz. "Can you imagine that as an operating principle here?"

Why does that sound like a threat?

Kaz let a long silence grow between them, to see if Thompson would say anything else. When he didn't, both men tipped up their bottles and drained them.

The basketball watchers suddenly yelled, and Kaz spoke above the noise.

"Nope, I can't imagine that." He stood, picked up the two empty bottles and set them on the counter by the sink. "Thanks, Bill. You've given me lots to think about in the ten seconds it's going to take me to fall asleep."

As he walked down the hall towards his room, he noticed that light still showed under Sascha's door.

You've got much to learn, my Russian friend. Kaz went into his bedroom, turned on the light and shut the door behind himself.

And so do I.

31

Moscow, 1970

As was normal at this time of the early morning, there were very few people riding the Moscow subway.

He listened to the familiar, rhythmic clacking as the Blue Line Metro carried him away from the city center, marking the change in echoes when the rails led aboveground. As the car slowed and rattled to a stop at Izmailovskaya station, he stepped quickly through the automatic doors out onto the tiled concrete platform, and descended the steps towards the exit, taking two at a time.

When he pushed through the station's heavy glass doors, he took a moment to adjust from the fluorescent interior warmth to the dark coolness of the predawn morning. As usual he'd stretched on the metro, doing isometrics against the handrails, loosening his thigh and calf muscles with deep squats and extensions. His tracksuit was thick enough to ward off the chill and he wore light leather gloves to keep his hands warm. He reached with both hands to sweep his hair back and began jogging, slowly at first, then picking up the pace to his normal running speed.

The exaggerated black figure of his shadow grew and shrank beside him as he ran, swiftly moving from lamppost to lamppost in the dark of the woods. The clattering sounds of the subway receded as he got deeper into Izmailovsky Park.

It was one of the oldest and largest parks in the city, a time-honored place for the common people to escape from the demands of urban life. He knew these paths well as a good place for off-hour running. And for concealment from the scrutiny of others.

He spotted the man three streetlights ahead. A dark figure sitting sprawled on a wooden park bench, with a mismatched collection of items next to him indicating that he'd slept the night there.

The runner shook his head. *Loser*, he thought. *The dregs of society*. He eased towards the left to give the derelict a wide berth. But the figure had spotted him approaching, and yelled as he drew near, sticking out a hand.

"Hey, athlete, spare some change?" The man's street-roughened, red-leather face cracked into a smile, revealing several missing teeth. "Maybe there's something to drink in your pocket?" His voice was coarse and raspy.

The runner locked eyes with the drunkard. *Parasite*. His gloved hand brushed his pocket, checking the contents.

Not recognizing the danger, the man leaned hard forward to stand up, looking for a windfall to start his day. Anyone crazy enough to run for no reason might be willing to part with a ruble or two. His head swam dizzily as he wavered upright and staggered forward a few paces to intercept. There was no one else in sight, and he didn't want to miss the chance.

The runner's lips curled in disgust. The lowlife had staggered into the path to try to block his way. He could smell the sourness of his unwashed body, poisoning the air near where it had slept.

No one had noticed the runner get off the train, and the two men were alone on the dark path in the park. Wrinkling his nose at the stink, he pulled up and stopped.

"You want money from me?"

Uncertain at the tone but still optimistic that this was an easy mark, the drunk nodded, and decided to act respectful. "Da, tovarisch." Rich people liked titles.

The runner glanced ahead along the path and then back over his shoulder, listening. Nothing. It was early. He looked back at the man and pointed past the bench with his left hand while digging into his pocket with his right.

"Come with me." He strode towards the bordering copse of trees, following a narrow footpath that led out of sight.

Greed outweighed caution and the drunk followed. Experience told him there couldn't be anything heavy, like a gun or a knife, in a runner's pocket. Or even the heavy metal of loose change. This was going to be paper money!

The athlete had stopped in the dim light ahead of him. As the drunk came nearer, he saw that the man was holding something in front of him, raising it now and nodding, an invitation to come close enough to take the gift.

The drunk stepped closer and reached out as the runner's hands opened and swept up, a metallic flash briefly visible in the obstructed lamplight. Then came a strange, cold feeling of something touching his neck as the runner's hands made a fast, twisting motion, followed by the instant alarm of a deep, choking pressure cutting in on all sides. The drunkard reached to pull whatever it was away, but he couldn't get his fingers under it. He moved to grab the runner, but the man had stepped agilely back, and was watching. The sudden pain was intense, making the drunk see stars. He tried to scream but was silenced by the tightness of the choking wire. His brain flared brightly without oxygen, whiteness filling his vision, and he felt himself falling, hitting the ground. Then he felt nothing.

The runner waited, watching, listening. He'd learned his lessons well: the execution had been near-silent, as always. He knew death wouldn't take long, and he used the seconds to look down at the prone figure in the half-light. A leech, sucking on the productivity and goodness of others, contributing nothing. A life no one cared about, one that the world was better without.

He bent, untwisted the wire and coiled his garrote back into his tracksuit pocket. As he stood, he realized he had an urge. He spread his legs to avoid spatter, lowered the front of his track pants and pissed on the body.

He jogged to where the path met the running trail. Glancing left and right to verify that no one was in sight, he retrieved the drunk's soiled paper and plastic bags from the bench and returned them to their owner, dropping them on the body. He brushed his gloved hands off, walked back out onto the paved path, took a deep, cleansing breath and resumed running.

Two lamplights farther, he ran past a billboard with a large, faded poster tacked in place. He knew it well and smiled slightly. It showed a muscular man in an armless workout shirt, smiling at an admiring boy sitting in his lap. The perfect father, an example to his son to never stop improving. To become the best he could possibly be.

He picked up the pace, pushing himself to get the maximum result, listening above his deep, controlled breathing to the distant mechanical sounds of a passing metro car.

32

Houston

The Aeroflot flight from Moscow to New York had been comfortable enough, stopping once to refuel in Paris, something for her to endure. The connecting Eastern Airlines nonstop to Texas was Svetlana's first time on an American carrier, and she'd taken her cues as to how to behave from her crew commander, Alexei Leonov. Minus the in-flight cognac.

A NASA delegation had met them at Houston Intercontinental Airport and driven them the hour south to Clear Lake, the home of Johnson Space Center and Houston Mission Control.

Svetlana had wondered how the Americans would treat her. Her first spaceflight had gone terribly awry, with a Cold War confrontation between an Apollo crew and the Soviet orbital space station Almaz; her crewmate cosmonaut and two astronauts had died. The Soviet space program had tightly controlled what the public was told. TASS had reported that there had been regrettable, accidental loss of life, but stressed the triumphant bottom line: Svetlana had walked on the Moon. The Russian people had celebrated that, and Brezhnev had made her a Hero of the Soviet Union at a ceremony at the Kremlin.

In Star City, they'd told her that part of the purpose of this initial Soyuz–Apollo training trip to the United States was going to be public relations. President Nixon had wanted her to visit the White House, but he was being investigated for illegal Watergate activities and had just fired his vice president for corruption. The White House handlers and NASA had agreed that appearing in public with a cosmonaut would be a mistake, so instead they'd booked her to do interviews with journalists. A photographer from *Life* magazine would be following her and the crew throughout their training, including the full-scale mock-ups today.

Svetlana hated the media side of a cosmonaut's life. It was nothing but a distraction from the real work, and she was thankful to see that the American crew members felt the same way.

The Johnson Space Center impressed her. It felt like the Lomonosov University campus where she'd studied in southwest Moscow, with large, widespread buildings and quietly busy people moving between them with purpose. Today they were in Building 9, and she felt almost at home. Hardware was the same everywhere, and training was training.

"So, let's go through the docking sequence again. Which ship is controlling attitude?" The Apollo commander, Tom Stafford, was standing next to a mock-up of the American and Soviet spaceships, reaching a long arm into the complex mechanism that would physically attach the Soyuz and Apollo capsules together.

"Each ship will have independent control until this sensor"—the NASA instructor pointed to a rocker switch on a large metal alignment petal—"is depressed by contact. Then both ships will automatically go to Free Drift, backed up by commanding from Mission Control in Moscow and here in Houston."

Stafford looked at Leonov, his Soviet counterpart, as the interpreter translated what they were saying. The men had instantly liked each other and respected what they each had accomplished; Leonov had done humanity's first-ever spacewalk, and Stafford had been to the Moon on Apollo 10.

Stafford said, "Alexei, I'm sure you agree, we need a crew override in case the automatic systems don't work."

Leonov nodded. "Da, the Soyuz has a manual backup option."

Svetlana looked at the two men, Stafford tall and lean, Leonov compact like the gymnast he once was, both prematurely balding. Their faces were intent as they methodically worked to understand this new machine, as they had so many before it, the complexity of the aerospace equipment providing them with a language all its own. But the objective was simple: how to make it work properly and keep it from killing them.

The other two American crew were standing, watching, and she glanced at them, trying to fix their unusual names in her head. The older one was Donald Slayton, but everyone called him Deke; she mouthed the name silently. He had a graying brush cut and deeply lined face. He had apparently been an astronaut since the time of Gagarin but had just recovered from some sort of medical problem. This would be his first spaceflight. The other astronaut was closer to her age, with blue eyes and a genial American smile. His name came easier to her, as it was just two guttural syllables: Vance Brand. He was also a rookie, and she'd realized with pride that of the six crew members of Soyuz–Apollo, only Leonov, Stafford and she had spaceflight experience.

Stafford conveyed the ease of longtime command and made the decisions for the group. Svetlana knew that when the Americans came to Star City to train, Leonov would naturally assume that role. She was also seeing that this was going to be a simple spaceflight: launch, rendezvous, dock, open the hatch, and show the world a clear example of direct cooperation between the two superpowers. There'd be a few experiments and too much media focus, and then they'd undock, the Americans to deorbit into the sea and the Russians to land back on the steppes of Kazakhstan.

Compared with the stakes of her first spaceflight, this one was almost trivial, especially since they had three cosmonauts in the Soyuz to share the tasks. But no matter—spaceflights were rare, and this was unlikely to be her last. There was a new Salyut space station being built, with plans for more in the future. For now, she would focus on doing this one right.

There was a pause in the instructor's explanations, and the *Life* magazine photographer took advantage of the moment.

"Can I get everyone on the crew in front of the simulator?" The six of them dutifully lined up, the Americans in light-brown flight suits, the Russians in pale green.

"Svetlana, please move to the middle."

Alexei winked at her, and she reluctantly stepped between him and Stafford.

Bloody media.

"Here's to the crew of Apollo–Soyuz!"

Tom Stafford had bought a round of beer, and the six of them clinked the brown bottles together. They were seated around a small table in a bar he'd brought them to, near the Johnson Space Center.

Tastes like kvass, Svetlana thought, the standard fermented Soviet farm drink. She'd heard about beer, but it wasn't common in Russia. She shrugged at its thinness. *Vodka's better.*

They'd dismissed the translator, relying on goodwill and the few words they'd learned of each other's language to communicate. Since her spaceflight, Svetlana had been studying English intensely, and was happy to have a chance to use it.

Alexei spoke. "Tom, that is mistake." He was frowning but in an exaggerated way to show he wasn't serious. "Is not Apollo–Soyuz. Our mission name: Soyuz–Apollo!" His eyes twinkled, and he raised his beer. Stafford laughed, and they all clinked bottles and drank again, toasting Alexei's version.

Stafford turned to Svetlana. "So, what did you think of the Moon?" He'd been taking language lessons as well, and added a few words of

Russian to clarify, his Oklahoma accent strong. "Kak Luna?" The other men quieted, and all looked at her.

She decided to try in English. "Very beautiful." She rolled the *r* and pronounced the three syllables of "beautiful" distinctly. "So big, and . . ." She hunted for the word and found it. "Unknown." She found herself looking down, remembering. "A sad place."

Tom Stafford nodded. His Apollo 10 crew had been the precursor to Neil Armstrong's Apollo 11; they had skimmed low over the surface, proving the technology but not landing. "Da," he agreed. "Beautiful, and somehow sad too."

The bar was called the U-Joint, and it was the preferred astronaut hangout, its walls decorated with NASA photos. Stafford pointed his beer at a separate collection of portraits—astronauts who had died. "We lost Luke Hemming and Chad Miller on your mission." The two men's smiling faces looked at them from the wall, oblivious to what the future had had in store for them. "We need to get a photo of your crewmate up there too. What was his name? Mitkov?"

Svetlana understood most of what he said. She raised her beer. "To Andrei Mitkov. And Luke, and Chad." She felt much bitterness at what had happened to Andrei, but everyone at the table was also a military aviator who had lost close friends, and so they all drank deeply.

Alexei broke the mood by jumping to his feet and walking over to the bar, asking the bartender loudly, "Young lady, beer is okay, but you have vodka?" He pointed at the shelf of hard liquor behind her, and she lifted out a large bottle of Gordon's with "vodka" written large on the label. Alexei smiled and said "Da!" making a circular motion with his hand and then pointing at his table.

The bartender nodded. These Russians were easier to understand than her typical crowd of drunken NASA engineers. "Six vodkas, coming right up."

As Alexei returned, triumphant, Tom Stafford was smiling broadly at him. "You know, Alexei, it occurs to me . . ." He paused. He'd noticed that Svetlana understood the most English and he gestured for her to help translate what he wanted to say. "Deke, here, was Chief Astronaut for many years. He and I have been thinking about an adventure, and we are pretty sure we can swing it."

Svetlana's English failed her. "Swing it?"

Tom clarified. "Manage it. Make it happen. Do it."

She worked through the words, hastily translated for her crewmates, then asked, "Do what?"

Tom smiled. "We figure it would be a shame if you traveled all the way to America and all you got to see was the space center and this bar." He looked at Deke and smiled even wider. "Vance, Deke and I need to keep current as pilots. We fly jets as part of our training, and NASA's T-38s are two-seaters."

Svetlana shook her head. With the Okie accent and fast talking, she'd only caught a few words.

"Never mind," Tom said. "Let me cut to the chase." He paused, making eye contact with the three cosmonauts.

"Today is Thursday." He raised his eyebrows at Svetlana, and she translated the familiar vocabulary. "This weekend—Friday, Saturday—we're going to go flying." He waved his finger in a circle, including the six of them.

"Flying?" Svetlana asked, now excited. "What aircraft? To where?"

The waitress arrived with a tray of full shot glasses, and Tom grabbed one, raising it to the group.

"In NASA jets, to the most American place there is." He smiled at Alexei. "The crew of Soyuz–Apollo is going to Las Vegas!"

33

The Strip, Las Vegas

It was Sinatra's name on the tall marquee along Las Vegas Boulevard that brought them in.

CIA officer Bill Thompson had announced that he'd decided to turn Alexander's request into a graduation reward. The Russian defector had been cooperative and apparently genuine, and the proximity of the Las Vegas Strip had been too hard for any of them to resist. Especially after the quiet monotony of Spring Mountain Ranch. Kaz had made a shopping trip into town the day before, and he and the Russian were wearing new Levi's and Ban-Lon shirts for the occasion.

Thompson parked in the vast, half-full lot next to Caesars Palace, and as he turned the key to shut off the car, he made firm eye contact with Grief to emphasize his concerns.

"Sascha, this is intended as an introduction to your new life, and as a thank-you for the depth of detail you have given us in the debriefings. We're going to try our luck at the casino, catch Sinatra's matinee and then get dinner. The three of us will stay together at all times, and any use of the Russian language will be kept quiet. Understand?" He translated quickly for Kaz's benefit, and Kaz nodded.

Grief was also nodding and asked, in Russian, "What about money?"

"The casino uses chips, and I'll get some for each of us." Thompson smiled thinly. "Uncle Sam will stake us to a modest amount. Part of your American indoctrination and cultural training."

They exited the car and walked along the tall Italian cedars and spurting jet fountains towards the sweeping semicircle of pillars mimicking an Italian piazza. Topless marble statues bracketed the covered entrance, with multicolored flags fluttering high above in the hot desert wind.

Stepping inside was like entering another world. It was instantly dark and cool with air-conditioning, the smoky glow of slot machines and gambling tables receding into the distance. The sounds of traffic on the Strip had been suddenly replaced by the competing muted cacophony of one-armed bandits and Muzak.

A young woman in a toga approached them, smiling. "Welcome to Caesars Palace. I am your slave. Can I take you into the Lion's Den?"

Kaz looked at Bill Thompson, his eyebrows raised.

Bill shrugged. "Why not?"

They had stopped in El Paso to refuel, halfway between Houston and Las Vegas. Just two long flight legs across the dryness of the American Southwest in three NASA T-38s—a geography lesson for the Russian back-seaters to absorb, staring out through their curved plexiglas canopies, seeing America like Tom Stafford wanted.

Texas is like the Kazakh Republic, Svetlana thought, wondering if there were any camels down below on the dusty farmland. As they crossed into New Mexico and then Arizona, she was fascinated by the fissured, rugged emptiness. It looked much more textured and three-dimensional than her impression had been from orbit.

After landing at McCarran airport in Las Vegas, the three jets taxied in together, Tom Stafford leading, Deke Slayton and Vance Brand tucked in tight on each wing. They'd packed overnight bags in the luggage pods mounted under their jets and changed out of their flight suits in the fixed-base operator pilots' lounge. Stafford ordered two taxis, and as the six of them piled in, he told the drivers where to take them.

He'd been thinking about it while flying and wanted to show his Russian crewmates a definitively good American time.

Bill Thompson glanced at his watch. He'd had a string of bad luck and blown through his own chips, but both Kaz and the Russian still had small, neat stacks of blue and purple on the green velvet in front of them. After he'd listened to Bill's explanation of the rules of playing blackjack, and observed Kaz's tactics, Grief had been holding his own.

The woman in the toga had initially led them to the slot machines, but after watching for a minute, Grief had shaken his head and spoken quietly to Bill. "That's just random, and the machine must win." He pointed at the card tables in the center of the room. "I want to be able to make choices, have some control of my fate."

Bill pulled three tickets out of his pocket and looked again at his watch. "Sinatra's show starts in fifteen minutes, gentlemen. One more hand, then time to go."

Kaz picked up his chips and thanked the dealer. Grief touched his small stack with his fingertip to count them. He was up six American dollars from what the CIA officer had given him.

Even here, in this strange place, I know how to win.

He carefully turned up the corner of the cards the dealer had placed in front of him and placed one more bet.

So this is true capitalism, Svetlana thought, looking across the Caesars Palace lobby. She smiled at herself. *Kind of exciting*.

Tom Stafford came back with room keys. "Alexei, you and I are bunking together. Deke, you're with Valery. And since Svetlana needs her own room, Vance, you luck out and get your own too." He looked at the group. "What's everyone feel like? Grab a late lunch and then try our hand with Lady Luck?"

The three Russians looked at him, uncomprehending, so he decided to stop asking and just command. He pointed past the slot machines to the elevators in the distance. "Go to your rooms, and we'll meet back here in twenty minutes." He looked at Svetlana to translate.

She nodded, repeating, "Dvadtsat minoot, syuda," for her Russian crewmates. Holding her key, she followed Vance into the noise of the casino.

The designers of Caesars had carefully considered how to extract as much money as possible, especially from the visitors who had committed to staying at their hotel. The brightest and most alluring slot machines, the ones that returned the maximum 25 percent profit steadily to the house, were closest to the entrance and all along the walkway to the elevators. They'd placed the high-rise of guest rooms at the back, which meant people had to run the gauntlet of craps, blackjack and roulette tables on the way. Simple marketing: let 'em know what they don't want to miss.

The concert hall and restaurants were built off to the left, with their own lobby and space for people to line up for the attractions. Kaz was standing next to Grief, looking around idly, as the matinee show line slowly shuffled towards the entrance to Sinatra's performance.

It was Tom Stafford's height and balding head that caught Kaz's eye. The cigarette smoke obscured him somewhat, but his lanky gait was familiar. Kaz smiled in surprise. *What the heck is Stafford doing here?* He looked at the group trailing Tom as they walked towards the elevators, and spotted Deke and Vance, plus two men he didn't recognize. And a woman, who was looking directly back at him.

"Kaz!" Bill Thompson's voice cut through his distraction. Kaz realized the line had moved several feet forward, and the people around him were waiting for him to catch up.

"Sorry, Bill, just thought I recognized someone." Alarm bells ringing in his head, Kaz acted swiftly. He walked to the Russian's left and spoke to get his attention.

"Sascha, have you heard of Frank Sinatra?"

Kaz flicked a quick glance over Sascha's shoulder, towards the group now waiting for an elevator. They were all chatting with each other, except for the woman, who was still staring at him.

Grief understood what Kaz meant, and answered in English, per Thompson's instructions. "Yes, Frank Sinatra very famous." His back was now to the elevators.

Kaz needed to hold his gaze. "Have you heard him sing 'Fly Me to the Moon'?"

Grief frowned, not understanding. Bill quietly explained, singing the chorus of the song.

Grief looked at Kaz, smiling now, and shook his head. "No, don't know that music."

The elevator doors had opened, and Stafford was calling the woman to get her attention. She turned at Tom's voice and joined the group, the doors closing behind her.

Kaz turned to the CIA officer beside him.

"Bill, we need to talk."

As the six of them looked at the elevator lights, waiting for their floor, Tom Stafford smiled at Svetlana.

"Sinatra fan, are you?" He'd noticed where she'd been looking.

Svetlana looked at him, not understanding.

He shrugged. "I got us tickets for tonight's show when I checked us in." He glanced at Deke and Vance. "Ol' Blue Eyes is as American as it gets!"

The doors opened, and as they found their rooms, Tom called down the hallway to remind everyone. "Twenty minutes, downstairs."

—

Svetlana closed the door behind her, walked across the room to set her small duffel bag on the bed and then stood, stock-still, her mind whirling. She was pretty sure that the taller man standing in the theater line was the American that she'd had a confrontation with during the tumult following splashdown after her spaceflight.

How can that be? It's ridiculous! The population of the United States is over 200 million people!

She thought it through. She'd only seen the American briefly, and under stressful and action-packed circumstances. She could easily be wrong about him.

But it was the shorter man standing next to him that had truly startled her. She'd initially seen his face head-on, then in profile, and finally the back of his head as he'd turned away. She was certain. This was someone she'd met on multiple occasions, who had been one of her instructors, someone she'd flown several airplanes with. A senior Soviet test pilot she'd last seen when she'd left Ramenskoye to join the cosmonaut corps.

What on earth is Alexander Vasilyevich Abramovich doing in a casino in America? How is that even possible? The thought banged in her head, echoing, until a new one took its place.

And what am I going to do about it?

34

Las Vegas

"It makes sense," Kaz said. He and Bill Thompson were sitting beside each other in a steakhouse half a mile down the Strip from Caesars, talking quietly in English as the Russian tucked into his meal on the other side of the large, round booth. "Before I left Houston, I'd heard they were going to send a crew over to start training with Tom, Deke and Vance for Apollo–Soyuz. Putting that woman on the crew not only rewards her, but makes the politicians look good."

When Kaz had quickly explained to Thompson that he had spotted three Soviet cosmonauts, including Svetlana Gromova, they'd aborted seeing the show and immediately left Caesars Palace. On the way out, Kaz had phoned Tom Stafford's room from the front desk. No, Tom said, he and his crew hadn't spotted Kaz, and he had quickly agreed that he would keep an eye on Svetlana. And he'd keep the group at Caesars all evening. As a military man, he'd immediately accepted the explanation that Kaz was in Nevada on a classified assignment, and promised to reassure Svetlana, if she asked, that she must have been mistaken.

Kaz hadn't mentioned the defector.

Bill Thompson tipped his head discreetly at Grief. "Would any of the three cosmonauts recognize our boy?"

Kaz nodded. "Very possibly. The test pilot community here in the States is pretty small, and I bet it's the same for them. Most of our astronauts used to be test pilots, so we have to assume that's also true for them." He thought for a second. "Though from what I've read, Yuri Gagarin was just a regular military pilot, and Valentina Tereshkova was mostly a parachutist. But I'm not sure about their Apollo–Soyuz crew."

Bill pushed his steak around his plate with his fork, his appetite spoiled by what had happened. And the amount of explaining and paperwork that was now going to follow. But first things first.

"We need to get backgrounds on all three cosmonauts to evaluate the likelihood that one of them may have known our friend. I'll need to talk to General Stafford ASAP about that and brief him to watch out for odd behaviors on his crew. I'll put him in touch with our Houston office in case he needs help."

He glanced at the Soviet, who was finishing his steak, and then back at Kaz. "Did you see any sign that he spotted or recognized the cosmonauts?"

Kaz shook his head. "No, he was looking at me the whole time. I'm sure he didn't see them."

Bill pushed his plate away. "Okay, enough for now. We need to get back to Spring Mountain and start preparing Sascha's transfer up to Groom Lake." He looked at Kaz sardonically. "And no more trips into the big city."

Bill looked away. "Damn, I was really looking forward to seeing Sinatra!"

To Svetlana, the evening seemed to last forever. She thought gambling was stupid—couldn't everyone see that the money they were steadily losing paid for the opulence of this place?

At the Americans' urging she had taken her turn at a slot machine and was unsurprised when her tokens quickly ran out. She demurred at the card table, choosing to watch Stafford and Leonov play and laugh together. Her engineer crewmate Valery Kubasov declined as well—good to let the two commanders bond.

As soon as they'd come down in the elevator, she'd excused herself by saying she had to go to the ladies' room, walking instead to where she'd seen Abramovich and the American. But the line had disappeared. She carefully read the theater entrance sign, noting showtimes, and checked her watch, guessing when the audience would be coming out. She looked around for a good place to be able to scan the crowd's faces, and decided on the theater gift shop, before rejoining her group.

Dinner was in an ornate cafeteria with the clumsy-sounding name of Noshorium. She asked Vance what it meant, but he just shrugged, smiling, and said he didn't know. *Odd,* she thought. He helped her order, and she watched carefully as salad arrived and the Americans ate all of it, well before the meat dish was served. *Why do they wait to serve all the food?*

She'd declined dessert, having anticipated the large size of the cheesecake slices that were set in front of the men. She checked her watch, quietly excused herself again and walked quickly to the theater shop, slipping into position just as the exit doors opened.

Standing behind a rack of postcards, she scanned faces as they passed, watching intently until the initial flood of people had dwindled to the final few, but she saw no one she recognized. *Chyort! How did I miss them? Could I have been wrong in what I saw?*

Stafford had given each of them a ten-dollar bill, and she used hers to buy two postcards, returning to the restaurant just as the men were getting up. She showed them her purchases: an exterior view of the building and a showgirl, and Tom smiled. "Souvenirs!"

Svetlana nodded. It was the same word in Russian.

Tom Stafford checked his watch. "Everybody ready for a little blue-eyed music?"

—

During the show, Svetlana had maneuvered to sit next to Alexei. In a lull between songs, she had quietly asked if all three cosmonauts could meet in her room at the end of the evening. He'd looked at her for a moment, puzzled, but had shrugged and nodded. After the show, Stafford insisted on them all going to the Cleopatra Bar for a nightcap, but Svetlana had declined, saying with the long day she had a headache.

In the quiet of her room, she turned on the light above the small desk, grabbed the pad of paper and ballpoint pen that were provided, and made herself notes. It was how she'd clarified her thoughts throughout her training, and she sought the certainty of how it felt, now, to have the facts written before her.

Alexander Abramovich, she wrote, in Cyrillic. Next to it she put *Moscow 1970?* Was that the last time and place she remembered seeing him? Then she wrote *Same American as at splashdown?* Again with a question mark, which she didn't like. Underneath, she hurriedly penned *Why not at theater exit?* During the show she'd surveyed the room and saw there were signs marking other exits, but she guessed that they were only for emergencies, and that everyone should have come directly past her into the casino. She listed a few possibilities: *missed them, other exit, not the same people*. She frowned at the last one. She didn't like being wrong and she was confident in what she'd seen. A thought struck her, and she added *They saw me and left before the show*.

Svetlana closed her eyes, picturing it. The American had definitely made eye contact with her. She opened her eyes and wrote a new line. *Would he recognize me?* They'd only seen each other in scuba gear, in and out of masks. Her hair had been wet and slicked down. She shrugged, and wrote *I recognized him*.

She chewed briefly on the end of the pen, and then added *Who does the American work for?* She wished she knew more about American government organizations, but she pictured who in the Soviet Union would have been doing the things he'd done at splashdown. She wrote: *Military? Spy? Maybe both?*

She started a new section. *Why here?*

It was the core question. How could a senior Soviet test pilot be in Las Vegas? Maybe he was here on some sort of international exchange program. She knew that Brezhnev had made a goodwill visit to America in June, and she'd heard they'd even opened a new Soviet consulate in San Francisco. Could this be some sort of Air Forces' easing of tension, like Apollo–Soyuz was going to do in space?

She pictured the United States as she'd seen it from orbit, focusing on the area around Vegas. There were many military airports in the region, including America's main flight test center at Edwards Air Force Base—she and her colleagues had been tasked with photographing all of them. She straightened in her chair as she visualized the most remote and secret part of the whole country, which was just north of here: the US nuclear test range. She wrote the words on her paper, hoping it would help her to see a link.

Svetlana paused, scanning her room, and was happy to spot what resembled a glass teapot on a shelf. She got up and went to inspect it, also finding small packets of instant coffee and two tea bags. She puzzled out how to add water to the boiler, slid the glass pot under the spigot and turned it on, relieved to see a small light glow red. Within a few seconds it gasped, and then started spitting boiling water into the pot. She dropped in a tea bag and sat back down to review her notes.

When Alexei and Valery joined her, they would want to know that she was certain of whom she'd seen. She pictured the moment again, like a tableau. Even though she'd only had a glimpse of Abramovich's face, she'd recognized him, and she'd seen the American full-on for many seconds. She wrote on the paper: *One, maybe just resemblance, but two together? Must be!*

The boiler suddenly began wetly snoring, and she saw with satisfaction that the glass pot was now half-full of steaming brown liquid. She carefully poured some into the hotel mug and examined the little containers beside the tea bags. They were clearly labeled with a picture of a cow, so she peeled one's paper lid open, sniffed the contents, shrugged and poured it in. There was a small wooden stick on the tray, and she used it to stir until the tea was a familiar creamy color, then took a tentative sip. *Not bad.*

Svetlana checked her watch.

They'd be here soon.

35

Caesars Palace

Alexei Leonov frowned, trying to focus carefully on what Svetlana was saying.

He and Valery had had several drinks with the Apollo crew, and the blur of alcohol made her even harder to believe. He was seated in the hotel room's only chair, and Valery was perched on a corner of the bed. Svetlana was standing by the curtained window.

"So how far away were these men from you?" Alexei worked hard to keep the incredulity out of his voice. She was a member of his crew, and he needed her to know he was taking her seriously. No matter how far-fetched her claim.

Svetlana spoke calmly. "About fifty meters. It was when we were walking down the corridor towards the elevators."

Valery spoke. "Fifty meters! Faces are small that far away." He had decided to take on the role of devil's advocate, freeing his commander to appear fair. "For how many seconds did you see them?"

"I first spotted them through the cigarette haze, and then they became clearer when we got nearer to the elevators." She considered. "All told, about thirty seconds." She looked squarely at Valery. "Plenty of time to become certain."

He pursed his lips and exhaled through his nose, the vodka he'd drunk making him bolder than normal. Yes, Svetlana was qualified, but he fundamentally didn't like or trust women in the cosmonaut program. They were too emotional and bound to cause problems. Like this one.

"So fifty meters away, for just half a minute." He said it flatly, as if laying the simple facts of her story open for Alexei to interpret.

Alexei took a different tack. "If this was the American who was at your splashdown, he must have something to do with NASA, and our NASA crew might have recognized him. Did you see any sign that they saw each other?"

Svetlana shook her head. "No, all three were distracted, and I don't think any of them noticed. And the American made no effort to get their attention." She pictured the expression on Kaz's face. "I'm convinced this was an encounter he didn't want. I think he was trying to distract Sascha to keep him from looking at us." A pause. She was the only test pilot in the group, the only one Abramovich might recognize. "At me."

Alexei considered. If what she was saying was true, no matter how unlikely, it was important. The question was how to deal with it. He sat quietly for a few seconds, and then decided.

"Let's not trouble our crewmates with this matter. It will only be a complication. And if we run into this American, it's best you behave as if you didn't see him, and don't recognize him. If he has a secret to keep, we should let him keep it, for now."

He looked at Valery, and then back at Svetlana.

"But as soon as we get back to Houston, I want you to brief our embassy handler on what you saw. He can then pass the information securely back to Moscow. If there is some reason why Soviet test pilot Alexander Abramovich is in America, they will know about it."

Svetlana nodded at his logic, glad to be taken seriously.

Alexei watched her face and saw acceptance. *Good*, he thought. *Enough of this nonsense*.

—

During the NASA jet flight back from Las Vegas, Svetlana had gone over every detail in her mind, realizing that she, alone, was going to have to be persuasive enough to spur their embassy contact into action. Alexei had accepted her story, but Valery was unconvinced. She needed to do better, passing word to Moscow, if she wanted to be believed.

Even though it was late on Sunday night by the time they'd landed at Ellington Field in Houston and returned to their hotel, Svetlana and Alexei had knocked on the attaché's door to explain what she'd seen.

Alexei hadn't told the attaché where the crew was going that weekend, and brusquely ignored his shocked reaction, saying the trip had been important for crew bonding, and that it had been kept quiet from NASA too. Such things were also common in Russia, he reminded him. And only because they'd gone there had Svetlana stumbled across potentially important information.

On hearing Svetlana's story, the attaché had been dubious. But he listened attentively—these two people in his room were, after all, the first Soviets to walk in space and to walk on the Moon. The woman's clarity and certainty were strong enough to make him realize that he would need to report what she had said in detail, so he asked her to write it out in longhand. He wanted to be sure he had the specifics correct when he transmitted to his superiors.

36

Ministry of Foreign Affairs, Moscow

The Soviet Union was the biggest country in the world and had an outsized bureaucracy to match. When word of a possible sighting of a Soviet military pilot in the United States reached the Motherland, the wheels turned officiously. And slowly.

When the attaché returned to the Soviet embassy in Washington after the cosmonauts' training week in Houston was over and they were flying back to the USSR, he briefed Ambassador Dobrynin, who quickly read the cosmonaut's report as well as the attaché's summary of all circumstances. The ambassador had heard no rumors of a test pilot being in America, but he allowed the report to be sent, just in case. Probably a case of mistaken identity. But his long years as a diplomat had taught him that there was no harm in being thorough.

The information made its way to the Ministry of Foreign Affairs in Moscow in the twice-weekly diplomatic pouch, carried on the Aeroflot flight from New York. The distribution codes on the envelope were read by the filing clerk on the third floor of the towering building, and the report was routed up to the twelfth floor, to the desk of the Assistant Deputy Minister for Military Liaison.

Nine days and six thousand miles distant from what Svetlana had seen, the envelope was slit open and carefully read. Then read again.

On the left corner of Vitaly Kalugin's desk the beige phone rang, its shrill bell making the entire rotary dial vibrate. Still eyeing the report he was reading, Vitaly lifted the handset and brought it to his ear.

"Kalugin," he said. Anyone phoning this number would know he worked in the First Chief Directorate of the KGB—the State Security section responsible for foreign espionage.

On the line was someone in Foreign Affairs that he knew slightly, a man of roughly equal rank to him, whom he'd talked to before. He listened carefully as the man explained why he was calling.

Vitaly understood. He'd been responsible for running an American Air Force officer who had become an astronaut on Apollo 18, and who had died during an armed altercation after splashdown. Vitaly's contact at Foreign Affairs had recognized a common name on a new development and had rightly followed up with him in case there was a link.

Vitaly pulled his green baize notebook closer and took notes as he listened. In neat Cyrillic he made bullet points for Major Svetlana Gromova, for Las Vegas, and then for Colonel Alexander Vasilyevich Abramovich. He asked his counterpart to repeat a couple of details about the American that Major Gromova thought she'd seen, and then ended the conversation, but not before extracting a promise that a copy of the report would be sent to his desk. They were of equal rank, but the KGB had primacy.

After he put the handset back into its cradle, he studied his notes and then, below them, wrote a short list of actions, drawing small, neat, empty squares next to each, to be ticked off as they were accomplished.

Vitaly sat back and thought his way through the possibilities, double-checking his logic. He nodded again. It wouldn't take long to see if this amounted to anything.

He flipped to the back of his notebook and ran his finger down his list of contacts in other departments. Picking the handset back up, he pinched it against his ear with his shoulder so he could stabilize the phone's base with his left hand as he spun the rotary dial.

When his call was answered, Vitaly asked a few simple and direct questions. His counterpart asked him to wait while he checked. Vitaly's fingertip idly touched each of the empty boxes on his page. His job was to solve puzzles and occasionally look into the future. He was good at both, and his recent success with the American astronaut had gained him a promotion within his department. But odds were that this issue would turn out to be nothing.

"Vitaly, are you there?"

"Da, listening."

"I found the file. Test Pilot and Hero of the Soviet Union Colonel Alexander Vasilyevich Abramovich was killed in action. He was shot down in a MiG-25 off the coast of Israel on 5 October this year. No body was found, but the Israelis handed over confirming pieces of the wreckage." A pause. "Does that answer your question?"

Vitaly's forehead creased in a frown. This was going to take more work.

"Da, thank you." He hung up for the second time, and placed a small, neat X in one of the boxes. And then wrote out two more tasks for himself. Two more empty boxes to complete.

If Abramovich had been killed nearly a month ago, who had Major Gromova seen? She'd recognized two people together, which added credibility to what she had reported.

He looked at the last thing he had written on the page and checked his watch. It was still early enough in the day that there was probably time.

He needed to take a trip out to Star City and talk to Major Svetlana Gromova himself.

37

Star City, USSR

"Vitaly Kalugin," he repeated to the Star City gate guard. "KGB," he added, holding his propusk badge up for inspection.

That elicited an instant response, with a stiffening of posture and a salute. "Izvineetya, tovarisch. Please pass through."

Vitaly had phoned ahead to make sure the woman was available, and then had taken the metro and the elektrichka commuter train out to Tsiolkovskaya station, next to Star City, the cosmonaut training center. An early snow had fallen, and the trees were already laden in white, dampening all sound as he walked inside the compound. It was only 50 kilometers from his Moscow office, but it felt entirely different. A tightly knit community, people moving with purpose. A place that existed to prepare cosmonauts for spaceflight.

The dezhurny duty officer in the headquarters building was expecting him, and escorted Vitaly down the corridor to a small, empty conference room. Vitaly checked his watch and accepted the offer of tea and sukhari; the hot liquid and hard dried bread were welcome after the walk through the late-fall cold. He'd arrived a few minutes ahead of time and sat patiently. The little-used room was unheated, and he kept his coat on.

He hadn't announced his presence to the Star City commander, though he was certain word would have been passed. If the KGB wanted a quiet meeting with one of the cosmonauts, there was no reason to make a fuss by formalizing the visit.

Vitaly was used to it.

The door opened at the arranged time, and a woman strode in and stopped, facing him. She was wearing a pale-green flight suit and jacket and carrying a satchel. Her expression was wary, but respectful. She nodded at him.

"Good afternoon. I'm Major Gromova."

"Kalugin, Vitaly Dmitriyevich. Major in KGB Counterintelligence, Special Service Two. Good afternoon. Thank you for meeting with me."

Svetlana nodded again, saying nothing. She hadn't really had a choice. The Chief Cosmonaut had passed word that the KGB wanted to meet with her, and here she was.

"Sit, please," Vitaly said. "Would you like tea?"

"Nyet, spasiba." She was, in fact, thirsty, but this wasn't a social call, and it wasn't a KGB officer's job to get her tea. She took a seat opposite him at the conference table and waited.

Vitaly looked at her, his expression impassive. He decided to start obliquely.

"How well do you know the test pilot Colonel Alexander Vasilyevich Abramovich?"

Svetlana shrugged. *This is how it is going to be.*

"He was one of my instructors and then a fellow test pilot when I was at Ramenskoye. We flew together a few times. I didn't know him socially."

Vitaly nodded. "When was this?"

"Three or four years ago. My time at Ramenskoye overlapped with his by about a year." *Asking questions we both know the answers to.*

"How would you describe him?"

Odd question. "About 1.8 meters tall, dark hair, fit, quiet, professional. Good pilot."

"Anything remarkable or distinguishing about him?"

"If you mean could I easily recognize him, then the answer is yes. He was a coworker I saw regularly, so I know what he looks like."

Vitaly stared at her for several seconds, then said, "Tell me, in detail, what you saw in Las Vegas."

Svetlana took a slow, deep breath, and then recounted, in sequence, what she had seen, including returning to the hotel theater to try to see the group of men exiting.

Vitaly leaned forward, rested an elbow on the table and cupped his chin. The KGB had lost an experienced agent in the altercation after this cosmonaut's splashdown, and the Americans had naturally not publicly shared any names or details of the personnel who had been involved. "Tell me about the American you recognized."

Svetlana frowned. "Your people debriefed me in detail after my spaceflight. Have you spoken to them?"

Vitaly just looked at her, waiting for an answer to his question.

She sighed. "I only encountered him briefly, inside the Apollo capsule underwater after splashdown, and then, later, I saw him above water from a distance. I think I heard one of the Americans call him Kaz, but I'm uncertain—they were speaking English. But if so, he may have been the same person in their Mission Control that I had spoken with from space. The names were similar."

When the KGB man didn't respond, she continued. "But I already debriefed all that, many months ago."

He decided to give a little. "Znayoo." I know. A pause, then he asked, "With wet hair and face masks and the armed conflict, how certain are you that this was the same man you saw in Las Vegas?"

"Very certain. There was no question, I just instantly knew it was him."

Vitaly had been watching her face closely. Her response to this question was the main reason he'd taken the time to come to Star City. To personally gauge her certainty.

He picked up his cup, tipped it to drain the last of the now-cold tea and set it carefully back on its saucer. He had one more key item he wanted to study her response to.

"Did either of the men recognize you?"

Svetlana looked squarely at him. "Colonel Abramovich did not—he never looked at our group at all. But the American and I made eye contact, so he may well have."

"Did he show any reaction to seeing you?" This was important.

"Not that I saw, no."

Vitaly sat back, and mentally reviewed the neat, open boxes he'd drawn by the list in his notebook. All checked off now.

He stood, cinched his coat's belt and started moving towards the door. "Spasiba, Major Gromova."

Sitting on the elektrichka commuter train, riding back into Moscow, Vitaly absently watched the white of the countryside snow turn gray with the soot of the approaching city, and considered what he now knew. And more importantly, the unknowns.

Major Gromova hadn't known that Colonel Abramovich had been reported killed in combat. That was good, as it muted her level of discord with what she'd seen. For Vitaly to do his clandestine job, the less noise she made the better. Especially as she would be in further contact with Americans during her training.

But most significantly, he now had reports of this one American showing up in three very different locations. In Houston Mission Control, talking to the crew in orbit. At the splashdown site north of Hawaii, in physical combat with the Soviet forces there. And recently in Las Vegas, escorting a Soviet whom, if Gromova's story were true, the Israelis had gone to great lengths to prove was dead.

Several new puzzles to solve.

From the KGB files, Vitaly had the American's name and a sketch of his military record. But going forward, Vitaly Kalugin was going to make it his job to learn all about Commander Kazimieras Zemeckis.

—

As soon as she got back to her kvartira on the seventh floor of Dom 2, Svetlana put the kettle on. The extra talking, plus her walk home in the dry, cold air, had redoubled her thirst. As she filled her steel mesh tea ball with leaves, her cat rubbed against her leg and meowed, looking up.

"You are hungry, Orbita? Would fish be good tonight?"

She had a dried perch in her small fridge, and broke a section of it onto a plate, setting it down next to the cat's water bowl. The cat purred as it considered and then picked at the offering, and the kettle began to whistle. Svetlana poured the boiling water over the ball, into her cup. She took it with the rest of the fish and a small block of hard white cheese into her living room, and sat at her dining table, overlooking the oblong rectangle of Star City Square. The late October sun had already set, and the streetlights drew long shadows as people walked from the training territory towards their apartments.

Typical KGB, she thought. *All secrets and closed-mouth self-importance*. She reviewed what he had asked, and what she had answered. A waste of her time, just so that he—*what was his name? Kalugin*—could make it look like he was doing something, to impress his bosses in Lubyanka. Like most of Soviet officialdom, just going through the motions, a pretense of actual work, with no necessity for actual purpose or accomplishment.

But the KGB, nonetheless.

She carefully pulled some of the flesh off the bone with her teeth, took a small bite of the cheese, and chewed as she opened her satchel and pulled out the study materials for the next day's Soyuz training. As she washed down the mouthful with a sip of hot tea, she smiled wryly, looking at the cat who had jumped onto her lap and was now cleaning itself.

"Eh, Orbita? Secret spy cat? That's no life for women like us."

She took another bite and opened the textbook.

That's why I'm a cosmonaut.

38

Ulitsa Gorkovo, Moscow

"Allo? Allo?"

A man had answered, and Svetlana could barely hear his voice on the other end of the phone against the noise of the street traffic.

She'd taken the elektrichka commuter train into the city, ridden the subway downtown to Revolution Square and then walked to a TAKSOFON pay phone. She was planning to treat herself to an oversized hot chocolate and a pastry at Café Filippov, and then buy some luxury items for herself and her cat farther up Gorky Street at the Eliseevsky grocery. But the real purpose of her rare midweek morning trip into Moscow was this phone call.

She'd put in a two-kopek coin, dialed the number from memory and had mentally rehearsed what to say. Now if the Soviet phone system would just allow her to hear the voice on the other end of the line.

She spoke again. "Allo! I'm calling to talk with Colonel Alexander Vasilyevich Abramovich. I went to school with him, and I am trying to get back in touch." Specific enough to be put through to him, she hoped, but vague enough to be hard to trace, if anyone tried.

There was no response. Svetlana pushed the pay phone's handset harder against her ear, until she could hear the low hiss of the connection. She thought she could hear someone breathing.

She prompted, "Menya slishitye?" Do you hear me?

"Da, slishoo," the man's voice responded, guardedly. "Colonel Abramovich is . . . not here." A pause. "Say again who is calling?"

Svetlana had anticipated this. "Natalya Surayeva. We were schoolmates in Stalingrad, and I'm in Moscow, hoping to see him while I'm here." Adding a note of concern: "Will Sascha be back soon?"

Another pause, and the man's voice took on a kinder tone. "Comrade Surayeva, I am a colleague of Colonel Abramovich's here at the Mikoyan Design Bureau. I'm afraid I have very bad news for you. Our friend Sascha has died. He was doing what he loved, flying the world's best airplane, and he was lost in combat, defending the Motherland. I'm very sorry to have to be the one to tell you this."

Svetlana's sharp intake of breath was real, as she rapidly thought about what this meant. Hearing the sound, the man added, "My deepest condolences."

What would Natalya say? "That's terrible news! When did this happen? Is there to be a memorial service?"

"Unfortunately, he perished in early October and the services were nearly a month ago." His unpleasant job complete, the man's voice became more officious. "Is there anything else, Comrade Surayeva?"

"Nyet, spasiba. It's just that the news is a shock. Thank you for letting me know."

"My condolences again. All the best." The man's voice was replaced with a buzzing dial tone.

Svetlana slowly replaced the handset. If Abramovich had died in early October, who had she seen in Las Vegas? Could she have been mistaken?

She realized she was still standing in the phone booth, and that a man was impatiently waiting for her to be done, glaring at her. She turned and exited, feeling oddly clumsy from the unexpected news, and stiffly turned towards the café.

She stopped as another thought struck her, and an aged babushka carrying a bag in each hand bumped into her from behind, grunting in displeasure. Svetlana apologized, and started walking again, faster now.

No, she thought. *I was not wrong.*

She had definitely seen Abramovich.

The KGB visit to Star City was proof of that.

39

Area 51, Nevada

The dismembering of the Soviet MiG-25 jet inside the Area 51 hangar had been clinically methodical. It was as if an alien had somehow landed on an earthbound operating table, and a team of eager research surgeons had been allowed to cut deeper and deeper into it, revealing more and more detail. The big difference here was that, afterwards, the doctors had to put all the pieces together again and bring the body back to life.

A Mach 3 Humpty Dumpty.

The team was a mix of Air Force and Lockheed Skunk Works technicians. The quick autopsy that the Israeli Air Force had done had helped; the wings and stabilizers were already removed, and things were always easier to take apart the second time around. At maximum disassembly, the laid-out, labeled and photographed components were spread over most of the hangar's floor. Like the exploded parts diagram that comes with a model airplane kit.

A separate team, headed by Colonel Irv Williams, had been focusing specifically on the cockpit. Irv and his pilots were going to have to fly this bird, and they wanted every scrap of info they could get on engine starting procedures, flying speeds and emergency responses. They'd built checklists for the earlier MiGs and used those as a starting point. But the MiG-25 had two engines, and was a much bigger, heavier and faster plane than their earlier specimens.

All the cockpit labels were written in the Cyrillic alphabet and the gauges were calibrated in foreign units such as meters and Celsius and kilograms per cubic centimeter. As part of their familiarization training, the American pilots had learned how to read the Cyrillic, but for key items they'd been using a Dymo label maker to put neat tape strips with English names next to the switches and instruments.

Eventually they'd want to evaluate all the radar and sensing systems, but for now, Irv had them prioritize what the pilots would need to safely fly it. He tried to keep his emotions to himself, but he was excited—there were very few airplanes in the world that could go three times the speed of sound, and as the boss, he would get to do the first flight on this one.

A test pilot's dream.

What he wanted most of all was a chance to talk to someone who had already flown the beast. There hadn't been that opportunity with the previous MiGs, and everything had had to be self-taught. But this time, Washington had passed word that the pilot who had landed the plane was defecting to the US, and at Irv's insistence, he was going to be spending time at Groom Lake as part of his test and development team. As soon as the CIA was done with the formal vetting and debriefing, the Soviet pilot would be released with a handler/translator to become a civilian advisor to Irv's unit under the USAF 57 Fighter Weapons Wing. Learning from an experienced MiG-25 pilot would save a tremendous amount of time and reverse engineering and would undoubtedly help fill in the gaps on flying some of the older MiGs as well.

The team had just finished putting the MiG-25 mostly back together, and were nearly ready for full electrical power-up, and then engine starts and taxi tests. Irv had pushed his engineering evaluation group to meet the expected date the CIA had told him the Soviet pilot would arrive at Groom Lake.

That date was today. He'd checked with the control tower, and the regular unmarked staff commuter plane up from Vegas had called ahead with their standard Monday flight plan. It would touch down in a few minutes.

He walked out of the hangar to watch them land on the Groom Lake runway.

"Why can I not look out window?"

Sascha sounded both puzzled and irritated. If they were going to be mining him for information on the MiG-25, and trusting him as a new citizen of the United States of America, why were all the curtains drawn, blocking the view out of the twin-engine King Air's side windows?

Sitting beside him, Kaz just shrugged. The crew had been explicit: no one in the 11 passenger seats got to survey the terrain on the 30-minute flight from Las Vegas McCarran airport up to Groom Lake.

Kaz knew why, but he wasn't about to enlighten his seatmate, even if he was newly cleared as a legitimate defector. Glancing at Thompson, Kaz saw that the CIA handler was fine with leaving Sascha's question unanswered as well. Their flight path would be skirting the restricted flying area of the entire Nevada nuclear test site; flying MiGs wasn't all the US government was up to in the region. The people on the plane would have different levels of security clearance, so it was easier just to have a blanket policy for everyone.

"You won't be in the dark much longer," Kaz said. Sascha appeared to accept this when Bill translated, and he leaned back in his seat again.

Both Kaz and Sascha recognized the pressure building on their eardrums as the plane started to descend, and the longtime pilots unconsciously moved their jaws to equalize the pressure, easily popping their ears. Around them, the other passengers—Bill and the weekly cleaning and support workers—were pinching their noses and blowing to clear the uncomfortable feeling. Attuned to the plane's subtle movements, Kaz and Sascha sensed as it steadied onto a planned descent rate, and listened to the rattle, whine and thump of the landing gear being lowered. They felt it as the pilots lowered extra flap and flared for landing. The tires squawked with the instant spin-up, and the King Air was on the ground, the smoothness of flight replaced with the rattling roughness of taxiing on pavement.

Since the transport's pilots were just dropping passengers off, they only shut down the left engine, allowing a security guard to climb aboard and confirm all the passengers' identification. When the guard got to the Russian, he paused after taking the proffered brand-new blue US passport. He leafed through it, noting the lack of stamps and recent date of issue. As he compared the photograph to Sascha's expressionless face, he shouted slightly to be heard above the single running engine.

"New passport?" He and the rest of the security team had been briefed that a former Soviet was arriving, and he didn't like it. His job was to keep Area 51 safe, and now the idiots in Washington were inviting a Commie fox into his prize henhouse.

The Soviet nodded, once. "Yes." His careful pronunciation of the single syllable made it sound very un-American.

The guard grunted, and held the Russian's unblinking gaze for several seconds, trying to get a read on the man that he could convey to his fellow guards. An odd coldness flowed down his back, but he ignored it and concentrated on what was in front of his eyes: a middle-aged, bland and balding but fit-looking guy whose identification met the entry requirements. He handed the passport back, checked Kaz's Navy ID card, ticked off both their names and moved on to Bill in the next row.

Sascha glanced at Kaz and lifted an eyebrow. The Soviet Union thrived on petty officialdom, and it seemed America was no different.

Having finished his screening, the guard walked to the front of the cabin, hunched over with the low ceiling and turned to address the group.

"When you get off, walk directly into the hangar." He pointed through the plane's open door at the giant V-roofed building next to them. "There'll be someone there to sort out your transport." He shot one last look at the Soviet and ducked through the door.

Kaz turned to Sascha and smiled slightly. "Welcome to Groom Lake."

—

"These are your new digs," Irv Williams said.

He'd met them as they got off the plane, helped load their meager luggage into his Jeep, and driven them past a mismatched series of low metal buildings to a long row of rounded trailers on the other side of the base. Kaz, Grief and Thompson climbed out of the Jeep and followed Williams towards a silver Airstream travel trailer, one of many parked in a long row, tied down securely and neatly aligned. Mounted on the roof was a large square box, which Kaz knew from experience was a type of air conditioner that blew air across evaporating water. Given the perpetually dry desert climate, it would cool the trailer, but also give it a distinctive smell common to many southwestern buildings, a smell that had earned it the nickname "swamp cooler." Inside, the slightly mildewy odor confirmed it.

"Each trailer is set up for two folks, with a bedroom at each end and a shared kitchen, living room and restroom here in the center." Irv looked at the three men. "Kaz, I have you and Alexander in this one so you can maximize shop talk." He turned to Thompson and pointed out through the small curtained window at the next trailer in the row. "You're in there."

Kaz saw a sourness cross the CIA man's face at the news that he would be separated from the Russian. *Fair enough*, Kaz thought. Thompson was on the hook for the defector for the foreseeable future. But this was an Air Force operation now.

The walls were paneled in grayish oak veneer, and a small TV sat on a high wooden corner shelf. There were silver bar stools around the kitchen counter, and the living area featured a velvet painting of a topless Hawaiian maiden sitting next to a waterfall. Three brass swivel lights mounted in the acoustic tile ceiling illuminated the painting.

Irv walked to the refrigerator, the trailer shifting slightly on its suspension as he moved. He pulled the door open wide enough for all three men to see a dozen cans of Pabst Blue Ribbon beer cooling inside. He smiled and let the fridge door swing shut. "I stocked it for you."

"Thanks, Irv," Kaz said. He dropped his bag on the living area coffee table and nodded at Sascha to do the same. Ever since he'd first seen the missile streaking upwards from the beach in Israel, it felt as though everything had been building towards today, and he wanted to finally get at it. "What's the plan?"

Irv glanced at his watch. "After the four of us grab lunch in the mess hall, I've set up a one o'clock briefing with all members of the detachment. That way, we can introduce Alexander to the whole group and give you two a chance to see all that we're up to." As he walked to the exit, Irv spoke more quietly, directly to Kaz. "Thompson told me you two will be here with our pilot for a few weeks at least. Seeing how it goes, before they decide on a long-term resettlement plan?" He raised his eyebrows for confirmation.

"Yeah, that's what he told me as well," Kaz said, and passed Irv to take the short steps onto the desert sand. "Have to wait and see how long I can stay. But, definitely, they want to keep Alexander here and useful, and out of sight, while they build him a new identity and find him a job somewhere."

As they walked to the Jeep, the Russian trailed them, looking around at the dry, rugged landscape, occupied with his own thoughts, with Thompson following behind.

Irv started the Jeep's engine and turned to the men as they climbed in, Kaz up front with him and the other two in the back. "I thought I'd give you a quick tour, get everybody oriented to what's here, before we go eat." He waited as Thompson filled the Russian in and saw him nod.

Quiet one, Irv thought. *But then again, how would I act if I were in his shoes?*

He smiled. "Let's start with the dump."

Thompson frowned—was he joking?—but translated the words anyway. Irv accelerated rapidly along a packed dirt road towards the south, skirting the base of a high, rocky ridge to the west. A large blackened area was smeared into the lower hillside.

Irv shouted above the driving noise. "We've had a base out here since the mid-fifties, and that's where we burn our trash and jettison the remains of old projects." He turned left, pointing towards the south as he went. "Down there you can see our fuel tanks, those silver-and-white cylinders, and here on the left is the base power and steam plant." He turned the Jeep left again, and drove past the two industrial-looking buildings, heading back north towards the main hub of the base.

Kaz had noticed something. "Just the one paved runway—does the wind always favor it?"

Irv smiled. "It's always windy here in the desert, but the ridgelines on either side of Groom Lake tend to channel it mostly north-south." He pointed to the salty-white flats to the northeast. "When the wind gets too bad, we can land any direction we like, out on the smooth lakebed. Assuming it hasn't been flooded. After it rains, it can take several days to dry out before the salt is hard enough to land on again."

In the back seat, Alexander asked a question through Thompson, who leaned forward. "He wants to know what that is."

Irv glanced right, to where Thompson was pointing. It was an area of raised mounds around a low building at the end of a taxiway. Kaz recognized the distinctive shape and suspected that Sascha did too.

Irv spoke. "Those are weapons bunkers, placed there so they're out of harm's way, but ready to load bullets and missiles onto the jets when we're running specific tests."

Alexander nodded, and commented to Thompson, who passed it on. "He says they do the same thing."

Kaz and Irv exchanged a quick glance, sharing a thought. *Interesting thing for a defector to remark on.*

They'd just passed several utilitarian-looking structures surrounded by a mixture of older military vehicles when Irv abruptly turned left into an unpaved parking area. He stopped, shut off the Jeep's engine and tipped his head towards the white, single-story, whitewashed building in front of them. Men were walking and bicycling towards the entrance.

Irv smiled. "Who's hungry?"

40

Base Headquarters, Area 51

"Gentlemen, if I could have your attention."

Irv's pilots and senior maintainers were gathered in the briefing room of the base headquarters building, next to the Groom Lake mess hall. On the front wall behind Irv were dusty green chalkboards, and through the long side windows the men could see the fire station and the original U-2 aircraft hangars, built nearly 20 years earlier. A large communal coffee urn burped quietly in the corner, and most of the men held a Styrofoam cup in their hand.

Their informal posture and easy confidence lent a ragtag uniformity to the group. They were wearing a mix of flight suit colors and coveralls, reflecting their various military and civilian backgrounds. Haircuts varied from tight brush cuts through to the ponytails and beards of the civilian maintainers and Lockheed contractors. Irv's hair was thinning on top but flowed over the tops of his ears and into full black sideburns.

He pointed to Kaz and Sascha, sitting in the front row.

"You've no doubt heard the scuttlebutt that the Russian pilot of our newly acquired MiG-25 might be joining us here at the Ranch. I'm happy to report that those rumors were true, and he's here with us today, and for the next few weeks."

Over lunch, Irv had quizzed Sascha about his flying background, and now he beckoned the Soviet to come stand beside him while he summarized it for the group.

"He's a combat veteran, a top test pilot holding several world records, and he did much of the developmental work on the Foxbat and other Soviet fighters."

The room was quiet as each man closely inspected the Russian pilot facing them. Normally, any Soviet would be treated as a nonspecific but hated enemy. The crowd was reserving judgment.

Thompson had briefed Irv on the CIA's ground rules, and he laid them out now for the team. "No need to get into the politics of why he's with us, or what our spooks in Washington's plans will be for him in the future. For now, we have daily access to the rare asset of a deeply experienced MiG flier. I want us to squeeze everything we can out of the opportunity, while at the same time welcoming a newcomer into our little flying club."

Irv smiled. "Let me introduce Colonel Alexander Abramovich. Call sign, Grief."

There was an uncomfortable tension when no one spoke in response to the introduction. Grief's eyes flicked around the room, making contact.

Irv continued. "Alexander is still learning English, so the USAF has thoughtfully provided an interpreter." He nodded towards Bill Thompson, who raised his hand and waved. No need to announce that he was CIA.

"We also have Navy Commander Kaz Zemeckis with us, acting as our MiG pilot's liaison with Washington. Zemeckis is no slouch either, a Pax River test pilot, currently detailed to NASA."

Kaz half turned in his chair and nodded at the group.

"My plan is to tap all of Abramovich's expertise. He'll be in one of the offices out at the Red Hat hangar for full-time engineer access, as we finish jet reassembly and get into the engine and taxi tests. For the pilots, he'll be evaluating and helping rewrite our systems books and checklists, as well as available for any of your questions that come up. We'll get him kitted out and flying back seat in the T-38 chase plane ASAP."

Irv smiled again. "Zemeckis, Abramovich and Bill Thompson here are already set up in their trailers, but they have a lot to learn about Ranch life. I'm counting on you to indoctrinate them on our little slice of Americana, starting tonight." There were matching smiles around the room. Men had been living and working at Groom Lake long enough for it to have developed a distinctive lifestyle. And since funding came through largely unseen black sources, the spending on keeping the troops happy could get lavish.

Irv turned to the Soviet. "You have anything you want to say?" Thompson quickly stood to translate for the group.

Sascha spoke in measured Russian. "Thank you, Colonel Williams. It is very good to be amongst pilots again, after all the intelligence debriefings." He shrugged. "I'm ready to go flying."

The strangeness of the situation echoed in a protracted silence. The foreign sound of the Russian words clashed starkly within this purposefully secret corner of America. Kaz decided to help break the ice by asking a fighter test pilot question. "Sascha, why don't you tell the group about your record-setting altitude flight in the MiG-25?"

The Russian shrugged again. "It was not a complicated flight. We stripped the jet of everything it didn't need, to save weight." He smiled slightly. "I even took my winter jacket off and emptied my flight suit pockets."

He closed his eyes, picturing the cold Moscow day.

"We loaded just enough fuel for the flight profile, and I took off into a good wind, staying in full afterburner. I pulled up immediately into a big half-loop, leveling off at ten kilometers, accelerating straight ahead to just under Mach 3. Then I pulled back at three g to set seventy degrees nose high, and just let it climb."

He paused. The room was silent as the men imagined what the power of that flight profile would have felt like.

"When the air got too thin, I shut the engines down to keep them from overheating. Eventually I peaked out at a little over thirty-seven kilometers." He repeated the math conversion that he'd done for Kaz. "Over 120,000 feet."

There were whistles of amazement. A few of the test pilots had taken a rocket-powered F-104 to nearly that height, but this Soviet flight had been done using regular, air-breathing engines—in a jet like the one that was being reassembled in their hangar.

One of the pilots asked, "When you shut the engines down, did the cockpit hold pressure?"

Grief nodded. "I was wearing a pressure suit, as usual, but the engines kept"—Thompson stopped him, to confirm the correct word—"windmilling, enough to spin the compressor and hold cabin pressure." He decided to add a boast. "The MiG-25 regularly flies at 25,000 meters—80,000 feet. It needs a good pressure system."

A second pilot raised his hand. "How did the jet behave in the very thin air?" The USAF had had to install small hydrogen peroxide thrusters on the wingtips and nose of the rocket-powered F-104 to allow the pilots to keep it from tumbling.

"Like a truck. The big twin tails were enough to keep it flying straight."

Kaz looked around the room. Now, instead of suspicion on these faces, he saw engaged curiosity. Irv caught his eye and nodded as the group peppered the Soviet with ever more detailed questions. Some of them were going to be flying this airplane and had realized that his experience was invaluable.

When the questions started getting too specific, Irv raised his hand.

"Guys, we don't need to solve all the problems right now. This afternoon we'll get our pilot set up at the hangar, and tomorrow morning we'll do a detailed walkaround of the new jet together."

He pointed out to Kaz and Grief the men he'd put in charge of the various tasks such as checklist development and aircraft systems manual writing. He singled out a pilot with a flattop haircut and dark complexion, seated in the front row. "George, once we get these two settled, I want you to brief them on the local flying area and procedures."

Captain George Claw nodded. He was a USAF test pilot and had flown at Edwards and Groom Lake for several years. "Will do, Boss."

Irv looked around the group, and then at the Russian. "Good to have you amongst us, Alexander. We've got ourselves a new jet to fly. Let's all get at it."

Late that afternoon, Kaz, Grief and Thompson sat in a small room at the Red Hat hangar. The walls were papered with topographic and airspace maps, and George Claw was pointing to a government drawing of the Groom Lake facility itself, spread on the table in front of them.

"Field elevation here is 4,500 feet. It gets very hot in the summer, so we have an extra-long runway to allow for the thin air." He tapped the center of the paper. "The main part, next to the base here, is concrete. But as soon as we get to the edge of the lakebed itself, the runway transitions to asphalt, poured on the salt pan." He spread his fingers along the map to show the extent. "The concrete's 8,600 feet long, with a 5,500-foot extension on the lake. So, 14,000 feet total available, one of the longest runways in the world." He looked at Thompson. "Is he okay with feet and miles?"

Grief nodded without waiting for the translation. Numbers were just numbers.

Claw pointed at the Groom Lake salt flat itself. "The lakebed serves as an emergency landing strip too. It's what initially got the attention of the Army Air Forces when they set up shop here and on other lakebeds as auxiliary airfields during the war."

"Which war?" Grief interrupted.

"World War II," Claw answered. When Thompson translated it as "the Great Patriotic War," Grief nodded at the more familiar Soviet name.

"Even though it's a desert, we occasionally get rain, and then the low part of the lakebed, here"—he indicated the center of Groom

Lake—"gets too wet to land on for a while. But the edges stay dry and hard." He glanced at Grief, who nodded.

Claw stood and walked to a wall map. "This is the flying area."

It was a typical topographic rendering, with brown shading for dry areas, green-blue for wetter valleys, and yellow for urban buildup. Las Vegas was a yellow blotch to the south, with a pale-green finger following the Pahranagat Valley up to the east. In the center was a black square surrounding the white circle of Groom Lake. Narrow contour lines showed the elevation changes, getting closer together near cliffs and steep valleys. The jagged hills surrounding Groom Lake stood out clearly.

Claw pointed at the central black square. "This is Restricted Area 4808A, our little piece of the big 4808 flying area that covers most of the Nevada Test Range. We call it the Box. For obvious reasons." He pointed to the left, where cross-hatching on the map marked other oblong squares. "Those are R-4807 and 4806, and we need special clearance from Nellis Control to fly in there."

He reached towards the large pie-shaped area that covered the right half of the map. "That's the MOA." He pronounced it *mo-ah*. "The Military Operating Area, our main flying airspace. In there we're cleared supersonic with no altitude restrictions, right down to the surface, and up to outer space." Claw smiled at the Russian. "Or at least as high as your MiG-25 can get us."

Grief got up and approached the map, peering closely at small numbers printed in various locations. "Those are frequencies?" he asked, with Bill translating.

Claw nodded. "Yep. We use UHF and VHF." He glanced at Thompson. "Ultra High Frequency and Very High Frequency." He looked back at Grief. "In the MiGs I've flown, you have UHF only." He raised an eyebrow.

"Yes, we use UHF for radio communications," Grief confirmed. "In the MiG-25 we also have HF for long-range when needed. Our civilian airliners use VHF."

"Same here," Claw answered. "But since we're so close to Vegas, there's lots of civilian traffic skirting the edge of our airspace, so we use both in the jets that have it."

The Russian ran his finger across the wall chart, tracing the blocky, irregular crosshatched outline of the R-4808 airspace to the southwest. "This is your nuclear test range?"

The question startled Kaz, Claw and Thompson. Nobody had mentioned the true purpose of the area west of Groom Lake. But on reflection, no real surprise that a Soviet MiG-25 pilot would know about it.

Kaz answered, "Yes." As a postdoc analyst in electro-optical sensing in Washington, he'd studied the Soviet equivalent nuclear range via space-based photographs. "Similar to your facilities in Semipalatinsk."

Grief looked back at him, expressionless. Semipalatinsk was not publicized or well-known, even in the Soviet Union.

Points taken by both men. Strange new world.

George Claw reached into a wooden tray by the door and pulled out two stiff, pale-blue pages, postcard-sized, covered with dense printing, and handed them to Kaz and Grief. "These are the pilots' frequency and airspace summary sheets, for when you go flying."

Kaz scanned the names and numbers, flipping the card over to see the condensed map on the other side. It had been a while since he'd flown in an operational test unit, and he was looking forward to it. "Thanks," he said. He looked up at their host. "Claw is an unusual family name. Where's it from?"

George Claw smiled. "I think part of the reason Irv asked me to brief you on the local area is that I'm originally from near here." He pointed at the upper-right corner of the wall map. "My family is native to the southwest, up towards Four Corners. The Navajo people. My dad served as a code talker in the war." His smile broadened. "The Japanese could never figure out what messages my dad and the others were passing on the radio. He was a Marine, and their work helped take Iwo Jima."

Grief had been looking closely at the summary card, comparing it to the wall chart, ignoring the side conversation. Thompson, sensing his distraction, had ceased to translate.

Now Grief turned to Claw, pointing at a sequence of numbers on the card, and then back at the wall. "You have a frequency wrong."

The American frowned, and then looked back and forth, comparing. "Heck, you're right. We must have transposed those two numbers." To Grief, he said, "Impressive you caught that."

Grief nodded, once. He took flying seriously, expected accuracy and loathed incompetence. Small mistakes killed test pilots.

Kaz thought, not for the first time, *It would be a mistake to underestimate this man.*

He glanced at his watch. "George, how about we go see the other MiGs, and any other planes Sascha and I might have a chance to fly in while we're here?"

41

Hangar 220, Groom Lake

In the dim light of the hangar, Grief stood stock-still for a moment, taking in the strangeness of the sight. Even though he had just walked across American soil, past an American flag whipping noisily in the wind in front of the base headquarters building, he felt as if he had been instantly transported back to Russia. The wooden hangar was familiar in its size and age, and in the way it smelled of old machines and jet fuel. And there, parked tidily next to each other in front of him, were several MiG fighters. Just like on so many flying mornings at Ramenskoye aerodrome, along the Moskva River on the southeast outskirts of Moscow.

The only difference was that it wasn't cold enough to see his breath.

Fighter pilots feel at ease with heavy machinery, and Grief immediately walked up to the nearest plane and placed his bare hand on the familiar cool metal curve of its side. He glanced fore and aft, noting the small details, and bent to look under the fuselage at the landing gear, antennas, and up at the single NR-30 cannon. He straightened and spoke to Kaz and Claw through Thompson.

"A MiG-21 F-13 model." He thought for a moment, imagining his way past the American insignia newly painted on the side. "You must have gotten this one from the Iraqis."

Claw smiled easily. "The exact source of these jets, and details on how we acquired them, are kept quiet. The military and the CIA prefer it that way." He shrugged. "It'll be the same with your MiG-25. We can't inadvertently repeat things we don't know, so it protects guys like you."

Grief listened to Thompson and nodded. It made sense. He raised his chin towards the cockpit. "I'd like to look inside."

Claw wheeled a ladder over, carefully positioning it flush without bumping into the fuselage. "Be my guest."

The Russian nimbly climbed the ladder and leaned over to inspect the cockpit. He turned and asked, "Okay to get in?"

"Is the seat safed?" Claw wanted to verify that the steel pin that keeps the ejection seat from accidentally firing was inserted into its slot in the pilot's right thigh guard.

"Yes." Grief had already checked for the unmistakable long red cloth tag attached to the steel pin, with REMOVE BEFORE FLIGHT printed on it.

Claw raised a thumb, and Grief reached across to the far cockpit sill. He swung his two legs up and in, like a gymnast on a pommel horse, and lowered himself into the ejection seat.

He felt at home for the first time since he had landed at Lod airport. His initial flight in a MiG-21 had been 15 years ago, when he'd been selected as a Mikoyan Experimental Test Pilot, and his hands reached on their own to hold the throttle and stick. He noted the relabeling and avionics changes to the original cockpit, but confirmed that most everything else was in place.

Good, he thought. *I could fly this, anytime*.

"Another lobster, Sascha?"

Claw's dark-brown eyes were twinkling as he stood next to the wide barbecue. The contractor kitchen staff had parboiled the lobsters, split them lengthwise and brushed them with seasoned butter, so the airmen could grill them themselves. It was a clear, cool night, and a handful of the group stood outside, talking and drinking on the patio of Sam's Place, the recreational facility at Groom Lake. The rest were inside eating, drinking, playing cards and pool, and setting up a screen to watch a movie.

Grief shook his head slowly, looking at the evening silhouette of the surrounding dry brown hills, and the glint of fading light off the lakebed. His shadow, Thompson, was there to translate his question. "How do you have fresh lobsters in this place?"

Claw gestured with his tongs towards hangars they hadn't visited. "Some of our American planes here fly real fast, and the boys need training sorties, so they go to Loring air base in Maine and back." He smiled and looked down at the assortment of red crustaceans. "A crate of these extra-large beauties fits perfectly into one of the side instrument bays, and the cold air at altitude next to the avionics keeps them fresh." He smiled even wider. "Amazing how those training flights often happen on the days we're planning a barbecue."

Grief considered. "How far?"

"A little over two thousand nautical." Claw calculated. "Just under four thousand kilometers."

Grief smiled slightly. To Thompson he said, "Tell them we used to fly from Moscow to Baku for Caspian Sea caviar. Only two thousand kilometers." He shrugged. "Also good training."

Kaz pointed west towards an incongruous field of green next to Sam's Place. "How long has the baseball diamond been there?"

"Almost since the beginning, I understand." Claw moved the grilling lobsters to the side of the central heat of the charcoal. "It was here long before I arrived." He pointed beyond the field into the darkness. "We also have a swimming pool, and riding stables too. A dozen horses or so, good for touring the hills, and for hunting."

Grief's ears pricked up as Thompson finished translating. "What do you hunt?"

"Small stuff mostly—quail, partridge, desert hares. But occasionally we go after bigger game. There are pronghorn antelope, bighorn sheep, even black bear." He looked at Grief. "You a hunter?"

Grief frowned slightly, as if the answer was self-evident. "All fighter pilots are hunters."

Claw pursed his lips. "True enough. We'll go together, next chance, if you like."

"Yes, I would like that, thank you."

Claw used the tongs to lift the last of the lobsters off the grill and onto a waiting platter, ready to carry inside.

"How about you, Kaz? You ride?"

"I do, and if I'm not in Houston, I'd like to come along."

Claw turned towards Bill. "Want to saddle up and join the party?"

"I'm more comfortable running on two legs than four," said the CIA man, turning to look out at the gathering night, tired of translating. "Besides, I prefer to hunt alone."

Odd response, Kaz thought. *And why did they send Bill, and not just a translator? Is the CIA confident about Grief being legitimate, or not?*

Sensing the tension, Claw said, "A lot of Navajo hunters do too." He picked up the plate of lobster and started moving towards the entrance. "You guys coming? I think the movie tonight is *Dr. Strangelove*, a favorite here." He looked at Grief and smirked. "You ought to find it entertaining."

42

Las Vegas

Eugene lived alone and had no family stateside, so to get a package in the mail was exciting. Especially this package, which he'd been anticipating for weeks.

He was assistant manager at the 7-Eleven on Las Vegas Boulevard. Despite the name, the store was open 24 hours a day. With his backup shift work schedule and odd-hour deliveries, it had taken Eugene a couple of days to be able to respond to the notice he'd received from the post office, and to get there in time to pick it up.

But at last, the thick envelope was sitting on his Formica kitchenette table. He was delaying opening it, savoring the anticipation.

In truth, he couldn't really believe it. A big, official-looking, light-brown envelope, with NUFOC written in large print in the top-left corner. A globe had been substituted for the O in NUFOC and there was an oval around the whole word like it was in orbit. *Just like* NASA, he thought. He ran a pointer finger along the return address to feel the distinctive printing.

Eugene turned and got himself a Pepsi from the fridge, pried off the pull tab and took a deep swig, his eyes locked on the package. He burped from the carbonation, and it snapped him out of his reverie. He flicked the tab into the trash under the sink, got a sharp knife from the drawer, set the can down on the table and picked up the envelope.

He cautiously slit the long edge, being sure not to cut anything inside. Then he reached in and eased the stack of papers out onto the table.

On top was a letter from NUFOC itself, addressed directly to him. *Dear Mr. Eberhardt,* it said. They'd even spelled his last name right! *Welcome to membership in the National UFO Committee, America's preeminent UFO experts and investigators. In your membership package you will find . . .*

He scanned the list while verifying that he'd received the items, one by one. There were several recent newsletters, an official field investigator's instruction book, the exam package he'd have to fill out to become fully qualified as an investigator, and a pale-blue membership card, embossed with the NUFOC logo and his name. There was even a name tag, with *Eugene Eberhardt* printed on it in neat letters, for him to wear at the next convention. He held it up to his chest at the place where he would pin it on.

So cool!

He took another deep swig of Pepsi and burped again, loudly this time. He opened the envelope wide to make sure he hadn't missed anything, then sat down and picked up the field investigator's book. That's what he really wanted: to be a man of action, out in the countryside, seeing and recording UFO activities for everyone to marvel at. As he read, he looked at the exam questions, immediately mouthing a couple of the answers.

He could do this. Eugene Eberhardt was going to be an accredited NUFOC field investigator. So exciting!

And it provided the perfect cover.

—

Eugene slowed and pulled off the pavement of State Road 25 at the precise location the latest NUFOC newsletter had specified. There were no signs, but Eugene had measured the distance on the odometer and was certain this was the right spot. He turned to follow the dirt track, pretty sure his Datsun 510 sedan had enough ground clearance to handle the rutted path. The steering wheel bucked a little in his hands, but he kept the speed at a jogging pace as the unmarked road led him across a valley towards the brown hills. A thin trail of dust followed the vehicle.

He was tracking southwest and had just crossed a dry arroyo. He glanced at the newsletter map on the passenger seat, getting his bearings. The hand-drawn chart showed him approaching the Jumbled Hills, where he'd have to park and proceed on foot. He'd bought a new Kodak Instamatic camera and notebook at the 7-Eleven, using his employee discount, and had put them, along with two cans of Pepsi and an apple, in his backpack. He'd also bought used binoculars at a pawnshop; the beauty of a gambling town like Las Vegas was that pawnshops were plentiful. It was a late autumn morning, so not too hot, and the desert air was always dry. He was wearing his orange-and-white 7-Eleven ball cap, a light jacket and his Adidas running shoes.

Practical. And, just in case he ran into anyone, he wanted to look the part.

The track climbed and curved and then petered out just short of the crest of a ridge. Eugene stopped the car, grabbed the newsletter and his backpack, locked the doors, pocketed the keys and started hiking. The ground was graveled dust with spiky creosote bushes every few yards, easy to walk around. Low, bushy junipers and pinyon pines spotted the hillside. As he climbed, rock outcroppings started pushing their way up through the dirt, but he could easily follow the footpath that snaked its way between them. The newsletter had mentioned pronghorn antelope, and he figured this might be one of their trails. It also warned about horned rattlesnakes, and he made sure he scanned ahead carefully as he walked. He'd heard the snake's rattle on TV and didn't want to hear that sound in real life.

The ground began to flatten under his feet, and then he was at the ridgetop, able to see clearly into the valley to the west. It was windier here at the top, and he tugged his ball cap down more solidly on his head. Fortunately, the wind wasn't strong enough to disturb the dust, and the air was clear. He held up the NUFOC newsletter map and compared it with what he could see before him.

He was standing on a ridgeline that ran mostly north-south, leading to a higher peak to the north. He checked the map: Bald Mountain. In the distance to the west were matching lines of parallel hills, the Papoose and Belted ranges. They looked close in the clear air, but the map said the nearest was 12 miles away. He took out his Kodak and took a panoramic shot of the whole vista.

But what he'd really come for, what the newsletter had written about, lay spread before him in the broad valley. Below and to the right was the wide, near-white salt flatness of Groom Lake. Butted up against Papoose Ridge on the lakebed's far side he could see a collection of buildings, with runways and a water tower.

Eugene was looking at Area 51.

Of the thousands of UFO sightings that NUFOC had tracked, a large proportion were in Nevada, and the majority of those were centered here, at Area 51. The remoteness and secrecy of the location only added to the intrigue. NUFOCers had established that the military security that kept people out began where Bald Mountain descended to the lakebed. Eugene squinted, but he couldn't see the guard post that the newsletter had warned was there. He looked carefully around the hillside near him, spotting a sparse barbed wire fence, and searched for any dust trails indicating that a vehicle might be headed his way, but saw nothing.

He reached into his bag for the binoculars. They were good ones, Jason Commanders 7x50s, with wide field of view and seven times power magnification. He raised them to his eyes, focusing on the road leading down from Bald Mountain. Bracing against the wind gusts, he tracked along the road until he spotted a square metal structure and a parked white pickup truck. Eugene nodded. The guardhouse. Air Force security contractor, no doubt. No motion visible on this Monday morning. He pointed the small Kodak at the location and snapped a picture. *I need a better camera*, he thought. But maybe he'd see something important if he studied the print with a magnifying glass.

He pointed the binoculars to the left and began a methodical survey of Area 51's buildings. He pulled his notebook out of the bag and sketched what he saw, annotating what he guessed each building might be. The water tower was obvious, and he spotted a control tower amongst the large hangars at the north end of the flight line. He could see the smudge of buildings beyond, but he couldn't figure out what they were for. There were several planes parked on the ramp, but all he could make out was the glisten of their metallic skin.

Farther left, against the upslope of the Papoose Range, he could just distinguish the low, regular shapes of multiple identical-looking buildings. *Housing, maybe?* A road led up to squat white rectangles: probably fuel tanks. North of the fuel tanks there was a jumbled, dark spot. He shrugged. *That many people with no one watching? Probably the dump.* A couple of roads led south, around the end of the lakebed. He swung the binoculars back north, making sure he hadn't missed anything, checking for any movement.

Above the rustling and keening of the wind in the underbrush, Eugene now heard the distinctive, distant sound of a jet engine. He lowered the binoculars and scanned with his naked eyes. *Not one engine, but engines*, he decided. He looked at the runway orientation and raised the binoculars to scan to the south.

There! A bulbous silver shape, wheels already down, descending for landing. He looked closely as the magnified image grew and recognized the broad black nose and white/silver fuselage: a US Air Force C-5A Galaxy. *Big plane*, he thought, but he couldn't make out the numbers on the tall tail. *Wonder what they're delivering?*

Like a small toy, it landed, and he saw the puff of smoke where the wheels spun up on the pavement to support the behemoth's weight.

A quick glance at the map showed the runway was 14,000 feet long, but 4,500 feet above sea level. He watched as the pilots took advantage of the extra length in the thin air, slowly coasting to taxiing speed. He grabbed his camera and took another photo, watching the plane make an elephantine turn and taxi towards the hangars.

When he realized he'd been completely focused on the distant activity, he hastily double-checked the near side of the lakebed and the slope leading up to his position, and then back to the east, to see if anyone besides him might be coming for a look today. All was still.

Perfect, he thought. He sat down on a jutting rock, put the binoculars back into the backpack and popped open one of the Pepsis. He watched the big plane ponderously turn in front of the hangars and slowly taxi until its nose was inside, out of sight. The faraway whining of the engines wound down, and once again the only sound was the desert wind.

Entertainment over.

He methodically surveyed the nearby ridgeline on the other side of the barbed wire, as he steadily sipped from his can of Pepsi. The NUFOC guide had warned about the dry Nevada air, and he was thirstier than he'd realized. He spotted a couple of likely locations and pictured how he could step over the wire and place the package the way he'd been so carefully taught. He tipped his head back to get the last few drops of caffeinated sweetness, put the empty can into the bag, checked that he'd left nothing behind, took one last, thorough look around to make sure he was alone and started walking down towards the Datsun. To retrieve what he'd hidden with the spare tire in the trunk.

His real purpose in coming here.

43

Earth Orbit

It looked like the end nozzle of a giant's garden hose: a 15-foot-long, lumpy cylinder, tapering to a smooth metallic cone at the tip. It was traveling at over 18,000 miles per hour and had launched from Earth ten days earlier. Its orbit carried it 185 miles high as it maneuvered, then swooped down to just 128 miles above the surface of the Earth to do its work.

It was a Zenit-4M robot satellite, and it was taking pictures.

At working altitude, the Zenit could sense the first faint brush of the wispy upper edges of Earth's atmosphere. Racing along at five miles every second, the impact of each air molecule created heat and slowed the satellite down. But the camera needed to be as close to the subject as possible to get good pictures, so the Soviet designers had added thermal insulation. They needed to be able to position Zenit exactly where their masters wanted it to be, and so they'd installed a small, efficient engine in the silver nozzle to fight the thin air's drag.

It was an expensive new modification, and the Moscow military analysts were impatient to see it work.

On this orbit, Zenit had arced well south of Australia, nearly over Antarctica in the midnight darkness. Following a path up the east coast of New Zealand, it had descended across the Pacific in just 30 minutes. Lining everything up to be perfectly in position at sunrise.

Sunrise meant long shadows. Shadows revealed secrets that could be seen from space.

A garbageman working for Los Angeles Public Works grunted as he lifted a heavy silver trash can up onto the sill at the back of his massive truck and tilted the bottom higher to dump the contents into the already full hopper. He tossed the dented can back beside its lid on the driveway, careless of the early morning clatter, and reached for the lever to activate the hydraulics that scooped and compressed the waste into the truck's main storage area. He and his partner had been working since four a.m., and he was happy for the brief break from manual labor.

As he idly looked up in the predawn light, his eye caught the movement of a white star across the sky. He watched it intently, frowning while listening to the truck's mechanism grind. *What the hell is that?* He craned his neck. *No flashing lights, so not an airplane.* The truck's machinery stopped, finished. He shrugged and made a wish. It wasn't a normal shooting star, that's for sure, but it was close enough. And he could use a few wishes to come true.

Zenit's tracking sensors knew they were getting close, and started their final, rapid mathematical calculations. The infrared horizon sensor had given the computer the exact alignment vertical, and Moscow had updated the onboard clock less than an hour prior. Star sensors and magnetometers added precision. The weather was forecast to be cloudless. This was going to be a perfect pass, and everything was optimized for the Ftor-6 camera to start doing its work.

Sunrise had hit Las Vegas at 06:06, and at 06:29:30 exactly, Zenit was overhead. The camera's lens cover, designed to protect the glass from direct sun and micrometeorite impacts, snapped open. Earth's light entered the lens and was magnified and focused by 1,000 millimeters of carefully ground lens, filling the entire width of Zenit, reflecting off a mirror to shine the image onto the 30-by-30-centimeter film. The Ftor-6 advance mechanism whirred, rolling frame after frame of unexposed film rapidly into position, cycling the shutter and then winding it onto an exposed roll.

In 60 seconds, the pass was done. Zenit now had a series of crystal sharp images of American terrain ready for developing. The camera lens closed, power was removed, and the satellite patiently waited for the Earth to turn enough so that its ground track was aligned with the open steppes of western Kazakhstan.

Crossing the coast of Africa, the small thrusters on Zenit fired and turned the satellite so that its main engine pointed in the calculated direction. At the precise moment, valves clicked open, and pressurized hypergolic fuel rushed through tubes, mixed with oxidizer and exploded in the combustion chamber, a yellow-gold flame shooting out of the large nozzle. Timing was critical, and after 256 seconds the valves snapped shut.

Zenit was now going too slowly to hold orbit—committed to a fiery re-entry.

As the air thickened, it slowed Zenit further and heated it more. A small accelerometer sensed the deceleration and sent a signal. Pyrotechnics fired, and Zenit exploded into pieces, the engines and solar arrays tumbling and burning up with the friction, a tough, insulated ball emerging from the carnage.

Inside that radiation-shielded ball was the camera, and the precious, delicate film.

A man-made meteorite, the surviving remnant plummeted ballistically towards the Earth—a cannonball coming home from space. The rapidly thickening air slowed it ever more violently, the fragile camera components inside at eight times their normal weight. Flame enveloped the ball, burning off the tough sacrificial skin, raising the temperature within.

But the design was good. By the time the skin was nearly burned through, the friction had slowed the ball to parachute speed, a pyrotechnic blew a small door open, and a tough drag chute snapped taut in the supersonic air. There was a harsh jerk, slowing the ball further, yanking out a larger parachute. The lines pulled taut, the ball was thrown sideways as the whip cracked, and suddenly the violence was over; the sphere now descended gently under the circular chute, a steel thistledown carrying its precious seed of exposed film.

With a bang, the ball hit a hard-stubbled wheat field in Kazakhstan, rolling to a stop as the last sensors sent the final signal to cut the parachute lines and transmit a beeping noise. A waiting Mi-8 helicopter detected the radio signal and homed in on it, soon landing beside the ball. The crew hustled out into the raw wind, deactivated the ball's self-destruct charge now that it was in safe hands, retrieved the parachute, hooked cables to the still-hot metal of the Zenit, and took off, the ball now suspended below the helo. It flew directly towards Baikonur's Krayniy airfield, like a giant bee returning to the hive with a load of precious pollen.

The waiting groundcrew waved their hands, guiding the helicopter into position over a specially designed cradle, and disconnected the lifting cables, strapping the ball down tight. A forklift carefully slid under the cradle, lifted it and drove up into the back of a waiting Antonov-26 cargo plane. The flight engineer guided the cargo inside, waved the forklift clear and strapped the ball into place. The pilots started the engines and took off, headed for Moscow's Chkalovsky airport.

After landing, another forklift loaded the ball onto a waiting Air Forces panel truck, which pulled out through the gates and turned left towards the OBK-1 factory in Korolyov, on the northeast side of Moscow.

After backing through large metal sliding doors, the truck was relieved of its cargo by a team of technicians, and the ball was set onto a test rig. They hooked up sensors to an access plate, checking the pressure and humidity inside the ball. With luck, the expensive camera could be used again. A lab-coated figure climbed the platform, twisted the recessed handle and opened the hatch. Two photo techs reached past him to unclip and retrieve the film canister, all 1,500 images tightly wound onto the spindle. Given the size and heft of the high-resolution film, it took two of them to carry it across the floor and into the film processing lab.

A LOMO large-format film developer was waiting for them, ready and full of fluid, the room dark except for red light. The techs let their eyes adjust and then opened and loaded the roll of film by hand, meticulously aligning the guide sprockets with the matching holes in the film, and threw the switch, watching the mechanism pull the cellulose off the reel, listening as it produced each negative, a color positive and then a developed color photograph of each. The negatives and positives slowly rewound onto take-up reels, and the prints fell onto a long rack to dry.

When the processing was done, the technicians turned on the white lights, and loaded the roll of positives and racked prints onto a trolley. They wheeled it down the corridor and into a room with a large glass-topped table, lit from below. They mounted the positive roll into a feeder at one end of the table and pulled the processed film smoothly across, into a matching receiver roll. The prints were left in their racks on the trolley.

Zenit's work was done. Military photo analysts stepped up to the table's edge, magnifying glasses in hand, and began their work.

Chief Analyst Konstantin—Kostya—was an expert in American geography. The twists and turns of the continent's ocean coastlines were familiar to him, and he could recognize at a glance the distinctive pattern of every US major city. He'd studied topographic maps intensely and had trained with endless satellite and ground-based photographs.

Kostya took great pride in knowing the features of a land he'd never visited better than most of its residents.

He rotated the handle on the reel, advancing the next positive image onto the light table. The analysts would go back over every photo in detail eventually, but for now they were looking for something specific. He adjusted his bifocal glasses and read the time stamp on the film's edge.

"3 November, 23:00 Decreed Moscow Time. Dima, tell me again, what's the pass we're looking for?"

Dmitri, his assistant analyst, checked the printed list. "Target time 5 November, 17:30 DMT."

Kostya nodded and rapidly advanced the roll, images moving swiftly under his eyes, his brain clicking and cataloging for future reference. The time stamp jumped to 5 November.

"Totchna! Here we go." He'd overshot and rewound a few frames, finding the exact start time on the filmstrip.

The initial image showed a 56-kilometer square of rugged terrain. He could see where the darker rocky hills were cut by arroyos, their low peaks pushing up through the paler dirt and sand. The white of salty lakebeds revealed the valleys.

Kostya grabbed his magnifying glass and focused on an area dotted with black specks. "Pawlin," he muttered—sagebrush—happy to see how clearly the early morning shadows made them stand out. This new version of the Zenit took good pictures!

He looked all around the image to get his bearings, then glanced at Dima and nodded, confirming. "Death Valley," he said in English, his accent making it sound like "Dett Walley." He advanced to the next frame.

Zenit's Ftor-6 camera had moved the film through at one frame every two seconds. With the satellite flying at five miles per second, that meant each image advanced across the Earth by 10 miles, ensuring that three or four photos of any specific location would be captured in subsequent frames as the satellite raced overhead.

Kostya easily stitched the 10-mile jumps together in his head, and he nodded as the pictures followed the ground track north and east. He'd seen this part of Nevada many times, but never this clearly. He had to pace himself not to leapfrog ahead. Photo analysts needed meticulous patience, in addition to intense attention to detail.

At 17:29:56 a highway came into view, snaking across the frame in the right upper corner. The rising sun cast a long shadow to the left of Little Skull Mountain, the focus crystal clear. The Nevada nuclear test site—this was going to be good.

Kostya advanced another frame. Jackass Flats came into view, and he carefully followed the roads and train tracks, looking for changes from the last imagery he'd seen. A smudge in the middle looked different, and he carefully raised and lowered his handheld lens, picking out the detail. He clicked forward and back, looking at the same spot from slightly different angles.

That's interesting, he thought. *They're still moving radioactive things into outdoor storage.* He used his lens to look closely at all the visible buildings, and made notes in his large green notebook.

The next few frames showed the familiar pockmarks left by multiple nuclear tests, like burst pimples against the arid pale brown, crisscrossed with the glinting hint of dirt tracks. He considered. Nothing different.

He rolled a couple of frames further until the edge of a dry lakebed came into view. He spotted the first half of a runway, the taxiways giving it a familiar gray kite pattern against the beige desert. He focused to make out the white "32" painted on the runway. Blurry, but there.

One more click, and half of Groom Lake was in the frame, the paved runway extension cutting across the corner, the ghostly salt lakebed runways outlined in white. He advanced three more frames until the runways had disappeared out the bottom of the frame, and then backed up, searching for the best of the images.

He read the info beside his choice. "Dima, get the print for images 5 November, 17:30:04 and 17:30:12." Dima riffled through the photos in the trolley rack, plucking out two foot-square color images and carefully handing them to Kostya.

Kostya placed them beside the backlit positive images, looking back and forth. From a rack on the table, he selected a small instrument that looked like a squat saltshaker. It was a jeweler's loupe, a high-magnification glass perfectly focused so that he could set it directly on the photo. He centered it on the image. Dima peered over his shoulder, grunted and pointed. "What's that?"

Kostya set his loupe on the darker spot and stared for several seconds, shifting the glass slightly.

"I'm not sure." He leaned to his right for Dima to have a look.

The younger officer peered through the loupe for several seconds. "It's fuzzy, but I see an oblong shadow next to an angular dark blob, like maybe a new, good-sized fighter is parked there."

Kostya nodded. "New is good in our business." He looked again, trying in vain to pick out any distinguishing features to help identify the type. *Might be an F-15*, he guessed to himself.

"Go to the lab and blow these images up, centered here"—he pointed at the change in Jackass Flats—"and again on this blob, so we can pass them up the chain ASAP." He turned back to the filmstrip on the table, relishing the work in front of him. "I'll see what else I can see."

As Dima left the room, Kostya grabbed his notebook, rewound the reel to 17:29:56, leaned back over the loupe for a more systematic look and started making more notes.

44

Restricted Flying Area 4808, Nevada

"You have control." Kaz's voice was clear and crisp in Grief's headset.

Magic words in a cockpit. There had been too many cases in two-seat airplanes where each pilot thought the other was flying, and the airplane had gone uncontrollable or crashed. Or worse, where both pilots were unknowingly fighting each other while maneuvering, *thinking* the airplane was out of control. The simple phrase was offered by one pilot and repeated by the other to show acceptance.

"I have control." Grief had learned the English phrase in the preflight briefings and placed his gloved hands confidently on the stick and throttles of the Aggressor T-38 Talon, giving the stick a slight shake to make it clear that Kaz could release his grip. Grief pushed the throttles forward with his left hand and eased the stick forward with his right. Time to get low, and fast.

Kaz took note of the Russian's sure, aggressive handling of the jet as he descended and prepared for the simulated combat engagement. Sam Phillips had asked him to personally keep an eye on Grief and the MiG-25, and since Kaz had passed his medical and was current in

T-38s, Irv Williams had agreed to have Kaz fly front seat for today's test exercise: his first chance to truly see Grief in action.

Ahead, above them in the airspace, was the new pride of the US Air Force fighter fleet: the F-15 Eagle, conceived and built to counter the threat of the MiG-25 Foxbat. The F-15 was a twin-tailed, Mach 2 interceptor fighter, with a huge planar array radar and Pratt & Whitney twin-spool, afterburning F-100 turbofan engines. The Air Force had begun test-flying the Eagle 18 months ago at Edwards AFB, 175 miles from where Kaz and Grief were flying. The latest variant had been detailed to Groom Lake so Irv's detachment could evaluate its intercept capabilities against Soviet aircraft and low-observable helicopters. Several miles ahead and low down in a dry valley, one of the Red Hat pilots was flying a modified Hughes OH-6 500P helicopter, very hard to detect due to its radar-absorbent skin. Grief and Kaz were flying the desert camouflage T-38, simulating a small, fast, ingressing MiG.

The F-15's task was to detect both aircraft, identify them using her radar's new non-cooperative target recognition software, and simulate shooting them down with her suite of radar-guided or heat-seeking missiles, or, if need be, at close range, using her M61A1 six-barrel Vulcan machine gun.

Kaz and Grief had briefed extensively prior to the flight, studying the airspace charts and local terrain, planning ingress and egress routes.

Grief had a key section of a topographic map clipped onto his left thigh and glanced down now to remind himself of what features to look for. A thick black grease-penciled line showed his desired track, and he looked ahead to confirm that the peaks and arroyos matched. He knew exactly where he was, and where he was going.

They'd briefed an ingress speed of 420 knots, at an altitude of 200 feet above the rough terrain. Grief glanced at the airspeed and radar altimeter, and he was exactly on both. But the ingress run would last 90 seconds or so, with the waiting F-15 ahead, above them, radar sweeping that whole time. Hunting for them, and the helo.

They brought me here to learn how the best Soviet pilots fly, Grief thought. *Now I'll show them.*

He pushed the throttles into afterburner and moved the stick forward, rapidly descending.

In the front seat, Kaz spoke into the intercom. "Easy, Grief. This is low and fast enough." With his hands hovering near the controls in case he had to take over, Kaz glanced down to the instruments: 100 feet and 480 knots. Just below them, the exposed rock and scrub brush flicked past at a mile every 7.5 seconds.

Grief said, "Ponyal." He didn't get all the words, but Kaz's tone was clear, and he understood.

He focused intently, craning around Kaz's helmet in the front cockpit, judging his height by the flashing blur, aggressively following the nap of the earth. Making it as hard as possible for the F-15's radar to find and lock on to them amongst all the background radar reflections. Especially while it was also searching for the low, slow, near-invisible 500P helicopter. He'd been told the *P* stood for Penetrator, after its ability to get deep into enemy territory, proven during Vietnam special operations.

Terrain suddenly rose ahead of them, and Grief slammed the stick right and pulled, instantly loading them to 6G, following the winding valley on his map, as planned. The thin, short wings of the T-38 tortured the air, making the plane shudder with the high-speed stall. *Just like MiG-21*, Grief noted.

A voice came through their headsets. "Fox One, Fox One, target low and fast, range eleven miles."

The F-15 had managed to lock on to them and had reached in-envelope release parameters to simulate firing an AIM-7 Sparrow radar-guided missile. Grief grunted, knowing what Fox One meant. The only way to beat it now was to break the Eagle's radar lock before the missile arrived—a matter of seconds. He slammed the stick left, reversing direction to follow the narrow valley, and forced the jet even lower, focusing everything on terrain avoidance. To succeed, he needed to get low enough to confuse the radar return, overwhelming it with ground clutter.

Kaz was now beyond uncomfortable at the speed and height. "That's enough, Grief," he said. Just as he was putting his hands on the stick and throttle to take control, they both heard "Lost lock! Lost lock!" in their headsets. Grief didn't know the words but recognized the tone of a pilot who had failed. He pulled the throttles back and eased the jet up, away from the ground, leveling the wings. In an easy, conversational tone, as if he hadn't been working hard at all, Grief said, "You have control."

Kaz took the throttle and stick and reflexively said, "I have control."

Pushing the transmit button with his thumb, Kaz called, "Knock it off, knock it off," the universal acknowledgment that this training exercise had completed. He glanced at the fuel gauges; the high speed and use of afterburners had rapidly drunk through the T-38's small reserve. "MiG is Bingo, headed back to base." Bingo meant all operational training needed to cease, as the remaining fuel was required for safe return and landing.

"Copy, knock it off, knock it off, and copy MiG is Bingo. Eagle will follow you back to the Ranch."

In the back seat, Grief smiled into his neoprene mask. The F-15 was America's newest, best fighter, with all the most modern technologies, and he had just defeated it, purely through his piloting skill.

The Eagle test pilot stood next to the blackboard, where he'd drawn the racetrack oval of his airplane's ground track in blue, and the ingress routes of the Red Hat T-38 and 500P helo in red. Kaz, Grief and the helo pilot sat in the briefing room, tipped back on their chairs, confident in how they had performed.

"Initially I saw the MiG on radar here." The Eagle driver drew a fat red chalk arrow at the bottom of the blackboard. "At that low altitude, it was just outside missile range, so I stayed in multi-target search mode to keep looking for the helo." He pointed at the second red line and shook his head. "I never saw anything, which surprised me given the big rotating blades."

The helo pilot did his best to keep smugness out of his voice, and almost succeeded. "The work the Hughes boys did on the blades surprises a lot of people."

The Eagle pilot nodded. In the back of the room, the test engineers were writing notes. They would be getting the downloaded data from the jet's digital onboard system, to review in detail what exactly had happened.

"As the MiG came into range, I locked it up, verified a good solution and pickled off a Fox One. Initial data was good, but then the signal started to diverge, and broke lock." He looked directly at Grief. "I don't know what you did, but it worked, and the missile went stupid."

Thompson, drinking coffee next to him, leaned close to explain what had been said, and the Russian responded. "I just used the small size of my jet and the natural terrain to confuse your radar. Hopefully, it helps with your evaluation and test program." To be offhand and non-self-congratulatory in victory was the most effective of daggers in a fighter pilot debrief.

"Yeah, well, it worked." The Eagle driver glanced at the helo pilot as well. "Between the two of you, we got handed our hat here today."

As detachment commander, Irv was also attending the debrief, and he now stood and moved next to the Eagle pilot, smiling to signal the end of the lesson. "We executed the test exercise well today, no one got hurt, and the value of realistic training with Aggressors was clearly demonstrated." He nodded at the engineers in the back. "I'm certain the F-15 is going to be a better fighter from the lessons we're learning here." He glanced at Grief, then added, "But it's nice to see that even a simple plane like the T-38, in the right hands, can be a formidable adversary."

As the Eagle pilot erased the board and his team of engineers started getting out of their chairs, Kaz watched Grief, who was still sitting calmly beside Thompson.

That Russian has been in real world low-altitude combat before, Kaz thought. *I wonder where?*

45

Nuclear Rocket Development Station, Jackass Flats, Nevada

Isaac Acklin didn't like his work anymore.

For one thing, it was hot. He'd known when he took the job that the Nevada desert was going to be far hotter than Avalon Park in Chicago, where he'd grown up. But he'd come to Las Vegas as a young truck driver seeking work and refuge from the cold of the Illinois winter. So hot wasn't so much the issue as how unpleasant the heat felt out on the sun-baked, dusty hardpan of Jackass Flats. And at night, the desert still got unfairly cold.

But really, the worst part was that the work was petering out into nothing, and he was mostly alone doing it now.

When the guys in white lab coats had been busy with their testing, it wasn't bad at all. Lots of people to talk to—construction and maintenance guys, vehicle operators like himself, ex-military. And plenty of downtime between the test firings of the nuclear engines the nerds were working on. Good pay too, with the extra security requirements and danger component of that type of work, and a results-oriented schedule that led to him picking up lots of overtime.

But fucking Nixon had stopped all that. *So stupid,* Isaac thought for the umpteenth time. The scientists here had been having real success. Even a driver like himself could see that. He'd heard that one of the most recent tests had run for hours, and at nearly full power. What a dumb time to shut it all down! But now that the government had pulled out of Vietnam and ended NASA's Apollo Moon program, they didn't see the need for these types of engines anymore, or at least Uncle Sam wasn't going to pay for them.

Just dump the problem in some future president's lap, Isaac thought. *Typical.*

Now he'd been reduced to a glorified trash collector. EG&G, the main nuclear test site contractor, had given him two strong-backed morons (he called them "the Twins" in his head) to help with the heavy lifting. And all the three of them had to do was work through a long list, collecting shit from one place and putting it somewhere else.

The bigger pieces went to the sandy open dump in the middle of Jackass Flats, where the heaviest of the machinery had been rolled out on the local rail track. Every time Isaac drove by flatcar after flatcar loaded with massive engines and test structures, he shook his head. All that work, silently corroding into dust in the Nevada sun, surrounded by the red-brown hills of the Skull and Shoshone mountains. Not to be salvaged or even touched until some safety wonk in Washington looked at a chart and decided the radioactivity levels had probably bled down low enough that his boss could get reelected.

The real pain was collecting all the small stuff—tools and books and notes and everyday things—that needed to be verified, cataloged, and then shelved into long-term storage inside the R-MAD, the Reactor Maintenance Assembly and Disassembly building. Anything that the safety inspectors had categorized as "mildly contaminated" was there on his job list, page after page of ridiculously specific tedium.

He and the Twins had driven out to Engine Test Stand One and loaded today's items into bins, filing cabinets and portable railed shelving. The four-story R-MAD building at the other end of the Flats was deemed suitable and large enough to house it all, and he'd backed the panel van up to one of the roll-down unloading dock doors. His job was to get the Twins to load everything onto pallets so he could then forklift it all into the designated rooms inside the facility. Once they'd unloaded it in place, he'd tick the items off on the clipboard list and then drive back for the next load.

As he watched the Twins unload, Isaac thought, *I used to be a heavy equipment operator. Now I'm a goddamned accountant!*

There were designated shelving units in some of the rooms for the endless sheaves of handwritten notes and printed reports, and others for bound books. He watched the Twins closely to make sure they didn't fuck it up. And he also watched the round, black-and-white, government-issue clocks that were on at least one wall in most rooms. All sense of urgency had long since departed the project, and any hope of overtime gone with it. No way was Isaac working one second longer than he had to every day.

Isaac Acklin didn't like it, but it was a job. An easy job, really, and still with premium pay, given most people's fear of lingering low-level radioactivity.

And with all the stuff he and the Twins still had to mothball, the job was going to last awhile.

46

Groom Lake

Grief really liked these shoes.

They were made of leather, mostly white with a sweeping red trim shape that reminded him of a wing. Kaz had bought them for him during the debriefings in the west Vegas hills, and he'd been running in them ever since.

He pulled the first shoe on over his white sock. He liked that it had seven rows of eyelets, so he could control local tightness. He preferred to leave the toes loose, pull the laces tight across his instep to cinch into his underside arch, and then to not use the last eyelet, for extra ankle flexing room. He grunted slightly as he sat on the corner of his bed in track pants and T-shirt and pulled the shoelaces tight.

The darkness of night was just lifting, the sunrise still hidden by the hills to the east. He held the second shoe up to see it better. Whoever the designer was, they'd been thoughtful, providing a grippable leather flap at the back to pull the shoe on, like a built-in shoehorn. The zigzag pattern of the sole was starting to wear away from the weeks of daily running but still gave him good traction. He'd puzzled out the letters of the maker's name, which was printed in lowercase on the shoe's tongue, realizing he recognized it as a Russian word: *nika*, the Greek goddess of victory.

He smiled into the growing light as he pulled the second shoe on. It was a good omen.

Battle was coming.

Unlike at Spring Mountain Ranch, Grief was allowed to run on his own inside the confines of Groom Lake base. He'd soon settled into a running route he liked, and that anyone who might be watching him had grown used to—including Thompson, running his own loops around the site. This morning was no different, the CIA handler lacing up by his trailer and nodding blankly at his charge. Ignoring him, Grief stretched briefly, then ran west to join the graveled access road, where he'd turn south on the long straightaway past the dump, left at the fuel farm tanks onto paved road, back north again by the base power plant, and then follow the edge of the taxiways to complete the square at the headquarters building. If he pushed it, he could make the five-kilometer route in 21 minutes, but no need to wear out his knees and hips: he usually completed it in 23. The shoes helped and were better than the Russian-made ones he'd left behind in Syria.

This morning he felt good. He never knew for sure until he started running and the various body parts checked in, but as he picked up speed approaching the dump road, everything felt solid and energized. He turned left and picked up the pace slightly from his norm. You only got stronger when you pushed yourself.

The wind was light from the west, as usual at this time of the morning, and he smelled the dump as he approached it, an unpleasant mixture of chemical and rotting odors. He looked closely as he passed and, apart from a circling buzzard, saw nothing moving. A satisfied smile crossed his face as he settled into his runner's breathing pattern.

He'd given himself specific goals for today's run, and he varied his route slightly to meet them. There was an access road closer to the hulking white cylindrical jet fuel tanks, and he followed it, looking more closely than usual at the plumbing lines and valves that led towards the airfield. At one point the lines crossed the road in a square arch, up and over, high enough for the tanker trucks that delivered the fuel to clear. As he ran underneath, his eyes traced the lines into the distance.

He nodded. They were exactly as he had sketched them out in his head.

Turning towards the power plant, he ran along the fuel lines that he'd reasoned supplied the diesel to run the generators, reminding himself of the exact location and access valves. There was a steady rumble and high whining noise from inside the building, and a low roar from the exhaust stacks in the roof. As he ran past, he looked carefully at the maze of wires and transformers where the power lines emerged. There was a high fence around the densest part, with warning signs for electrocution.

As the sound of the generator faded behind him, he listened to the steady rhythm of his shoes on the pavement, and then heard the familiar distant, growing whine of a jet engine starting. He glanced at his watch—07:00. That would be the daily weather check, the duty pilot taking a T-38 airborne to determine wind and visibility, bringing the Groom Lake operation to life.

With a little over a kilometer remaining, he did a quick internal inventory, realized that nothing hurt and that he had plenty of reserve. He accelerated, deliberately pushing himself. He increased his breathing rate and was rewarded by a visceral response from his body: a warming rush of blood, an increasing roaring in his ears, a sharpening of vision.

As his trailer came into sight, he visualized a finish line and pushed to hold his sprint speed steady until he crossed it, then slowed to an easy pace to cool his body gradually. A quietening jog to Dump Road and back, stopping at the steps that led up to his end of the trailer.

A good run. He stretched, bending at the waist, extending the tendons and muscles along the backs of his legs. He lifted one foot onto the step, leaning forward, and looked again with satisfaction at the white and red of his shoes.

His run had reconfirmed his visualization. It was almost time.

He was ready.

47

Moscow, Seven Months Earlier

The cold April rain was rattling off the high leaded windows, the noise rising and falling as the gusts unevenly gathered and then lost strength down the twists of the Moskva River. General Secretary Leonid Brezhnev absently noted the sounds as he sipped his tea and prepared his thoughts for his next meeting. Spring rain was welcome after the cold, dark gray of winter across his vast country. And it helped wash the streets of Moscow clean.

The word "Kremlin" meant "fortress within a city." Since before recorded history, petitioners had come to this particular rise of high ground, naturally protected and easily defended, inside a broad curve of the riverbank where the smaller Neglinnaya flowed into the Moskva. The visitors' purpose had always been the same: to beseech the leadership to hear their concerns and, hopefully, to grant their wishes.

It was no different today.

Brezhnev had sent no less than Nikolai Podgorny, his second-in-command and chairman of the Presidium, out to Vnukovo airport to greet this latest visitor. Often what Kremlin supplicants really wanted was not a decision, or money, but simply public recognition from the supreme ruler. Brezhnev and Podgorny had judged that such recognition was what this man had traveled so far to receive, and it was important to honor it. Especially since they needed something from him in return.

They'd ensured there was a long row of uniformed soldiers with their rifles held at attention on the runway to receive him as he came down the steps from his red-and-white Aeroméxico DC-8. No special government aircraft for him: Mexican President Luis Echeverría Álvarez was a man of the people, and he visibly traveled on the same airline as everyone else.

They'd arranged a motorcade, as befit a head of state, but only three cars, as it was merely Mexico. Brezhnev knew Echeverría had come directly from Great Britain and France, and he would be traveling on to Peking. But the Soviet Union was the crown jewel of this international tour. Mexico, publicly meeting face-to-face with the USSR, one of the world's two great superpowers.

Sitting in his office on the third floor of the Council of Ministers building, Brezhnev purposefully kept the Mexican waiting. After carefully reviewing his briefing notes, he glanced at the large digital clock on his desk and nodded. Twenty minutes was enough to make his point.

Pushing on the arms of his chair, he levered himself up. He'd always been stockily built, but at 67, the fatty foods and vodka were thickening his short frame. He smoothed his oiled, receding hair with both hands, walked around his desk and along the long meeting table to the double doors at the end of his office, and opened them, stepping back in clear invitation.

A personal touch that the visitor would, no doubt, recount to everyone. On the left breast of his dark suit Brezhnev wore his two highest medals, Hero of the Soviet Union and Hero of Socialist Labor, to signify the occasion.

The men shook hands and introduced themselves through interpreters, smiled broadly for the photographers, closed the door and sat—Echeverría at the table opposite Podgorny, Brezhnev once again behind his desk at the table's head.

After the formalities, the Mexican president visibly wanted to speak, and the two Soviets let him. Echeverría looked back and forth between the men as he talked, passionately expressing his vision of a global order that included the Third World, equably sharing resources and giving power to the people. The interpreter had no trouble keeping up, as the words had been said before in London and Paris. Brezhnev and Podgorny nodded gravely as the president made his points.

When it was finally the Soviet leader's turn, he complimented Echeverría on his leadership, talked of the long history of cooperation between the two nations and their shared goals of empowering their populaces, and promised future collaboration and financial support, details to be discussed with his staff as the day progressed.

As Brezhnev finished with the pro forma, he paused, and Podgorny recognized it as his opportunity.

"President Echeverría, we have one small favor to ask."

After the magnanimous nature of his welcome, the Mexican president smiled, looking at Podgorny expectantly. "Yes, of course, Mr. Chairman. What is it?"

Brezhnev was the one who answered. "Later this year, we may ask permission for a transport airplane to make a short flight from Cuba through international airspace to your airport in Mexicali. It would only be on the ground for a few hours and then return to Havana." He smiled, turning his full charm on the bespectacled visitor. "We'd like to keep it quiet."

Echeverría's mind raced at the unexpected request. *What does the most senior leadership of the Soviet Union want in Mexicali?* There were Russian settlers in the area from long ago, and low-level trade in cotton and manufactured goods. Unlikely that was it. Mexicali was also a border town with the United States.

He considered that fact. Still, granting landing clearance to an international flight was no big deal. And saying yes now would help him in his remaining dealings in the Soviet Union.

He smiled again, so widely his eyes crinkled behind his tinted glasses. He liked the implied equality of a superpower quid pro quo.

"Mexico's tequila must be even more world-famous than I thought, General Secretary! Consider it done. And we look forward to loading a few cases onto your airplane."

48

KGB Headquarters, Dzerzhinsky Square, Moscow

It was a bizarrely ugly building. The flat planes and oppressive pale bulk of New Soviet architecture had been unforgivingly grafted onto the ornate, graceful angles of the 1898 headquarters of the All-Russia Insurance Company like a crazed vivisection experiment. A transformation of elegance and commerce into brutal functionality and espionage.

Lubyanka. The headquarters of the Committee for State Security, the Komitet Gosudarstvenoy Bezopasnosti.

The KGB.

Vitaly Kalugin was at his desk in the old part of the building, leaning on his elbows, reading intently. After his trip to Star City, he'd put in a requisition for background documents on several topics, and the multiple folders had arrived in his inbox overnight. His half-smoked Belomorkanal cigarette in the ashtray in front of him trailed a thin, vertical thread of gray as it turned to ash, and the tea in his cup had gone cold as he methodically worked his way through each of the folders, rereading key sections, his thick finger occasionally tracing the margin of the paragraphs. He paused often to pick up his pen and make neat summaries, capturing transient thoughts into his green baize notebook.

After a careful second read-through, he closed the last folder with a snort of dissatisfaction, setting it back on the stack in his inbox for when he needed to refer to it again. He stared unfocused for many seconds across the room, took a long pull on the cigarette and exhaled the smoke through his nose. He drained the last of the cold tea, centered his notebook in front of him and reviewed what he'd learned.

Until now, the American, Commander Kazimieras Zemeckis, had only barely caught the attention of the Soviet espionage apparatus. The documents had shown that he'd been a Navy combat fighter pilot in Vietnam, the top graduate of his test pilot class at Patuxent River in Maryland, selected into the military Manned Orbiting Laboratory astronaut program, and then badly injured in a flying accident that had cost him his pilot status. He'd gone on to do a PhD in electro-optics at MIT and had subsequently disappeared from the Soviet records. A disappointingly thin file.

Vitaly took one final drag on the cigarette and stubbed the butt out in his ashtray, careful to fully extinguish its flattened cardboard rolling tube.

Where had Kazimieras Zemeckis disappeared to? Someone had assigned him to support Apollo 18 at NASA, to work in Mission Control and talk to the crews on the Moon. They'd also sent him to the splashdown in the Pacific where the KGB had lost an agent. Had Zemeckis killed him? And who was he now working for?

Vitaly pondered the differences of Apollo 18 from the previous Moon missions. It had been kept quiet in the Western media, publicly listed as a classified spaceflight with an all-military crew. It made sense to him that the US Joint Chiefs would have wanted a trusted agent deeply embedded within NASA during such a spaceflight. Given Zemeckis's flying operations and his academic background, it was logical that he had been the one they'd choose, still active-duty military but in a civilian role. Vitaly reviewed his thinking and nodded. That piece fit. And worth remembering for future joint NASA/Department of Defense projects.

He reached for his pack of Belomorkanals, tapped the bottom and pulled out a fresh cigarette, pinching both ends to keep in the tobacco. He struck a match, inhaled to make sure the flame caught properly and considered the other half of this morning's problem.

Why had this same American been spotted with someone who had been potentially recognized as a Soviet test pilot, in Las Vegas of all places? And if he truly was with Colonel Alexander Vasilyevich Abramovich, twice Hero of the Soviet Union, how could that possibly be?

Vitaly frowned deeper. *A yashick Pandory*—a Pandora's box of complications.

As in many countries' intelligence services, the KGB had various levels of security, from Unclassified, or Gray, to Top Secret, or Red, as well as special access levels beyond that. As a counterintelligence officer with the newly acquired rank of major in the First Chief Directorate, First Department, specializing primarily in the United States and Canada, Vitaly had access to files up to Top Secret.

He reached to retrieve the top folder from his inbox and opened it again. It had been prepared by the Third Chief Directorate with the Soviet Armed Forces, which dealt with military counterintelligence and covered Abramovich's most recent assignment. He'd been deployed in Syria, but apart from the cover page with the basic details of date and place of assignment, a copy of the posting orders, and a page listing the bare facts of his shoot-down and death on October 5, 1973, the file contained just one other piece of paper. Block letters were stamped diagonally across the page: SECURITY CLEARANCE INSUFFICIENT FOR ACCESS.

Vitaly turned to look out his window, then pushed his chair back and stood, picking up his cup to get more tea. He put his hand on the teapot and judged it still warm enough, setting his cup down on the small table to pour. His recent promotion had moved him to his own small office, and he liked the privacy. The chance to think on his own.

His wife had packed some kozinaki honey nut bars on top of his lunch box, as usual. As he sat back at his desk and carefully set the teacup on its saucer, he opened the lower drawer on his right side to retrieve the treat. He held a hand under his chin to catch the crumbs as he took a bite, brushed them into his tea and took a loud sip to wash it down.

Why would the Third Directorate have assigned a special security classification to a pilot's posting in Syria? Why were the final details of his life so meager? The day after Abramovich was shot down and reported killed, the Yom Kippur War had broken out between Israel and its neighbors, including Syria. Was that timing just coincidence? *Likely*, Vitaly thought, but he hated coincidences. He chewed and swallowed the last of the bar and took another sip.

Given that the cosmonaut was sure of what she'd seen, had Colonel Abramovich survived the crash and defected to the West? If so, why hadn't the First Directorate, *his* Directorate, been informed? A new security risk in his territory, the Americas, should have automatically triggered an alert to KGB officers of his rank. It was normal procedure between the Third and the Second, to try to track a defector's location and to be on the lookout for newly leaked information.

Vitaly turned and looked out the window again, at the blank wall of the building facing his, now just catching a bright ray of morning sunlight. How exactly might this pilot have defected?

He took another deep lungful of cigarette smoke, holding it in to extract the maximum nicotine as he thought. That extra page in the folder spoke volumes. Someone in the Third Directorate knew enough about what had really happened in the skies over Israel on October 5 to assign a special access security clearance to it.

Vitaly exhaled slowly, the smoke curling up in front of his face. He blinked.

Keeping internal secrets was nothing new. He certainly didn't hurry to share information when it might be useful later for his department's tactical advantage. Or for his own.

And, he suddenly realized, no one else was tracking this. The convoluted link between the Soviet test pilot Abramovich and the American test pilot Zemeckis was now his to untangle. And turn to his advantage.

For the first time that day, a small smile touched Vitaly's lips. He bit into his second kozinaki bar, thinking, *I love my job*.

In a corner office in the Kremlin, the black phone on the broad mahogany desk rang, clanging jarringly into the quiet. The man looked up from the briefing he'd been reading. He stared at the telephone for one full ring cycle, then picked up the receiver.

"Andropov," he said. Anyone who knew his number knew he was the KGB chairman, and full member of the Politburo.

He listened to the clear, urgent voice for nearly a minute, his thick black eyebrows furrowing under his receding gray hairline at the unexpected and unwelcome development. He asked a few questions, thought for several seconds, gave clear direction to stop the investigation without explanation, and replaced the handset in the cradle.

He looked through his facing window across the triangular inner courtyard, thinking. All the pieces were still in place, but this particular operation had very high stakes and an unusually small circle of awareness.

He needed to keep it that way.

49

Sredmash—Ministry of Medium Machine Building, Moscow

Sometimes names deceive.

When the Viking known as Erik the Red was exiled from Iceland in 982 for murder, he fled in his longboat to settle on the cold, rocky shores of a much larger island to the west. Disingenuously, he called it Greenland. It was a far from accurate name, but one that he chose for his own purposes: to help draw generations of Norse settlers. The misdirect worked.

In the central administrative circle of Moscow, just south of the Moskva River on Bolshaya Ordinka Street, was a location with a name that was similarly misleading. Behind a high fence and wrought iron gates loomed a massive white-columned building, its square, 12-story bulk filling an entire city block. By the main entrance, an unobtrusive metal plaque announced the edifice as the Ministry of Medium Machine Building. Or, as it was commonly known, Sredmash, a short form using the first syllables of the Russian words for "medium" and "machine."

The ministry's actual function was far removed from its bland name. These were the headquarters responsible for the Soviet Union's nuclear capability.

The Ministry of Medium Machine Building did not just direct Soviet nuclear research, but espionage as well. Its first objective had been to win the race with the United States to split the uranium atom for use as fuel, and for ever more capable weapons. In 1944, a German physicist named Klaus Fuchs and several other Soviet spies had been infiltrated into Los Alamos in New Mexico, right in the heart of the American Manhattan Project, developing the world's first atomic bomb. They fed invaluable information to Sredmash at the end of the Great Patriotic War, speeding development of the first Soviet atomic bomb, Device 501, detonated on August 29, 1949.

Detonated at Semipalatinsk.

Since then, Sredmash had built nuclear power plants for cities, nuclear reactors for submarines and icebreakers, and nuclear-tipped missiles for the military. And on the windswept, slightly radioactive steppe of the Semipalatinsk Test Site, Sredmash was now responsible for building a nuclear rocket engine at Baikal-1.

The ministry's longtime director was Efim Slavsky. On this gray November day, on the twelfth floor of the hulking building, in the conference room that adjoined his office, he sat at the head of the table, scowling in anger at Vladimir Kryuchkov, head of the KGB First Chief Directorate.

Slavsky was a big man. He'd been a farmer, coal miner, metal factory worker and Revolutionary soldier, who had begun as a junior engineer at Sredmash and eventually risen to the positions of chairman and minister. Even now, at 75, the raw strength of his wide, square shoulders and long arms was undiminished. His prominent jaw and the gravelly depth of his voice added to the unmistakable impression of power.

"So you cannot control your own officers?" Slavsky accused Kryuchkov. Slavsky had summoned Kryuchkov—responsible for all KGB operations abroad—to the meeting.

Kryuchkov stared impassively back, his thick glasses resting on his misshapen nose, broken long ago. He'd been a fighter and a prosecutor and a diplomat before being hand-picked to lead the most influential directorate within the KGB. He was unafraid of big men.

"I cannot control secrets that have been deliberately kept from me, Comrade Director."

Slavsky snorted, the deep lines angling down either side of his nose exaggerated by the sour downturn of his lips. "Your whole job is secrets. You should know how to contain them."

Another big man, with wiry gray hair and pendulous earlobes, sat across the table from Kryuchkov, on Slavsky's right. He was wearing the brown tunic and khaki shirt and tie of the Soviet military, his shoulder boards denoting him as marshal, the highest rank in the Red Army. His name was Andrei Grechko, Minister of Defense of the Soviet Union. Grechko now spoke to the KGB man.

"How much has been revealed, and to whom?"

It was the key question.

Kryuchkov looked calmly at Grechko, his erect bulk silhouetted against the flat light of the tall windows. "The information has been contained, General. Our internal system worked just as it should. It was only the keen intelligence of one of my senior officers that connected seemingly unrelated facts and recognized that there might be a link. As soon as he spotted it, he followed protocol and reported it directly to me."

Kryuchkov glanced at Slavsky, and then back at the marshal. Both of these men outranked him. Marshal Grechko was a full member of the Politburo, the highest policy-making group in the Soviet Union, and both he and Slavsky were trusted advisors to General Secretary Leonid Brezhnev. Kryuchkov decided he needed to reinforce that he had his own power base and support. "I immediately alerted Chairman Andropov, and fully briefed him on what had occurred."

There was a pause as Slavsky and Grechko considered. They were the ones who had hatched the original idea 11 months previously. Satellite imagery had revealed that the Americans had secretly developed an asset that could be of great value to the Soviet Union, and that it was being held in one of the most inaccessible locations in the United States. When Slavsky had first suggested the plan, Marshal Grechko had thought it outrageous, but on closer analysis he'd agreed the risk might be worth it. After painstaking discussions between the two of them, they had met privately with key Politburo members to brief them and ask for input, and then they had taken the plan to a main Politburo meeting.

The Politburo was not a democracy. All the work was done in advance, so that each member could come to the meetings secure in his facts, ready to see which way Chairman Brezhnev was leaning. Brezhnev would listen to each man as he stated his position, and then he would summarize in a way that made it clear what he had decided would be done. There was never a vote and no majority rule.

After Grechko and Slavsky had spoken and others had fully expressed their opinions, Brezhnev had asked the pivotal question. "Can I assume that this plan is approved?" No one around the table spoke, and Brezhnev had concluded for them all. "The plan is approved."

Andropov had been at that meeting and his direction had been clear. Only the very highest level would know the full operation. No senior section heads and military commanders would be briefed. It would be a KGB-led operation, with the information siloed so that not even the specific individuals needed to execute and achieve the objective would grasp the whole picture.

Until today, everything had proceeded according to plan. But if rumors of what was actually happening leaked to the various agencies involved, it would spread like a cancer, destroying any chance of success.

The original idea had been Slavsky's, and he now spoke to the KGB officer. "I assume you have a way of communicating with your man in America?"

Kryuchkov nodded.

Slavsky looked at Marshal Grechko. The two large men, both lifetime soldiers, stared at each other for several seconds, then Grechko shrugged, his large ears shaking slightly with the motion.

He said, "This development doesn't change the military position." With the Americans already flying their next-generation F-14s and F-15s, and with the new Soviet designs for the MiG-29 and Su-27 well under way, the marshal knew just how much the tactical significance of the MiG-25 had been diminished. The technology had never been as good as they'd made the West think, and the fighter was a deceptive pawn to trade in this high-stakes gambit.

Slavsky nodded, still holding the marshal's gaze. As head of Sredmash, he knew more than anyone the importance of what they were attempting. This new KGB activity had been unwelcome, yes, but it was not entirely unexpected. And Andropov had dealt with it, and with this underling, properly. Time to soften the tone slightly and finish the meeting with a feeling of shared purpose.

To Kryuchkov he said, "Thank you for coming, Vladimir Alexandrovich. Your actions make sense. We are very close to something that will give the Soviet Union a tremendous advantage."

He looked back at the minister of defense. "A capability that will surpass any nation's in the world."

50

Above the Greenland–Iceland Gap

It was a long, long flight.

The Antonov-22 heavy military transport had taken off into the early winter darkness from the northern Soviet Severomorsk-3 air base near Murmansk, on the frozen Kola Peninsula. Initially the crew had steered their big plane directly north towards the Pole, then turned left to skirt Finland, Sweden and Norway's North Cape, eventually easing south to pass between Greenland and Iceland. The navigator, seated inside the glass nose of the plane, below and ahead of the pilots, had plotted an ideal course, like a piece of string pulled tight in a great circle on the globe between Murmansk and Havana, to minimize distance and save fuel. But as a military flight they needed to stay in international airspace the entire way, and so he'd dodged north instead, around Scandinavia, and added an easterly dogleg to steer clear of Newfoundland in Canada and the New England seaboard of the United States. When the nav had tallied it up for the captain, the route was just a titch over 9,000 kilometers, about 5,000 nautical miles—close to the plane's max range, even with the extra fuel bladders installed inside the cavernous fuselage.

The An-22 was a giant of a thing. The cockpit and nose bubble had seats for six men, the 200-foot wings held four huge Kuznetsov NK-12MA engines with throbbing double counter-rotating turboprops, and to keep the bulbous fuselage flying straight, there were tall twin tails mounted on wide booms at the back. It took a long, ponderous time to climb to its maximum cruising altitude of 30,000 feet, and it didn't go fast when it got there. It was going to take a little over 15 hours from the moment the wheels left the Arctic runway until they touched down on the Cuban asphalt. There were bunk beds and a small galley for rest and refreshment, as the crew took turns slowly flying nearly a quarter of the way around the world.

Seated uncomfortably in the back on the troop transport benches was a small team of aircraft technicians. They had been hand-picked for their specific knowledge and skills in anticipation of what they were going to be asked to do when they got to Cuba. Close inspection of their mismatched uniforms showed them all to be more senior in rank than run-of-the-mill technicians; they had also been chosen for their reliability and discretion. During the long transit, these men found comfortable places to stretch out, play cards, read and sleep, covering themselves with rough blankets against the damp chill of the massive cargo transport.

November flights to Cuba were coveted. A chance to escape the cold darkness of the sun-starved north and bask in the tropical Caribbean warmth. They'd also be able to bring back Cohiba cigars and Havana Club rum to sell on the Soviet black market, a well-known small sideline to help improve the upcoming New Year's celebrations.

Droning along, the icy blackness of the ocean nine kilometers beneath them and the endless dark and twinkling stars of the universe above, it felt as though they were suspended in the air, going nowhere. The crew hadn't been briefed on the specifics of their mission yet, but it didn't really matter. They had sunglasses in their pockets and rubles to spend, and were ready to welcome the first direct heat through the cockpit windows when their southerly flight path helped lift the Sun high into view.

Daydreaming of palm trees and a little beach time before their true mission began.

51

Building 1, Johnson Space Center, Houston

The headquarters building at the Johnson Space Center was the tallest of them all. Nine stories of white stucco over concrete with recessed tinted windows, built to resist the Texas heat, standing proudly above the flat Houston floodplain and the greasy brown bayou waters of the misleadingly named Clear Lake.

Kaz had been called from watchdogging the defector at Groom Lake to a NASA meeting in a ninth-floor corner office. He'd chosen the hard, pale-green government-issue sofa, diagonally next to the large mahogany desk of the Director of Flight Operations, Bill Tindall. Kaz had arrived five minutes early, and the secretary had ushered him in to wait for Tindall and for NASA's Chief Astronaut, Al Shepard.

Tindall had been part of the original team that created Mission Control, and the images of Gemini and Apollo spacecraft on his walls reflected his NASA career as he'd worked his way up to running all of flight ops. On the credenza behind Tindall's desk were mismatched models of space capsules and a Moon-themed snow globe. On the desk, next to a penholder and an oversized glass ashtray, was a skinny upright light with a fan of plastic branches protruding from the top, festooned with small balls. A miniature, sparkling solar system as a reminder of NASA's business.

"My wife bought that for me."

Kaz hadn't heard Bill Tindall come in and, slightly startled, got up to shake his hand. Bill was tall and round-faced, with a cowlick of sandy blond hair atop his receding hairline. During the Apollo 18 mission, he and Kaz had had many urgent meetings to solve the endless problems, and they respected each other. Bill leaned a haunch on his desk as Kaz sat back down on the sofa.

"Happy to be back flying T-38s?"

Kaz smiled. It had been Tindall who'd worked the NASA system to approve Kaz's one-eyed-pilot status. The Navy had decided not to fully reinstate him as a military pilot, but NASA was its own separate organization, and Tindall had been the one with the power to decide.

"I sure am, Bill. The Ellington instructors put me and my eyeball through the wringer, but it seems like it's been long enough since the accident that my brain has figured out new ways to judge distance. I just kept landing at the right place on various runways until they let me do it on my own." He paused, looking directly at Tindall. "It feels great to be flying jets again, and I have you to thank."

Just then a new voice broke in. "Yeah, well, flight privileges come with a cost, you know. Word has it your new call sign's gonna be 'Cyclops.'"

Al Shepard, the first American in space and Apollo 14 moonwalker, was leaning on the doorjamb, grinning widely at Kaz, his crooked front teeth glinting. As NASA's Chief Astronaut, he'd also been key in returning Kaz to flying status.

Kaz stood again to shake Al's hand. "I sure hope that's not true, Al," he said. Bad call signs tended to stick. "Just 'Kaz' is fine."

Shepard smiled even more broadly and added a wink. "I made that up, but you never know." He nodded at Tindall. "But Bill and I do have something to talk with you about."

Kaz turned and looked at Tindall, who said, "We got a classified briefing yesterday of some of the stuff you're up to in Nevada. Pretty amazing, and it sounds like a lot of fun as well."

Kaz nodded, saying nothing. Secrets were best when kept.

Tindall continued. "With the type of work you're doing there, and the Soviets assigning their woman cosmonaut, Svetlana Gromova, as one of the crew of Apollo–Soyuz, we think you're the right guy to be the crew's official liaison here at NASA."

Kaz held Tindall's gaze for several seconds, and then turned to Shepard. Taking care of the three Soviets training in Houston would be interesting, but complicated.

Shepard read Kaz's mind. "We already know Tom Stafford took the whole crew to Vegas, and he told us the woman might have unexpectedly seen you there. Given that you were also at her Apollo 18 splashdown, why not confront the situation head-on?"

Kaz thought hard. Having a foot solidly in with the Soviet crew at NASA and with the defector in Groom Lake would give him room to minimize any rumors or inadvertent overlaps like the one in Vegas. And it would keep all the Soviet presence with one NASA point of contact: him. Also, he admitted to himself, the cosmonaut Svetlana Gromova had intrigued him since he'd spoken with her from Mission Control during Apollo 18. And even more after she'd outwitted him during the tumultuous Pacific splashdown.

He nodded. "Good that I'm front-seat again, if you two can spare an occasional T-38 for me to commute between here and Nevada."

Shepard said, "Absolutely. The Russians are due here at JSC tomorrow morning to get their preliminary training finished, and it's likely the only way you can balance the two jobs."

Kaz had one lingering concern. "I can't say yes until I call General Phillips about this."

Shepard smiled. "Don't you worry, Kaz, we've already talked with Sam at some length." His eyes twinkled. "In fact, it was his idea. And you better get cracking. The Soviet crew is arriving tonight."

—

Kaz looked once more at his wristwatch and then out through the tall, runway-facing windows of Houston's Intercontinental Airport. The barely understandable public address system had echoingly announced that Delta Flight 353 from New York had landed, but he hadn't yet seen it pull up to the gate.

During his hour's drive up to the airport from the Johnson Space Center—in the eight-passenger, blue-and-white NASA Dodge Maxivan he signed out to transport the group—he'd been thinking about how to get off on the right foot in his new official role as the Soviet crew's NASA liaison. He'd been told they would be accompanied by their own Russian-national interpreter, plus a US State Department escort who had met them when they'd landed at JFK airport earlier in the day. Six people total; Kaz figured cosmonauts would travel with minimal luggage, the way astronauts do, so there'd be enough room in the van.

Movement caught his eye, and he simultaneously heard the growing whine of the three jet engines as the 727-200 turned to taxi into its assigned jetway. He could see the pilots peering over their instrument panel to follow the directions of the marshaler, the light from their cockpit bright against the evening darkness. The marshaler crossed his lit batons over his head, the jet bobbed slightly as the pilots pushed on the toe brakes, and the engine noise suddenly dropped as they cut the throttles to off.

Kaz walked to where he could see down the unloading ramp, and watched the distinct mix of Texans in cowboy boots and New Yorkers in shiny suits getting off the plane. He was sure he'd recognize Svetlana, but he'd checked NASA photographs earlier in the day, reminding himself what the male cosmonauts looked like.

First he spotted the balding head and short stature of the Soyuz crew commander, Alexei Leonov, striding up the jetway. Next to him was a tall man in a dark suit, peering ahead to try to pick Kaz out in the small crowd of people waiting. Kaz waved, and the men came towards him. The dark suit held out his hand to Kaz, smiling.

"John Sorenson, State Department. You must be Commander Kazimieras Zemeckis. I let the crew know you'd be waiting for us."

"Call me Kaz." While shaking hands, Kaz noticed Svetlana coming up the ramp alongside her dark-haired crewmate, Valery Kubasov, and a young, fair-haired man.

"How was your flight?"

"Routine," Sorenson said. His dark suit accentuated the paleness of his face and his prematurely balding head.

The Russian crew commander spoke in thickly accented English as he took Kaz's hand in both of his. "My name—Alexei. Good to meet you, Kaz." He said the words as a learned phrase, no doubt taught by an instructor in Star City.

"Good to meet you as well, Alexei."

Still holding on to Kaz's hand, Alexei nodded at the remaining trio. "Kubasov, Valery Nikolaevich, Flight Engineer Number 1. Gromova, Svetlana Yevgenyevna, Flight Engineer Number 2." His eyes twinkled. "I think you know her?" At last, he let go.

Kaz smiled back but thought it best to say nothing.

Alexei shrugged, maintaining eye contact, and then tipped his chin towards the young blond man, lowest in the pecking order. "Polukhin, Vladimir, perevotchick."

The younger man nodded his head to Kaz and dutifully translated, "Interpreter."

Svetlana was staring at Kaz intently. He nodded at her and said, "Svetlana," careful to match the tone he'd used with Alexei. She nodded back, her expression neutral. He turned to the third cosmonaut and said, "Valery," and shook his hand. Better to keep things even until he'd sussed out who knew what, and how they were all going to act.

Greetings completed, there was a slightly awkward pause. Kaz broke it by turning and pointing ahead, along the wide airport hallway towards a descending escalator. "Let's go get your bags."

—

In the NASA van, Alexei naturally chose shotgun, instructing the interpreter to sit between himself and Kaz on the bench seat. The others settled themselves in the rows farther back, faces visible in the rear-view mirror.

After Kaz had pulled out of the airport and headed south on Interstate 59 towards Houston, Alexei asked through the interpreter, "So you are a pilot, Kaz?"

Kaz nodded. "Yep. Navy pilot. Now I fly T-38s with NASA."

"They let you fly jets with just one eye?"

Observant guy, Kaz thought. "Yep, I lost an eye in a flying accident, but once I showed them that I could still land, they gave me my medical back." He paused while the interpreter translated, and then asked, "What would they do in the Soviet Union?"

Alexei shook his head. "To fly jets, pilots need to be perfect." He smiled broadly. "For cosmonauts, even worse. During selection they check our whole bodies for scars. Any visible ones, patooey, you were out."

Kaz nodded, smiling at Alexei's deliberately silly word. *A simple but harsh policy*, he thought. *Hard to find a pilot who's never been injured.* He glanced across at Alexei. "What all did you fly?" A common-ground pilot question, good to build a friendship. He flicked a glance in his mirror. Svetlana was clearly paying attention to their conversation.

"I started with simple gliders, then propeller-driven Polikarpovs and Yak-18s, then on to jets—the MiG-15." He smiled again, and Kaz realized that Alexei smiled at everything, which made it hard to read what he was thinking. "Perhaps you know this jet fighter plane, Kaz?"

"Yes, though I've never seen one up close." Both men knew that, with the war in Vietnam, that was a lie, but an acceptable one. "Fun to fly?"

Alexei chuckled. "All airplanes are fun to fly, no?"

Kaz laughed as well, agreeing.

The cosmonaut tipped his head towards his two crewmates in the back. "Valery Nikolaevich is a space engineer, an expert in orbital mechanics, but Svetlana Yevgenyevna is also a pilot." He raised his eyebrows in respect. "A test pilot."

Kaz raised his eyebrows as well, finding it hard to resist mimicking Alexei's theatrical expressions. "Yes, with her walking on the Moon, Svetlana is pretty well-known here in America." He stole another glance in the rearview. She was looking out the window as the skyscrapers of downtown Houston loomed. Her profile was double-reflected in the glass—upturned nose, high cheekbones, strong chin.

Kaz returned his eyes to the road and steered the heavy van onto the I-45 entrance ramp, south towards NASA.

52

NASA Johnson Space Center

Kaz spent the next morning watching the Apollo and Soyuz crews train on the spaceship docking system in Building 13. The full-scale mock-up of the Soviet and American hardware looked like a huge double-lobed metal spider, and the intricacies of sensors and mechanisms, especially for failure cases, were vital for the crew to fully understand. As liaison, Kaz expected that he would eventually be their CAPCOM in Mission Control during the mission itself, another reason to closely audit their training.

Kaz spoke up. "Ready for a lunch break?"

Tom Stafford looked up on hearing Kaz's voice and checked his watch.

"Gosh, time sure flies when you're having fun." He looked to Alexei and tried out one of the Russian words he'd learned. "Obyed?" He pronounced it with a thick Oklahoma accent: *Ah-bee-yed.*

Alexei smiled, happy to use some English phrases in return. "Yes, lunch! Why not?"

After the crew extricated themselves from the test apparatus, Kaz led them out a side door into the bright Texas November sunshine. With the astronauts in orange-brown flight suits and the cosmonauts in pale green, they were a colorful group walking across the central quadrangle towards the Building 3 cafeteria. As the Russian interpreter stayed closest to the two commanders and the other men moved as a group, Kaz found himself walking next to Svetlana.

Kaz glanced sideways to find her studying him. Evaluating. She spoke, in surprisingly good English. "That was you in the Pacific Ocean, in the capsule and then outside, under the water." A statement, not a question.

Kaz nodded. Pointless to deny it.

"And it was you on the radio, speaking with us during the mission?" A question this time, and he nodded again.

Unexpectedly, she reached out a hand to shake, saying, "It is nice to meet you here. Now. Kaz."

Kaz shook her hand awkwardly while they kept walking. Her small hand was dry, her grip strong. Had she recognized him in Las Vegas too? *Definitely no point in asking that.*

He said, "Congratulations on being assigned to Apollo–Soyuz, Svetlana."

"Thank you."

He looked for something else to say. "Did you sleep well?"

The corners of her eyes crinkled slightly. "Yes. But did you, after seeing me?"

That startled Kaz, and he hoped to hell it didn't show. *Does she mean what I think she means?*

"Yes, I did, thanks." He was relieved to see the low steps to the cafeteria in front of them.

"Ah, here we are," he said. "I have someone who wants to meet you."

—

After guiding the Russians through the cafeteria line, Kaz led them to a table. He took the seat across from Svetlana, both remaining quiet as the rest of the crew around them chatted via the interpreter. When he spotted Laura, he waved and was greeted by an answering smile as she strode towards them. Svetlana's eyes followed Kaz's gaze, and she raised an eyebrow.

Kaz stood, kissed Laura on the cheek and turned to introduce her to the Russian crew.

"Alexei, Valery, Svetlana, this is my girlfriend, Dr. Laura Woodsworth. She's a planetary geologist here at the space center."

Laura held up a brown paper bag and looked directly at Svetlana. "Okay if I join you?"

Svetlana nodded and said, in English, "No problem."

Laura took the empty chair at the end of the table. As she opened her lunch bag and pulled out her sandwich, she spoke rapid-fire to the only other woman in the group. "Major Gromova, I've been very excited to meet you. It's a huge honor just to be sitting at the same table as the first woman to walk on the Moon. I have a million questions, but maybe I should let you eat your lunch first."

Svetlana blinked at the verbal onslaught, and then sorted through what she'd understood as she swallowed a mouthful of tomato soup. She asked, "So you are a doctor?"

"Yes, a PhD. I have a doctorate in planetary geology—cosmochemistry."

Svetlana thought. "You study the Moon?"

"Yes. All the rocks and regolith the Apollo program brought back from the Moon are kept here at the Johnson Space Center, stored in an inert nitrogen atmosphere so they can be studied. I work in the Lunar Receiving Laboratory."

Careful, Laura, Kaz thought.

Svetlana considered Laura for a few seconds, then asked, "What have you found?"

Laura took a quick bite of her sandwich to think about how to respond, and Kaz covered. "We brought back around a thousand pounds of rock—half a ton or so. From it, we now know the age of the Moon."

Laura directed a small glance of thanks at Kaz. "We've been analyzing oxygen isotopes sealed in the Moon rocks, and they match those of early Earth, so we're pretty sure there was a huge collision four and a half billion years ago, and the Moon was ripped from the Earth itself."

Svetlana nodded. "Our scientists think that also."

Laura shifted the subject to more personal ground. "NASA's maybe going to allow women to be astronauts for their new project, the Space Shuttle, in a few years. I really admire you and Valentina Tereshkova for leading the way."

Svetlana tipped her head to one side, assessing. "You want to fly in space."

Laura blushed. "Is it that obvious? Yes, I sure do!"

Now Svetlana smiled, glancing around the room. "That's good to hear. There are too many space men."

After lunch, Tom Stafford offered to lead the crew back to the sim so Kaz could escort Laura back to her lab. As soon as the two of them were out of earshot, walking along the quadrangle, Laura said, "I'm sorry I almost blew it, Kaz. I got carried away just meeting her. Do you think she knows we found radioactivity on the Moon?"

The Department of Defense had confiscated the fragments of radioactive rock that the Apollo 18 crew had brought back; the existence of the larger rock, and who had ended up with it after splashdown, had been kept highly classified. He answered Laura truthfully, though incompletely.

"Probably, yes. She helped collect the samples on the surface, and she was in the capsule with them during the three-day return, with a radiation detector onboard. I bet her government is keeping it quiet as well."

Laura nodded, reflecting on the lunchtime conversation. "She's a sharp one."

"Given what she's accomplished, she'd have to be," Kaz said.

53

State Road 25, Nevada

It had been so long since she'd been left by the side of the road that she could barely remember her earlier life. A vague recurring dream of a time of warmth and a full belly, with her mother and siblings nearby, had become more of a feeling of something lost than an actual memory.

Since then, Alma's life had been outside.

When the pickup truck that abandoned her had spun its tires and pelted her with gravel, she'd been confused and scared. Fleeing the rush and noise of the fast-moving traffic on State Road 25, she'd run as long as she could, eventually slowing to a lope, and then a walk, down the smooth surface of a dirt road leading to the west. When an occasional truck came dustily past, she hid in the surrounding low greasewood bushes.

Thirst had been her first problem. Alma had smelled the air, hunting for the familiar scent of water. Her nose led her to the low part of the valley, where she found a shallow slough; she cautiously sniffed and tasted the greenish water, and then drank her fill.

Hunger came next, and the westerly breeze brought faint but unmistakable smells of food. People food. Alma followed the road towards them, stopping to evaluate when she saw two buildings at a crest in the road and motion around them.

She'd been hit many times in her short life, so Alma sat, watching and listening intently. The food smell was strong, and her mouth wet itself with anticipation of the taste of it. After a while the people disappeared inside, and her stomach urged her to do something. She knew she could outrun them on the open, empty land if she needed to. She got up and slunk closer.

Staying downwind just in case, she crawled under the multi-strand barbed wire fence easily. Next to the larger, rounded building that was making a steady hum, she could see two metal cans. Her nose told her that's where the smell was coming from. The sun was setting, and she knew darkness would be to her advantage. Alma squatted to pee, moved to a good observation point, lay down and waited.

A door on the rounded building suddenly opened, casting an oblong of light onto the open ground. Alma stiffened, ready to run. The person who came out was carrying something square. He walked to the cans and threw the object inside, forgetting to replace the lid.

Alma sniffed carefully. The man had brought a new food smell, even richer. She watched him go back inside and close the door, the ground between them instantly darker.

She waited a little longer and then moved closer, keeping low, her bushy tail between her hind legs. The smell got stronger as she sidled up to the cans.

Alma was mostly boxer and Labrador, with a black nose, brown coat and white flash on her chest. She had both breeds' long legs, a useful asset in raiding garbage cans. She carefully reared up, put her paws on the can's edge and smelled.

The scent was intoxicating on an empty stomach and prompted a hasty decision. Moving back quickly, she pulled the can over, bit securely on the box that came tumbling out and ran.

Within seconds of the clanging metallic noise, the door of the building opened and the man came out again, shouting. He looked at the spilled mess, and then into the darkness. Yelling again, he walked to the can, kicked the loose items into it and stood it back up. This time he secured the lid, scowling once more at the darkness and muttering before going back inside.

As soon as she judged that she was safely clear, Alma stopped and worried her prize open. A bonanza—several pizza crusts, and two full, triangular, uneaten pieces. She devoured them all, licking the crumbs and flavor from the box when they were gone.

Sated, she looked back at the lights of the two buildings, and then ahead, down the road to a larger collection of twinkling lights in the distance. More lights would mean more people, and more options for food. Taking one last lick of the box, Alma turned and started descending the road into the valley of Groom Lake.

She settled in the junkyard. It was far enough from the people to feel safe, with plenty of hiding spots, and there were daily drop-offs of uneaten food and garbage from the mess hall. Water was readily available at the drain for the power plant, and often oozed from the waste of the dump. There was shade in the many abandoned metalworks and under the rock overhangs in the nearby hills.

There was also competition. The large black buzzards' beaks and talons were to be avoided, there were rats in the dump, and nomadic coyotes would sometimes challenge her. But Alma's familiarity with humans gave her an advantage; she learned the daily pattern of when food would arrive, she didn't spook when people were in sight, and her size made her a worthy opponent when it came to the other scavengers.

Alma was inevitably noticed by the Groom Lake residents, and sometimes someone who was homesick for their pet would leave scraps and water out for her, near their trailer home. She was wary, but occasionally at night, when all was quiet, she would steal in and take the easy food, as a treat.

There was also one man who regularly ran past the junkyard at dawn. He would look in her direction as he passed, the rising sun shining onto the hillside, and she'd heard him whistle too, as if he were calling her. During one run she watched him stop, place something he'd been carrying onto a flat rock inside the dump's entrance and then continue running.

Alma was curious. She waited until he had run into the distance, and then moved close enough downwind to smell what he had left.

Meat. The unmistakable scent of unspoiled meat.

An early-flying vulture or hawk would claim the prize for breakfast if she didn't hurry. She carefully looked around for more people, and saw none, then verified that the runner was too far away to be a threat. Darting out of hiding, she grabbed the morsel and ran back up to safety to devour it.

It was spicy meat, a section of salami, gratifyingly dense and pleasurable to chew.

The next day the runner did the same thing, and again the next. By then Alma was watching for him. She noticed that the runner now stopped in the distance to watch her eat. Closer than he'd been, but still far enough that she felt safe.

Alma began to count on the morning treat and became bolder in retrieving it, not waiting until she was back up the hillside to stop and eat. She got used to the man watching her too, confident that he was too far away to be a threat.

Until she felt unwell. After two days of particularly large pieces of the meat, her shoulders and hips started to ache, and she developed a cough. On this, the third morning, she did not feel like running down the hill to grab the treat, but she went anyway, slowly, unable to resist the texture and flavor. As she moved back up the hill, she stopped, stricken with sudden, painful diarrhea. When she turned to inspect it, she smelled blood. Her coughing grew worse, deep and lung-racking, and she tasted blood coming up into her mouth.

Alma suddenly felt overwhelmingly tired. She moved painfully to her normal shaded resting place, stopping to cough or have more spasms, panting heavily, feeling less and less able to draw a full breath. As she lay down, her body squirted another foul jet from her anus, the liquid full of blood. She was already too weak to move clear of it. Her coughs became almost continuous, and her nose began to bleed. Something was terribly wrong, but she was powerless to stop it. Each breath became harder, and she could feel her heart racing in her chest.

Staring across the flatness of the lakebed at the rising sun, Alma felt her vision gray and fade. With one final, desperate cough, the air poured wetly from her lungs, full of blood.

Alone, on the junkyard hillside, Alma died.

The runner, who had stopped to watch the dog's last painful movements, listened as the coughing subsided. When he heard nothing but silence, he smiled, then turned and began to run again.

54

Groom Lake

There had always been animals on the farm Grief grew up on near Stalingrad, and he had learned to ride horses when he was young. It had taken him a few minutes to figure out the differences of the western saddle and neck reining, but it wasn't complicated. He'd borrowed cowboy boots from a selection on a long shelf in the Groom Lake stables, and a heavy, oversized jacket from several hanging on pegs. Claw had pulled a .22 rifle off the rack for Grief to slide into the long leather saddle holster behind his right leg. The horse was a reliable American paint, and with Claw beside him on a large brown quarter horse the two men set out on an early morning familiarization ride. Kaz was away in Houston, and Thompson had stayed behind to go for a run. The two pilots figured they could communicate well enough on their own.

"Where do you want to go?" Claw raised his hands, palms up, a universal gesture.

Grief looked at the low hills next to the base, and then across the edge of the lakebed to the north, towards the more rugged mountains there. He pointed in that direction, and said, "Mozhno?" Can we?

Claw looked at his watch and nodded. “Yep, no problem, we’ve got all morning. That’s where some of the best hunting is, anyway, by the old mine heads.” He turned his horse, made a clucking sound and leaned forward in the saddle until it had settled into an easy trot. Grief did the same, the horses raising a salty dust trail as they headed north, skirting the western edge of the lakebed.

The daily desert winds hadn’t yet begun, and the sun was just rising over the ridgeline to the east. Grief settled in, using the time to better observe the lakebed runways and the surrounding territory. He noticed a strange structure sticking out above the salt pan to his right, with a paved road leading to it. It was a long, tapered pole, maybe 15 meters tall, that looked like an obelisk. Claw saw him staring at it and called the answer out over the noise of the trotting horses.

“Radar test stand.”

Grief pondered each word and then understood. The engineers would mount a new, full-sized aircraft on that pole in different orientations and bombard it with radar from all directions, measuring the strength of the reflected signal. From that they could develop tactics to minimize radar detection. They had a similar rig at Ramenskoye, and it had been used to test new radar-absorbing sections on the MiG-25, making it less visible.

He nodded at Claw and gave a thumbs-up. “Ponyal.” Understood.

As the edge of the lakebed curved to the right, towards the base of the low mountains, they crossed an access road, obviously well used, with tire tracks and good fresh gravel. Grief’s eyes followed it up and around to where it disappeared through a low cleft in the ridgeline towards the east. He realized that this must be the main artery for truck-borne resupply of the base. It would be the shortest distance to the north-south civilian highways that lay beyond the hills.

Good to see, he thought, as well as to compare with his memory of the satellite photographs he’d studied in detail many months ago, in Moscow. He looked for other expected landmarks and picked out two distinctive promontories, orienting himself. He called out, “Claw!”

When the other rider turned, Grief pointed farther east, just south of where the access road climbed towards the ridge.

"Mozhno?"

Claw shrugged. "Why not? It'll be pretty over there, looking down at the base." He reined his horse to the right, heading directly towards the rising sun. He'd gotten them both cowboy hats at the stable, and now he tipped his brim low to shield his eyes, Grief doing the same.

Claw decided to cut the corner across the hard, flat lakebed itself. Once they got into the hills, the horses would be walking, with more of a chance to rest. Time to go fast.

"C'mon, Russian, let's see what you got!" He dug his heels into his horse's flanks, urging it to a gallop. Grief did the same on his paint, and the two raced across Groom Lake, the horses happy to have the freedom to run.

As they reached the scrub brush of the far side, Claw reined his horse in, but Grief kept going, flashing past in victory. He called back over his shoulder, "I win!"

Both men laughed at his competitiveness, and let the horses settle into a walk as they began to climb the shallow arroyos into the hills.

"Wanna take a break, maybe walk around a bit or just have a sit?"

The horses had climbed most of the way up the eastern ridge, picking their way around the sagebrush and low, spiky shrubs until they'd almost reached the barbed wire that marked Area 51's border. Claw's thighs were in need of a stretch.

During the climb, Grief had moved his horse out in front and had been looking around with interest at the roughness of the terrain and, behind them, at the ancient sweep of the land down towards the lakebed. Claw had let Grief lead, unconcerned about exactly where they went. He reached into his saddlebag and pulled out a thermos. "Water?"

Grief looked back at him and nodded. "Da. Voda." He reined up, swung his leg over to dismount and flipped up the leather saddlebag to retrieve his water bottle as well. Claw took both sets of reins, tied the horses to a stunted juniper tree and then sat on a low, flat rock, facing west. He took a sip and raised his chin towards the view.

"Look at that."

Grief wiped his mouth, screwed the cap back onto his bottle and sat. The entirety of Groom Lake was in front of them, with the dark runway markings apparent on the pale salt of the lakebed, and the buildings of the air base clearly visible on the far side. On cue, a pair of T-38s accelerated on the paved runway and climbed, turning right towards them, the sound trailing far behind them with the distance.

"Pretty, isn't it?"

Grief nodded, understanding. "Da. Prekrasna." He meant it. It was beautiful in its austere ruggedness.

He glanced at Claw. "Nuzhno possat." I need to piss. He moved his hands in front of his crotch to explain.

Claw shrugged. "Be my guest. I'll do the same."

Grief got up, walked around a small turn in the ridge until he was out of sight, and then looked intently for the marker he knew would be nearby. The pre-briefings had been clear on exactly what to expect, and his keen eyes rapidly scanned the ground, looking for and then spotting it. He grabbed a loose rock, dug quickly and retrieved the square, oilskin-wrapped package. Glancing quickly back towards Claw to make sure he was still unobserved, he tucked it into the broad inner pocket of his coat.

He stood, kicked the ground to cover the hole, unzipped his fly and pissed on the disturbed ground.

As he relieved himself, he looked across at Groom Lake, feeling a rush of victory.

I am winning, he thought.

55

Grief's Trailer, Groom Lake

Darkness. The nightly blanket that provides a time of rest for the innocent and concealment for the villainous.

Grief had hidden the package he'd retrieved on the upper shelf of his bedroom clothes closet after returning from the ride. Then he had patiently waited. He had the trailer to himself when Kaz was away, but he'd noticed that everyone's doors were normally unlocked, and he couldn't risk someone like the CIA man or Claw blundering in unannounced.

A habitual light sleeper, he woke every hour on the hour to listen for activity around him. Now, the glowing hands of his bedside clock read two a.m.—well after the last of the serious drinkers had finished at Sam's Place and returned to their trailers. He listened for a full minute. Nothing but the wind and quiet of the November desert.

None of the curtains on the trailer's windows were made for a blackout, and if he turned on a light, its glow would escape around their edges, easily noticed by anyone who happened to be awake. Grief reasoned that the small bathroom was the one place where he could have a light on during the night without sparking any curiosity. He retrieved the flashlight provided in his bedside table drawer and rolled out of bed in his underwear. He quietly opened the closet door, reaching up in the darkness for the package and then down into the sheath pocket of his flight suit for the USAF-issue jackknife that had come with it. He padded barefoot into the bathroom, closed the door, ensured the small, high window's curtain was pulled into place, and turned on the light.

He sat on the closed toilet lid and set the package, the flashlight and the knife on the small countertop surrounding the sink. Whoever had hidden the bundle on the ridgeline for him had carefully sealed it in taped plastic. He paused once more to listen for 30 seconds. Hearing nothing, he picked up the package. It was rectangular and as heavy as a hardcover book, wrapped in a heavy plastic bag surrounded by beige packing tape. The light over the sink was low wattage, so he used the flashlight to study how best to get it open with no damage. He set the flashlight down, picked up the knife and clicked open its main blade.

He slit the tape at both ends, and also up the sides where it had been double-wrapped. The end of the plastic bag had also been taped closed, and he slit that too, then ruffled open the bag and peered inside.

A letter-sized envelope, along with a couple of heavier items wrapped in cloth. He pulled each of them carefully out and set them on the bag, which he'd spread on his lap like a napkin.

Information first, he thought.

The envelope had nothing written on the outside. He used the tip of the blade like a letter opener and gently slid out a single sheet of folded paper. On it was a handwritten table of cryptic Cyrillic and numbers. He studied it under the beam of the flashlight for over a minute, until he'd figured out what it all meant.

He sat back for a few seconds and then scrutinized the table again, running a finger along it until he found what he sought, about halfway down. He checked the next few entries, looked up as if he could see the sky through the trailer roof, nodded, and then refolded and slid the paper back into the envelope.

He unwrapped the smaller of the two cloth-wrapped objects, which was about the size of a child's shoe. The shiny metal object inside was a camera, with built-in reusable flash and a lens cap. He shone the flashlight on the small window on its back, verifying that it was loaded with film, and carefully set it on the counter.

Grief smiled thinly at himself, realizing that he was proceeding just as he always had at Novy God, the New Year's celebration of his childhood—first opening the card, and then the small presents from his mother and grandmother, saving the biggest for last. His smile faded into a frown. Never a gift from his father, the drunkard gone from his life by the time he was 13.

The final package felt heavy in his hands. He unrolled it and found the radio he was expecting. A silver, Hammerite-painted metal box, with several knobs and a folded antenna.

There were switches for power and the operating band, thumbwheels to control frequency and volume, a toggle for recording/sending, and two attached cables for recharging and the earpiece/mic. There were no instructions, but that didn't concern him—this radio was similar to the model he had trained with in Moscow.

He carefully plugged the charging cord into the side of the radio and the other end into the outlet above the sink. He was gratified to see a small, recessed yellow light glow for a few seconds and then be replaced by the green one next to it. Whoever had prepared the radio for him had left it fully charged.

Checking that the power was off, he unclipped the antenna and methodically extended it. It moved smoothly to its full one-meter length, ready to receive a signal. And send his transmission. He moved the volume thumbwheel, feeling the click that powered the radio on, and turned it just far enough to hear a hiss through the small built-in speaker.

It worked.

Grief turned the radio off, unplugged the charger and retracted the antenna. For want of a better option he replaced everything in the plastic bag. It was dark green, and he figured it was as innocuous to a casual observer as anything else he might choose. He closed the jackknife and got up, ready to go back to bed, but then turned, lifted the lid and pissed. Not wanting to make any unnecessary noise, he didn't flush.

Shutting off the bathroom light, he padded softly back to his room, where he returned the items to their places in the closet and bedside drawer. After climbing back into bed, he lay on his back, arms behind his head, thinking and planning. The table had said 04:17. Confident that he would awaken, he rolled on his side, closed his eyes and fell into a dreamless sleep.

With no clouds to reflect the warmth of Earth's soil back downwards, desert nights were always colder than it seemed they should be. Grief had donned the jacket he'd borrowed from the riding stable and was crouched outside, partially against the cold and partially to keep hidden in the shadowed lee of the trailer, as far as he could get from the adjoining trailer where Thompson lay sleeping. His eyes had clicked open at 04:00, and the radio was now on, antenna extended, the earpiece clipped into his right ear and the volume set.

He was about to talk to a spy satellite that was a distant grandchild of the original Sputnik, launched 16 years earlier, and far more sophisticated. When it received a specific encoded signal from a ground transmitter, a small tape recorder inside its pressurized hull would start to turn, playing back the most recently recorded message and then instantly resetting itself to record. Grief checked his wristwatch, listening intently, looking to the sky on the off chance that the satellite would be visible as a high, sunlit white dot crossing the Nevada predawn sky.

His earpiece got a sudden burst of static and he looked down at the radio, his thumb quickly spinning the knob, fine-tuning the volume. He held his breath to listen better and was slightly startled to hear a familiar voice start speaking. He paid close attention, totally focused on remembering the details and questions. When the voice stopped, he spoke quietly into his microphone, responding to the questions and providing preplanned dates and exact timings. He mentally counted as he spoke, easily keeping within the time allotted. Next, he heard brief static, and then a repeat of the earlier message in case he'd missed it. He listened again, looking skyward.

This time he spotted the satellite, directly overhead, one medium-brightness star moving past the twinkling stillness of the others. When he'd heard the whole message again, he reviewed what he'd already said in response and decided nothing further was needed. He clicked the radio off, pulled the earpiece away, bundled the wire, retracted the antenna and slipped it all into his coat pocket.

Grief stood and took a slow look around, seeing no movement. He gazed skyward once more at the now-retreating satellite, carrying his recorded voice over the horizon, ready to replay it for the first ground station that knew the right combination of frequencies and codes. Somewhere over a picket communications ship, or perhaps the Soviet Union itself.

None of the new information had surprised him, and soon Moscow would have the details they needed back from him.

He visualized the wheels that were in motion and felt a rush of pride. They were counting on him, and he was about to deliver. All his life he had worked to refine himself, done whatever was necessary to overcome lesser people and to gain the myriad skills that allowed him to be entrusted with this mission.

The final prize was getting very close, and Grief was ready.

56

1945—Near Stalingrad, USSR

It had to be done.

A thin trail of dust followed Sascha, kicked up as he ran along the narrow dirt road. Barefoot, he rapidly passed the orchards, fields and wooden farmhouses of his kolkhoz—his collective farm.

Or what was left of it. His quick glances left and right revealed more of an overgrown battlefield than farmland, as the wild natural growth of the fertile southern Volga floodplain began to reclaim the recent scars of bomb-crater subsoil, shattered trees and countless unmarked graves.

Sascha had been eight when the Great Patriotic War started, and was just turning 11 when the Battle of Stalingrad began. The invading Nazis had been beaten, but at a punishing cost to Mother Russia and her children. Within earshot of his kolkhoz, over two million men, women and children had been killed in just six months. Even now, two years later, the rebuilding in Stalingrad had barely begun, the city's ruined buildings sparsely occupied by the equally shattered survivors.

Sascha ran. He was the fastest runner at the kolkhoz.

The demands of war had brought out the best in some people, tested their mettle, forged the war heroes that Sascha idolized. The now-legendary medal winners who had pushed Hitler back and turned the war's tide: sapper Vladimir Chekalov, sniper Vasily Zaitsev, Colonel General Alexander Rodimtsev, a hero who shared his first name. These were the New Soviet Men he had decided to emulate—true masters of their feelings, learned, healthy, muscular, a higher biologic type. Sascha was already a runner, and he was going to make himself a superman.

But for his father, the war had been the latest in a lifelong series of personal injustices. He'd grown up a peasant on the Czar's land and then became a lowly bednyak on the collective, a weak and jealous man who blamed faraway Moscow for all he'd failed to accomplish. The war had only made him more of an abusive, drunken tyrant, a man who beat his wife and only son to make himself feel he was the master of something.

But Sascha was 13 now, and puberty was giving him adult strength, and adult ideas. Newfound speed and endurance, and the growing ability to do what had to be done, here on the collective and in the world beyond. As he ran, his right hand brushed his pocket, checking for what he'd placed there. He looked ahead, down the road, towards the sod-roofed wooden shack where he'd grown up and the bushland behind it, where his father hid daily from the required collective work. To drink.

Sascha's feet carried him past the shack, down the overgrown track and into the cover of the trees that had survived the shelling. As he approached the lean-to where his wastrel father spent his days, he slowed to a walk. He noted with pride that he was barely even breathing hard, despite the pace of the run. His bare feet were quiet on the naked soil of the path.

"Why are you here?" his father slurred as he spotted Sascha approaching. He sneered at his son as he reached for a half-empty bottle propped on an upturned log next to his wooden chair. "You should be working in the fields!"

Sascha kept his silence and evaluated what he saw. Bloodshot, unfocused eyes above a red-veined, swollen nose. A slack, unfit body thick with fat and a bulging drunkard's belly.

Not my father, Sascha thought. *A lowlife thing. Filth. Scum.* His right hand was in his pocket.

"Why are you here?" the thing repeated, and then laughed, a noise like he was clearing his throat to spit, his open mouth revealing missing and rotted teeth. The same laugh Sascha heard every time the rough red hands had slapped and punched his mother. And him.

But no more. Sascha withdrew his hand, the loop he had tied on one end of a length of wire already secure around his right pointer finger. He had heard of this simple method of execution and had practiced the motion. That's what heroes did. They got fit, they studied and practiced, they made themselves better. And then they removed filth from the world.

Sascha quickly circled the bloated figure, his left pointer finger finding the loop he'd made at the wire's other end. He stepped close and dropped the wire over the man's head, crossing it once then jerking it tight and twisting the wire into place. Simple, easy to do. Just as he had practiced.

He stepped back and walked around to witness what he knew would happen.

The drunk was pawing at the wire with both hands, unable to pry it up to relieve the pressure. His eyes bulged and he struggled to draw breath, the brain starving for oxygen. A face contorted with anger turning to fear, and then desperation, the tongue coming out of the foul mouth, the body writhing and twisting and pitching forward out of the chair onto the ground, knocking over the nearby stump on which rested the bottle of vodka. It flipped onto its side in the dirt, the remaining clear liquid leaking out.

The body thrashed, the hands futilely trying to reach behind the head to untwist the wire. A few spasms, one last kick, and then it was still.

Sascha watched, unmoving and unmoved. As soon as he was certain that death was complete, he untwisted the wire, yanked it free of the loathsome neck in one smooth motion, pulled it through a handful of leaves to clean off the bits of gore and wound it around his fist to stash neatly back in his pocket.

All that was left was to drag the body into one of the old shell craters in the forest, use the shovel from the lean-to to cover it with dirt and fill in the low depression, and hide the dragged trail with leaves. Then continue running.

One more death in a land that reeked of it. But this was a death that was just, one that made the world a better place. One that had to be done.

And now Sascha knew how.

57

Warfarin

The usual first indication of a problem was a cow, lying dead in a pool of blood.

When Midwestern cattle ate sweet clover hay, especially if the clover had been put up wet, they would sometimes develop severe gut pain and start hemorrhaging internally, with blood eventually coming out of their nose, mouth and anus. Far too often, by the time the farmer found them, it was too late.

A French research pharmacist had discovered the root cause—a chemical in a mold that grew on the plants. Its symbol was $C_9H_6O_2$, but when he first found it on tonka beans, he called it coumarin.

Karl Link, the American biochemist who'd found that same chemical in dank clover, realized that such a reliable mammal killer would make a marketable rat poison. Inspired by his funder, the Wisconsin Alumni Research Foundation, he chose a name for the new product he developed.

Warfarin.

When rats and mice ate it over a few days, the warfarin gradually decreased the amount of vitamin K in their blood, which slowed its natural, necessary ability to clot. Once they'd eaten enough, they simply bled to death.

The US military used warfarin extensively as a simple, reliable way to eradicate vermin, and mandated that it be provided and stored in service buildings and under sinks on bases around the world.

It was an odorless, tasteless, time-delayed poison. Very handy, readily available, and made even more potent by an amplifying interaction with caffeine. Perfect to deploy in a place where everyone drank coffee out of large communal percolators. Coffee at the morning stand-up meeting, coffee in the ready rooms during the day to keep sharp, and coffee to sip with whisky in the evening while playing cards at Sam's Place.

All anyone had to do was to be the quietly competent new guy on base who didn't mind volunteering to make the coffee.

THE

HUNT

58

New Orleans

Just outside Slidell, near the eastern end of Lake Pontchartrain, north of New Orleans, a huge radar dish was turning in the night, protected inside its white dome.

It was a civilian radar, used by the FAA to track airliners as they flew from hubs like Houston and New Orleans along the southern US coast, or out over the Gulf of Mexico to the southern Florida cities of Miami and Tampa. But it was also part of the USAF Southern Defense Network, providing air traffic control for the military forces stationed at New Orleans, Houston, Eglin and Tyndall. And, unknown to most Slidell residents, it was also watching and listening for unexpected flights, especially those originating in Cuba.

The spate of recent hijackings in and out of Havana had put the Defense Network on alert multiple times, but it was the undetected arrival of 19 Cubans aboard a Russian-built turboprop directly into New Orleans International in October 1971 that had highlighted the vulnerability of the US underbelly. Consequently, Congress directed the USAF to build better sensing equipment, and as a direct result, standing next to the big white Slidell dome, there was a new FPS-6 height-finder radar, providing more detailed information to Tyndall Air Force Base in Florida, which would scramble jets to intercept unidentified traffic. At Tyndall, NORAD had also built the world's first large phased array AN/FPS-85 radar, a huge, white, flat structure tipped towards the sky, to watch for southern threats in the atmosphere and all the way up into orbit.

On this November night, the radars were tracking a target that had taken off from Havana with no international flight plan and was now flying westward across the Gulf. The speed and altitude identified it as a probable transport plane, and the Defense Network technician watching on her radar screen had assigned it a tentative marker as an unknown Cuban/Soviet turboprop. It wasn't typical of air traffic between Cuba and Mexico, and it also wasn't following any standard route. But it was keeping to international uncontrolled airspace, well south of the US Air Defense Identification Zone, so none of the armed jets that were holding alert at Tyndall or New Orleans had been assigned to investigate.

The technician used one of her radarscope's features to draw a trace of the flight path thus far, and she laid her finger on the screen to extrapolate where the bogey was likely to fly on that course. Probably one of the northern Mexico airports, maybe Monterrey, or even all the way to Mexicali or Tijuana. That would be a long flight, but her primary concern was that it would get closest to the ADIZ when it was south of Texas. By her finger track, it looked as though it would remain just clear.

Mexico's Air Traffic Control would have to deal with it, not her, but she was definitely going to watch it as it plodded across the Gulf. There were always headwinds there, and her groundspeed readout showed a meager 340 knots.

Something slightly interesting to keep track of through the night.

59

Groom Lake Fuel Farm

Security is a funny thing. It's largely a matter of perception. The taller the barbed wire fence, the tighter the personnel clearance requirements; and the remoter the location, the safer and more relaxed the secured people feel once they are on the inside. Like a tough, impenetrable outer hide protecting the soft belly and fragility of flesh within. It's as if a mutual permission has been given when the compulsory sorting and winnowing is complete. By definition everyone behind the fence has passed through the tightest of filters, and has a shared sense of protection. Of invulnerability.

Until a destructive force is let loose on the inside.

Aircraft need fuel. When the first jet-engine-powered planes started flying, the US military decided on a blend of kerosene and gasoline, to optimize the benefits of easy ignition, availability, and simplicity of transport and storage. It came in various grades depending on the engine type, but the most common, and the one that was needed by most of the fleet of aircraft at Groom Lake, was called Jet Propulsion Fuel, Type 4. A simple 50/50 kerosene/gasoline mix.

JP-4 for short.

JP-4 was refined from crude oil pumped out of the ground, blended in refineries mostly in Texas and Louisiana, and delivered across the country via pipeline and tanker truck. At Groom Lake, the big USAF fuel trucks regularly offloaded into the large white aboveground tanks, where smaller fuel bowser trucks could refill on a daily basis, then deliver the jet fuel directly, pumping it into the aircraft parked out on the ramp.

Sometimes big airplanes landed at Groom Lake. For a complete top-off, a fuel-hungry monster like the B-52 bomber needed nearly 50,000 gallons—five or six bowsers-full. The smaller fighters held about 2,000 gallons, so a single bowser could service several at a time.

Standard military procedure was to fill each aircraft's tanks right after landing. The practice kept any humidity from condensing like dew inside the tanks overnight and adding unwanted (and corrosive) water to the fuel.

The same applied to the fuel bowser trucks. In the evening they were driven up to the large storage tanks, topped off and parked overnight, ready to be dispatched as needed during the upcoming flying day. Pretty much standard procedure at airports across the USA, and all around the world.

Grief's eyes snapped open.

He'd felt the trailer move as someone climbed the far steps, and now heard furtive noises through his bedroom door. He glanced at his bedside clock: 23:30. He listened intently, hearing the faint sounds of water running and the toilet flushing. Then nothing.

Kaz is back, he realized. *Blyat! Why tonight?*

Lying in the darkness, Grief reconsidered his plans. Changing the sequence now would cause serious problems. It was still more than two hours before he was planning to get up, and the American would have just flown in and would be tired.

Grief had been trained to move very quietly. The operation was still going to work.

He rolled onto his side and closed his eyes, listening to the silence.

At two a.m., Grief slipped silently out of the trailer into the darkness. As his feet touched the ground, he stopped, letting his night vision fully adapt, his ears pricked for any sound.

Nothing.

He did a quick personal inventory. Since he was about to do something that required extreme focus and fitness, he took a moment to check his personal state of readiness as a necessary step towards self-preservation. It was an old habit, honed by years of operational flying.

He carried a medium-sized drawstring bag in his left hand, and he nodded to himself as he patted his pockets with his right, ticking down his list. He'd gotten enough rest, and his body felt good, his head and vision clear. He'd gone over the plan in detail multiple times and had double-checked his gear. He figured there was a high probability that he would succeed, but he had backup options available in the unlikely case of failure.

He also took note of the familiar sensations of excitement: the rush of blood, a tingling of hands, the increased heart rate and depth of breathing. He was about to do something challenging, something for a higher purpose, something he was uniquely qualified for. And he was about to do it well.

It was what he lived for.

He stepped forward into the blackness, and as he rounded the corner of the trailer, he bumped into someone coming the other way.

Both men were startled, but Grief reacted faster, almost instinctively. His right hand drew a coiled wire from his pocket, and he pulled and looped it over the other man's head, yanking violently and cinching it into his neck, twisting it hard into place, then stepping back. The dark form staggered and fell, and Grief counted silently to 20, staring urgently into the night to see if anyone else was up. He opened his drawstring bag and pulled out his red-filtered flashlight, kneeling over the prostrate form. A quick on/off revealed who he'd just killed.

The light reflected off thick lenses and heavy frames. It was Bill Thompson, his lean face distorted, blood coming from his nose, tongue protruding in death. Grief looked up at the CIA man's adjoining trailer and could just make out that one of the doors was open. Why had he been outside? Did he somehow know of Grief's plan? Or was it just insomnia, maybe a need for fresh air?

No way to know. Grief reached under Thompson's arms and lifted, dragging the body with heels scraping across the sand towards the open door. At the base of the stairs he stopped, considering options, then decided.

He knelt beside the body, untwisted the wire, pulled it clear, and wiped and coiled it back into his pocket. Then he dragged Thompson parallel to the trailer's side, lifted the heavy rubberized skirting, and pushed and rolled the slack body underneath. The skirting flapped back down into place, and the Russian stood and looked and listened, aware that killing the CIA man had taken time he hadn't allotted.

Seeing and hearing nothing, Grief reached up to quietly close the trailer door, turned and walked swiftly towards Dump Road, the drawstring bag swinging in his left hand. As his feet gained the harder pavement, he turned left again and picked up the pace.

On his dawn runs he'd noted the stark cones of light beneath the occasional streetlights, and he now approached the fuel farm in the more shadowed areas, along a preplanned path of near darkness. He'd waited for a clear night that was expected to have a good northwest wind, common enough in the desert, to help carry any sound away from the main base and trailers. He listened carefully as he walked, and he could barely hear the power plant's diesel generators humming above the gusting rush of desert wind. He looked up: clear stars and only a sliver of the Moon.

Perfect.

The bowser trucks were parked neatly next to each other, like they had been every morning when he'd run by. Once, after double-checking that there was no road traffic, he had taken a quick detour in to verify a detail, and he was confident that what he'd found then would be the case now. He briskly approached the upwind truck, reached up to swing open the unlocked driver's-side door and pulled himself smoothly inside. A glance at the dashboard confirmed it: the key was in the ignition. Why lock a vehicle when you're already inside the fence?

Grief paused to take one last look around, making sure there were no unplanned circuits being conducted by a night watchman. He had his jackknife ready in his flight suit leg pocket, just in case.

Nothing. Just the harsh cones of the streetlights and the surrounding blackness. He pumped the gas pedal twice with his foot, reached forward and turned the key.

The big diesel engine rumbled reliably into life, and Grief watched the rpm gauge settle into a smooth idle. Truck drivers here took pride in maintaining their machines, just like in Russia. He opened the door, hopped down and walked back to the truck's left side. In the dim illumination from the nearest streetlamp, he could see that the panel framework was open, revealing a thick black hose wound on a large drum and some controlling machinery. He'd watched several times as the drivers had refueled the planes he'd been flying and had learned how these American bowsers worked. He reached in and pushed a large green button, the electricity from the big diesel responding to power up the drum reel and pump with an added high-pitched whine. He grabbed the heavy metal pump handle on the end of the rubber hose, pulled hard to start the drum rolling, and yanked on it until he had pulled out enough slack to easily point the nozzle at the adjoining truck. Squeezing the flow handle, he felt and saw the gush of JP-4 splashing in an arc on the side of the bowser and onto the ground, puddling blackly and beginning to flow away, following the slight grade under the line of trucks towards the main storage tanks.

He thumbed the locking feature on the pump handle into place and played the flow back and forth until he was satisfied that he'd soaked the adjoining truck, then carefully laid the gushing hose end on the ground. Turning, he walked along the rear of the other trucks towards the flowing fuel's destination.

To stay independent of the Nevada power grid and to give Groom Lake an extra layer of security, the civil engineers had chosen to generate its electrical power with diesel. The big motors of the generators burned the same fuel as the trucks, all supplied from a single cylindrical diesel tank propped on stilts next to the larger JP-4 tanks. As he'd run by, Grief had traced where the diesel line ran from the tank into the generator building, power cables and hoses efficiently co-located by orderly men for design, inspection and maintenance efficiency. As he watched, the first tongue of the flowing fuel surged across the ground and began to pool along the lines.

Grief checked his watch, confirming it was 03:00. He was on schedule. It would only take a few minutes to saturate the area with fuel, and then he could move forward with his plan. He looked back towards the main base, nodding to himself when he saw no moving lights. He glanced out across the lakebed and to the eastern hills beyond, picturing what should be happening there, assuming his radio message had gotten through.

The pool of fuel now lapped against the base of the JP-4 supply tank and flooded along the diesel connecting hoses. Grief counted slowly to 30, to be doubly sure there was enough, then walked back around to the running fuel truck. After one more fresh splash over the adjoining truck, he released the hose handle to stop flow, pushed the yellow button that rewound the hose onto the reel, and then hit the red button that killed the pump motor. A quick swing up into the cab to turn the key to off, and it was quiet again. He hopped back down, closed the door and took one last look around.

No obvious indication of sabotage for the first responders to see.

He reached into the drawstring bag still dangling from his left hand.

Showtime.

Though they had to fly the wood in, there was a stone fireplace burning in Sam's Place during the cold desert evenings to make Groom Lake feel more like home. Several boxes of wooden matches were kept stacked on the mantel above it, and Grief had quietly pocketed one.

He pulled it out now, knelt by the edge of the puddle and prepared to light a match.

A pool of pure kerosene won't ignite from just a small open flame. But gasoline will, and especially the more volatile vapors that rise off it—the ones that give it the distinctive smell. Grief knew this, and hunkered close to the ground to block the wind. Holding the box close to the surface of the spilled fuel, he struck the match along the abrasive red phosphorus strip and then held the resulting flame just above the liquid.

The wind gusted hard around him and blew the flame out before the gasoline caught fire. Grief stuck the wooden end of the used match between his teeth and carefully retrieved another from the box. Huddling even lower, he tried again, ready to yank his hands back at the first sign of ignition.

This time the flame caught with a low woof and spread rapidly downwind in a blue-yellow wave across the evaporating sheet of fuel. Grief stepped back, removed the other spent match from his mouth as he stood, and methodically replaced them both, along with the matchbox, in his bag as he watched.

The yellow-orange light of the widening, deepening flame reflected off the underside of the nearest truck and suddenly spread up the soaked surface. Grief surveyed the area around him by the light of the flickering flames, making sure he'd left no trace. The hard, scuffed ground showed no new footprints. He walked behind the now-burning truck to verify that the flame was spreading along the ground to the deep pool around the fuel lines and tanks, watched for a few more seconds, and then turned and started jogging up the road.

Step one complete.

60

Groom Lake Guard Shack

It was Joey Fanelli's turn to stay awake, and as usual, to pass the time, he'd been drinking coffee and reading a novel. When Karl was on watch, his preferred pastime was solitaire, but Joey was a reader, and enjoyed the night shift as it gave him plenty of time for the latest from John D. MacDonald's Travis McGee or Ed McBain's 87th Precinct.

Every 30 minutes since they'd started their shift at eight p.m., per the EG&G written instructions for Groom Lake guardhouse duty, Joey had put his book down and gone outside for a look and a listen down the hill, back towards the lakebed and then east, across towards State Route 25. Leaving Karl asleep in his reclining chair.

It was a ritual Joey was used to, and it also helped break up the tedium of the long night shift, as well as giving him a chance to take a leak, what with all the coffee. Each time he came back inside, Joey made a note in the ledger that sat on the main desk: Date, Time, Activity, and in the Comments space in the far right-hand column, ALL QUIET, the new block capitals joining the list of similar, neatly handwritten entries above it.

The EG&G instructions actually specified that both gate guards were to stay awake and alert throughout the 12-hour graveyard shift, but crews had long since realized that so long as one of them was awake, the other could doze with no harm, since there would be lots of time to wake him up if anyone approached. In fact, the guards had decided among themselves that it was better this way, as one of them would always be fresh. Just in case they both fell asleep, though, they kept a small alarm clock on the desk, set to go off every two hours. Part of the pattern was to do the quick outside inspection, note the details in the log, then reset the alarm clock.

Night traffic at Groom Lake was unusual. Down at the air base, only rare types of projects flew in the darkness. On the ground, the big semi tractor trailers that hauled in resupply were always scheduled during daylight hours, and the workers who arrived daily by bus tended to come around dawn. Sometimes, disassembled new planes being shipped from the Skunk Works in California would arrive in the wee hours to avoid any prying eyes, but those deliveries were planned well in advance and mentioned in the briefing that each crew got as they came on shift. None was planned for this night.

So lights coming up the road from the east at three a.m. were out of the ordinary. Joey spotted them when he was outside pissing, and he zipped up and hustled back in to rouse his fellow night guard.

"Hey, Karl, wake up!"

Karl remained soundly asleep, snoring with his mouth wide open, so Joey walked around the desk and shook his chair. "Hey, Karl, we've got company coming!" Karl snorted and sat up, blinking himself awake.

The men resembled each other. Late forties, big bodies going soft with inactivity, their brush cuts revealing the time they'd both spent in military service in Korea and then Vietnam. It was a natural transition from the Army to a paramilitary organization like EG&G, and their service records made security clearance straightforward. Most of the guards had served.

Running his tongue over the dryness of his teeth and then swallowing, Karl thickly asked, "What's up?"

Joey pointed out the window, down the gently sloping road towards the east, to the small, bobbing lights in the distance.

"Someone's coming."

Karl was the senior of the two, having been hired a little over a year earlier than Joey. As such, he stood beside the pivoting end of the lowered swing gate, on the approaching vehicle's driver's side. In his left hand he held a large, powerful flashlight, switched on and pointing towards the oncoming headlights. His right hand was empty, ready to be raised high and palm forward in the universal signal for stop. Also on Karl's right side was his holster, the leather strap unsnapped, his Colt M1911 Government pistol available to be grabbed quickly if needed. He'd never had to draw it.

Behind him and well to his left, on the other side of the road, Joey stood with the light of the guard shack at his back, making him a pure silhouette to anyone approaching from the east. He cradled a shotgun, the barrel pointed down and away from Karl, but ready to be turned and raised at the first sign of trouble. The two men were following the procedure and positioning prescribed in the EG&G handbook for unexpected traffic, exactly as they had practiced it many times before.

Just lights in the night. SOP. Nothing to be alarmed about, yet.

Joey had called it in to the central Command Post while Karl had been retrieving the weapons, and the bored night voice on the other end of the phone had replied, "Roger, keep us apprised of what 'n who it is." Generally, late night traffic was a delivery that hadn't been scheduled properly or was late. The anti-nuke protesters usually made their fuss at the test range's south gate, closer to the comforts of Las Vegas. The entrance road off SR25 was deliberately unmarked to help maintain Groom Lake's anonymity. Might just be a couple of teenagers from Rachel or Ash Springs looking for a place to make out.

But the lights kept coming, bouncing up and down on the unpaved gravel surface.

Karl raised his right hand to arm's length and moved the flashlight, cycling it left and right as the vehicle got close to be sure to get the driver's attention. The pole-mounted searchlights shining down beyond the entrance barrier revealed a nondescript, four-door, tan-colored sedan with no front license plate. Imported, maybe a Toyota or a Datsun.

A Jap car. Karl didn't like that. Joey didn't either, and he raised the shotgun, braced and ready to blast at the first sign of trouble.

Per the manual, Karl was preparing to shout "Halt!" and lower his hand onto the heel of his pistol then gesture with his chin for the driver to roll down the window.

But the car stopped about 20 feet short of the gate. An unusual thing to do. With the overhead floods glinting off the windshield, the two guards couldn't see who was inside the car or, more importantly, how many there were. It raised their hackles, and Karl pulled the pistol out of his holster and pointed it at the car. Joey's shotgun was now aimed at the center of the hood.

"Open your window!" Karl commanded. Best to establish communication, in case this was an innocent mistake.

No response.

Karl tried again, louder, pausing between words. "Open . . . your . . . window!"

Just as he was about to step around the end of the swing gate and move towards the car, Karl saw a slight change in the reflected light off the driver's-side window and heard a voice from within. A man's voice, slightly high-pitched.

"I'm on public land!"

Karl squinted, frowning. The words were not the response he expected, so he decided to go by the EG&G rulebook.

"This is restricted federal property. Unless you have official business with the US government, turn your vehicle around and return to the main road."

Joey nodded. It was exactly what Karl was supposed to say.

The car didn't move, and the high voice repeated, "I'm on public land!"

Karl glanced at Joey. Both figured it must be some type of protester.

"You may still be on public land," Karl shouted, "but you're obstructing a government road and this facility's main entrance. I'm asking you for the last time: turn your vehicle around and return to the main road."

Silence.

Karl decided to silently count to 10, and if the car hadn't moved, he'd call for reinforcements. No sense escalating the situation when this car hadn't really done anything threatening.

As he got to seven, he saw a hand emerge from the driver's-side window and wave. The high voice carried through the darkness. "Okay, we were just out driving—we'll turn around." The hand disappeared and the car lurched slightly as the driver shifted gears, the white of its backup lights suddenly glaring across the road and the scrub brush behind it.

We, Karl thought. *At least two people in there. Maybe just a make-out couple after all.*

The car bumped on the raised road edge and pivoted back onto the flat beyond, paused, and then started moving slowly forward, the front wheels turning. The guards' tension palpably lowered. Then Karl and Joey saw the driver's hand reappear across the top of the car as if to wave, but instead it made a throwing motion, hard to make out in the shadowed darkness of the verge. The small engine whined louder as the driver accelerated rapidly, the car fishtailing slightly and squirting gravel.

No rear license plate, Karl noted with growing alarm. *But wait—did the driver just throw something?*

To his left, Karl heard a thud and spotted a quick blur of motion. Something rolled to a stop on the road between himself and Joey. Both men looked at it, and with horror recognized exactly what it was.

A grenade. An olive-green M26 fragmentation grenade, nicknamed the Lemon, the safety pin long since pulled, and the arming handle pivoted up and sticking out at a near right angle. Karl and Joey had both been taught that the fuse time was somewhere between four and five seconds. They'd trained with them, thrown them in practice and knew exactly what was about to happen.

The central delay fuse down the center of the grenade was about to ignite its surrounding waxy mixture of RDX and TNT, just under six ounces of high explosive that would rapidly expand and shatter the enveloping coil of metal, hurling pieces of it in all directions. It was a weapon designed to seriously injure any living thing within a 50-foot radius.

Joey and Karl were each about a dozen feet from the center of the dirt road. They were in the process of dropping to the ground as the hail of metal reached them.

Several fragments tore directly through the bone of Karl's forehead and into the softness of his brain, twisting him onto his back as he fell. He died instantly. Above him, one of the floodlights flickered, a shower of sparks falling as it shorted and then died.

Joey was luckier. He'd been slightly turned, and the barrage of shrapnel hit him mostly on his right arm and leg, knocking him down, his shotgun clattering metallically onto the hardpan and gravel beside him.

The concussive noise rang in Joey's ears as he lay on the ground, trying to sort out how hurt he was. He tried to push himself to his feet, but his right arm shrieked in pain. He rolled to his left, pushed hard with his good hand and pried himself up onto his left leg. When he went to stand, his right leg started to buckle, but he grabbed the shotgun by the barrel and precariously got his balance.

"Karl!" Joey tried to yell, only managing a raspy shriek. The motionless lump of his friend did not move. He glanced down and saw that his right pant leg was now darkening with spreading splotches of blood. Leaning heavily on the shotgun, he hobbled towards Karl, only managing a step or two before being hit by a wave of weakness. *We need help*, he thought, and turned for the guard shack, noticing that the facing window had been broken in the blast. The door was still open, and he tottered inside, letting go of the shotgun and grabbing the edge of the main desk instead. He half hopped around the end to the wooden chair, twisting and mostly falling into it, yelling in pain. He brushed away small shards of glass on the desk as he scrabbled for the phone, knocking the handset out of its cradle. He had to blink and concentrate to remember the number and then fumble left-handed to spin the rotary dial. Grabbing the handset, he held it to an ear still half-deafened by the blast. He barely made out a bored female voice.

"Command Post."

The familiar formality of it helped prod him into speech.

"This is East Gate Guardhouse! We've been attacked by a grenade, and Karl is down! Send help!"

The effort cost him, and he fell back sprawling in his chair, his head lolling to the side. The shattering blast through the window had knocked his paperback novel onto the floor. He was staring at it as he lost consciousness, just as he heard an odd booming sound echoing up from the direction of the lakebed.

Joey's eyes rolled up into his head and he slumped, his good arm falling to swing beside the chair, a small, tinny voice still coming from the now-dangling handset, urgently demanding more details.

61

Groom Lake Aircraft Ramp

In the hills of North Vietnam, just east of the muddy Cầu River and not far from the long coast facing the East Sea and the Chinese island province of Hainan, a single thick telephone line rose up a steep bluff, over an exposed ridge and back down again, trailing on concrete poles towards the north. It connected North Vietnam's military war commanders with the communications centers farther into the heartland—a vital intelligence link between the front and the decision-makers in Hanoi.

In the fall of 1972, as President Nixon tried to make good on his election promise to end the war, his national security advisor, Henry Kissinger, hadn't trusted what he was hearing from North Vietnamese leader Lê Đức Thọ at the Paris Peace Accords. He'd strongly suspected that the moment the US withdrew their forces from South Vietnam, the North would invade. Kissinger wanted reliable intelligence on Thọ's actual plan, preferably a wiretap of conversations between the North's leadership and its deployed generals.

Aerial photographs collected during the war had revealed that single, vital telephone line, but its location made a land-based special operation extremely problematic. What Kissinger needed was a way to get commandos in and out securely, by air.

The United States needed a stealth helicopter. Such a thing didn't exist yet, but the DoD's Advanced Research Projects Agency had been working on it.

ARPA had secretly contracted with Howard Hughes and his Hughes Tool Company to find ways to modify an OH-6 utility helicopter to make it as quiet and radar-invisible as possible. To do this, Hughes added a fifth blade to the main rotor and converted the tail rotor to four blades, decreasing how hard each blade had to work and thus the noise it made. They muffled the engine exhaust, swapped the transmission for a quieter one, added acoustic blankets and coated everything in flat-black, radar-absorbent paint.

When they were finished and NASA did the sound tests, they found the modified OH-6 was far quieter; enemy listeners had to be six times closer to hear it coming. They officially called the helicopter the 500P Penetrator, code-named it the Quiet One, and Kissinger's wiretap mission was on.

During the night of December 6, 1972, an all-black Quiet One flew along the nap of the earth across North Vietnam to the target, dropped two commandos beside the telephone line, spread a camouflage solar-powered communications relay on a nearby tall tree, and landed in a dry streambed to wait. The commandos took 20 minutes to install and power the wiretap and make it back to the Quiet One, which safely lifted off and returned to base, undetected. The intercepted conversations immediately started flowing to Kissinger in Paris, and he quietly thanked the CIA for the excellent intelligence. Seven weeks later, he and Thọ signed the peace treaty, and US forces in Vietnam—and the Quiet One stealth helicopter—returned to the United States.

It was still a test aircraft, so it was immediately detailed to Groom Lake to keep the technology away from prying eyes and to undergo further radar detection testing. And on this November night in 1973, as the fire burned and expanded at the south end of the base, it was parked in its usual place on the edge of the north flight ramp.

Grief had flown several Soviet helicopters as part of his test pilot training. He didn't like them. He found them clumsy and slow, and felt that the designers were allowed to be too easily satisfied with poor control harmony, which increased the pilot workload unnecessarily. But a patient senior test pilot had taught him the basics of hovering and autorotation, and Grief decided to treat it as just another skill. After he'd studied the satellite photographs of Groom Lake assets, he'd done some refresher helo training at Ramenskoye a few months earlier. Just in case.

The ramp was pitch-black, and the dark helicopter was near-invisible. Grief walked to where he had seen it parked, then fished his flashlight from his bag. A quick look to remove the Quiet One's engine air inlet and exhaust plugs, and the pitot tube cover, and to verify there were no tie-downs. He opened the pilot's door on the right-hand side, chucked the loose items into the back seat and climbed in, his flashlight gripped between his teeth.

The red glow illuminated the simple cockpit. He searched and found the light switches, ensuring they were all off, and then turned on the battery. His left fingertips found the clearly labeled START switch, and he did one last look-around, his feet on the pedals, his right hand cross-armed on the collective.

Time to go.

He pushed and held the starter, listening to its low whine rise in pitch. All turbine engines need to get spinning before you add fuel, and he waited until it sounded right then turned the throttle handle on the collective to the idle position to add fuel and spark. He could hear the immediate change, and watched the temperature and rpm climb into their green ranges on the simple gauges in front of him. Once the sound started to stabilize, he released the starter, transferred his right hand to the cyclic, his left to the throttle on the collective, and did a quick inventory as the engine warmed and came up to speed. He could feel the vibration of the blades spinning up on the tail and main rotors above him. Normally he would wait for the oil to warm up, but these weren't the circumstances to worry about being kind to the engine. Despite the Quiet One being low noise, he wanted to get off the ramp and out of earshot as quickly as possible.

Grief centered the cyclic, anticipated the torque with gentle pressure on the pedals, and then twisted and raised the collective to drive the main blades to lift him off the ground. He felt the familiar lurch and unwanted rotation as he rose into hover, overcorrected with his feet until he sensed the helo would hold heading into the northwest wind, and then eased forward on the cyclic to start moving.

Moving north, and west, immediately. To get clear of the ramp and hangars, steering directly away from the buildings and eyes and ears of Groom Lake. He eased back on the throttle as soon as he had airspeed, to help minimize the noise. The white of the salt pan lakebed was easy to see in the starlight, and he set his initial heading to skirt its edge. His night vision was fully adapted, but gauging height was hard. He moved his lips and teeth to shine his flashlight on the radar altimeter, and nodded: 20 feet, about 6 meters, easy to maintain over the flat and scrub brush as he turned towards the west.

Looking to the left, he could see the low, dark bulk of the ridgeline that backed the base, and continued his slow left turn to fly down the west side of it. He'd studied the terrain extensively in satellite photographs, and had rechecked the distinct local features on the topographic charts in the Groom Lake pilots' ready room.

Grief looked back towards the base as it disappeared behind the ridgeline. No sudden floodlights near the hangars, no flashing lights of an interested or alerted security car. If someone had heard the helicopter, they would likely assume it was part of the emergency response to the fire.

He shifted in his seat, settling himself for the flying task. He had to cover the 40 miles to his destination flying as low and quietly as this aircraft would allow. At cruising speed, he'd calculated it would take 20 minutes.

Time to concentrate on navigating in the faint moonlight.

62

Groom Lake

Kaz awoke to the sound of sirens.

He'd decided to fly his NASA T-38 from Houston Ellington Field to Groom Lake the previous evening, stopping once in Albuquerque for gas. Claw met him at the jet as he shut down, and they'd had a late dinner and drink at Sam's to get each other up to speed. Kaz finally made it to bed in his end of the trailer long after the defector had retired and later than he'd wanted, especially with the two-hour time difference.

The bedside clock hands were now glowing 03:25, and he shook his head groggily.

Sirens at a secret air base were bad news. *Grief first*, he thought.

He reached up and flicked on the little built-in reading light above his bed, with no response. *Bad bulb?* In the darkness he hastily pulled on jeans and a T-shirt, walked to the door and threw the light switch.

Nothing.

He squinted hard to clear the grit from his good eye as he pulled open the door and stared into the blackness of the trailer's central living room. He picked his way around the furniture until he reached Grief's closed door and knocked loudly, the sirens still whining.

"Grief, you up?"

No answer.

Kaz yanked the door open. He could see the dim shape of the bed and rumpled covers. "Grief, wake up!" He walked closer and saw that the bed was empty, then glanced at the open bathroom door.

Grief was outside somewhere.

Kaz hurried to the large living room window and pulled the curtains apart. The rows of trailers blocked any open view of the runways or hangars to the north, so he crossed to look out the smaller, south-facing window above the sink. He could see the disjointed cycling of vehicles' revolving lights in the distance, as if a few emergency trucks were parked near each other. The source of the sirens. There was also a reddish glow, but he couldn't tell if it was just the residual glare from the beacons on his eyeball in the darkness.

He considered what was down at that part of the base: fuel tanks and the station power plant. He glanced around the nearby trailers and saw no lights at all.

A big transformer must have blown.

He saw a couple of shapes moving in the shadows outside and went back into his bedroom to grab his flying boots and jacket, along with the flashlight from his bedside drawer. Outside, he sat on the steps to lace up his boots.

A figure loomed out of the black, briefly flicking a flashlight on him. "You got power?"

"Nope." Kaz squinted to see who it was but didn't recognize the man. The intermittent red emergency lights reflected off his face, making it look like the man had a nosebleed.

"You headed over to help?"

The man shook his head and sighed. "Nah, the fire guys and security are already there. I'd just be in the way. Gonna try to get some more sleep instead." He turned and walked down the alleyway between the trailers.

Kaz watched the indistinct form disappear into the darkness.

Where is Grief?

Fully awake now, and with his boots on, he pushed himself off the steps and headed for Thompson's trailer. The CIA man would be concerned about what was going on.

Kaz rapped on the door, and when he heard nothing from within, he pulled it open and yelled Thompson's name. No reply. He shone his flashlight inside and saw that Thompson's bedroom door was open. A quick check showed that the bed and the bathroom were empty.

Sirens, and now both the CIA handler and the Russian were missing. Were they together? Was Thompson looking for Grief too? Where would they go?

Towards the flashing lights, he reasoned. He turned for the door and was stopped by another thought. *Maybe they were the cause*.

Kaz hurried back outside and saw headlights coming down Dump Road, and sprinted in that direction. The November desert air was cold, and he zipped up his Navy Nomex jacket as he ran. There was a gusting, late-night wind from the northwest, curling past the mountain and down the road, and it made him feel even colder now that he was out of the lee of the trailers.

Raising a hand to shield his eye, he held up the other to catch the driver's attention. When the vehicle braked to a stop, he saw it was a Jeep, with the detachment commander, Irv Williams, at the wheel.

Going around to the driver's side, Kaz asked, "What's going on?"

"There's a fire down at the fuel depot, and a power outage. Don't know what caused it yet. There's also some sort of trouble up at the guard shack. Wanna come with me for a look?"

As an answer, Kaz jogged around to the far side and clambered into the passenger seat. Irv let out the clutch and accelerated hard towards the glowing and flashing lights.

Kaz said, "Grief and Thompson are both out here somewhere too. I checked and their beds were empty."

Williams shrugged. "Those sirens are too loud to sleep through."

Kaz considered that, looking ahead at the glowing red, and asked, "Does the county fire department get called in?"

Irv shook his head. "No, with all the classified ops here, we man our own base department fire 24-7." He lifted his chin, gesturing forward as they approached the lights. "They're there now."

"What's happening at the guard shack?"

Irv squinted as he slowed the Jeep, well upwind of the fire trucks. "It was confusing. They reported the lights of a vehicle on the approach road, weird at this time of night, then some sort of garbled message, and now they're not responding. Might be the power failure. I want to see what's going on here first, and then I'm gonna zip up there to check it out." He looked left at the diesel generator building, which looked intact. "We've got to get base power back on ASAP."

The two men climbed out of the Jeep, their arrival ignored by the firefighters who had unrolled hoses from their large, square truck and were spraying a wide jet of thick white AFFF foam across smoldering refueling trucks and tanks. A second fire truck was parked crosswind, spraying the sides of the large, still-intact JP-4 tank with what looked like water. The men closest to the fire were all wearing silver suits and hoods; the ones farther back were in a mismatched assortment of boots, coats and helmets, some in what looked like hastily donned civilian clothes.

"Looks like they called in the off-shift guys too," Kaz said. He didn't see Thompson or Grief anywhere.

Irv was staring past the men at the damage the fire had already done. Three of the four fuel bowser trucks had burned and exploded, and the firefighters had doused the fourth with foam and water to protect it. The skeleton of the diesel tank on stilts was in the center of the conflagration, barely recognizable as it had split and melted in the heat.

A man spotted them and approached, redly silhouetted by the flames behind him. He was wearing heavy rubber boots, a thick black-and-yellow rubberized coat and a fireman's helmet, tipped back on his head.

Irv greeted him by name. "Looks like you're getting it under control, Russ?"

Russ nodded. "Yep. Good thing the boys responded as quick as they did. Way too close to the big JP-4 tanks. We're cooling them down now." He glanced towards the base water tower. "Should have enough supply."

Irv glanced in the same direction. "Any idea what caused it?"

Russ shook his head. "Looks like it started at the third truck, but we're not sure how. Likely a battery short or something, and then the wind blew the fire across into everything else."

Kaz studied the hulk of the farthest-upwind burned truck, considering the odds of a sudden short in the night.

Irv pointed at the diesel generator building. "Any idea how long until we can get the power going again?"

"My guys'll have this fully contained in the next few minutes, but then we'll need some time to get everything cooled down and safe." Russ considered. "We're going to be short of diesel, but we've got what's in the last truck's tank, and of course we have our own supply tank over at the firehouse. We'll sort out a way to get that tank moved over here and plumbed into the generator. Hopefully get the lights back on by"—he moved his left arm awkwardly inside the heavy sleeve to expose his wristwatch—"oh, five thirty or so." He looked squarely at Irv. "Best case."

Irv nodded. "That'll do until we can get resupply and a permanent fix." He looked at the burned-out truck hulks. "We're going to be slow refueling for a bit. Need me to call in any extra help here?"

Russ said, "Nah, we've got it under control. I've already sent a guy to wake up base services to start figuring a plan for the generator."

Irv nodded, glancing at Kaz. "Great, thanks, Russ. We're going to take a run up to the guard shack."

Russ shrugged. "Just your friendly neighborhood firemen, doing what we do best."

Irv drove fast around the northern curve of the lakebed, with Kaz hunkered down in his seat, trying to keep warm against the whipping wind. The Jeep's small, retrofitted heater fan was whining loudly on full HOT, without much effect.

They could see no floodlights as they approached the guard shack at the top of the ridgeline. Irv pulled in beside the security truck that was parked at an angle, and he left his engine running and headlights on to illuminate the scene. A serious face appeared around the corner of the building, checked to see who had arrived and then disappeared again. Both men got out and walked quickly around towards the guardhouse.

Kaz stopped short, taking in the whole tableau. Swing gate in place, but with a crumpled body on the right and what looked like an angular black pistol casting a low shadow on the ground beside it. The window of the guardhouse facing the road was broken, and inside, the two men of the security detail were bent over, their faces bottom-lit by the flashlight one of them held. Irv was already at the door.

Kaz heard one of the guards shout, "Do you have any more first aid packs?" He pivoted and ran to the Jeep, unclipped the kit he'd noticed between the seats and hurried back.

Irv was kneeling behind the main desk with the others. "Man down here, Kaz, multiple wounds, lost a lot of blood. Any compresses in there?"

Kaz had clicked the box open and handed Irv the four neatly rolled bandages from within.

"Worth me looking at the other guy?"

The guard holding the flashlight responded. "Nope. Looks like shrapnel wounds to his face and forehead. No pulse."

"Shrapnel?" Kaz and Irv said the word simultaneously. They both reached a conclusion immediately, and Kaz said it out loud. "Grenade?"

The guard who was kneeling grunted as he applied the bandages onto the downed man's right thigh. "Sure looks like it. It got them both, but this one still has a weak pulse." He glanced up at them. "I'm just an emergency medic. We need to get him some blood and a doctor pronto." He nodded at the tabletop, where a portable radio was sitting upright. "We called down to the Command Post to hustle and get us some help, but they didn't respond."

Irv grabbed the radio. "Command Post, Colonel Williams here, how do you copy?"

No answer. Not even static.

"Damned power outage!"

Kaz's mind was racing, thinking about a possible common cause. He said, "Irv, you going to stay here or head back down?"

Irv was standing again, looking out the broken window into the night, assessing the probability of continued threat. Kaz saw blood on his face.

Irv spoke, summarizing the situation for his own clarity. "There has been definite hostile action here, and we have two men down, one deceased." He turned to Kaz. "I'm staying with these men until more help arrives. We'll use their truck as needed." He saw the shotgun on the floor, picked it up, cracked it open to check the load and started to move outside. "Go ahead and take the Jeep, Kaz. Give a full update in person to the Command Post and get them to call me ASAP and send help. I'm going to have a look around."

Kaz said, "Wait a minute, Irv, I think you're bleeding."

Irv scowled. "I'm what?"

Fresh blood was spreading below Irv's nose. Kaz said, "Looks like a bad nosebleed."

Irv brought his hand up to his face, wiping at his nose and mouth. He stared in surprised disgust at the red wetness on his palm and fingers. "Shit, I never get nosebleeds!" He tipped his head back and pinched his nose between his thumb and forefinger as Kaz checked the contents of the first aid kit. There was a blue roll of cotton batting, and he tore off a couple of small pieces and handed them to Irv, who jammed them into his nostrils.

Shaking his head, Irv said, "I don't like coincidences. Kaz, don't worry about me. Just get going." He frowned angrily, the two wads of cotton already turning red with fresh blood.

Kaz nodded and headed out the door, jogging over to pick up the pistol on the ground beside the guard's body. He popped the mag out to make sure it was full, snicked it back into place, shoved the pistol into his pocket and ran to the Jeep.

He didn't like coincidences either.

63

Jackass Flats, Nevada

The flight took Grief across a hellish moonscape.

Hundreds of nuclear blast craters, some as big across as a football pitch, monochromatically rolled past in the half-light below him. Decades of deep scars, eroding slowly now in the sere high air of the Nevada desert. Gradually releasing their radiation into the wind and occasional rainstorms that swept across the barren land.

From his careful study of the satellite images, Grief had expected it to look the way it did, and he had used his pilot's perspective to pick out hills, ravines and craters that he'd be sure to recognize day or night, airborne or on foot.

He permitted himself a small smile. He'd dealt well with the unexpected complication of the CIA man, and quickly thinking to hide the body had helped guarantee that his actions stayed undetected amidst the other multilevel confusion he'd created.

The route from Groom Lake to Jackass Flats was a naturally flowing one, following a connected series of valleys carved by the upheaval of tectonic forces and Ice Age erosion. To Grief it made navigation simple.

He only needed to follow the valley center, keeping the high ground even on both sides, and recognize the few ridge-cresting turning points. When he spotted a particularly wide, deep bomb crater, 400 meters across, he nodded. The analysts had told him it was from the biggest of all the American bombs, exploded in 1962. He didn't care whether it was the biggest or not; what mattered was that when he saw it, he knew exactly where he was.

Moving slightly in the helicopter's downwash as he quietly flew past, growing and thriving along the broad crater's edge, was a spiky tumbleweed with a name that would have made him smile at the irony had he known: the Russian thistle. The only plant tough enough to survive the fallout.

Grief followed a narrow arroyo that opened into a sand-bottomed valley, with a single dirt road down its center that he knew would soon lead him into a sloping open plain, and his destination: Jackass Flats. The instructors in Moscow had smirkingly explained to him the double meaning of the American name.

As the wide valley came into view, Grief concentrated on flying even lower, easing open the throttle for more speed. He was confident there would be no more sudden ridges and was aware that even the muffled sound of his helo would carry far across the open expanse. If there were roving night security patrols, the buildings and artifacts in this part of the nuclear test range would be of high priority. He wanted to minimize his exposure: get in, find what he was looking for and get out.

Undetected.

A clock in his head was automatically counting the seconds since he'd come through the ridgeline, and he glanced at his airspeed indicator. Being constantly hyperaware of time was a fighter pilot habit, cultivated because knowing how much time was passing made it easy to calculate how much distance was being covered. He strained his eyes to look ahead, knowing a crossroad and a potential power line were coming. As he saw the paler glint of the road, he eased the Quiet

One up high enough to cross at the barely visible telephone pole. Standard technique: don't look for the wires, go over the poles.

He started counting again and checked his magnetic heading. He had two stops planned, and the first one should be visible very soon.

There! He altered course fractionally to the right and eased up on the controls, to start to slow. His eyes ran along the lengths of train cars that had loomed into sight, and he counted, confident that nothing would have been moved in this decaying graveyard of nuclear rocket engine test equipment. He spotted the distinctive shape of the railcar he was seeking, brought the helo to a quick hover, set it down and let the engine briefly idle. As soon as the blades had slowed to his satisfaction, he cut the switches and the Allison turboshaft engine rapidly wound down into silence. He threw the battery switch to OFF, unstrapped, grabbed his small bag and climbed out.

A Soviet Russian, standing alone on Jackass Flats.

Grief ran through the prioritized list in his head and walked with clear purpose towards the railcars. Glinting in the moonlight on the nearest flatbed was a high, shed-sized square box with a large silver barrel on top, fluted at its uppermost edge, like a giant metallic Grecian urn.

The Russian reached into his bag and retrieved the camera. He carefully framed and took one overall picture, then strode swiftly around to get photos of each side, as the briefing team in Moscow had requested. Large white block letters spelling "PH-2" gleamed on the slab sides of the lower structure, reflecting in the camera's flash. He nodded.

Phoebus 2A, the largest nuclear rocket engine the Americans had ever built. Now abandoned, to slowly rust and shed its radioactivity into the emptiness of the Nevada desert.

He climbed the ladder that led to the structure on top, holding the camera carefully as he ascended. He'd been told that the plumbing that led from the tanks up to the Phoebus engine was of extreme interest to the Soviet researchers in Semipalatinsk, and Grief carefully photographed it from all angles, using his flashlight as a second light source, for depth.

He saw there had been corrosion at some of the connections, where the dissimilar metals touched. He grabbed a long section of pipe and shook it, hard; the heavy-gauge metal flexed very slightly. He braced his feet and heaved, but nothing bent far enough to break. He got his footing and tried a solid kick, jackknifing his leg and striking right next to the connection point with the heavy sole of his flying boot, twice. No luck.

Only surface corrosion, he concluded. *No matter*. They'd built in a backup plan.

Grief climbed as high as he could on the external piping that led up to the nozzle on top, pausing to get close-up photographs of fluid routing and any printing he saw. He took one last walk around the raised platform, confirmed that he had images of everything, and then stopped for a slow, careful look and listen in all directions. He saw no lights and heard nothing but the wind.

Climbing back down the ladder, he looked over his left shoulder along the glinting rails, to orient himself in the darkness. As soon as his feet touched the ground, he strode confidently in that direction. The satellite photographs had given him two other locations to search, and in the moonlight he followed the paler-colored dirt path towards them.

The first was another railcar. The Soviet analysts had used their satellite images to build a time sequence of this distant nuclear dumping ground and they noticed that a car that had arrived late was parked nearest the entrance. It was of special interest because, from what they could discern from the fuzzy images, it contained a hodgepodge of pipes and final cleanup items. Grief walked along the edge of the track until he saw it, and then climbed up on top and directed his flashlight beam down at the contents, kicking aside loose items as he went.

Blown sand had drifted into the gaps between the long tubes, making them hard to shift, but at the far end was a square metal bin, hastily welded into place to hold bits and pieces. He peered inside, then vaulted up over the lip, landing on the jumble of loose parts with a rustling metallic crunch. Getting down on one knee, he started sifting through the various-sized parts.

During testing a few years previously, the Americans had blown up a nuclear rocket engine, fracturing key components and revealing the internal structure of dewar insulation and cryo valves. The logical place for the radioactive bits to be dumped was here somewhere. By the light of the borrowed flashlight, he rapidly sorted through the pile, stopping occasionally to photograph details of larger objects and setting small pieces aside.

Several items were too heavy to lift, even with both hands, so he kicked and pushed them out of the way to make sure he didn't miss anything. Satisfied, he surveyed his small pile. He had five metal objects, all of the type that was needed, all small enough to be carried. Straightening up, he threw them one by one out onto the sand and climbed out himself.

One last place to search.

Jogging now along the dirt road, he looked for the long, straight tracks to his left where successive dump trucks had emptied their contaminated loads. He knew there were about 30 piles, but the satellite photos hadn't given enough resolution to know which might contain what he needed. Time to move fast.

He came to the first jumble, played his flashlight up and down it, and frowned. It looked more like scrap iron than engine hardware, just an angular heap of large pieces of dryly corroded metal. Grief kicked briefly around the base of it, looking for components small enough to carry, but found nothing. He glanced at the glowing hands of his wristwatch—almost 04:20. He did a slow scan of the horizon, confirming that nothing was moving, then turned to jog to the next dumped pile. He had time for a quick look at each, then he needed to get back to the helicopter.

Before he could be on his way to the rendezvous in Mexico, he had one more destination, here on the windswept plains of the Nevada Nuclear Test Site.

64

Jackass Flats

If there was one thing Isaac Acklin found even easier than supervising moving items into storage at the Nuclear Rocket Development Station, it was night shift. EG&G was contracted to provide regular patrols across Jackass Flats, and the crews assigned to daytime cleanup were also required to rotate night duty as part of the deal. This week it was Isaac's turn.

It wasn't that bad. Vegas was a night owl town, and he tended to stay up late anyway. Swapping his schedule around to support night patrols one week out of four was just part of Sin City life. And it was something to brag quietly about to the women he chatted up: Isaac Acklin doin' solo patrol across the restricted nuclear facility to the north, in an armed vehicle.

The reality, like everything in Las Vegas, was a lot less glamorous. He would sit in the duty shack at Mercury by the south gate, shooting the shit with the guards there. Twice a night he would get into an aging white EG&G pickup with an M14 rifle mounted in the gun rack behind the driver's seat and drive the prescribed route up and around the test site. Back when there was active testing and nuclear material on location, the patrols each had two crew and were continuous. But now EG&G was just going through the motions, and the government no longer really cared.

Isaac's patrols were sporadic and alone.

There weren't many choices of route to take, especially for the inbound and outbound portion. EG&G also had the road maintenance contract, and they'd let that slip too. The truck would bounce along the cracking asphalt, up Road Alpha through the pass at Skull Mountain and then down to the crossroads by the old Reactor Control Point. That's where Isaac decided either to turn left on Road Hotel towards Engine Test Stand #1 and the outdoor Radioactive Materials Dump or to turn right on Road Golf and beeline straight across to the R-MAD building.

Tonight was fairly clear and cold, and he wasn't planning to get out of the truck, so he opted for a third choice: straight ahead on Road Foxtrot to swing up by the remains of Test Cells C and A, and then do a quick counterclockwise drive around the R-MAD's perimeter road. As familiar to him now as the Avalon Park streets he'd grown up on.

Mostly he was looking for wildlife. He'd seen coyotes occasionally, and fairly often he came across a herd of pronghorn antelope. Isaac boasted in town of using the M14 to bag a pronghorn, or maybe even a brown bear, but he knew he never actually would. What would he do with one anyway? Put a dead antelope in his car somehow and take it to a butcher in Vegas?

He'd read somewhere that headlights spooked animals, so he mostly drove by moonlight. The darkness of the pavement showed up well against the pale sand, and the suddenness with which things appeared gave him the feeling of going really fast. Like he was flying maybe.

Tonight, as he traversed the high pass and suddenly had all of Jackass Flats laid out before him, he reached forward and pushed the headlights knob in. He had to slow down a bit until his night vision kicked in, but then he accelerated again, flicking his eyes left and right now to look for the telltale flash of movement of an antelope.

Exhilarated and all alone, he was Isaac Acklin of south Chicago, protecting the nation's nuclear rocket test facility.

65

Mexicali Airport, State of Baja California, Mexico

Landing at the Mexicali airport had been straightforward. Apart from the boredom of the six-hour night flight across the Gulf of Mexico from Havana, there'd been nothing remarkable. For the return leg, at least they'd have a tailwind.

The An-22 captain had received a detailed ops briefing from the senior Soviet Air Forces general in Cuba, including what to expect on the ground and which frequencies to use when contacting Mexican Air Traffic Control. The Mexicans had provided someone on the radio who spoke good enough Russian to handle the vectors, descent and clearance to land at the long, well-lit runway. He'd touched the big plane down gently, taxied it back in the darkness on the single runway to the parking apron, and shut down at the pre-briefed spot.

It was 04:25, and there was no visible movement on the airfield until headlights came on by one of the buildings and a fuel truck drove out to the plane. The captain tasked his crew chief with making sure they got a full load for the return leg.

No customs or immigration officers rode out with the fuel bowser. Word had come down to the airport authority that this was a special flight, authorized by President Echeverría himself. A matter of national security. Give the visitors gas and whatever else they needed, then leave them alone. They'd only be on the ground for a few hours.

Once the truck driver finished the fueling and retracted his hose back into the bowser, he unloaded a wooden crate from the passenger seat of the cab, brought it around and set it carefully on the tarmac, per his instructions. He gestured at the crate with open hands, and then at the plane's crew chief, making it clear that the box was for him. Then he got back into the truck and drove away. The Russian shrugged, picked up the heavy crate and walked it up the side steps into the Antonov.

The captain had kept the crew in the cargo hold, after briefing everyone on the salient points of what they were there for. A fighter jet would land, they'd remove the wings and tails per usual, load them into the transport crates they'd brought from Russia, winch the main fuselage up the aft ramp inside, strap everything down and take off. The crewmen nodded. All work they'd done before, many times, hauling jets and parts around the Soviet Union and to foreign destinations like Syria.

None of the technicians asked where the jet was coming from. It didn't matter, and no one had told them where they were now, anyway. Just get the job done and get back to the palm trees of Havana for a couple days' rest before the long flight home.

The crew chief pointed at the box the bowser driver had given him and asked, "What should we do with that, Commander?"

The pilot considered. "Let's open it up, then decide."

The chief nodded and retrieved a crowbar from a toolbox. He knelt to pry up the wooden slats across the top, and then used his pocketknife to slit open the sealed cardboard box within. Lifting the top flaps out of the way, he peered and then reached inside, and stood to hand the captain an envelope that had been lying on top.

He smiled, tipping his head towards the box. "It's what I guessed it was, from the weight."

The address on the letter was handwritten in Spanish, which the captain slowly deciphered, and he was startled to realize it said "General Secretary Leonid Ilyich Brezhnev." He carefully returned the envelope to its spot in the crate, then gingerly lifted one of the bottles inside far enough to read the label. Blue agave tequila, Jalisco premium *añejo*. He slid the bottle back down and closed the flaps.

He smiled back at the crew chief. "Hammer the crate closed again, carefully, and stow it somewhere safe."

66

R-MAD, Jackass Flats

It took Grief three trips with his hands full, but he had allowed the time. He'd picked out some promising valves and broken metal pieces in two of the dump sites, and he wanted to put them together with what he'd found in the railcar, to photograph and then choose the best ones to take with him. As he'd expected, once he laid them next to each other, the best two cryogenic valves and two samples of metal insulation were readily apparent. He loosened the strings on his carry sack and put the four prize items inside, nestling them carefully next to the camera where they wouldn't damage it. He still had some key photographs to take.

As he approached the Quiet One, Grief stopped in his tracks. Above the noise of the wind and his footsteps, he thought he heard the distant whining sound of a vehicle. He tried to narrow down where it was coming from, but the best he could do was somewhere north, upwind of where he stood. He looked and listened intently, holding his breath as he scanned the horizon, but he heard and saw nothing more.

Best to stay on track. Opening the helicopter door, he climbed in and placed the bag carefully onto the other front seat, closed the door beside him and went through the process to start the Quiet One for the second time that night.

He only had a short hop this time, just the five kilometers due east to the largest remaining building at Jackass Flats, a place his briefers had told him was called the R-MAD—the Reactor Maintenance, Assembly, and Disassembly building. They'd told him that in English "mad" meant either crazy or angry, and had laughed that in this case it was probably a bit of both.

He spun the collective's throttle in his left hand, balanced the cyclic delicately in his right and eased the Quiet One back into the air.

What is that? Isaac let his foot off the gas in case he had to brake. He was careful not to touch the pedal yet, though, to keep from lighting up the local area and spooking the wildlife with the red glare of his brake lights.

As he coasted slower, the familiar pale brown and bright white of a pronghorn antelope crossed quickly in front of him, followed by another, and then several more, all running with a bouncing gait. He figured they'd been spooked to leap across the exposed narrow road by the low noise of his engine. Ingrained in them was the necessity to avoid anything new or noisome, and Isaac's truck in the night was another potential predator.

Isaac peered hard through the windscreen, waiting to see if another one would pass, then decided that was it and accelerated towards Test Cell A.

The R-MAD was a hulking, angular shape in the darkness, slab-sided with multilevel flat roofs, like a giant's pile of cement blocks haphazardly stacked together. Grief shut the helicopter down in the parking lot, close to some large doors. He grabbed the camera from his bag, put it in his flight suit leg pocket, and reached into the back seat for the gun he'd taken from the rack at the Groom Lake stables, just in case that engine noise he'd heard turned out to be anything. He'd had enough surprises for one night. In addition to the .22-caliber rifles there, they also kept a Stevens 12-gauge pump-action shotgun, and that's what he'd grabbed on the way to the helicopter.

If he needed a gun, he wanted close-range lethality.

As expected, the twin man doors beside the tall garage entrance to the building were unlocked. Why lock a door to an abandoned building inside a secure facility? Grief took one last slow listen and look-around outside, turned the knob and entered, leaving the door ajar behind him.

The interior was completely dark, so he clicked on his flashlight, and the illumination revealed the unmistakable growing jumble of a place that used to be busy and cared for, and now was neither. The industrial tile floor had dust piled up towards one wall, and there were cables and mismatched tables and chairs next to a wheelbarrow. Empty water jugs sat on the tables, and long-outdated notices were peeling from a corkboard on the wall. The air smelled musty and stale.

Grief wasn't sure where the things he was looking for would be stored, but his briefing team in Moscow had expected that the bulky, heavy items would be on the main floor and the smaller stuff one floor up: minimal labor to meet the objective of long-term low-level radioactive warehousing. Stairs were visible through an open door at the end of the corridor, and he walked swiftly down the hall to climb them, shotgun in his left hand, flashlight in his right.

The stairs led up into a messy open room, laid out in a makeshift intentional order. Plying his flashlight left and right revealed rough racks and shelving that had been installed along three of the four walls, piled with varying heights of loose papers, bound folders and books. The fourth wall was lined by a wide collection of filing cabinets of different sizes and colors, butted tightly against each other, with small labels glinting on some of the drawers.

Grief frowned. Searching all this would take more time than he had, especially by flashlight. The room had no windows, so he closed the door and hunted until he found several light switches. He flicked them all on and the overhead fluorescents buzzed and lit up, making him blink and squint in the sudden harsh brightness. Shielding his eyes, he strode to the nearest rack of shelving, leaned the shotgun in the corner and started rapidly leafing through the papers.

He was looking for schematics, photographs and any personal notebooks containing hand drawings or equations. As he flicked through the stacks, he kept in mind several images they'd shown him. When he found something interesting, he turned to get good, unshadowed lighting and took a photograph. The camera held an oversized magazine of film, and he rapidly cranked the advancing mechanism between shots.

After several minutes Grief glanced at his watch and surveyed the remaining papers on the shelf, gauging his progress.

More of the same, he judged, all printed texts and reports in no particular order. *Let's see what they've hidden.*

He walked to the first of the filing cabinets and opened it.

Empty. He slammed the drawer shut and opened the one below it. Also empty. He tapped the outside, listened to the hollow sound and started tapping other drawers until he heard a more solid thump. He pulled it open and smiled at his luck.

Notebooks. A stack of them, hastily piled into the drawer.

He lifted out the first and thumbed through the pages. It looked more administrative than technical. He grabbed the next and did the same, and then the next. The fourth gave him pause, and he slowed to examine it. Messy handwriting, pages of equations, and the asterisks, circles and arrows of someone using the book to develop their thoughts. He started to photograph it, but the book wasn't very thick, so he dropped it on the floor behind him to take with him when he left.

More tapping, opening and riffling revealed several more notebooks and two folders of interesting photographs. He quickly judged what to photograph, wanting to use up all his film, and what to bring with him. He rechecked his watch. He'd been in the room for 20 minutes and had gathered all he could prudently carry. With the hardware he already had in the helo, it was enough.

He put the red filter on his flashlight and, holding it in his teeth, picked up the bundle of notebooks and folders under one arm, retrieved the shotgun and killed the lights.

Grief stood in the darkness with his eyes wide open and counted slowly to 60, allowing his night vision to begin to return. He knew full dark adaptation would take 20 minutes, which he figured would be about right for when he'd need it most. As soon as he could see the details of the door frame and the knob in the dim red glow from his flashlight, he leaned the shotgun against the wall, opened the door, picked up the gun and headed down the stairs.

Time to fly.

"What the fuck?" Isaac said the words out loud.

As he began the patrol past each of the buildings—first Test Cell A, and then C, and now the R-MAD—Isaac had turned his headlights back on again. There was often loose metal or debris on the pavement that he didn't want to blow a tire on. And the only animals he'd ever seen near the buildings were rats, and he didn't want to come across any of those in the darkness.

Several smaller buildings, purpose-built for flammables storage and higher-radiation operations, skirted the edge of the large fenced area, all joined by a ring road. By habit he followed it. There was never anything new to see, but he knew this part of his job was clearly specified in the EG&G security instructions, since the R-MAD was being used as the main low-level radiation material repository.

He turned the wheel a little to illuminate each shed-sized structure as he slowly drove past, looking for open doors or weather damage. As usual, he saw nothing but slowly decaying loose junk and corrugated iron.

But then he came around the corner of the R-MAD itself. Sitting in a place where there should be nothing but old asphalt and tumbleweeds was a helicopter.

He jammed on the brakes.

What the fuck is a helicopter doing here?

No one had said anything about it back at the Mercury guard post. He glanced at the portable radio in its holster clipped to the dash. It was off, because he knew from experience that coverage across the hills was spotty, and there was never anything to say anyway.

He looked back at the dark shape lit by his headlights, put the truck into park and tried to figure it out. The helicopter was all black with no insignia markings. It looked military—definitely not like some civilian sightseeing chopper. There was no sign of movement around it, and he saw no lights at all.

Isaac pulled the radio out of its holster and clicked it on, heard the standard quick burst of static as it warmed up, and checked it was on the right frequency. He pushed the thumb button.

"Mercury Base, this is Isaac, can you hear me?"

Nothing. He turned the small squelch knob on top until he heard the static feedback, set the volume and tried again.

"Mercury Base, you there?"

Just an uninterrupted low hiss. He grimaced. *Fucking EG&G, they can't even provide radios that work!*

He decided there was still a chance Base was hearing him, so he transmitted a quick summary, shut the radio off and slid it back into its holder.

Isaac took a deep breath. Time to go have a look. But first he twisted to pull the M14 rifle out of its clips. He pushed the button to pop the 15-round magazine out and confirm it was full, clicked it back into place, pulled the slide lever back and released it to load a round into the chamber, moved the safety lever to OFF with his pointer finger and reached for the truck's door handle.

The gusting wind grabbed at Grief's clothing as it whistled around the concrete building, drowning out any subtlety of noise. The idling pickup truck's headlights lit the helicopter starkly, the long black shadows crossing the tarmac and projecting up onto the white walls of the building beyond.

He skirted the light to stay hidden, holding the gun firmly in his left hand. Moving to his left around the helo, he tucked in tight against the darkness of the high building wall, crouching behind some rusting 45-gallon barrels.

Assessing.

How many people were there? That was the key question. When he saw movement, silhouetted against the light, he resisted the urge to rise and shoot. He watched as a single man walked cautiously forward, staying out of the light, noting he also held a gun.

Time was ticking, but Grief needed to be sure. He quietly slipped past the barrels and obliquely approached the truck's open door. A quick glance inside showed loose items piled on the right seat and a radio in its holster by the dash. There was no back seat, and no one would have been riding in the bed.

Grief's adversary was alone. It made the next part simpler.

As Isaac moved stealthily past the helicopter, he saw that one of the doors to the R-MAD was partially open. The threat now localized, he crouched. Whoever the crew of the aircraft was, they had gone inside the building. He could see through the upper glass of the door that the interior lights were off. The idea of walking into that darkness, alone, scared him. He knew from his day shifts that the entrance opened on a long corridor with multiple side doors, which meant many places to hide. It would be like walking into an ambush.

He glanced at the helicopter, trying to think of how to stop the intruders from leaving while giving himself a safe way to escape in the truck and go get help.

How do you disable a helicopter? Do they have keys?

He moved closer and squinted through the Perspex, seeing none.

Can I shoot the instrument panel?

He tried to think of the most fragile part of the machine and looked at the blade above his head. The sound of the M14 would alert whoever was in the building, but with a wrecked rotor blade, they wouldn't get far. He raised the rifle, aimed carefully at the thicker part of the blade towards the hub where the .30-caliber bullet would do the most damage, and moved his finger to the trigger.

The shotgun blast took Isaac completely by surprise.

Grief had moved close to ensure the spread pattern of the 12-gauge buckshot wouldn't hit the helicopter. He'd aimed for the upper body and head, raising the stock hard against his shoulder and firing quickly, before the man could do his helicopter harm.

At such close range the effect was devastating. The eight heavy lead pellets from the double-aught shell hit Isaac in a five-inch grouping in the center of his upper chest, tearing through his heart, deflecting and deforming on the bones of his ribs and spine, knocking him violently backwards. His M14 flew from his hands as he fell, clattering onto the asphalt. Grief moved forward in case the man was still alive, picked up the fallen rifle, checked the safety was off and fired a round into his head.

He wasn't sure how many more shells were left in the shotgun's magazine, and he wanted to save them for later, in case he needed them. He quickly put the rifle on the helicopter back seat, pumped the shotgun's action once to load the next shell, and put it on the seat as well.

Ignoring the body, Grief ran to retrieve the loose items from inside the building, where he'd dropped them when he saw the truck. He strapped the papers and photos onto the passenger seat of the helicopter and swiftly buckled himself in. His night vision was still shot, but he counted on it to return during the transit time back to Area 51, and he started the Quiet One's motor for the third and final time that evening. He glanced at the fuel gauge, nodded and moved quickly to lift off the ground, turn and accelerate away, staying higher this time and watching his radar altimeter until he could pick out more detail in the darkness.

The pool of light from the truck's headlights and the low shadow of the body, lying in its pool of spreading dark blood, receded into the night behind him.

The clock on the instrument panel showed 05:00.

67

Groom Lake

Kaz braked hard in front of the base headquarters building, leaving the engine running and the headlights on. He jumped over the low side of the Jeep and ran up the steps. As he'd driven back onto the base, he'd seen no lights on anywhere, and sunrise was still barely a glow on the eastern horizon. He opened the door and followed the beam of his flashlight inside.

The Command Post desk was empty. A portable radio was on the countertop, and Kaz picked it up to call Irv. The grip felt oddly wet in his hand, and when he shone his light on it, he saw it was red with blood.

What the hell? Kaz instinctively wiped under his own nose and looked at his hand to make sure he hadn't started bleeding too. *Where did the blood come from?*

He pushed the button. "Guard shack, this is Kaz at the Command Post, Irv, how do you hear?"

A slight pause, then the voice of the medic crackled back.

"Loud and clear. We need help. The gate guard's vitals are getting very weak. Colonel Williams's nosebleed hasn't stopped, and now he's down with some sort of severe gut pain."

Frowning, Kaz pushed the button and said, "Roger." He heard a muffled shout from down the hallway and flicked his flashlight beam in that direction. He saw the sign for the restroom and hurried down the corridor.

"In here!" The voice was strained. Kaz pushed the door open and shone his light inside.

Lying on the floor was an Air Force officer whose face Kaz recognized from the morning briefings. Her face was covered in blood, and she was moaning, holding her hands to her stomach.

"What happened?" Kaz asked urgently.

She spoke in short bursts, obviously in pain. "I don't know! My nose started bleeding, and it hasn't stopped." She groaned. "Now my stomach hurts something fierce, and I think I shit myself! I tried to call the doc, but no answer." She twisted her face up towards Kaz, eyes desperate. "I need help!" Blood was flowing steadily from her nose, adding to the pool on the floor. Kaz grabbed a roll of toilet paper and tore off some lengths, rolling them and helping her jam them into her nostrils.

"I'll go for the doctor!" he said, then realized he didn't know where to go. "What's his trailer number?"

"Seventeen," she gasped. "But he may be with the firemen." She let out a long moan.

Kaz nodded. "Hang in there—I'll get you help!" He ran back down the hall, out towards the Jeep, thinking rapidly.

Something had poisoned both Irv and this woman, and maybe the crewman he'd seen by his trailer, which very probably meant that more people across the base were afflicted as well. But not everyone—the firemen and medics had been fine. And so was he.

What was causing it?

As he reversed quickly and spun the wheel of the Jeep in a U-turn, headed for the line of trailers, he mentally added in the attack at the guard shack and the fuel truck fire at south base. No way it was random.

Something, most likely someone, had to be behind these things happening simultaneously.

Someone at Groom Lake who couldn't be fully trusted.

As Kaz drove, scanning the numbers on the corners of the trailers, a new thought entered his head.

Was all this just to create mayhem? That didn't make any sense. There had to be a core reason, some purpose.

Trailer number 17 loomed in his headlights, the number painted in black on the brushed silver, and he slid the Jeep to a halt. Vaulting again over the side, he stopped, suddenly, almost overbalancing, and looked in the other direction, across the open airfield towards the flight line.

Holy shit, he thought. *Could that be it?*

He didn't bother knocking, just threw open the trailer door. Climbing inside, he shone his light around and yelled.

"Doc, doc, you here?"

Silence.

Kaz strode to the nearer bedroom door and pushed it open, seeing nothing but rumpled sheets on an empty bed. He turned and walked fast through the central living area to the other bedroom, but that bed was stripped. He doubled back and checked the bathroom. Empty, but plying his flashlight across the sink, he saw splatters of blood.

Shit. Him too?

Kaz stood still for several seconds, figuring it out, weighing priorities. The doctor would have responded to the blaring of the sirens, and if he saw he had a nosebleed, so what? Most likely he was with the firefighters, probably debilitated with whatever had afflicted Irv and the woman. No help to anyone.

Kaz flung open the trailer door and jumped into the running Jeep.

Headed for the ramp where the F-15 was parked.

68

Groom Lake North Ramp

As he flew the Quiet One around the end of the long, rocky promontory that led back to Groom Lake, Grief strained to see ahead. His plan now hinged on how well the fuel farm fire had done its job, and whether the base was still blacked out. As the white of the salt lakebed came into view, and then the dark of the paved airplane ramp and hangars, he could see no lights. He gave it several more seconds of flight, confident that at this distance and low altitude he was unlikely to be detected by anyone on base. No lights at all showed, behind the hangars or beyond, as far as he could see.

Excellent, Grief thought. *No need to land in the desert and walk in.*

He pointed the helicopter directly at the near edge of the north ramp. It was 05:20, and the glow of predawn was tinting the eastern sky ahead of him. Soon there would be enough light for the next phase of his plan, but still plenty of dark to conceal what he was doing.

He smartly pivoted the Quiet One into a quick, low hover above its customary spot, set it down, chopped power and killed all switches. As the spinning blades slowed above him, he unstrapped, gathered his things, opened the door and stepped down onto the ramp.

Listening alertly, looking for movement, in case the fire and warfarin poisonings and the guard shack distraction he'd radioed for hadn't been sufficient.

Nothing.

With both the M14 and the shotgun cradled in his right arm, and his tote bag, now full and heavy with its metal and paper contents, in his left hand, he walked quickly across the asphalt pavement towards the second of the large hangars, looming blackly in the dark, ahead on his right.

Normally the groundcrew used electrical power to open the heavy hangar doors, but as at military airfields everywhere, there had to be a backup plan to get airplanes outside in case of emergencies. Grief entered the hangar through the nearest man door, walked to where the jet loomed tall in the cold darkness, set down the two guns and climbed the portable ladder that was pre-staged by the open cockpit. He placed his bulky drawstring bag on the bare metal floor ahead of the ejection seat, tucked in just clear of the control column's base. It was a normal place for pilots to carry clandestine items, not approved in case they had to eject, but usually overlooked. His left leg would be high enough to clear the bag and still rest on the rudder pedal.

He climbed back down the ladder, picked up the guns and walked straight ahead of the jet to the point where the center hangar doors opened. He set the guns down on the cement floor, released the latch holding the doors together and grabbed the bare metal with both hands to pry the sliding hangar doors apart.

They ran on rollers high above, and Grief had to overcome both the inertia of the tall slabs of metal as well as the friction of the small metal wheels on their tracks. For a moment nothing moved, and then the door started shifting left, slowly gaining speed and eventually collecting the door next to it, both of them rumbling open as he leaned and pulled. He glanced back inside the hangar, judging when the opening was wide enough to clear the jet's left wingtip, and pushed the doors slightly farther. He walked across and repeated the effort for the right-hand doors, thankful for the cold wind gusting and cooling the sweat off his face.

The doors had made their distinctive rumbling and squealing sound, so he paused again to listen and look out across the ramp to make sure he hadn't alerted anyone. He glanced at his wristwatch, and then at the sky to the east. It was 05:25, and he could see a distinct change of color where the sun was going to rise.

Right on schedule. Just one more thing to do.

Carrying the weapons, he strode quickly out of the hangar towards the sleek gray shape of the F-15.

There were many ways to disable a high-performance fighter aircraft. Grief had considered firing the shotgun into the instrument panel or cockpit canopy or sending a couple of rifle rounds down into the intake of the engine, but he wasn't certain of the effect that would have. He'd decided to opt for something much simpler and more familiar.

The F-15 had straightforward, heavy landing gear, with a single tall rubber main tire on each side. The safety of the rifle he'd shot the man with at Jackass Flats was still off, and he was confident that the magazine mechanism would have loaded another round into the chamber. Grief knelt by the left tire of the American jet, carefully aligned the barrel, glanced around once more to make sure no one was visible, braced the rifle and fired.

The 0.308-inch bullet passed directly through the nearer rubber wall of the radial tire and out the opposite side, leaving two neat holes. Grief had aimed it so there was no chance of the round hitting metal and ricocheting back at him, and despite the very high pressure of a jet fighter tire, he was confident it wouldn't somehow explode and tear apart. He listened as the 340-psi dry nitrogen gas inside hissed rapidly out and watched the wing of the jet above him perceptibly settle towards its left.

Grief wanted one more level of insurance. He looked up at the underside of the wing, carefully pushed the muzzle against it between the flush-riveted lines of supporting struts, braced himself and fired again.

He knew the metal skin on the underside was probably titanium, but it was a large-barreled rifle, and the bullet punched cleanly through it. He waited a few seconds and was gratified to see fuel start dripping out of the hole.

If someone now tried to fly this machine, they'd need to take the time to change the tire first. Otherwise, it would shred while taxiing, with the rubber fragments likely getting swallowed by an engine and causing so much drag the plane would be unsteerable to take off.

The bullet hole in the wing was small enough that it might easily get missed in a hasty inspection, but as soon as the fuel system pressurized after takeoff, there would be a significant, unstoppable leak.

Simple precautions against the very low probability that anyone would try to catch him in the only plane on base that was fast enough. Grief stood, turned and jogged back towards the dark, wide-open mouth of the hangar.

And saw headlights in the distance, approaching.

Kaz parked the Jeep by the first hangar along the flight line. He leapt out, pulling the pistol from his pocket, and headed for the F-15. As he cleared the building, he stopped to assess.

No movement by the jet. Just the sound of the wind across the tarmac.

As his eye adjusted, he saw an odd darkness across the north face of the other hangar, and realized its big doors were partially open, where they should have been closed.

All senses on alert. Quickly rethinking what Grief was doing.

He edged along the sheltering dark of the nearer hangar, watched for a few seconds, and dashed across the open space between the buildings. He crept to the edge of the tall, open hangar door, listening intently.

Small sounds of footsteps from within, and then metal scraping on metal, and a creaking. Like a ladder touching an airplane and someone climbing up into a jet. Kaz moved quickly around the corner to duck inside.

Grief fired the shotgun at the silhouette beside the door.

—

The sudden numbness of his leg and foot told Kaz he'd been hit. He turned and ran. *At least the leg's working,* he thought, as he dodged around the hangar corner and ducked down behind a bulky transformer, peeking around it, pistol ready.

Cursing that he'd been shot. Waiting for Grief to come finish the job.

He reached behind himself until his fingers found gravel. He picked up a larger stone and awkwardly flung it towards the adjoining hangar, gratified to hear it loudly strike metal. He picked up another stone and waited, hoping to draw the Russian out.

Searing pain suddenly hit him, and he felt down his leg as he kept watch for the Russian. He expected some blood, but the cloth he touched was soaked, and his boot felt warm and slick. A wave of nausea passed through him.

Shit. The shot must have hit a major artery. He fumbled to undo his belt, yanked it out of the loops, and set the pistol down for a second to cinch the belt at the widening of flesh just below his knee, using both hands to pull it tight. The belt was made of woven canvas, and he pushed and pulled on the prong until it popped through, holding the makeshift tourniquet securely in place. He pulled and wound the loose end under the flat of the belt a couple of times, maximizing the tension until he was satisfied it was all he could get. The lack of blood flow would eventually do serious damage to his lower leg and foot, but it would have to do for now. Wiping his bloody hands on his thighs, he picked up the pistol again and risked a quick peek around the edge of the transformer.

He didn't see anything new, and rapidly assessed options. Grief didn't know how well armed he was, or even if he was alone, and would be hesitant to come for him blindly. Whatever Grief had shot him with had had a bigger flash than a pistol—likely a shotgun. That probably meant one more shell ready to fire, and maybe more.

But why were the hangar doors open? He had guessed that Grief would try to steal the F-15. Only the MiGs were parked inside this hangar. Why would Grief go to all this trouble to steal a MiG? And where would he go with it?

Maybe there's something about the MiG-25 we haven't discovered?

Another thought occurred to him. *Maybe he's destroying all the MiGs?* But that didn't make any sense.

He bobbed his head around the transformer's corner again, and still saw nothing. Whatever Grief's plan was, he was going to be executing it now. Kaz decided he needed another way into the hangar, less exposed, and looked for the nearest entrance. It was time to move. He got up from his crouch to run and the leg immediately buckled under him. He fell and rolled, seeing stars from the sudden pain.

Shit! Is the bone broken?

He felt for the familiar hardness of his tibia from knee to ankle, finding nothing unusual. The fibula deep under his flesh he couldn't be sure of, and the torn upper section of his calf muscle burned in fiery agony when he touched it. He took a deep, gasping breath, carefully rolled back to his feet and hobbled towards the door, more hopping than running, knowing how exposed he was if Grief came around the corner.

Just as he grabbed for the doorknob with his blood-slicked hand, he heard the unmistakable grinding whine of a jet engine starting. Coming from within the hangar.

And then the light above the door came on.

His eyes instinctively shut against the sudden glare. As he pulled himself inside, he couldn't see a thing. His good eye's night vision was instantly shot, and none of the interior lights were on. The firemen must have finally been successful in getting the transformer powered back up: all the lights that were normally left on at night, like those at the hangar entrances, were now on. But the room he was in, and the hangar itself, was still dark.

The sound changed to a deep-throated roar as the jet engine transitioned from start mode to running. He only had a matter of seconds before Grief would be able to taxi clear of the hangar.

He fumbled beside the door until his fingers found light switches and flicked them on, then he hobbled as quickly as he could down the entrance corridor. He threw the door open, spilling light into the cavernous blackness. With Grief's jet already running, there wasn't time to worry about more light. He stepped through, steadied himself in as stable a stance as his injured leg allowed, and raised his pistol to fire.

From the front of the plane he saw a muzzle flash, and heard the zip and clanging thwack of a high-speed bullet hitting the wall next to him, and then another. He dove, groaning in pain, and rolled to his right, up against the covering bulk of a parked start cart. With the pistol in his left hand, he reached blindly around it, squeezing the trigger a couple of times at where he knew the jet was. The noise from the engine rapidly increased, and there was the added banging and thudding of debris being thrown around by the jet wash.

Grief was rapidly moving out of the hangar.

Now or never, Kaz realized. He pulled himself up on the start cart, leaned across the top of it to stabilize his aim, and fired the remaining five rounds at what he guessed were the most vulnerable parts of the Soviet jet.

As the pistol's slide locked aft with the magazine emptied, the MiG-25 pulled free of the hangar, the engines now at near-full military power, and turned hard to the right, to the east, towards the runway and the Groom Lake lakebed.

Towards the brightening light of sunrise.

69

F-15 Eagle

Kaz crab-ran, limping badly, towards the F-15. Of all the jets at Groom Lake, it was the only one that had a weapons load of any sort in it. Claw had mentioned that the test team was doing aerial gunnery qualifications, and so it should have a full bay of 20-millimeter rounds loaded for its Vulcan cannon.

The MiG-25 had already cleared the parking ramp and was moving fast, crossing a taxiway towards the runway. As Kaz reached the F-15, he saw in the half-light that it was sitting crooked, with the left main tire flat.

Shit. With no other option available to him, he bent carefully on his good leg and pulled the heavy rubber chocks clear of the tires.

He hurriedly yanked the intake covers out of the engines and slid the pitot tube covers off, throwing them downwind. He reached up below the cockpit and pushed in the flush door that covered the built-in boarding ladder release. As it telescoped out and down, he popped open the adjacent canopy control, twisted it hard to the UP position, watched as the canopy pivoted open in the wind, then re-stowed the handle.

The F-15's internal ladder was just a skinny central shaft with a few hand- and footholds, designed for fit men to clamber up into the cockpit when there wasn't a more substantial groundcrew ladder handy. Kaz reached up and grabbed with both hands, balanced on his good leg, and swung his injured foot into place on the first rung.

This is going to hurt.

Pulling hard, he moaned as he pivoted on the bad leg, scrabbling to get his good foot on the next higher toehold. Reaching up, he grabbed the cockpit sill and did an overhanded chin-up, hopping his solid leg one rung higher and pushing. With most of his upper body now high enough, he leaned hard into the cockpit, twisted and flopped into the seat, his injured calf banging painfully into the lower instrument panel, smearing it with blood.

But he was in.

He glanced around, trying to sort out the cockpit. He'd never flown an F-15, but it was built by the same people who had made the F-4, and as a test pilot he'd learned that all planes were essentially the same. You just had to figure out how to get them started. He threw on the master and starter-ready switches and was about to pull a nearby black handle labeled JET FUEL STARTER when he remembered the still-dangling ladder, just in front of the left engine intake. Grabbing the sill with both hands, he leaned over, stretching to reach the top rung. Pulling hard, he nestled the telescoping sections into each other, slammed the last piece flush and snapped the covering door into place. He fell back into the ejection seat, feeling sick with the pain and the effort. *And blood loss.*

Time to focus. He pulled the JFS, cranked the right and then the left engines by raising their finger lifts and bringing the throttles to idle, and closed the canopy against the screaming engine noise. He didn't have a helmet or oxygen mask, but Grief was bareheaded as well. Neither of them would be able to fly very high without extra oxygen, and there was no way to talk on the radio.

Unimportant. He had to get the jet flying, ASAP, and with a flat tire.

Ahead and to the right he saw the MiG-25's afterburners, bright orange reflecting off the lakebed, rising above the extended paved section of the runway where Grief was just going airborne. It was still quite dark, but Kaz pictured what was straight ahead of him: a run-up apron and then a service road that led directly out to the lakebed itself. He needed to minimize turns on the flat tire so the tough rubber sidewalls would last as long as possible. A quick glance showed his screens had powered up, and the green of the heads-up display, the HUD, glowed in front of him. Looking through it, he saw the MiG-25 turning left, climbing and gathering speed in full afterburner across the lakebed.

He had to go now. Disregarding all normal procedures he slammed both throttles to full afterburner, and as the Eagle lurched forward with the sudden onslaught of power, he used the pedals to steer to the right, ignoring the burning stab of pain and muscle spasms in his calf, aiming for the apron and service road. He'd decided to take off on the bare salt of the lakebed.

Full of gas and bullets, with no missiles or external tanks, the F-15 weighed 40,000 pounds, the weight split between the two main tires and the single nose wheel. Kaz slapped the flaps down and jammed the stick full right and forward to offload the bad tire as much as possible, but until the airspeed got high enough, most of the 10 tons on that side kept crushing and further deforming the radial-stiffened rubber. As the speed rapidly increased, the flexing bulge tried to keep up with the accelerating rotation of the wheel, putting more and more stress on the tire itself. Just as the plane was crossing from the black asphalt of the service road out onto the hard white salt pan of the lakebed, the tire had had enough, and started to rip. With that first flaw it instantaneously self-destructed, the centrifugal forces of the high-speed spin tearing it to pieces, heavy chunks of steel-reinforced rubber flying in all directions from under the left wing root.

Most of the debris slammed up into the lower fuselage and underside of the wing or bounced down onto the lakebed, leaving black skid marks and minor dents in the aluminum and titanium skin. Several fragments flew directly aft, one of them hitting the slanting leading edge of the horizontal stabilator, leaving a deep, jagged dent before it bounced off into the dawn. But it was the forward-flung pieces that were the highest threat. Just 15 feet in front of the spinning wheel was the huge square intake for the F100-PW-100 engine, acting like an enormous vacuum cleaner head, trying to pull in enough air to feed the max-power afterburning turbofan.

Several tire pieces were sucked into the engine.

Caught by the power of the inrushing air, the fragments slammed into the first stage of the multibladed compressor fan that raised the pressure high enough for the engine to run. The titanium blades were tough, designed to take the impact of near-supersonic rain, dust and small birds. But it was a crapshoot whether they could handle something as unpredictable as radial tire shards.

Kaz got lucky. The pieces struck the spinning blades without breaking any of them off at the root, which would have caused wholesale destruction. Instead, the sharp edges chopped the rubber into digestible pieces, and for a few seconds the afterburner exhaust color changed slightly as the engine burned not only JP-4 and air, but rubber and metal as well.

The loss of the tire caused a whole new problem, though. All that remained after the rubber shredded off was the metal rim, about half a foot shorter without its tire, and causing much higher drag across the hardpacked salty sand of Groom Lake. Kaz held the stick full right and eased it back as the jet rapidly accelerated, the left aileron and stabilator pushing down hard on the air to lift the drooping wing. He bulled through the pain of his injured leg, pushing on the right rudder pedal to keep the nose pointed straight, forcing himself to tap the toe brake a couple of times until the airspeed was high enough to dominate.

And suddenly it was sufficient. The big twin engines had rammed the balky machine up to a high enough speed that the lift from the wings was greater than the weight of the jet, and the F-15 pivoted nose up, clear of the flat white ground. Kaz raised the flaps to accelerate and, praying that it wouldn't foul, slammed the gear lever up. He rolled hard to the left to start an immediate turn, and focused on the glowing red flame of the distant MiG-25 afterburner exhaust, accelerating away towards the south.

Below and behind him, the landing gear was cycling up. The long white shaft of the oleo strut began pivoting forward, the mechanism rotating the wheel 90 degrees to fit properly and the high-pressure hydraulics ramming it all into place, flush up against the F-15's belly. Within a second the covering gear door slammed shut, enclosing it all. No trailing pieces of shredded rubber snagged in the mechanism, and the bare metal wheel, smaller than the normal tire, slipped into place. The underside of the Eagle was now slick and smooth, ready to go fast.

At the same time, as the weight came off the gear, microswitches clicked and sent a signal to pressurize the fuel tanks, to help feed JP-4 to the engines as the jet climbed and the air got thinner. What had been a slow, leaking drip suddenly turned into two narrow fountains, squirting fuel out through the bullet holes in the top and bottom of the wing. The Eagle carried 3,000 gallons of jet fuel total, now rapidly burning up in the engines and spraying out into the morning twilight.

The fight was on.

The five shots that Kaz had taken at the fuselage of the MiG-25 as it cleared the hangar had all struck home. But the Colt 1911 45-caliber pistol was not designed to disable a heavy metal machine from nearly a hundred feet away.

Kaz had first targeted Grief in the cockpit and then the fuel tanks and engines as the MiG moved forward. The half-ounce spinning bullets had mostly splatted into or deflected off the nickel-steel skin. One had buried itself in the titanium structure surrounding the hottest aft section of the engine. But the only one to do any real damage had struck the heat-resistant plexiglass of the cockpit canopy, punching a starred hole to Grief's right, passing just in front of his face, showering his exposed skin with small plastic shards, and blasting another hole in the plastic on his left where it exited, just aft of the metal rail. A small wound, but a significant one, as the cockpit now couldn't hold air pressure. And Grief had no helmet or mask to feed him oxygen.

The Russian was going to have to fly his high-altitude interceptor at an even lower altitude than he'd planned.

The designers of the F-15 had purposefully built the machine for air combat. It had a huge, powerful radar dish concealed inside the gray nose cone, and the pilot's most-needed controls were all mounted on the throttles and control stick, where they could be actuated by feel while the pilot searched the surrounding airspace for threats. As Kaz pulled the jet hard around to point at the MiG-25, he played with the switches, watching through the HUD and glancing at the display screens, teaching himself the plane. He cycled through several radar options until he got what he wanted, and a small green glowing box appeared, superimposed on the afterburning orange-red of his adversary.

Radar lock.

The airplane's computers started doing the math, and showed him range, closure and potential weapons solutions. With no heat-seeking or radar-guided missiles loaded, all Kaz had was guns, and he'd have to get very close to use them.

From Grief's debriefings at Spring Mountain Ranch, and from the Red Hat test pilots who had flown it, Kaz knew the MiG-25 had low maneuverability, especially when it was still full of fuel right after takeoff. The placard limits were just a little over two g, but Grief would be max-performing the jet to try to get away, unworried about bending the wings.

Kaz had to cut across the wide left turn Grief was flying to get the F-15's gun into lethal range. He assumed his pistol shots hadn't done any damage, so he had to close the distance before Grief could climb and accelerate, where the big Tumansky R-15 engines could push the Soviet interceptor up to its optimum design speeds of nearly Mach 3. Faster than the Mach 2.5 limit of the F-15.

Kaz needed more thrust. Suddenly, something popped into his head that a bragging Eagle test pilot—they'd already earned the moniker Ego Drivers amongst fighter pilots—had mentioned to him at the bar one night. There was apparently a switch in the cockpit to allow the engines to run hotter in case of vital tactical need. Though it would quickly burn the engines up, it had been included to give extra power for the critical purposes of one flight. Kaz looked urgently around the cockpit as he maneuvered, hunting for a guarded switch, probably specially colored. His eye flicked past the black and yellow canopy jettison and ejection handles, until finally he saw a small red-covered switch tucked under the left sill, marked V MAX.

Bingo!

He hooked his finger under it, pulled hard to break the safety wire that kept pilots from flipping it inadvertently, lifted the pivoting cover and clicked the switch into position.

Nothing. Kaz felt no change in performance.

Maybe V Max means it only engages when I get to higher speeds? No matter. Doesn't hurt, might help. Pay attention!

All dogfighting is a trade-off. How to maneuver to a weapons-firing envelope while maintaining enough speed and energy, and to get there before the adversary shot you or reached their tactical target, or you ran out of fuel. Kaz pulled smooth and hard on the stick, adjusting his nose position to point out in front of the MiG-25, the numbers in the HUD showing his range rapidly closing as he cut across the circle.

He looked beyond the green box highlighting his adversary, at the lights of Las Vegas now visible in the far distance. Grief was rolling out on a heading that was going to pass well west of town. What was his target? Was he planning some sort of kamikaze maneuver to damage something on the nuclear range? *Or maybe the Hoover Dam?* Kaz shook his head. Even if it was hit by a MiG-25 at high speed, all that concrete and metal would only take minor damage. And why do it? It didn't make sense.

He's running, Kaz realized. Racing to get somewhere straight south of Groom Lake. Kaz pictured the geography, trying to remember exactly where Vegas was in relation to San Diego and the Salton Sea and Yuma and Phoenix.

Mexico!

Grief was racing to take the MiG-25, the fastest jet available, across the border into Mexico with whatever secrets this clever double agent had gathered. Leaving behind the havoc he had created at Groom Lake.

In the F-15's HUD, the afterburning MiG-25 was getting big as Kaz approached from the left rear quarter. He looked quickly down to the left at the ARMAMENT panel, saw that the gun was in HIGH rate with 940 rounds showing on the small digital counter. There was an over-center locking switch that he pulled out and flicked up to ARM. A glance back up at the HUD now showed a large circle with tick marks at each hour position, and a long, straight line leading to a cross. As he rolled and maneuvered to align with the MiG, he could see that the line was a bullet prediction path, and he worked his hands and feet to center the target in the circle. His right leg now felt numb when he pushed with it, as if it was dead below the knee.

Over his shoulder, Grief saw the approaching F-15 getting close to a weapons solution, and instantly reacted. Slamming his stick to the side, he rolled the MiG-25 inverted and pulled hard, burying the nose towards the Earth, diving for the safety of the twisting valleys of the Shoshone Mountains. In the growing light of dawn, he chose a narrow arroyo and judged it exactly, pulling the MiG to its structural limits as he leveled off 20 meters above the ground. Staring fiercely ahead, he rolled left and right to follow the winding, rocky contours, daring the American to follow.

Kaz cursed as his flight path overshot and he pulled hard up, rolled and yanked the F-15 back down to regain track on the MiG. The glow of its afterburner was still visible, but disappearing as it turned to follow the deep, narrow valleys. Kaz jerked back on the stick to stop his descent and strained forward, craning his neck to see where the MiG would reappear.

There! He caught a glimpse of glowing red, and his eye tracked ahead along the valley's shadow, predicting where it would open onto the wider plain. He rolled and pulled to cut off the distance, and dropped his nose to accelerate to be within his guns' range.

The MiG-25 Foxbat came racing out of cover in full power directly in front of Kaz, flying even lower now as the ground flattened out. Too low for a descending shot, Kaz realized, and he eased the F-15 down to co-altitude, just a few yards above the rolling desert floor. Trying to yaw the jet with his lifeless foot, he had to shift in his seat and straighten his whole thigh to push on the pedal and get his nose on target.

Two transonic 20-ton machines, roaring as their torches of exploding fuel burned out the back, hugging the hummocking curves of the Nevada desert, trying to gain advantage. With no helmet, the cockpit noise was a relentlessly deafening high-pitched whine. Not being strapped into the ejection seat made Kaz feel like he was riding a crazed bull bareback.

The MiG in front of him was rolling and jinking left and right, spoiling Kaz's aim. He felt it going oddly out of focus and saw his vision graying. *Lack of blood!* he realized. He fought it, shaking his head and squeezing his leg and gut muscles to force blood to flow to his brain, focusing everything to concentrate.

Without weapons and with the F-15 in close pursuit, Grief had only one real option left. As he raced across the desert floor, he slowly eased his jet to the correct roll angle and yanked the stick full aft, pitching the MiG as hard as it could turn, directly into the other fighter. To cause a collision and count on the MiG's titanium-framed toughness to survive it. And saving one last maneuver to guarantee the impact.

Kaz saw the Foxbat go suddenly planform, directly up in front of him, visibly yawing to the right. To avoid slamming into it, he was tensing his good leg to stomp on the left rudder when a voice screamed in the back of his head: *You've seen this before!* Fighting his instinctive reaction, he pushed instead to the right, seemingly headed towards an inevitable crash.

The MiG suddenly yawed the other direction, somehow reversing and pointing exactly back towards Kaz in a wild, seemingly out-of-control maneuver. The same thing Kaz had seen eight years earlier over North Vietnam.

"You bastard!" Kaz yelled.

But this time he wasn't flying an aging, ponderous F-4. He knew the MiG would be out of energy after the violence of that gyration, so he snapped the F-15 hard left and pulled the stick with both arms, wrestling the jet around at over eight g, grunting and straining with everything he had to stay conscious. His body felt crushed as he forced his back against the seat to take the load straight down the rigidity of his spine, and his vision narrowed to gray, and then black, but he could still hear and think, and he counted the seconds until he knew the two jets would be aligned. He released the heavy stick, his vision snapped back, and the MiG was there in front of him, still twisting and falling and trying to accelerate.

Now! Kaz extended his right pointer finger to wrap around the trigger on the stick and pushed once more with his bad leg to bring the pipper sight squarely over the target. As he saw it centering, he squeezed his entire right hand and the jet vibrated, a harsh metallic buzz filling the cockpit as 100 rounds a second were fed through the M61 Vulcan cannon's six rotating barrels.

They spit out from Kaz's right wing root, the yellow-white of the muzzle flash visible in the dawn's half-light. As he fired, he moved the controls slightly to let the pipper track forward and back, left and right, until he saw an explosion from the MiG, and an instant, heavy trail of thick black smoke. Kaz pushed hard and rolled to clear the sudden debris, releasing down and under the damaged Soviet jet.

The MiG-25 instantly lost speed as the engines failed and came apart, pieces of high-speed turbomachinery shredding the aft end of the airplane. It began plummeting towards the desert floor, and Kaz pulled hard left to stay with it and follow it down.

The MiG-25 tumbled violently, no longer a sleek flying machine. Inside the cockpit, the drawstring bag of papers and heavy metal valves had slammed from floor to canopy and rearward into the ejection seat, a projectile gone wild in the confined space. In his hurry to take off, Grief hadn't stopped to don his gear and strap into the seat, and the ferocity of the gyrating fall threw him around as well, smashing him alternately into the metal and plastic, cutting flesh and breaking bone.

Yet he'd put countless aircraft out of control as a test pilot and had learned early on to stay detached from the wild movements around him. Even now, in this fatally wounded beast, he watched as the Earth grew rapidly bigger, and saw the dial on his altimeter spinning down. His last act was to hook one arm and then the other under the flailing shoulder straps, twist his body to get roughly centered over the seat, and then pull the large, ear-shaped red handle, commanding ejection.

The endless brown desert sands came rushing up, and the MiG-25 Foxbat added one more crater to the Nevada nuclear testing site.

A pilot's death, even that of an enemy combatant, always shook Kaz. When he saw the bright explosion of the MiG hitting the ground, he closed his eyes for a few seconds, forcing himself not to imagine what that last instant of violence and fire would have been like. His own personal nightmare.

Then the reality of his own situation reassumed control of his thoughts. He was flying a heavy jet that he'd never landed, with one tire missing, a wounded, bleeding and numb leg, and no way to radio the ground. He looked around the instrument panel and found the FUEL QTY gauge on the right-hand side, and his eyes widened when he saw the pointer buried far counterclockwise—reading near-empty. Beside it on the warning lights panel he read the orange-lit words FUEL LOW.

Shit! Where did my fuel go?

He turned instantly back towards Groom Lake and was relieved to see that, even after the extended dogfight, it was just to the northeast over the ridgeline. He had to get back on the ground, ASAP.

He eased the throttles back to mid-range to save fuel, and briefly took stock. He felt dizzy, and his right leg was giving him a strange combination of intense pain and numbness, a pins-and-needles sensation gone wild. He wasn't sure he could be precise in steering the jet on the ground after touchdown. He knew that the F-15s, even though they weren't Navy planes, had been designed with an arresting hook, mounted between the engines at the back. He looked past the gear lever, found a hook-shaped lever marked HOOK and slammed it to DOWN. There was no reassuring clunking feeling through the airframe, like in Navy planes with their heavier arresting gear, but he saw a small HOOK caution light come on. *Good*, Kaz thought. Now he needed to attract the attention of Base Rescue before he ran out of gas, and get them to raise the emergency cable across the approach end of the runway.

He flew low across Groom Lake base, from south to north, wagging his wings left and right, cross-checking his dwindling fuel supply. He saw that the fire trucks were no longer parked by the fuel farm and spotted them driving up the access road towards the fire hall. He eased right and flew directly over their heads, letting his altitude drop down to 50 feet so they could clearly see his lowered hook. He pivoted around to look after he passed and was gratified to see them turning hard right onto the desert scrub, back towards the runway threshold. He circled once, feeling increasingly sleepy with the loss of blood and fighting it, then saw them clearing the tarmac, holding up their thumbs as he passed. He turned onto an extended downwind to give himself time to get properly lined up, just like he was doing a long, flat carrier approach. His gas needle was nudging against zero, but this was one cable he didn't want to miss.

When his head bobbed, he realized he'd momentarily blacked out. He shook his head and hauled the jet around to the right, one last turn to final.

Pushing the landing gear out into the slipstream caused a lot more drag, so he'd delayed it as long as possible. When he was lined up and nearing the end of the runway, he reached with a shaking left hand and lowered the big red gear handle, relieved when the three square lights behind it read NOSE, LEFT and RIGHT.

Three wheels down and locked. But only two with rubber on them.

He flicked the flap lever down, and then put both hands on the stick for strength. The F-15 handled ponderously but well enough at approach speed. An airplane symbol in the HUD clearly showed where his velocity would impact the ground. He glanced at the airspeed and angle of attack, content to hold 130 knots. Since he was not strapped into the seat, he braced with his legs and back as best he could for the impending sudden deceleration.

Wham!

He hit the ground solidly just before the cable. The bare wheel crossed it in a shower of sparks without snagging, and Kaz jammed both palms against the instrument panel just at the moment the hook took the cable. He shifted hard forward in the seat, twisting and shuddering along with the jet as it was violently yanked to a stop, and suddenly all was still. He reached across with both hands to lift the finger guards and pull both heavy throttles all the way aft to off, sat back and collapsed, feeling tiny in the hard ejection seat, dizzy and completely drained. As the adrenaline left his body, he felt a wave of nausea, a sudden shivering coldness, and then everything went black.

Behind him, the fire trucks rolled into position, their flashing beacons blinking red and yellow against the brightening light of the early dawn.

EPILOGUE

Nellis AFB Medical Facility, Las Vegas

Kaz was running.

Ahead of him, through the brief gaps between the trees along the winding dirt path, he caught glimpses of his quarry, fleeing hard, never looking back at him. Kaz pushed himself, leaning into his sprint to close the gap, digging in harder with his toes, his breath coming in gasps.

Each stride shortened the distance between Kaz and his prey, until he could clearly see the strong legs and pumping arms just ahead of him. When there was only a body length between them, Kaz reached hard with his left hand, gave one final surge and grabbed the shoulder, pulling and twisting to stop the other runner, to reveal them.

As the other head turned, the runner squirming to get free of his grasp, Kaz was shocked to recognize who it was. Not who he expected.

Svetlana. With a quick, hard pivot she shook her shoulder free, accelerated rapidly away from him and was gone.

Kaz stared after her, wondering how she had disappeared so suddenly. Then came the creeping realization that this wasn't real, that he was dreaming, and that now he was swimming deliberately towards the surface of consciousness. Waking himself up.

Kaz tried to open his eyes. The lids felt strangely gummy, the left one sticking on the dry surface of his glass eyeball. He blinked several times to wet it, and then opened both eyes, hard, raising his eyebrows and reaching with his fingers to pull down on the lower lids to help. The air felt cool on his exposed good eyeball as he looked around the room, finding reassurance in the rectangular reality of his surroundings.

The lights were off and the venetian blinds closed against the brightness of a large window that covered most of the wall to his left. A metal gantry next to him held an IV bag that dripped clear fluid into his left forearm. He was in a bed with shiny metal rails, and there were two doors to his right, both closed. All was quiet, except for the low, distinctive rumble of jet engines on takeoff somewhere in the near distance.

I'm in a military hospital. His brain was working slowly. *What the hell happened? And what was that dream?*

He heard three quick knocks on the door, and a muffled male voice saying something unrecognizable.

"Come in!" Kaz called. Or tried to. He cleared his throat and tried again, louder this time. "Come in!"

The door opened and bright light from the hallway spilled in, revealing the silhouette of a man who stopped before he came all the way in. "Okay to turn the light on, Kaz?"

"Sure, go ahead." Kaz squinted as he heard a wall switch being thrown and the quick, humming crackle of fluorescent lights. Even so, the sudden blare of brightness made him grimace, and he took his time reopening his eyes.

The familiar figure now standing at the foot of his bed was tall, thin and mostly bald, wearing a pale-blue shirt and darker-blue pants, with ribbons and a name tag above his left breast pocket. He had a blue forage cap tucked under his arm and was smiling at Kaz with concern.

"How you feeling, cowboy?"

General Sam Phillips, World War II fighter pilot, NASA Apollo Program Director, and now commander of Air Force Systems Command. Kaz's mentor, and the person who had assigned him to work with NASA and to oversee the MiG-25. And its pilot.

Kaz tried his voice again. "A little dazed, General, to be honest." Forcing his brain to work, he made a guess. "Are we at Nellis?"

Sam Phillips smiled. "Yep, in their base hospital." He nodded at the tented sheet covering Kaz's right leg. "You lost a lot of blood. Nellis air base had the nearest supply."

Kaz frowned. "Washington is at least a five-hour flight from here. How long have I been out?"

Phillips sat in the bedside chair, setting his cap on his lap. "Long enough for the medevac chopper to bring you here, and for the docs to top off your fluids and sew up the damage to your lower leg," he said. "I spoke to the surgeon, who said it was a straightforward repair job. He expects you'll have no lasting damage, apart from some interesting scars."

Kaz nodded slowly and tried wiggling his toes. His calf and foot still felt numb, but he saw reassuring motion under the blanket. "So . . . how long?"

"Twenty-six hours. They gave you painkillers to help you rest." When Kaz kept looking at him, Phillips added, "It's Saturday morning."

Something that had been worrying at Kaz surfaced out of the mental blurriness. "Irv Williams and the ops desk clerk were both bleeding from the nose. I think maybe the Groom Lake doc was too." He looked at the general, his earlier guess trickling back into his head. "Was it warfarin?"

Phillips nodded. "Yep. Many of the personnel at Groom Lake had similar symptoms, with nosebleeds and gut pain. It turned out that the communal coffee pots in the flight ops briefing room and the pilot ready room had both been laced with it. They tell me you can't taste the poison over the coffee, and after a couple days it builds up and starts to take effect." He paused. "Not the first time that Soviet agents have used warfarin as a weapon." Phillips had also been director of the National Security Agency, dealing with foreign intelligence.

Kaz had flown into Groom Lake Thursday night and hadn't drunk any coffee. He asked the vital question. "How are Irv and the others?"

A slow nod. "Irv and all personnel who were poisoned are okay. The Nellis medics who came by helicopter to pick you up radioed back ASAP for help. Thank God warfarin poisoning is treatable. They got to everyone in time with fresh blood and extra vitamin K for coagulation, and they'll all recover. Several of them are here in this hospital too, plus the surviving gate guard who got hit by the grenade. The docs say he's going to make it, but it'll be a long haul."

Phillips looked hard at Kaz. "Bill Thompson from the CIA is dead. Killed by strangulation—looks like it was some sort of garrote. His body was hidden under his trailer."

Kaz slowly shook his head. "Shit, General, that's terrible." A pause, then a flat statement. "So Grief was a Soviet double agent." He tipped his head to one side. "Where was he headed with the MiG-25? Mexico?"

General Phillips nodded. "An Antonov-22 heavy transport was on the ground just across the border at Mexicali, staged there out of Cuba—we'd tracked it across the Gulf in international airspace. A few hours after you shot the MiG down, it flew back to Cuba. The An-22 is big enough to carry a MiG-25. We're confident they were planning to take it and the pilot back home to Russia."

Kaz frowned. "I don't get it. Why the whole ruse about handing us a MiG-25? Just for the intel Grief had gathered about Groom Lake? Why didn't he take the F-15 instead?"

"We think the Soviets decided that would have caused too big an incident. Someone defecting with an older asset is one thing, but deliberate, sanctioned theft of our newest fighter would have caused unacceptable repercussions." Phillips paused. "And it turns out that's not what they were actually after."

Kaz waited.

"Yesterday they found a security guard shot and killed out on the nuclear test range, next to a secure storage facility building. Putting the pieces together, it looks like while everyone at Groom Lake was dealing with the fuel farm fire and the grenade attack at the guardhouse, the Soviet flew the Penetrator helicopter down there and stole some secrets." He glanced at the hospital room door. "I'll tell you later exactly what, but our initial survey of the MiG crash site found the remains of specific, high-intel-value hardware."

He stared at Kaz for a few seconds. "That's what he was sent here for. Your quick actions saved us from a serious breach of key American technology."

Kaz shook his head. "But I didn't prevent us from being duped or stop him from killing people." He took a deep breath to center himself and thought for a few seconds. "Any leads on who attacked the guardhouse?"

The general shook his head. "Not yet. But now that we know there's some sort of sleeper mole here in the Vegas area, we'll be actively hunting. We've found what we think are the remains of satellite communication hardware and a camera in the plane's wreckage. Looks like the mole somehow passed that to the Soviet here as well." He frowned. "Groom Lake will be taking a hard look at their security."

Phillips sat back. "One weird thing. So far, we've found no trace of the body at the MiG crash site. Did you see anything?"

Kaz closed his eyes, picturing the final moments of the dogfight, watching the burning wreckage of the MiG-25 plummeting to Earth and exploding. He shook his head. "I didn't see him get out. But it was barely dawn, so I might have missed it."

Sam Phillips shrugged. "Yeah, what's left is mostly a smoking hole, and we figure the body just burned up in the violence of the impact. Still, our boys are having a very careful look around the area."

Kaz asked, "What's Washington going to do about it all?"

Phillips looked at him for a few seconds. "Fortunately, nothing was made public, so both sides will deny that a MiG-25 was ever here. The CIA will treat the loss of its officer with their usual security, and Thompson's family won't ever be told how or where he died. We'll explain the local deaths as accidental, tighten security and be thankful for all we learned about that Soviet jet." He paused. "We'll let the Israelis know, though. Their intel guys let them down as well."

Kaz nodded and looked down the bed at his covered leg. "Think this will impact the Apollo–Soyuz mission?" Some detail of his dream stirred in his head and was gone.

The general tipped his head, considering. "I don't think so. Nixon still wants to look good as a statesman. Heck, with Watergate, now more than ever." He smiled slightly. "After this mess here, we're gonna need you to keep an even closer watch on the cosmonauts."

Kaz felt a sudden wave of tiredness and laid his head back on the pillow. The general took the cue and stood.

"Those meds must be knocking you back some, Kaz. Get some rest, get yourself out of here and back to Houston, and we'll talk future plans then."

Kaz nodded slowly, his face drawn and thoughtful. "Thanks for coming all this way, sir."

General Phillips nodded back, his expression serious. "What you did out there yesterday was nothing short of phenomenal, Kaz. Your nation and I thank you." The men looked at each other for a few seconds, then Phillips turned and left the room, closing the door behind him.

It felt like a huge relief to let his eyelids close, and Kaz relaxed into the stiff comfort of the hospital bed. As he began to doze off, his thoughts flowed with stark images of the dogfight, with joyous satisfaction at truly flying again, and with waves of acute sadness about the men who had been killed.

When Kaz finally slept, he dreamed.

AUTHOR'S NOTE

The Reality Behind The Defector

The majority of the characters, events and things in *The Defector* are real. This made creating the plot both a thrilling jigsaw puzzle and an endless challenge to stay true to fact and history. Here's a quick summary, to save you bothering ChatGPT.

REAL CHARACTERS

Andropov, Yuri. Chairman of the KGB 1967–82, later General Secretary of the Soviet Union

Beregovoy, Georgy. Cosmonaut, Star City Director 1972–87, wounded during 1969 Brezhnev assassination attempt

Brand, Vance. US Marine Corps fighter pilot, Lockheed test pilot, astronaut, Apollo–Soyuz crew member

Brezhnev, Leonid. General Secretary of the Communist Party of the Soviet Union 1964–82

Carmi, Eitan. Israeli fighter pilot, shot down a Kelt missile at the start of the Yom Kippur War

Dayan, Moshe. Israeli Minister of Defense 1967–74, lost his left eye in 1941 when a sniper bullet hit his binoculars

Echeverría Álvarez, Luis. President of Mexico 1970–76

Elazar, Dado. Chief of Staff of the Israel Defense Forces 1972–74

Forsman, Billy. USAF Colonel, Air Attaché to Israel during the Yom Kippur War, key role in Operation Nickel Grass

Grechko, Andrei. Marshal of the Red Army, Soviet Minister of Defense 1967–76

Keating, Ken. US politician, Ambassador to Israel 1973–75

Kissinger, Henry. US Secretary of State 1973–77

Kryuchkov, Vladimir. Head of the KGB's First Chief Directorate 1971–78

Kubasov, Valery. Cosmonaut, flight engineer during Soyuz–Apollo mission

Kutakhov, Pavel. Marshal of Aviation, Commander-in-Chief of the Soviet Air Forces 1969–84, Battle of Stalingrad veteran

Leonov, Alexei. Cosmonaut, world's first spacewalker, Soyuz commander during Soyuz-Apollo mission

Marwan, Ashraf. Egyptian businessman and spy known by Mossad as "the Angel"

Meir, Golda. Israel's first and, to date, only female Prime Minister (1969–74), significant role in shaping the country, born in Ukraine, raised in Wisconsin, died in 1978 of lymphoma

Nixon, Richard. President of the United States 1969–74

Phillips, Sam. USAF General, Apollo Program Director 1964–69, National Security Agency Director 1972–73, USAF Systems Command Commander 1973–75

Sadat, Anwar. President of Egypt 1970–81, killed by assassination

Shepard, Al. USN Admiral, test pilot, first American astronaut, Apollo 14 commander, NASA Chief Astronaut

Slavsky, Efim. Director of Sredmash 1957–86

Slayton, Deke. USAF test pilot, astronaut, NASA Director of Flight Crew Operations, Apollo-Soyuz crewmember

Stafford, Tom. USAF Lieutenant General, test pilot, astronaut, Apollo commander during Apollo-Soyuz mission

Tindall, Bill. NASA Director of Flight Operations, Johnson Space Center

Veliotes, Nicholas. US Middle Eastern diplomat, Deputy Chief of Mission to Ambassador Keating

APOLLO-SOYUZ A 1975 joint project between the US and USSR for astronauts and cosmonauts to rendezvous and dock in space, demonstrating cooperation and peace. The Soyuz had only two crew, but it had previously flown with up to three.

AREA 51 / GROOM LAKE A highly classified CIA/USAF base in the Nevada desert, used for aircraft technology development and testing, including the U-2 spy plane and captured Soviet fighters. Also the subject of conspiracy theories, as many believe the base is used for extraterrestrial research. The US government did not officially acknowledge the existence of Area 51 until 2013.

BAIKAL-1 A secret Soviet nuclear rocket engine test facility within the Semipalatinsk Test Site (used for nuclear weapons testing 1949–89) in what is now eastern Kazakhstan.

CAESARS PALACE A casino hotel on the Las Vegas Strip, opened in 1966. It has several restaurants, including the Noshorium. Frank Sinatra performed there regularly.

EG&G Edgerton, Germeshausen, and Grier, a US national defense contractor and provider of management and technical services at the Nevada Test Site.

F-15 EAGLE A US air superiority fighter aircraft designed by McDonnell Douglas to counter the expected performance of the MiG-25, first flew in July 1972. Broke eight time-to-climb world records in 1975, including reaching 100,000 feet just 3:30 after takeoff.

KGB AND WARFARIN There are rumors that Stalin was killed by Soviet intelligence using warfarin in 1953.

KRASNY KRIM A Soviet destroyer deployed off the Israeli coast during the Yom Kippur War.

MIG-25 FOXBAT A Soviet supersonic interceptor and reconnaissance aircraft, designed to counter the U-2 and A-12 that were developed at Area 51. First flew in 1964, misinterpreted by the West as an agile air combat fighter. Set multiple speed and altitude records. Flew over Israel during the Yom Kippur War. In 1976, Lieutenant Viktor Belenko of the Soviet Air Defense Forces defected in a MiG-25 to Japan.

NERVA Nuclear Engine for Rocket Vehicle Applications, successfully tested at Jackass Flats on the Nevada Test Site from 1961 to 1973 by the Atomic Energy Commission and NASA, developing a nuclear thermal rocket engine. NERVA is seen as a potential power source for civilian vehicles and military vehicles including spacecraft, missiles, bombers, and even submarines.

NINFA'S A Houston restaurant opened in 1973 by Mama Ninfa Laurenzo, where she invented fajitas.

ONE-EYED PILOTS Wiley Post set a speed record flying solo around the world and was the first man to fly up to 50,000 feet. Adolf Galland was a Luftwaffe fighter ace with 705 combat missions. Saburō Sakai was a Japanese naval aviator and fighter ace. Flying Officer Syd Burrows flew a full military career with the Royal Canadian Air Force.

OPERATION NICKEL GRASS US airlift to rapidly deliver military supplies and equipment to Israel during the Yom Kippur War, ordered by President Nixon in response to Golda Meir's urgent request for assistance.

THE QUIET ONE A stealth helicopter based on the Hughes OH-6, developed by ARPA for CIA/Air America covert operations in Vietnam. Deconfigured after the war, the aircraft may now be flying with the Snohomish County Rescue Team in Washington.

SIX MILLION DOLLAR MAN An American TV series (1973–78) about a former military astronaut, injured in a test flight accident.

SPRING MOUNTAIN RANCH A 528-acre estate west of Las Vegas bought by Howard Hughes from actress Vera Krupp in 1967, now a state park.

SREDMASH Common abbreviation for Srednevo Mashinostroyeniya, the Ministry of Medium Machine Building, which supervised the entire Soviet nuclear industry, including activities at the Semipalatinsk Test Site.

STAR CITY The Gagarin Cosmonaut Training Center, 30 miles east of Moscow, where all cosmonauts have trained since 1960. The author trained in Star City, too, and was also NASA's Director of Operations there.

UFO GROUPS There are many organizations that study reported UFO sightings, such as MUFON, CUFOS and NUFORC, with field investigators and specialized teams to investigate possible physical evidence of extraterrestrial craft.

YOM KIPPUR WAR Begun by surprise attack on Israel on the Jewish holiest day of Yom Kippur, the three-week war (October 6 to October 25, 1973) was led by Egypt and Syria to regain territory lost during the 1967 Six-Day War, caused more than 15,000 deaths and helped precipitate the 1979 Egypt–Israel peace treaty.

ZENIT SPY SATELLITES Soviet reconnaissance satellites (1961–84) that used high-resolution cameras and film-return capsules, which were recovered after re-entry into the Earth's atmosphere.

ACKNOWLEDGMENTS

Writing this book took years of research, regularly demanding expertise I'll never have. I heartily thank each of these friends for their insights, ideas and corrections, and for patiently doing their best to help me get it right. Any mistakes that still managed to sneak in are all mine.

Aaron Murphy—finance and getting everything done
Alex Shifrin—trusted reader
Alla Jiguirej—Star City sage
Anatoly Zak—Russian Space Web
Andre Leblanc—NORAD combat flight controller
Aviv Bushinsky—Israeli insight and help
Barb Harris—schedule and support
Bob Civilikas—USN RIO
Cass Graham—NERVA expert
Charles R. "Chuck" Louie, Jr.—USAF heavy cargo/test pilot
Cheryl-Ann Horrocks—daily assistance and chief of staff
Dave Hadfield—aviation expert and beloved brother
George Abbey—NASA leader
Haim Divon—Israel's Ambassador to the Netherlands
Heather Reisman—Israel research and insight
JD Polk—medical expertise
Jeff "Canman" Canclini—F-4 RIO
Jeff Peer—Israel/US combat fighter/test pilot, Egypt POW
John Webb—NERVA videos/imagery

Kristin Hadfield—beloved daughter and key assistance
Larissa Okhrimovich—Star City history
Madison Doucette—schedule and support
Mike Bloomfield—F-15 fighter/test pilot, astronaut
Rob Wilson—weapons expert
Roger Hadfield—pilot/weapons expert and beloved father
Russ Wilson—firefighter
Scott Berg—F-4 fighter/test pilot
Shaun Kennedy—trusted reader
Ty Greenlees—National Museum of the USAF MiG-25 guide
Winston Scott—VF-84 fighter pilot, astronaut

My eternal, boundless thanks to Jon Butler for the key support and fountain of ideas, to Rick Broadhead for the tenacious attention to detail, and to Anne Collins for the good-humored clarity and enduring, unflagging, much-needed skills and support.

Most of all, gratitude and love to Helene for everything, here on this grand adventure together.

CHRIS HADFIELD is one of the most seasoned and accomplished astronauts in the world. He was the top test pilot in both the US Air Force and the US Navy, and a Cold War fighter pilot intercepting armed Soviet bombers in Canadian air space. A veteran of three space flights, he served as capsule communicator—CAPCOM—for 25 Shuttle missions, as NASA's director of operations in Russia, and as commander of the International Space Station. Hadfield's books *An Astronaut's Guide to Life on Earth*, *You Are Here* and *The Darkest Dark* have all been international bestsellers, and topped the charts for months in Canada. His debut novel, *The Apollo Murders*, became an instant #1 bestseller in his homeland.